Bev

Judas Playing Field

Sister From Another
Mother!

Love You !!

Patricia Deary

Also by Patricia Neary

Dr. James Blake, a highly respected chief medical physician at River Edge Mental Health Institution, wrestles with demons that would terrify the most dangerous patients on the dreaded fourth floor. Blake's social and professional distance conceals grim secrets: a sinister past, scheming ambition, and a brilliantly concocted lethal plan to destroy his patients. There is no antidote. Its execution is irreversible. And at last, acclaim will shine in the eyes of his greatest love and tormentor.

No one can stop him. . . until fifteen-year-old Franki Martin is admitted to River Edge and experiences his resident evil.

Website: www.breachofsanity.com
Available online at: Amazon.com,
Barnesandnoble.com & Xlibris.com

Judas Playing Field

PATRICIA NEARY

iUniverse, Inc.

Bloomington

Judas Playing Field

This is a work of fiction. All of the characters, names, incidents, organizations, and dialogue in this novel are either the products of the author's imagination or are used fictitiously.

iUniverse books may be ordered through booksellers or by contacting:

iUniverse
1663 Liberty Drive
Bloomington, IN 47403
www.iuniverse.com
1-800-Authors (1-800-288-4677)

Because of the dynamic nature of the Internet, any web addresses or links contained in this book may have changed since publication and may no longer be valid. The views expressed in this work are solely those of the author and do not necessarily reflect the views of the publisher, and the publisher hereby disclaims any responsibility for them.

Any people depicted in stock imagery provided by Thinkstock are models, and such images are being used for illustrative purposes only.

Certain stock imagery © Thinkstock.

ISBN: 978-1-4759-8548-1 (sc)
ISBN: 978-1-4759-8549-8 (hc)
ISBN: 978-1-4759-8550-4 (e)

Library of Congress Control Number: 2013906538

Printed in the United States of America

iUniverse rev. date: 5/31/2013

To my late mother, Elizabeth Neary, nee Campbell, for giving me my first insight into the wonderful world of imagination. I miss you always and love you forever.

Chapter One

Ellen glanced at her watch. It was exactly 4:33. She let out a sigh of relief. It was time to take her last walk out of River Edge. With the box of mementoes on her arm, she slowly made her way down the familiar corridor to the red exit sign hanging above the front door and strolled out into the glorious sunshine to her Lexus. She set the box down in the backseat and then drove out of the parking lot.

Arms filled with packages and happy as a clam, Ellen skipped up the coble stone pathway and entered the house. She bounced up the stairs, yelling Tom's name. No answer. Ellen put the packages down and sashayed out onto the deck. There he was bent over with his hands in the dirt, like she knew he would be.

"Hey, handsome." Tom didn't turn to acknowledge her compliment. *Why he won't wear his damn hearing aids is beyond me*, she thought. Down the flight of six steps she went. "Tom, do you have your hearing aids on?" Ellen lightly touched him on the shoulder, trying not to scare him. He keeled over onto his side. Ellen screamed, staring into rigid eyes. His fingers were still clutching his chest.

"Tom. Tom, honey this isn't funny. Tom. Tom, can you hear me?" she shouted, her voice getting louder with panic. Dropping down to her knees, she quickly checked for a pulse. Nothing. She placed both

1

hands on his upper body and began CPR, trying desperately to revive him. Seconds felt like minutes, and still no response. Ellen bolted into the house and grabbed the portable phone; she dialed 911.

By the time the ambulance arrived, it was too late. Tom Smith was pronounced dead. The deep purple markings around his nose and mouth indicated he'd been without oxygen to his brain for over an hour.

In a fog, Ellen was padding aimlessly around her house when she eyed the surprise gifts Tom had purchased for her retirement party. Seeing this only made her cry harder. This was not how she had planned her first day of departure from River Edge. A loving relationship snatched away in one cruel moment. Ellen reached for the phone and dialed her friend, Sandy's cell. No answer. She tried her house phone. A couple rings later, the machine picked up. Ellen left an urgent message for Sandy to call her back.

After catching up with Franki Martin at Teaser's Pub, Sandy stopped by Gilliam Grocery Store to grab a few things before heading home. Arms loaded with grocery bags, Sandy stopped to stare at the overgrown lawn. She could have sworn she'd mowed it only four days ago, and already it looked like a wheat field. She decided to give it another manicure once she put the groceries away. When the food was stored where it belonged, Sandy checked her phone. Her blood ran cold as she listened to Ellen's tearful message. She immediately dialed Ellen back.

"Ellen. Ellen what's wrong?"

"I came home and found … Tom." Ellen choked out the words.

"Found Tom? I don't understand."

"Sandy …" Ellen paused wiping a fresh batch of tears. "Tom's dead."

Sandy gasped, trying to catch her breath. "Oh my God. When? How? Never mind, I'm on my way."

Sandy dabbed her tears with the sleeve of her white shirt, leaving behind black mascara smudges.

"Thank you." Ellen hung up.

Sandy grabbed her keys and purse and flew out the door. She squealed out onto Vicor Road and sped across the city to 1213 Coble Road. The entire way, she fought back her own tears so she wouldn't cause an accident.

Chapter Two

Franki had just arrived home from a tiring twenty-four-kilometer bike ride through the trails of Victoria. After two months on the road doing a book tour, Franki appreciated being home again. She carried her mountain bike inside and up the stairs and was leaning it against the wall when the phone rang. She had just enough time to toss her helmet and grab the receiver before it went to voicemail.

"Hello," she answered, out of breath.

"Hey, girl, you sound out of breath."

"That's because I am. Sparkie, can you give me a second? I'm dying of thirst."

Franki put the receiver down and rushed to get a bottle of water from the fridge. She gulped half the bottle and returned to the phone.

"I'm back," she said.

"So how in hell are you?"

"I'm good, little worn out, but nothing too serious. And you?"

"Same shit, different day. When did you get home?"

"Yesterday morning."

"Do you have time for an old friend?"

"What did you have in mind?"

"I thought you and I could spend the night over here. We can gobble down some greasy pizza, drink some beers, and play catch-up. It feels like years since we've seen each other," Sparkie complained.

"A couple of months."

"Whatever! Get your ass over here, little Miss Famous, or is my offer too boring for you?" Sparkie laughed.

"Shut up. You know as well as I do no amount of money can change me."

"I'm jealous—that's all."

"Get over yourself. Need anything?"

Sparkie laughed, trying to hide her embarrassment. "Yeah, I invite you, but you have to pay."

"Not a problem. I'll see you soon."

"Hey, Franki."

"Yes."

"I've missed you."

"The feeling is mutual." She hit the off button.

Franki took a warm shower, dressed, and then jumped into her brand-new Jeep Wrangler and headed across town to visit her long-time friend Sparkie.

Thirteen stoplights and nine blocks later, Franki arrived at the apartment complex on Tuner Street. She leaped out of the driver's seat and looked up; the sky had begun to turn. Luscious colors of orange and pink grazed the baby-blue sky like arrows. She let out a contented sigh, thankful to be alive.

During the ride up to the third floor, Franki read the graffiti on the walls with amusement. *Everyone always has something to say*, she thought. She stepped out onto the third floor and walked to door number 311. It was ajar. Franki stepped across the threshold, placed the bags on the kitchen counter, and closed the door behind her.

"Sparkie?" Franki called out, looking around. "Sparkie, where are you?"

Sparkie came out of the bathroom and down the hall, wearing summer attire and a big bright grin. Franki's smile quickly vanished.

"Well look at you, Miss Writer."

"Hi." Franki gave her friend a warm hug. "What the hell happened to you?"

"Does it look that bad?" Sparkie tenderly touched the side of her face. "I've tried every shade of powder imaginable. Damn thing, can't hide it." Sparkie shrugged.

"Yes, it looks terrible." Franki furrowed her brow.

"Thanks for the compliment, buddy. Believe me if I told you I fell?"

"Not a chance." Franki shook her head.

"Aw … I screwed up three days ago."

"Want to elaborate."

"Old habits die hard, my friend."

"I'm waiting." Franki folded her arms across her chest.

"Okay, drill sergeant. I'm not like you, okay?"

"Please tell me you didn't go hooking."

"Yes and no. And don't lecture me. I don't need your holier-than-thou shit. Besides, he was cute and seemed pretty normal. Bad judgment on my part. Does normal even exist? I know it doesn't in my world."

"Where did you meet this asshole?"

"Evolutions—where else? Anyway, during our little meet and greet, he seemed really cool, like he was really, really into me. And I guess he was, to his standards. I invited him to come back here so we could keep the hot momentum going. That's when it all turned to shit. Mr. Cutie couldn't get the limp noodle up."

"And—"

"Long story short, the dude was a head case. He started playing rough. A little too rough for my liking, and that's got to say something. Then he started smashing me around, and that gave the freak a woody. I tried to fight back. I think I bit him, but I'm not sure. Everything went to crazy in seconds. He got what he came for, and this is the aftermath of me being stupid. Sometimes I forget where I came from. I'm more pissed because the color here"—she pointed to her shiner—"don't match my pink hair."

"Not funny," Franki scolded. "You could have been hurt worse or even killed. What's his name?"

"Terry, Larry. I don't remember."

"Please tell me you called the police."

"Nope!"

"Why not? The asshole raped you!"

"Yeah, and let's not forget I was the one who invited a total stranger to my place for a night of good wholesome sex. With my record, the judge would throw me in jail, not him."

"Give me a break."

"I was a fucking slave to the streets, Franki. You give me a break, please. You might have forgotten where we came from, sweetheart, but I haven't. Not all of us just walk away from a lifestyle we know!" Sparkie shouted defensively.

"No, I haven't forgotten the street, but I sure as hell grew up though. You choose the life you want to live, not the other way around. It doesn't matter what you did in the past; it doesn't give any asshole the rights to take what he wants at your expense."

"Hey, I'm over it. It happened—can't change a damn thing."

"We're you messed up on blow?"

"Drunk, yes. Cocaine, nope."

"Sweetheart, I wish you would be more careful when you go out."

"Yeah and if wishes and buts were candy and nuts, we'd all have a merry fucking Christmas. So now that we got my love life out of the way, enough about me. It's always the same shit different pile. I want to hear about the big book tour. And don't leave out any details." Sparkie danced to the kitchen to play hostess for the evening.

Chapter Three

The next morning, Franki lounged around in her leather recliner, sipping her morning brew. Her thoughts were on last night's evening with Sparkie and how it brought back memories she'd rather forget. Street life was hard and scary, never knowing from one minute to the next what would happen. She wasn't happy during her confinement at River Edge, but she sure was grateful to have Sandy and Ellen in her life. And when it was time to leave, Sandy stood up to the plate and took her in as her foster child and continued to teach her life skills that would take her to places of sanity and accomplishment. Franki was proud of who she had become today, all thanks to hard work and change.

Franki stared around her loft, feeling at ease to be back home. Two arduous months on the road, different hotel rooms, greasy food, uncomfortable beds, and empty pillows would make anyone appreciate the comforts of home. Until her dying days, Franki would never forget those cold nights huddled up in the alley on the concrete. It was a nightmare she was happy to have awakened from. A slow smile crossed her lips at the recent memory of the look on Ellen's face after she'd given Ellen a painting of the three of them standing in front of the Three-Mile Garden at River Edge, the one she strolled around a million times seeking answers for a better life.

Suddenly she was startled from her reverie by the telephone.

"Hello," she answered.

"Where have you been? I've been trying to reach you all night. Do you not check your phone or what?" Sandy said.

"And a good morning to you too, grouch."

"Franki, I've been trying to get a hold of you."

"And now you have. What's up?" Franki sipped her hot brew.

"I'm afraid I have bad news."

"What kind of bad news?" Franki sat up taller.

"I don't quite know how to tell you, so I'll just say it."

"This doesn't sound good."

"It's not. Tom had a heart attack, Franki."

"Say what?" She set her half-full mug back on the table beside her and leaped out of the chair. "When?"

"Yesterday. That's why I've been trying to get a hold of you."

"Okay, okay." She felt panic rising up in her body like pressure in a steam pipe. "Tell me what hospital, and I'll meet you there. I'm on my way."

"Franki, Tom died yesterday." Silence. "Franki, I'm sorry."

"No! Tom can't be dead, Sandy."

"I'm sorry, honey."

"Doc … Shit! Sandy, Doc. Is … How is Doc?"

"Franki, Ellen is okay. She's doing pretty good under the circumstances. I've been here with her since yesterday."

"I'm coming over."

"Do you want me to pick you up?"

"No, stay with Doc. I'll be fine. I'll be there shortly." Franki thumbed the off button and rushed to her bedroom to get dressed.

Sandy walked out to the patio and looked over the wooden railing. There was Ellen, bent over doing something she hated, gardening.

"Ellen?"

Ellen glanced up. "Hi."

"What are you doing?"

"Do you think Tom would like these lovely chrysanthemums beside the gaillardias?"

"I don't know. He was pretty picky." Sandy smiled, shaking her head.

"You're right. I should plant them next to the lanterns." Ellen paused, trying to decide where the flowers should go.

Sandy started down the steps. "Ellen, Franki is on her way over."

"How did she take the news?"

"As well as to be expected."

"Tom loved her as if she was his own grandchild."

"Franki knew that."

Sandy looked out and saw a white van pulling up the driveway. The logo, Roses Flower Shop, scripted on the side of the van.

At the front door, Sandy took the colorful bouquet from a very handsome, well-built, blond-hair, blue-eyed deliveryman. Her hormones hungrily danced at the sight of him. She quickly thanked him and closed the door before he had a chance to notice her dirty thoughts reflecting in her horny eyes. She then carefully rearranged the flowers in an antique vase and placed them in the middle of the dining room table.

Franki pulled into the driveway and shut off the engine before stepping out. In the few seconds it took Franki to make it to the front door, Sandy was already there with open arms. Together they cried, and then Sandy led Franki through the house and out to the backyard.

"Doc." Franki flew down the steps.

Ellen stood up at the sound of Franki's voice.

"I'm so sorry." Franki wailed in Ellen's arms.

The show of support should have been the other way around, but Doc was Franki's strength no matter what the situation was. Doc said nothing she didn't have to. The grief between them was as evident as the morning sun.

A short while later, Sandy returned to the patio, carrying a tray of goodies to eat. Cheese and crackers, grapes, strawberries, warm croissants, sliced ham, and yogurt. "Hey, you two, come get a bite to eat."

"I'm not hungry. You two go ahead."

"Too bad, Ellen. You're eating a little something, hungry or not," Sandy ordered.

"She can be a real pain in the ass, you know that?" Ellen said.

"Try living with her, Doc." Franki said.

Ellen laughed, following Franki up the patio steps.

That morning, all three sat outside under the beautiful, warm blanket of nature, sharing loving stories of their beloved Tom.

Chapter Four

The homicide detectives, Jim Masker and Dan Kape, were sitting in Jim's Camaro, sipping the newest fad of iced coffee. The Camaro was as unmarked as Jim was willing to go. This summer night was one of the hottest yet. They were dressed casually in shorts and T-shirts with firepower strapped inside their holsters. They did not look like the average detectives.

"How'd the son of a bitch escape from a locked-down mental hospital?" Dan asked more to himself than his partner.

"How in the hell should I know?"

"Sorry, my mistake. How in the hell would you know anything about this case? You were too busy watching strippers grinding on a pole." Dan shook his head.

"What's that supposed to mean?" Jim narrowed his eyes.

"I mean, while you were on vacation, I got stuck with the paperwork you didn't finish."

"Like what?"

"The McCarthy case. Mean anything?"

"Oh."

"Yeah, oh." Dan sucked the cold liquid into his mouth and quietly reviewed the file on his lap.

"You are such a crybaby. Anytime you want to fill me in on this current case, feel free, partner."

"I'll read the report when I'm good and ready. Call me a crybaby, will you."

"Wuss." Jim smirked, taking a loud slurp of his coffee.

Dan Kape had served with the Victoria Police Department for the last seventeen years. He was an honorable man and liked by his peers. His hard work and endless hours sped him through the process from rookie cop to homicide detective. This gave him the privilege of dressing down on hot nights such as this one. Over his seventeen-year career, Dan had experienced the aftermath of some horrific crimes, forcing him to emotionally close off.

Back when Dan was a rookie, he received a domestic violence call. He witnessed his first dead body and what people were capable of doing to one another. A man had killed his wife with an ax. Dan entered the home, saw the woman lying on the floor with an ax handle sticking out of her face, and ran outside and puked. The foul stench of a rotting corpse lingered in his mind for days. When he closed his eyes to sleep, the grizzly vision flashed back, sending him into an awake nightmare. But the violence on the city streets in homes and anywhere else didn't subside; he just learned to live with the scent of death cloying in his nostrils daily and the grizzly visions hidden behind his eyes. Murder clung to his soul like superglue.

Dan, now forty-one, wasn't all that impressed with his thinning hair, deep wrinkles around his eyes, and the excess bulge around the midsection. He had a light heart and loved to joke around, but no one mistook his kindness for weakness. He had a boundary line not to be crossed, and if you did, there were consequences. Like the night he went home early and found his wife in bed with a guy half her age. He beat the hell out of him before tossing his half-naked ass out his front door. Then he calmly packed his belongings and left for good. The next morning, Dan found a small one-bedroom apartment he now called home. His friends at the precinct tried setting him up on blind dates, but that only turned out to be a shit show. He couldn't get past the bitter betrayal of his ex-wife. Instead, Dan put every ounce of energy he had into catching bad guys while rising through the ranks until he reached homicide detective.

Dan's partner, Jim Masker, on the other hand, was known for his womanizing ways. Women to Jim were like an all-you-can-eat smorgasbord at a Chinese buffet. It didn't matter where Jim went; he always had a supply of beautiful women to pick from. He was a thirty-two-year-old adolescent with a Chip and Dale face and masculine frame women couldn't resist. Beyond his arrogant façade, Jim was one hell of a good detective. He could chase a bad guy six city blocks without ever breaking a sweat. And his keen sense for bullshit was remarkable. He could tell when a perp was lying before he or she ever opened their mouth. Like his partner, Jim also had a softer side to his aloof persona. A year and half prior, the two worked a missing child case. Zoë Black was her name. She was eight years old, blonde hair, blue eyes. One week after the abduction and endless man-hours, Zoë was found in a shallow grave eight kilometers from where she had last been seen. The little girl had been sexually assaulted and strangled. Dan and Jim apprehended the scumbag, but it didn't lessen the pain of having to tell Mellisa Black that her baby was never coming home again. That some monster with a sick mind chose her child to get his sick perverted jollies off on. That night, Dan got a call from Barney the bartender at Dooley's Pub, the local watering hole for cops. Dan arrived at the pub and drove his drunk partner home. All the while, Jim slurred he was giving his resignation the following morning. He'd had enough trying to protect innocent people from the scum that lurked everywhere. But Dan knew it was the pain and booze talking. The next morning, Jim arrived at work, feeling like shit and ready to face another day of fighting crime.

Jim slurped the last of his coffee.

"I'm ready." Dan held up his sheet.

"Take it away, maestro."

"This guy is a crafty piece of work. A real ladies' man. Thirty, medium build, blond hair, attractive. Kind of looks like you a bit," Dan mocked.

"Read the damn report, smartass."

"Up until yesterday this wackjob was locked up at River Edge for murdering three young women. Finds his victims in bars and gets them drunk, she goes home with him, and the rest is history."

"Sounds too easy, if you ask me."

"This guy is a major player."

"Okay, so I know how he gets his victims, but what does he do once he has them?"

"You name it."

"Sexual charge?"

"Sarah Miles was raped, beaten, and then stabbed three times. Tyra Field was raped and then stabbed twelve times. Third victim: Clara Howard. She was raped and found with her throat slit."

"I'd say it's sexually motivated. I think he generally hates women," Jim added.

"No shit." Dan lit a smoke.

"Why do you have to smoke in my car, man?"

"Why do you have to nag me?"

"It stinks, and you're polluting my lungs."

"Plug your nose and hold your breath." Dan smirked.

"Show some respect."

"Nag, nag, and nag." Dan flicked his smoke out the window. "That just cost me a quarter."

"You're worth it." Jim laughed.

"Do you want to hear the rest?"

"Continue please, before victim number four turns up dead. Give me a quick rundown on the pathologist report."

"Sarah Miles, contusions found on 60 percent of her body, sexually assaulted, but no semen found. Stabbed three times. This animal takes his time."

"Second victim?"

"Tyra Field, raped, again no semen found, and stabbed twelve times throughout the face, chest, and torso."

"Angry son of a bitch. Third?"

"Clara Howard raped; no evidence found. He cleans up. The animal slit her throat, almost decapitating her."

"What kind of knife?"

"Ivy Frost thinks it was a boning knife, according to her testimony."

Jim felt his stomach swirl. "What's the psychologist report?"

"He's a deranged freak that likes to torture his victims. What else can be said?"

"I am so sick of these money makers wanting to protect these pricks. Oh, he had a bad childhood, his mommy loved him too much, or not enough—bullshit. Try telling that sob story to a victim's family." Jim shook his head. "Anyway—"

"Before you get riled up, orders are to flash his pretty mug shot around, starting with this bar. Maybe we'll get lucky, and somebody has seen the prick." Dan opened his door. "Or he's in there having a cocktail."

"Yeah, right." Jim laughed and climbed out of the driver's side.

The detectives strutted inside Club Galaxy with attitude. They made their way to the bar. The bald-headed, long-bearded bartender with tattoos up his neck asked the detectives what they wanted to drink.

"Nothing for me." Dan flashed his badge.

"What, man? I'm not in violation of anything," he snarled, wiping the bar in circular motions.

"Relax. We're not here to close down your shop," Dan said.

The bartender tossed the rag behind him. "What do you want?"

"Have you seen this guy within the last twenty-four hours?" Dan handed over the photograph of Roger Taut. Bartender man took an uninterested glance. "Nope."

"How about her?" Jim pointed to the waitress, collecting empty glasses off one of the tables.

"Debbie!" Bartender man yelled. "Get over here."

Isn't this moron Mr. Personality, Dan thought.

Debbie crossed the bar, balancing an overloaded tray on her arm. "Hi."

She seemed friendly enough.

"Have a look at this guy and tell me if you recognize him."

She plunked the tray onto the wooden bar and studied the photograph closely.

"Sorry, I would have remembered seeing this one. What's he done?"

"He doesn't like women," Jim warned.

"Too bad! He's a real cutie." She popped her pink bubblegum. "What about you, tall, dark, and handsome? You like women?" Debbie winked. "Want a date?"

"Sorry, on duty." Jim smiled, relieved.

"Too bad." She shrugged.

Dan leaned against the barstool, feeling nauseated by another in-your-face flirtation. Before he threw up, he handed the bartender his card.

"If this guy shows up, call me," Dan ordered, and he and his partner walked out.

Once the detectives were no longer visible, the bartender tore Dan's card in little pieces and tossed it in the garbage.

"Why'd you do that?" Debbie cleared off her tray.

"Don't need the hassle."

"What if—"

"What if nothing. Get back to work."

"Yeah, like I'm so busy." She glanced around the almost empty bar. "Can I get a double rum and coke and a Canadian?" Debbie whispered, "Asshole," and walked away.

Jim leaned against his car, waiting for Dan to finish his cigarette. It was a beautiful night. All kinds of people strolled the city strip. Too hot to stay indoors without A/C.

"That was a lost cause," Jim said, placing his hands behind his head.

"Not for you," Dan teased.

"Give me a break, please."

"What? She was cute."

"Cling on, buddy. One date with Debbie, and she'd be out buying a wedding dress."

"The expert." Dan shrugged. "Come on, Dr. Phil, six bars to go." Dan stomped out his butt.

The detectives were heading a block north from Club Galaxy when Dan's phone rang.

"Kape, go ahead." Dan listened to the dispatcher give a code 187 for homicide. "We're on it."

Jim flashed his lights and sped along the main street doing ninety-five in a forty zone.

"My guess is the creep hasn't left." Dan tossed the folder on the backseat.

Chapter Five

The detectives drove into the apartment complex parking lot on Turner Road. It was located in the lower west side of the city. Dan and Jim jumped out and looked around. This was not a very nice area in the city. The streets were poverty stricken and had plenty of drug dealers, debilitated housing projects, and gang-related crime. The parking lot illuminated the darkness with flashing lights. An eerie dusk had settled in the sky like a sinister mist in a horror film. An unwanted ambulance waited for a body they would not be transporting to the hospital. This victim would be leaving for the morgue in the coroner's van. Nosey Parkers began gathering around the perimeter just waiting to get a sniff of what had happened.

The detectives entered the building and rode the elevator to the second floor. They walked down the dirty-carpeted hallway, stopping at door 202. Dan took out his handkerchief from his back pocket and held it over his nose and mouth before stepping inside where a violent homicide had taken place. The young woman was found dead in her bedroom. She'd been bound with silk scarves at her wrists and ankles. Blood spatters chased their way up the walls and across the ceiling.

"Was this victim sexually assaulted?" Dan asked, moving closer to the body.

"Over and over. I found this beside her battered body." Derk, one of the best forensic specialists on the force, held up a six-inch lead pipe. It had already been bagged in a forensic plastic bag and sealed with crime tape. "I dusted for prints with gentian violet. There may be a partial. I'll know more when I take the pipe back to the lab and place it in a fuming chamber. And I'll know even more when I get all of this evidence bagged, tagged, and back to the lab."

Dan leaned down for a closer inspection of the body. His stomach began to roll at the gruesome sight of the victim's broken body. Her nose and chin were shattered. Contusions and abrasions ran the length of her five-five frame. The deep, visible laceration to the throat showed the sternocleidomastoid muscle had been cut in half. The internal and external carotid artery had also been severed.

Inside the gaping wound in the victim's throat, Dan could see tiny wiggling larvae approximately two millimeters. Lucky for this victim, she'd been found approximately twelve hours after death. If the victim had been found anywhere between fifteen to twenty days after death, the larvae would turn to a pupa and then become an adult fly feasting on the flesh. Dan rose to his feet and coughed back a lump of tar in the back of his throat.

Derk glanced over his black-rimmed glasses. "You okay there, Dan?"

"Yeah, just a tickle in the back of my throat."

"He worked her over good, don't you think?"

"That's putting it mildly." Disgust twisted at the corner of Jim's mouth.

"I'm not trying to be insensitive. Being flip comes with the territory of spending more time with the dead than the living. The beating this woman received—the guy you're looking for hates women."

"You think." Jim sniffed.

"Actually, guys, this case reminds me of the one I worked about seven years ago. He raped, sliced, and diced. Nice fellow landed himself in River Edge for an extended holiday, thanks to that star psychiatrist. I believe her name is Dr. Smith. She was the expert who convinced the jury he was criminally insane. Who was that psycho?"

"Roger Taut."

"That's him." Derk snapped his latex fingers. "Isn't that animal supposed to be locked away at Funny Farm for Freaks?"

Derk guessed he wasn't in some padded room, by the cold expressions on the detectives' faces.

"Do we have an ID on the victim?"

"Josey Moran, twenty-four years young," Derk informed, looking up from the corpse.

"Next of kin?" Jim took out his notepad and scribbled some notes.

"That's for you guys to figure out," Derk said, not missing a detail of the inspection of the body.

"Who called 911?"

"Landlord. Came to collect his damage deposit and found her. Poor guy, he looks pretty distraught."

"Thanks, Derk. Anything else we need to know?" Dan asked.

"I'll give you the pathologist report once the autopsy's done. Or you can come down to the morgue and watch." He smirked under his mask.

"I'll pass; just fax the report." Jim walked to the door, grateful to get the hell out of there. "C'mon, partner, we've got grunt work to do."

Two hours later and more than half the complex questioned, the detectives were no further ahead. How could no one hear the piercing screams of a woman being tortured to death? He understood people were nervous around cops in this neighborhood, but a young woman died a violent death, and nobody helped her.

It felt good to be standing outside. The evening heat had cooled a couple of degrees, making it bearable. A warm breeze dried the sweat off the detectives' faces as they made their way across the parking lot to Jim's Camaro. Dan lit up and leaned against the passenger door. A little stress reliever, he justified.

"You okay?" Jim kicked a stone with the toe of his running shoe.

"I will be once we find psycho boy and throw his crazy ass in prison where he belongs."

"We will. We always do."

"He's one sick fuck—that's for sure." Dan pointed in the direction of the apartment building.

"You won't get an argument from me." Jim walked around to the driver's door and slid behind the wheel.

Dan opened the passenger door, heaved his heavy girth onto the passenger seat, and buckled his seatbelt. Jim, being the show-off, screeched out of the parking lot going way faster than he should have. The detectives headed to the station to begin paperwork and track down invisible leads.

Chapter Six

A round six-thirty that evening, Bill Cobie, a longtime friend and co-worker, walked the coble path to Ellen's front door and rang the bell. Sandy opened the door, wearing her usual pleasant smile.

"Hi, Sandy. Is Ellen awake?"

"Yes she is. Please come in." Bill followed Sandy up the stairs to the living room where Ellen was perched on the couch.

"Ellen, you have company." Sandy's voice carried into the living room.

"Bill." Ellen greeted him warmly. He kissed her cheek, wrapping his arms tightly around her, knowing exactly what kind of emotional turmoil she was suffering.

"Coffee, anyone?" Sandy asked, stepping back into the living room.

"Sure, if it's not too much trouble." Bill smiled.

"No trouble at all." She disappeared back into the kitchen.

Not five minutes later, Sandy returned, setting the tray quietly down on the table, not wanting to interrupt the flow of conversation between Ellen and Bill. She quietly exited the room.

"How are you, honey?"

"I'm not sure." Ellen began to cry.

"Cry all you want, darlin'." He patted her knee.

"I'm tired of crying, but I just can't seem to stop. I have brief moments when I feel like this is all a bad nightmare. Then a wave of reality hits me again, like gale winds in a tornado."

"I know." He spoke with experience. "Oh how I wish I didn't, but I do."

"This ache"—she placed her hand on her chest and took a breath— "is unbearable."

"Remember, I'm here for you."

Ellen blew her nose for about the hundredth time.

"Ellen, is there anything I can do?"

"No, Bill, Sandy is taking good care of me."

"This is a hell of a way to start retirement." Bill gave Ellen a little squeeze on the shoulder and shook his head.

Sandy came back into the living room. "I have a couple of errands to run. Do you need anything while I'm out?"

"Not that I can think of."

"Okay then, I'm off."

"Don't worry. I'll take good care of Ellen. Promise." Bill winked at Sandy.

"Watch out; she's a handful." Sandy laughed.

"Go on." Ellen waved good-bye.

Franki sat cozily curled up on her old tattered recliner. It was her first piece of furniture she'd purchased after leaving River Edge, and she had no intention of ever getting rid of it. Franki held up an old photograph of her family. It had yellowed over the years, but she could still make out the smiles on their faces. Ever so gently, she ran her finger along the outline of her parents and sister, wondering what life would have been like if her parents hadn't died. She let out a sigh of sadness and blinked back her tears. The news of Tom's death brought back a flood of emotions and regret. That relentless sorrow had almost ended her life. If it weren't for Ellen and Sandy's ongoing support, she'd probably be dead right now. Ellen's endless support during the trial of the Wilkins gave her the vindication to stand strong. Sandy adopting Franki gave her the love and stability to begin life anew. The two women loved her and helped her face life on life's terms. Her heart sank, knowing what Doc must be going through. Losing someone you love sucked, and there wasn't anything anyone could do about the longing. All that's left was memories. Franki wiped away the fallen tears, trying to accept the loss of her good friend, Tom Smith.

She glanced around the loft, itching for a distraction, when the easel in the corner caught her eye. A colorless canvas was begging to come alive. She rushed to her bedroom and changed into overalls and then slipped her bare feet into clogs that were speckled with countless colors. Franki tacked the photograph at the top left-hand corner of the canvas and began duplicating the memory with vitality.

Ellen and Bill were on their second cup of java, enjoying as best they could each other's company.

"Are you getting some rest?"

"Days are fine. Nights are hell."

"It's a matter of time, Ellen. Remember when I lost Betty?" Bill shook his head, still feeling the intensity of his loss.

"I do."

"I thought I would shatter into a million pieces. I didn't know how I was going to live without her. And there were times I didn't know if I could."

"You hid your pain well."

"I thought I had to. It's that manly crap, boys don't cry."

"Does it get easier, Bill?"

"Yes, after the initial shock wears off."

26 *Patricia Neary*

"You miss Betty?"

"Every minute of every day, but now I remember only the good times. I was a lucky man to have Betty. She was as much a part of me as I was of her."

"I had an awful dream this afternoon. Tom and I were out sightseeing on Bonger Mountain. Tom slipped, looking over the edge at the river below. I caught him by the wrist, but I couldn't hold on. He was too heavy. I watched him slip away until he disappeared in the river below."

"Ellen, I'm no expert, but I think it's your conscious mind working toward acceptance. You could not have prevented Tom's heart attack any more than I could save Betty from cancer. Do you hear me?"

"It's so damn hard to let go."

Ellen looked away, blinking back another round of grief.

"Time, honey."

"Yes. Time."

Ellen took a sip of her now tepid brew, feeling her stomach swirl. She'd had enough caffeine for one day. The stimulant was making her feel nauseated and jittery.

"Ellen, have the funeral arrangements been made?"

"Yes. Tom's brother and sister are flying in tomorrow morning. The funeral will be the following day."

"Would you like me to pick them up at the airport?"

"Thank you for the offer, Bill, but Franki's got everything under control. It's her way of helping me."

"How is she these days?"

"Relatively healthy, beautiful, and very successful. However, she's still full of piss and vinegar." Ellen chuckled.

"She was one of Blake's victims who are now HIV positive."

"Afraid so. It hasn't hindered her any, I can assure. The best revenge is to succeed in life. That woman is one tough cookie."

"I'm still trying to get my head wrapped around what he's done. Ellen, from the perspective of genius, he was a mastermind. He actually made the virus using sheep visna virus and cattle bovine virus, then combined his own herpes cells and put all three in some dish—or however the monster did it. And when it was ready, he injected the lethal toxin back into his body, knowing it would attack the T-cell, creating HIV or Aids. I mean, who does that?" Bill rubbed his face with his palms. "Then he goes on a sexual rampage destroying patients he took an oath to protect. I'm a forgiving man, but I won't forgive Blake for what he's done. I never will."

"Sandy wants to locate the grave, dig him up, and kill him again."

"Sounds like a plan to me."

"Let it go, Bill. I've had to."

"Okay then." Bill's stomach made a hungry growl. "I really must get going. You going to be okay?"

"Sure, sure. I think I'll go and rest. I'm not as young as I pretend to be." She yawned, trying to mask her pain.

Ellen walked Bill to the door.

"I mean it. You don't have to be brave. Everyone has a breaking point. You need anything—"

"Thanks, Bill." She opened the door and watched him walk along the coble path, head down. He drove out of the driveway before she closed the door and shut the world out.

Ellen placed the tray on the kitchen counter and went to lie down.

Chapter Seven

The following morning, Franki knocked on Ellen's door with her first delivery, Tom's brother Jack. She rang the doorbell again; it had become evident that Ellen and Sandy had slept in. Finally, she heard someone coming down the stairs. The door opened. Franki was right in her thinking. They'd slept in. Sandy's hair looked like she'd stuck her finger in a light socket, and Ellen's didn't look much better. Hers was glued to one side of her head. Sandy took Jack's luggage and placed it in one of the spare bedrooms and then went to the washroom to brush her hair and teeth and splash cold water on her tired eyes before returning to the kitchen somewhat respectable. Ellen, on the other hand, didn't bother.

Jack mirrored his brother, Tom. Ellen gave Jack a big hug and welcomed him to her home. Jack fought back his tears in time. Ellen stepped back to take a good look. Tears misted in her eyes. "Now come on," Jack said. "Don't start or you'll have me going all over again." He patted Ellen on the shoulder. "Is that fresh brew I smell?"

"Sure is," Franki said. "Want a cup of mud, Jack?"

"Certainly."

"Follow me."

All three followed Franki into the kitchen. She took charge getting mugs out of the cupboard, pouring coffee, and getting cream from the fridge.

"I think this girl was a waitress in a past life." Said Jack.

Sandy laughed. "She's a regular Poly Annie, that one."

"Oh, I'm sorry, Sandy, this is Jack. Jack, this is my good friend Sandy." Said Ellen.

"Please to meet you." The two shook hands.

"Thank you for taking such good care of Ellen in this time."

"My pleasure, Jack. I'm so sorry. Tom was a good friend to me and many others."

"He sure was."

Then came a weird, uncomfortable silence when no one knew what to say next. Sandy cleared her throat. "Why don't you guys go out to the patio? I'll bring more coffee and muffins out in a minute."

"C'mon, Jack. I'll show you the backyard. You won't believe your eyes." Ellen beamed with pride.

"The last time I saw the backyard, it was nothing but a bunch of weeds and crab grass."

"It's changed a bit since then," Franki piped up. "You'll be impressed."

Jack leaned over the balcony, and his mouth dropped open with envy; he could not believe his eyes. "My brother did all this?"

"Every flower, shrub, and blade of grass. I swear." Ellen held up her hands.

"Well, I'll be darned. I didn't know he had the patience, let alone the talent. Wow!"

"Chalk it up to retirement," Ellen said.

Jack snickered. "Was my brother that bored?"

"No. He loved being outside with nature. Come on. Let's have a seat, shall we?"

"Don't mind if I do."

Jack took off his ball-cap and placed it beside the chair. Reaching into his shirt pocket, he pulled out a pack of Player's filters.

"Haven't given up that filthy habit yet, I see."

"Don't start. You sound like Tom."

"Look what happened to him, and he didn't smoke." Ellen furrowed her brows. "How was your flight?"

"The coffee was cold, juice warm as piss, and don't get me started on the oatmeal. It could have been wall paste for all I know."

Everyone started laughing.

"So where's the flying nun?"

"Jack, be nice."

"What?" He smirked. "Anyone that dresses in black from head to toe, whatever that thing is called, and decides to give up sex, marriage, and everything else that's normal, I think has some issues. While she's here, maybe you can talk some sense into her."

"Dorthy is just fine; it's you that could use help." Ellen chuckled, placing her hand on top of Jack's.

"On that note, I'll get Jack here an astray." Franki jumped up.

Franki's laughter carried with her to the kitchen.

"Jack needs an ashtray," Franki said to Sandy, still laughing.

"What's so funny?" said Sandy.

"He just called his sister the flying nun. He means no disrespect; it's just the way he says things."

"Ellen wouldn't take too kindly to that."

"She's fine. Want some help?"

"Sure. Can you slice the cinnamon buns?"

"For you, buddy, anything." Franki took a knife from the drawer and began cutting squares.

"Today is the big day, kiddo." Sandy patted Franki on the shoulder.

"I know. I didn't sleep much last night. I'm way too excited and nervous. After all these years, I'm finally going to see my sister. Wow!"

"I am so happy for you." Sandy wrapped her arms around Franki's waist. "You deserve all the happiness and love coming your way."

"Thank you." Franki handed Sandy the cinnamon buns on a plate.

"You carry those please. I have the ashtray."

"Yeah, don't forget the butt tray. If he keeps picking on his sister, he may need it."

Once outside, "Here you go, Jack." Sandy handed him the butt collector and sat down next to Ellen.

"C'mon, Franki, have a seat by me." Jack gestured at the chair next to him.

"Can't. Have to go and get your sister."

"Jesus, you're a busy little bee. You won't miss her; she'll be the one in the pretty black dress with the lovely headdress thingamabob to match," Jack said playfully, rolling his eyes.

Franki popped Jack one in the arm for insulting his sister, telling him to be good before Ellen gave him a lecture he'd soon not forget. And then she dashed down the back steps and out the gate to her Jeep.

A couple hours later, Franki arrived with Dorthy in tow. Tears began flowing like a fountain; that's when Franki and Sandy decided to get lost, giving this brokenhearted family time to grieve.

After Sandy and Franki left Ellen's place, Franki drove her Jeep back to her loft. Sandy followed in behind a couple of seconds later. The two had plans to spend the rest of the afternoon together. They stopped at a local chip truck and picked up lunch before heading to the beach.

Chapter Eight

That afternoon, Franki stood just inside her walk-in closet, leaning against the doorframe, scanning her beautiful wardrobe. She called this space the rod of many colors. Her longtime dream of seeing her sister had finally materialized. A storm of emotions swirled in her stomach, ranging from excitement to calm. Franki was so ready to see her sister, Beth. She selected a Givenchy design to wear. A cream, pleated, short suit with matching open-toe sandals. Pantyhose were out of the question. Franki moved on to the bathroom to touch up her face with a smidge of makeup and smiled in the mirror at the result. She wasn't hard on the eyes, for sure. She took a deep breath and strolled out to the kitchen, where she retrieved her keys, purse, and the gift she'd painted for her sister.

During the drive to Monties' restaurant, Franki had time to think of all she had missed with her sister. It made her angry and sad, but what could she do. The present offered her a new beginning, and she intended to indulge every minute of it. She couldn't change the past; she just hoped Beth had a better life than she did. Living with monsters was a horrible tragedy of the past.

Franki drove into Monties parking lot, killed the engine, and glided across the hot pavement to the front door of the restaurant. The hostess greeted Franki with a welcoming smile. "You must be Franki Martin?" she asked with twinkle in her eye.

"I am."

"There is a beautiful and very anxious woman waiting for you outside on our patio."

Franki could feel her anticipation building with each step closer to the outside patio. The hostess led Franki through the restaurant and outside to Beth's table. The moment Beth spotted her little sister, tears sprang to her eyes. She leaped out of her chair and threw her arms around Franki and began to sob. It felt so natural in so many ways. The server gave them a moment before taking their drink order. Franki, not liking all the attention from the patrons around her, quickly let go of Beth's embrace, pulled out her chair, and took a seat across from Beth. And the two began to talk like when they were youngsters.

Chapter Nine

It was quarter after six when Sandy jolted awake to the sound of the phone ringing on the nightstand beside her head. She fumbled around on the nightstand for the earpiece.

"Yeah," she answered, still in a fog.

"Did I catch you having a nap, sleeping beauty?" mocked Franki.

"You could say that." She wiped drool off her cheek with the back of her hand and swung her legs over the side of the bed.

"Sorry, but I need a favor."

Sandy gave her head a shake and let out a yawn. "What's up, kiddo?"

"I need you to entertain my sister while I go pay my respects. Mind?" Franki never minced words.

Sandy sprang to her feet in one motion, hearing a loud crack at the backdoor. It sounded like someone was trying to force his or her way into her house.

"Franki … hang on. I think someone is trying to break in. Hang on."

Franki froze, fearing the worst. She and Beth had just finished watching the news. A serial killer, Roger Taut, had escaped from River Edge. He'd been incarcerated at the Edge for brutally slaying three women, seven years prior.

"Give me a second," Sandy whispered into the mouthpiece, throwing the receiver onto the bed. Halfway down the hall, she stopped mid-step, hearing the loud crack come again. Inside her chest, her heart crashed fiercely against her ribs, threatening to break a bone at any minute. She had to force herself to suck in air. She quickly moved into the living room and grabbed a metal poker from its stand beside the wooden stove. Armed and ready, she crept to the backdoor and crouched against the wall. "I'm armed, asshole!" she shouted as loud as she could.

Sandy waited for another bang to come, which would have taken the door off the hinges. Her imagination went into creepy overdrive. She envisioned a masked man breaking through the rest of the splintered door, wielding a six-inch butcher knife, with empty eyes and a thirst for murder. A disturbing wave of warning filled the air. Then silence. The seconds ticked by slowly, until finally she could uproot her feet from the floor. She was no longer frozen in a crouched position. She rushed from window to window, peeking outside. No one. She breathed a sigh of relief. She hoped she had scared away whoever it was at the door. Then she remembered that Franki was still on the phone. She hurried back into her bedroom and grabbed the phone off her bed.

"Franki." No answer. "Franki. Franki, are you still there?"

She pushed the on button a couple of times, trying to bring back the connection. Lifeless. *That's odd. I tell her someone's at my backdoor, and she hangs up,* she thought, shaking her head as she made her way to the kitchen for a drink of water.

Sandy had no idea Franki and Beth were racing across town to her place.

A twenty-minute drive over to Sandy's house turned into ten and a half.

Franki roared through the city like a fire truck. She ran one red light and nearly ran over a pedestrian crossing on the crosswalk. She cared but had no time to stop and apologize. She was on a mission. Once Franki Martin got something in her head, it was unlikely she would change her mind, be it right or wrong.

Franki roared into Sandy's driveway and jumped out of the Jeep, engine still running. She sprinted to the front door like an Olympian. Franki pounded hard on the door until Sandy opened it. That's when she grabbed hold of her foster-mom like she hadn't seen her in a million years. Sandy didn't know what the hell was wrong with Franki. She'd never seen her act this way.

"Jesus Christ, Sandy, you scared the shit out of me," Franki said.

"I'm fine. My question is why are you the one acting like a lunatic? It was my place that someone tried to break in to."

Meanwhile Beth, seeing Sandy in all her form at the front door, calmly shut the engine off and proceeded up the walkway to the front steps.

"You didn't hear?" Franki asked, looking more frazzled than Sandy.

"Hear what? I was sleeping, remember?" Sandy rubbed her tired eyes.

"I'll tell once we are inside." Franki practically pushed Sandy back inside the open doorway.

Once inside, Franki decided to do a sweep of Sandy's place first. Before trotting off, she yelled, "Sandy, this is my sister, Beth. Beth, this is my foster-mom, Sandy Miller." The ladies shook hands. Franki moved through the house, first checking the phone, and then made her way to the backdoor. Wood splinters littered the floor. It was clear someone wanted inside Sandy's house. Franki walked back into the living room where both Sandy and Beth were standing wide-eyed and bewildered.

"The phone is dead," Franki said.

"What do you mean dead? I thought you hung up on me."

"No, I didn't. The next time someone is breaking into your house, I strongly suggest you take the damn phone with you. What the hell were you thinking? I know you weren't. You need to call the police and report this. That backdoor is no joke."

"Well, you freaking out is not helping me, Franki." Sandy looked down and realized she still held the poker in her hand. "Relax. Whoever it was that tried to get in is gone now." She placed the poker back in its holder. "It was probably a bunch of kids with nothing better to do."

"Well, while you were taking a beauty siesta, Beth and I watched the six o'clock news. Not good. Did you know that a maniac escaped from River Edge a day ago? A Roger … someone or other." Franki waved a dismissive hand.

"His name is Roger Taut, Franki," Beth said, still as calm as she had been.

"You can't stay here. Not with the backdoor hanging on its hinges."

"I know it's a bloody mess. Now I have to buy a new door, damn it."

"That's it. If you're not going to call the police, I will." Franki took out her cell and dialed 911.

Franki was a little whirlwind. All Sandy had wanted to do was come home, take a nap, have a beer, and relax in peace. Ellen was in good hands with Jack and Dorthy staying with her. Neither of them had had a decent night's sleep since Tom's passing. Everything had happened so quickly she hardly had time to catch her breath when Storman Norman arrived to save the day.

"I need a beer. Care for one, Beth?" Sandy asked.

"Please."

Beth followed Sandy to the kitchen.

Franki put her finger over the mouthpiece of the phone. "None for me, thanks."

Sandy smirked. "I wasn't asking you. Besides, you're the one stressing the hell out of me. Racing over here like a madman with his ass on fire, and then you want me to give you a beer."

Beth started laughing; she understood Sandy's frustration all too well. Franki grew up separately from her sister since the tragic death of their parents, but the drama hadn't changed in Franki's life. She was the same hyper Franki she'd always been, just more rough around the edges than Beth had remembered.

"Let's not forget the red light she raced through or the guy on the crosswalk she almost took out," Beth said.

Franki gave her a look.

"Thank you … That will be just fine. We'll be waiting." Franki slapped shut her cell phone. "This is the appreciation I get for giving a shit. You are lucky I showed up when I did."

"Thank you for caring, Franki. It's just you need to take the concern down a notch. I'm fine." Sandy did a twirl in the kitchen. "No harm."

Franki left the kitchen and strolled back into the living room. She stood in full view of the front picture window trying not to lose patience. What the hell was taking the cops so long? *Glad no one was hurt or dying*, she thought. When it came to the people Franki cared about, she was somewhat pushy, but it was only because she couldn't bear to lose someone else in a senseless way. She'd lost enough loved ones in her young lifetime and wasn't about taking chances, no matter how small the crisis.

Beth and Sandy stood at the backdoor, staring at the undeniable evidence of a botched break-in. Splinters of wood littered the beige linoleum floor. A huge crack lined the middle of the door. The doorframe hung on a broken hinge, not to mention the lock was beyond bent.

"Forgive me for being intrusive, I know we just met, but by the destruction I see before me, it's not safe for you to stay here, especially alone," Beth said.

"I'll make my decision after I talk to the police."

"It's not the police you have to worry about." She smiled and took a sip of her beer. "Franki will not allow you to stay here, no matter what the police say."

"Don't remind me. Sometimes she thinks she's my parent, rather than the other way around. She can be such a pain in my ass." Sandy looked at Beth, an older version of Franki.

"Franki loves you. You saved her life," Beth said.

"Franki is the daughter I never had."

"She told me you adopted her after …"

"River Edge. I certainly did. And I don't regret a second of it. Franki needed to be given a break, and I was just the one willing to do it. She is a great kid."

"Thank you for helping my sister. I wished I'd been there for her."

"I know, but now you two have a lifetime of being there for each other." Sandy hugged Beth. "I think we should go see what grouchy is up to."

"Hide your weapons. We all know what she's capable of." Beth laughed as the two sauntered into the living room to wait for the police to arrive.

Chapter Ten

Franki was the first one on her feet when she heard a car door slam and then another. She looked out the picture window, eyeing a metallic Camaro parked behind Sandy's Beamer. She watched as two men slowly made their way to the front door.

"Tell me again, why are we taking a break in call when there is a serial freak loose in the city, perhaps killing women?" Detective Jim Masker groaned at his partner.

"Because the captain doesn't think we have anything better to do? How in the hell would I know? I'm just following orders." He shrugged.

"You'd think we were door-to-door salesmen. I thought we were supposed to be doing detective work, like finding the guy responsible for killing Josey Moran."

"Makes two of us." Dan knocked at the front door.

Franki did the honors and greeted the detectives.

"I'm Detective Kape, and this is my partner, Jim Masker."

"Can I see some identification please?"

The detectives pulled out their badges.

"Come in." Franki stood aside, allowing the two men to enter.

These two guys are as different as night and day, Franki thought, looking at the better-looking one.

"Okay, ladies, who is the owner of this home?" Dan questioned, taking out his notepad from his shirt pocket.

"That would be me." Sandy raised her hand.

All three gathered around the two men dressed in casual clothing. "And you reported someone trying to break in to the house?"

"I made the 911 call." Franki raised her hand.

"It's not a real break in. I mean whoever tried to get into my house didn't succeed." Sandy tried to explain.

"Oh." Dan appeared puzzled.

"I mean, I heard someone trying to get in, but ..."

"So you were home at the time?"

"Yes. I was taking a nap. I heard a big bang at the back of the house and went to check."

"So it wasn't a dream." Detective Masker smirked.

"No. I was awake at the time, talking to my daughter here on the phone." She pointed at Franki. "And that's when I heard it."

"Ladies, why don't you have a seat on the couch. My partner and I are going to take a look around and make sure no one is lurking around your house," Detective Dan said politely, seeing the tension in his partner's eyes.

"By all means help yourself. The damage is at the backdoor."

"Officers, I can't get a signal on any of Sandy's phones," Franki said. "Might want to check that out while you're at it."

"We will. And we're not called officers; we're detectives," Jim said.

"Excuse me," Franki spat back with the same irritation.

Isn't she a bitch, Jim thought, walking away.

"Looks like you've met your match, buddy. That woman is not only drop-dead gorgeous, she also seems not to like you. That's a good sign," Dan whispered and then laughed.

Sandy went back to pacing in front of the picture window.

"Franki, try and be nice," she said.

"Why?"

"Oh I don't know—because they're here to help." Deep wrinkles formed between Sandy's brows.

Franki plopped her ass down next to Beth and stole a swig of her beer. Sandy stopped pacing and went to the couch to join the other ladies. All three watched in silence as the detectives walked out the front door and returned the same way a short while later.

"So what's the verdict?" asked Franki.

"There are tracks leading from the woods at the back of your house to the backdoor," Detective Masker said. "We can't tell who it was, but no one is there now. The wire from the street pole that runs to your house supplying your telephone service has been deliberately cut from the outside. I've notified the company. They should be here shortly to reconnect the line, with of course a service charge added to your bill." Sandy rolled her lovely green eyes. "And no doubt, Miss Miller, you'll need a new backdoor. My advice is to find a place to stay tonight and order a new door as soon as possible. We'll have a police officer patrol the area and make sure all is quiet. We don't want whoever it was to succeed in his second attempt to rob you. Get a new door put on as soon as possible. For tonight, nail what's left of your door closed."

Dan made himself comfortable on the footstool. "Miss Miller, when you looked outside, did you see anyone?"

"No."

"Do you have any enemies?"

"Not that I'm aware of." Sandy shrugged her shoulders, surprised by the question. "Detectives, not that I'm trying to downplay this situation, but I think it was kids trying to get in and steal stuff. When I yelled, they took off."

"You may be correct, but it would take a whole lot of power to put a crack down the middle of the door. The concerning part is this: someone deliberately cut your telephone line. That's a warning to me that someone didn't want you having access to help. Kids looking to steal …" Dan shook his head. "They don't have criminal know-how to be messing with telephone lines."

Detective Dan Kape let his words hang in the air for a moment.

"So you're saying this is serious?" Sandy asked.

"I'd say so."

"I told you. Didn't I tell you?" Franki slapped her hand on her knee.

"Who would want to hurt me?" Sandy pulled at her sweaty hands, reality now settling in.

"You are not hanging around here to find out. You're coming to my place until that door is fixed with a thousand dead bolts on it." Franki's neck webbed with high blood pressure.

"Miss Miller, where are you employed?" Detective Kape inquired.

"River Edge Mental Institution. What does that have to do with this?"

Sandy's employment sent up red flags to the detectives.

"Are you familiar with a patient, Roger Taut?"

"Not personally. I work on the second-floor ward. Mr. Taut is housed on the secured fourth floor."

"Then you know he's escaped?"

"I'm afraid I had no idea. My friend's husband just recently passed away, so I've been taking care of her."

"But you do know why he was institutionalized?"

"Yes I do. Detective, what does his incarceration—or lack of, at this point—have to do with my current situation?"

Sandy took a swig of beer, trying to relax her nerves.

"We are covering all bases, ma'am," Jim piped up.

Franki crossed one leg over the other, trying to get comfortable. "Do you think this break-in has anything to do with Roger's escape and Sandy's employment?" she asked.

"Yeah, should we be scared?" Beth asked.

"My only advice is to be careful. A young woman was murdered last night in her apartment on the west side of the city. We can't say for sure if it was Roger Taut, but as of now, he is a person of interest," said Dan.

"How was she killed?" Franki asked.

"I can't comment on that."

Franki sat up straight, ready for the answer. "The anchorwoman said the victim found in her apartment had been brutally murdered."

"The media has a tendency to blow things out of proportion," Jim lied.

Sandy stood up off the couch. "Detectives, if there isn't anything else, I'll go pack some of my belongings. I'm not staying here tonight." She sighed.

"I'll come help you, Sandy." Beth tagged along.

Franki opened the front door to show the gentlemen out when Detective Jim Masker had a light-bulb moment at the sudden recognition. "Aren't you the author, Franki Martin?"

"In the flesh." She flashed her pearly white smile at Mr. Gorgeous.

"I've read one of your novels."

"Which one?"

"*Blackness Strikes Twice.*"

"What did you think?"

"I loved it. I could really identify with Owen. Maybe we could have dinner sometime and discuss the book in more detail," Jim said, stroking Franki's ego.

"Here," Franki said, "let me give you my card. It also has my e-mail address. You'll find the synopsis to my next novel, *Hidden Secrets.* Tell me what you think. And then I'll let you know about having dinner with you."

"I will," Jim said.

Franki stood in the doorway watching as Detective Masker nearly fell on the stairs. She had to admit she had a small crush on Mr. Attitude. She opened the door, trying not to laugh. "Hey, you okay?"

"Great, thanks." Jim's cheeks flushed red with embarrassment. "Bye for now." He gave a wave.

Franki shook her head and closed the door.

The detectives made it safely to the Camaro. Dan opened his door. "*I could identify with Owen.*" He had you're-a-bull-shitter written all over his pudgy face. "Have you even read *Blackness Strikes Twice?*"

"The synopsis." Jim grinned, sliding behind the wheel of his car.

"I've never seen you even pick up a book, let alone read one. You are one sly prick. But Miss Martin is a smart cookie; she'll catch on to you real quick."

"It's simple, Danny Boy. Now I'll buy the book, read the first couple of chapters of the beginning, middle, and end. Miss Martin will be putty in my hands."

"Don't count on it. Miss Martin has a whole lot of attitude, buddy. And she's not a pole rider."

"I'll bet you a hundred bucks I have a date with Miss Author by next weekend."

"Deal. I just scored an easy hundred bucks. That nice-looking young woman in there"—he pointed to the house—"will run rings around you and leave you choking in her dust."

"It's all in the approach, my man."

"I'll believe it when I see it." Dan buckled his seatbelt. "C'mon, there's a briefing in twenty-five minutes, and Captain Barlow will be pissed if we're not ready."

"Maybe he should stop sending us out like fucking errand boys. This call had nothing to do with Taut."

"And you can tell him that." Dan laughed. Jim liked to talk big when the captain wasn't around.

Once the backdoor had been secured with nails and rolls and rolls of a handyman's finest tool, duct tape, they were ready to leave. Sandy took her car, with Beth as her passenger, and drove across the city to the loft. Franki drove in the opposite direction to McKay Funeral Home to pay her respects to a man she loved and adored. Tom Smith, may he rest in peace.

Chapter Eleven

Back at headquarters and bagged tired, the two detectives sat behind their desks waiting to be summoned by Captain Barlow. Dan was on the computer checking to see who could have the means to harbor such a madman as Roger Taut. He checked and rechecked and then printed out a list of all Roger's relatives and anyone affiliated with him dating back seven years ago. The detective was trying to piece together where Roger would go to hide. The nine bars Dan and his partner went to turned up nothing. No one had seen a hide or hair of the suspect in question since his escape from River Edge. That didn't mean they hadn't seen him; it just meant they weren't telling the police anything.

Dan glanced up, eyeing his partner at his desk. His feet were on the desk, head leaning against the back of his chair, eyes scanning a book. He could not believe what he was seeing; nothing like the comforts of home. *No way*, thought Dan. The chair squeaked as he moved his pudgy frame out of his seat and rounded Jim's desk.

"Comfy?" Dan scowled, kicking his chair.

"Yeah, why?" He put the book on his lap and glanced up at the figure towering over him.

"What in the hell are you doing?"

"Reading." He smirked.

"Reading what?"

"*Blackness Strikes Twice*." He held the book up.

"On company time, no doubt."

"What are you, my chaperone now? I was just taking a glimpse."

"Yeah, why don't you take a goddamn glimpse at the case we're working on? You know, the criminal psychopath piece of garbage that destroyed that young woman over on the west side. Your love life can wait."

"What's gotten into you, grump?" Jim opened his desk drawer.

"In case you haven't noticed, Romeo, we—as in you and me"—he pointed at Jim and then back to himself—"have a killer to stop."

"I know."

"Then help me out and find us a lead, would ya? Jesus Christ, it's not like he's going to walk in here and turn in his sorry ass, now is he? Because if he does, so help me God, I'll kiss your hairy ass in front of everyone in this room. Now put your nose where it belongs."

Jim tossed the work of fiction inside the drawer and closed it with his foot. At that moment, Captain Barlow yelled from his office doorway.

"Don't forget the file," Dan barked at Jim and then grabbed the printout off his desk, sending papers flying to the freckled linoleum floor. He cursed, bending down to pick them up. Then he stomped across the room to the captain's office.

Dan closed the door and took a seat next to his partner.

"Any news on Taut?"

"So far nothing, sir. Taut is a ghost. None of his groupies have heard from him. I've made a list of all his relatives and friends from seven years back." Dan flicked the pages in his hand. "I'll check them out as soon as we're done here," Dan said.

"Sir, no offense, but no more sending us out on break and entry. It's a waste of our time," Jim said.

"Don't tell me how to do my job."

"Fine, it's just—"

"Nothing. What do you have to contribute to this case, since you know so much?"

"A date with an author." Dan groaned.

"That would explain why you have nothing for me except excuses. I have uniforms combing the city in search of this prick, and my two leading detectives are coming up with squat." The captain leaned over the desk. "Now get out of here and find me something."

"One more question, sir. Are Harry and Derk finished with Josey Moran?" Detective Masker asked.

The captain searched the papers and files on his desk.

"Nothing came in yet. Why don't you two leading ladies take a trip to the morgue and see how far Harry has gotten with the autopsy."

"I hate that fucking place. It stinks. It's dark. It's just nasty." Jim gave his head a shake and rose out of his chair.

"And I hate murderers, Detective. Now find this guy before another young woman ends up dead."

"Got it." Jim couldn't get out of the captain's office fast enough. Getting reamed a new asshole was enough for one day.

Dan rolled the sheets into a paper tube, and they made their way out the front door to the waiting Camaro parked in the underground lot. Jim hadn't wanted to spend another minute in Captain Barlow's office, but the morgue wasn't that appealing either. This case was beginning to grate on everyone's nerves. And no one had a lead to the whereabouts of Roger Taut.

Chapter Twelve

O nce the detectives arrived at the city morgue, Dan took the time to have a quick smoke before entering the edifice of eternity. Dan and Jim crossed the threshold through the gray iron basement door and proceeded down a labyrinth of eggshell-colored, aged brick walls and speckled tiled floors until they came upon Harry's office. Harry Barclay was Victoria's top pathologist and had a somewhat staid sense of humor. Then again, what could be funny about cutting into dead bodies every day? Dan paused, wondering if Derk might be assisting Harry with Josey Moran's autopsy. There was only one way to find out.

Jim knocked. No answer. He knocked again. The silence was creepy.

"Okay. Nobody's home. Time for the tour, shall we?" Dan motioned for his partner to take the lead.

"Why me?" Jim scowled.

"Because it was your idea to piss off the captain. If you hadn't opened that big yap of yours and bitched about the B&E call, we'd be sitting in someone's living room, probably being offered a cold beverage. Instead we're down here with the dead people. Asswipe." Dan shoved his partner down the corridor.

The detective grudgingly led the way to the end of the corridor and then took a right and a left. There at the end of the hallway stood a black steel door. Dan pulled it wide and descended down a flight of concrete stairs into the soulnessness of the building. The further down they went, the colder it felt. Goose bumps rose up like spikes on Jim's arms. The scent of death grew all around them like a Nova Scotia fog, thick as paper. Straight ahead at the end of the hallway stood a set of oscillating steel doors. The detectives glanced at each other and began counting the footsteps to their destination.

Dan opened the door and poked his head inside. The core of the autopsy area was a lot brighter than any of the ominous corridors the detectives had just traveled.

"Hey, Harry. Derk. You guys busy?" Dan yelled from just inside the door.

"Having a party with the dead. Why?" Harry looked up from one of the sparkling sinks.

"Any news on the Moran party?"

"C'mon in and close the door. You're letting out all the smell." Harry smirked.

"I'm just going to the cooler now, guys. Good timing." Derk walked away.

"Plan on staying for the party?" said morgue man Harry.

"You could say that," Jim said, feeling Dan's eyes burning holes in his skull.

"Suit up and you'll have the answers you seek before I take out her organs." Harry removed his mask. "How's that for satisfactory?"

"Got nothing else to do. Right, numb nuts?" Dan gritted his teeth.

Derk came out of the cooler, wheeling the body on a portable gurney.

"Here we go." Jim threw his up his hands. "Time to piss and moan. Like *you've* never pissed off Captain Barlow."

"Ah, lovers' spat?" Derk laughed.

"Nope. Dumb as a stump here decided to piss off the captain, so he sent us here," Dan said.

"If I didn't know any better, I'd say these boys are being punished, Harry." Derk jacked up the gurney.

Jim turned to his partner. "Are you going to be like this all day?"

"If you had kept your trap shut—"

"Yeah, yeah—I got it!"

"Can't you feel the love, Harry?" The pathologist laughed and shrugged his shoulders.

"Dan is such a bitch when he doesn't get his own way," Jim said.

"These two remind me of an old married couple," Derk said, rolling the victim onto the cold table.

"You two bitches go suit up. I don't have time for a therapy session. I have work to do," Harry ordered with authority and then smirked as he returned to the table where he gently placed the back of the victim's skull onto the head block.

In the room across the hall, Dan remained quiet as he suited up in plastic gowns, booties, and rubber gloves. Jim dabbed Vicks ointment below his nostrils and sealed the mask to his face. Dan never bothered; the scent of death blending with menthol only exacerbated the smell of the decaying corpse for him.

By the time both detectives reentered, Derk had the naked corpse prepped and ready. The forensic genius had just finished taking a second set of film. Harry was busy collecting any trace evidence left behind on the body. Then he clipped the victim's manicured fingernails, placing the tips in a white envelope.

The detectives watched closely as every piece of evidence was dexterously collected, bagged, sealed, and properly labeled for the forensic lab to view.

Now it was time for Josey to be sprayed down. Jim eyed the long, crimson streamers snake down the table and disappear into a drain at the end of the cold table. Dan found this procedure so unfair. Josey Moran was unable to defend herself against her attacker, and here one last time, she had succumbed to the powerlessness of strangers' eyes and probing hands. An ID tag tied to her big toe exhibited how methodical and unsympathetic these rooms seemed to be. It was contrary to popular belief; these seemingly strange men and women did care about the dead. That's what drove these devoted specialists to work day and night in search of answers the dead could not give. They gave up time with families, fresh air, and sunshine. Instead of happy faces in their dreams, they saw dead, blue faces with pleading eyes. All in the name of justice.

Josey had been digitally photographed at the crime scene. At the morgue, however, she would undergo two more rounds of film. These shots would be full-length images front and back. Also close up images of any injuries, cuts, and identifiable marks, such as tattoos or birthmarks. All evidence at the victim's apartment had already been collected, placed on white paper sheets, rolled, and taken to the lab to be analyzed.

Once the blood had been washed away, it became evident that Josey Moran had been tortured to death. Big, strong, nothing-bothers-me Detective Dan turned away. His mouth went as dry as cotton. Jim could feel the perspiration collecting inside his gloved hands. The victim's once beautiful face had been savagely battered. The monster responsible for her tragic end made sure Josey experienced mortal terror. Her upper and lower teeth were knocked out. He broke her nose, fractured her left eye. Lips cut, bruised, and three times the normal size. The contusions, abrasions from being dragged from room to room, and lacerations marred 95 percent of her body. Her throat had a wide gash, exposing her sternocleidomastoid muscle, severing the main carotid artery. Josey bled out.

Harry stepped up to the middle of the table. "If you want answers, now is the time to ask."

"Cause of death?" Dan asked.

"The pig finally killed her by severing the carotid artery. Detectives, this poor girl was alive when the animal violently assaulted her with the pipe. Even if she hadn't died when he opened her throat"—Harry swallowed a lump of anger—"she would have expired from internal bleeding. Do you gentlemen want to hang around for the dissection? I think we will find that her insides equal her outsides."

"Derk, were you able to get a full print on the pipe?" Jim asked, rocking on his heels.

"I found epithelial tissue and blood cells from vaginal tearing on the cervix wall. No prints."

"Facial fragments, such as zygomatic and ethmoid, are now floating inside her skull from the massive blows to the face." Harry was kind enough to show the images on the light box.

"The bastard tore her apart!" Dan's anger whirled like a potter's wheel.

"This is probably one of the most vicious beatings I've seen come through my morgue," Harry said.

"Jesus, Harry. Did you have to tell me that? Dan said while shaking his head.

"Did you find a hair, a piece of fluff, anything that could connect our escapee to the murder scene?" Jim asked, trying not to breath in corpse stench.

"Everything I collected at the scene has been taken to the lab. The samples just collected will be taken as soon as we're finished," Derk replied.

Harry picked up the scalpel. "If you guys are already feeling queasy, I suggest you step outside. The last thing I need in here is a pool of vomit." The pathologist was ready to cut a Y shape into the victim.

"You know what, Harry, Derk, I think I will leave now. Fax the rest of the report, will you. I have some people to check out." Dan quipped.

"Fair enough. I'll call over if we find anything special to report," Harry said, placing the blade below the clavicle bone.

The detectives went across the hall, undressed, and got the hell out of there.

Chapter Thirteen

ranki fought back the tears as she slowly made her way down the aisle to the casket. It had been a good many years since she stepped foot inside a funeral parlor. It had the ripe scent of flowers and bereavement that left her wanting to bolt to freedom. Freedom from pain, loss, and sorrow. Without warning, a vivid image of both her parents in closed caskets flashed across her mind, leaving her knees feeling like rubber. She stopped to take a breath before continuing on.

She gave her condolences first to Jack and then Dorthy. By the time she made it to Ellen, her bottom lip was quivering so much Franki thought it was going to vibrate off her face. Ellen held her like only Ellen could. Moments later, Franki settled down. The worst was over. It was time to step up to the shiny redwood casket. Tom lay still on a bed of puffy white silk, his black pinstriped suit tailored to perfection. She placed her hand on top of Tom's hand, flinching at the coldness of his skin. Tears spilled from her eyes and down her cheeks, dropping off her chin. She wiped them away with the back of her hand as fast as she could. But there was no keeping up with the stream of loss. Franki was going to miss her friend Tom. Their special nights sitting outside on the patio gazing up at the star-filled sky, talking about anything and everything. Tom, being the optimistic one, never let Franki give up hope on her life. He knew she had great potential. Before her final good-bye, she asked Tom when he got to the other side if he could tell her parents she missed them. Then pressing her finger to her lips, she touched his cheek and mouthed the words, "I love you, my friend." Tears flowed from her pretty sapphire eyes, expressing how much she would miss him.

Franki jumped when Ellen touched her on the shoulder.

"Sorry, honey, I didn't mean to startle you. Want to sneak upstairs and have a coffee with me?" Ellen whispered in Franki's ear.

"Sure." Franki wiped her nose on a tissue.

Arm in arm, away they went. Franki did the honor of pouring coffee into white Styrofoam cups, adding cream to Ellen's. After placing the cups on the table, she took a seat next to Ellen on the leather sofa.

"How are you holding up?" Franki asked, feeling composed.

"I'm doing the best I can. Is everything okay with you?"

"Sorry I'm late."

"Problem?" Ellen raised her gray eyebrows.

"I guess." Franki sipped her black brew and made a face. "Who made this shit? It tastes like … never mind."

"What do you mean, you guess?"

"Not now, Doc."

"Franki?"

Nothing ever got past Dr. Smith. It was as if she had invisible feelers that sensed when something was off beam.

"I'm not bothering you at a time when you need us. Christ, will you give yourself time to grieve?" Franki crisscrossed her legs.

"I'm grieving, don't you worry. I'll be the judge of what I can and can't handle in my time of need. Now stop stalling."

"Fine." Franki sighed. "Someone tried to break into Sandy's place. The backdoor is all smashed to hell. She's not allowed to stay at her place alone. She either stays with you or she stays with me. The police suggested it."

"Sandy's not hurt, is she?" Ellen's heart skipped a beat.

"Scared yes, hurt no. She tried to put on a brave face. You know how she gets. But I could see right through that bullshit. She was pretty shaken up. And someone cut her phone line. When I arrived, I called the police because she hadn't. You know her; doesn't want to bother anyone. I don't know what she was waiting for." Franki rubbed her neck. "It's not like the fairy police were going to float to her place and ask if she'd been robbed." A half smirk unfurled around Franki's mouth.

"What did the police say?"

"Don't stay home alone and order a new door."

"That's it?"

"Yeah pretty much. And they called the telephone company to come and hook up Sandy a new line."

"I take it Sandy's staying with you then." Ellen smirked at Franki's parenting skills.

"You bet. Hey, do you remember a patient by the name Roger Taut?"

Ellen swallowed hard, fearing what was to come. If Ellen lived a million years, she would never forget him. The fine hairs on the back of her neck bristled. Her eyes tried to hide trepidation, but it was no use. Franki saw right through Ellen's alarm.

"Where did you hear that name, Franki?"

"He escaped from the Edge. It's all over the news. They say he's one dangerous dude."

"When … when did you hear this?" Ellen had a look of seriousness Franki hadn't seen before.

"The six o'clock news. No joke. And the detectives that came to Sandy's place confirmed it and warned us to be careful. Watch your surroundings, don't go out alone, and stuff."

"Pay heed to their warning. Roger Taut is delusional and high-risk dangerous."

"The police didn't go into detail, but a woman was murdered in her apartment on the west side. They couldn't be sure it was that Roger dude, but they weren't saying it wasn't either."

"Roger was found guilty of murdering three young women seven years ago. The court sentenced him to River Edge for an undisclosed period of time. According to court documents, Roger was never to be released. This man is highly unpredictable and blends in well. The police no doubt will have a hard time catching him. What are the police doing?"

Franki spotted the glimmer of professional craving in Doc's eyes, like a window had just opened, letting in the soft, warm breeze.

"And you never mind, Nosey Nancy. Don't even think about what I think you're thinking. You are officially retired now, shrink. Your time has come and gone, my dear. Pay heed to my words now."

"Don't give me that speech, Franki," Ellen said. "I'm not getting involved unless I'm invited."

"And if you have anything to do with it, it might be as soon as you leave here. Doc, please, you need to get some rest."

"Thank you for all your love and concern." Doc placed her age-spotted hand on Franki's cheek. "I love you, kid. So are the three of you coming tomorrow for an early brunch before we go to the gravesite?"

"That's the plan."

"Okay then, I should get back down stairs. I'll have Jack escort you to the Jeep."

"Doc, please. I don't live the street life anymore, but I haven't forgotten how to survive either."

"I worry about you. Sometimes I think your confidence is a mistake for cockiness. Could that be possible?"

"I disagree," Franki said, opening her purse and exposing her 22-caliber handgun hiding at the bottom. "I travel, Doc. I need my own protection."

"Where did you get that?" Ellen whispered sharply. "And I suppose you know how to use it."

"I've taken lessons. I wouldn't want to be the asshole in front of the bullet; let's put that way." Franki laughed.

"Be careful tonight. I'll lecture you tomorrow."

"Don't worry, Doc. Cautious is my middle name." Franki leaned over and kissed Ellen on the cheek. "I know how to take care of me."

"Good to hear! Jack is still walking you out to the Jeep. Not a word about it." Ellen shook her finger at Franki.

"Not like I can win this argument anyway." Franki shrugged. "Tell the morgue man the coffee sucks."

"I'll put that on my list of priorities." Ellen rolled her eyes and patted Franki's shoulder. "Get going."

At the front door of McKay's Funeral Home, Franki said her good-byes with the promise of seeing them all tomorrow.

Jack opened Franki's door and lit a smoke.

"You guys still coming over tomorrow?"

"Wouldn't miss the pleasure of your company, Jack. What's the matter? You board with the two old dolls?" Franki smirked.

"As much as I love Ellen and Dorthy, they're way too serious."

"And you are the class clown. Great combination, Jack."

"What are you ladies up to tonight?"

"Getting drunk. Come on over if you like."

"I better supervise serious-lee and serious-lou. I'm like the balance between two thunderclouds."

"Like the rose between two thorns, you meant to say."

Jack laughed.

"Remember, my offer still stands."

"Don't get too drunk. Busy day tomorrow, kid."

"No shit, Mr. Responsible. Why do you think I want to get pickled." She leaped into the driver's side. "Hey, you okay?"

"It's not every day I lose a brother." He let out a stream of smoke.

"I'm really sorry, Jack."

"Thanks. Enough of this wimpy crap. Go. Get on with your night."

"You sure?"

"Yeah, I'm sure." He stomped his butt out on the pavement. Then he turned and went back into the funeral home. Franki beeped her horn and drove off toward home sweet home.

Chapter Fourteen

Franki drove into the driveway and killed the engine. Her mouth had become so dry she could taste the hops in the cold beer washing away the dehydration in her throat. It had to have been that shit coffee she drank at McKay's Funeral Home. Her day had been filled with an assortment of emotions, from the elation of finally meeting her sister again after all these years to having to saying good-bye to a dear friend. It had been a very tiring day for Franki.

Franki reached across the passenger seat to retrieve her purse and box of beer off the floor before stepping out into the night air. She closed the door with her hip and proceeded up to the front door. Franki was about to put the key in the lock when Sandy and Beth opened the door. They stood in the archway like two overzealous children, hoping for a promised treat.

"How did you know?" Sandy pointed at the box of beer.

"Call me psychic."

"Here, let me take that off your hands." Sandy handed Franki a cold beer in exchange for the two-four of beer. Franki was happy for the trade.

"Thanks." Franki gulped three quarters down her parched throat before letting out a very unladylike burp. "Now let's go inside and chill, shall we?"

"After you." Beth motioned for Franki to trail Sandy. Franki sat her beer down on the kitchen counter and went to change into something more comfortable. Sandy had already put the two-four of brown ale in the fridge by the time she'd returned. She was back in the spacious living room, chatting with Beth like they'd known each other forever. Franki smiled; her sister was fitting in well, just like she knew she would.

Franki flopped down in her favorite chair. "So how is everyone?" She took a swig.

"Franki, thanks for coming to my rescue earlier."

"Admit you were scared?"

"I was frightened. Wouldn't you be?"

"Damn straight. Someone tried to break into my place, I'd have the fucking SWAT team here. Not you, Miss Cool. No, you don't even call the police."

"We're not all like you, Franki. When I first heard the crack, I thought my heart was going to break a rib; it was pounding that hard inside my chest. I mean, there I was crouched down, legs shaking, feet literally fixed to the floor with fear. I was freaked."

"Couldn't tell with that poker still glued in your mitt." Franki laughed. "What were you planning to do with that weapon of choice?"

"Close my eyes and swing. What else?" Sandy shrugged.

"Oh, you are a real force to be reckoned with, Florence Nightingale."

"Yeah, well I'm glad it's over. How is Ellen?"

"She's okay. It's hard on her, no doubt." Franki choked back a sob.

"I feel so bad for Ellen, and I have never met her. I mean, the day of her retirement she finds her husband dead. God, it breaks my heart." Beth placed her hand across her heart.

"Ellen will get through this rough time. She always does," Sandy said.

"The woman is the epitome of strength."

"Here, here." They raised their glasses. "To Tom and Ellen." Sandy cheered.

Franki left her chair for another beer. "Anyone want another?"

"Bring it on." Sandy hooted.

"Sure, if you're buying." Beth laughed.

After a quick jot to the bathroom, Franki returned with cold beers. She handed her sister one and then gave one to Sandy before making her way back to her old, broken-down chair.

"Franki, why don't you tell us how you snagged a date with the hunky detective." Sandy giggled.

"Nothing to tell. He read my book and wants to have dinner."

"He's cute, but not the brightest," Beth commented.

"When a man looks like that, Beth, he doesn't need to be Einstein," Sandy announced. "He's probably great in bed. What do you guys think?"

"My guess is he's had lots of practice." Franki smirked.

"Looking the way he does, you can bet on it," Beth spoke with conviction.

"And all those ripples beneath his shirt. Yum, yum, yummy, ladies." Sandy licked her lips. Sandy was well on her way to intoxication, which happened maybe twice a year.

"You need to get laid. And, yes, he's cute. Now let's see how much personality he has," Franki said, shrugging her shoulders.

"Oh that would be my number-one priority. Making sure he's smart." Sandy rolled her eyes.

"How long has it been since you had a date?" Franki stared at her adopted mom.

"Never mind. I'm not the one he asked out," she said, trying to get out of the hot seat.

"How long?" Franki pressed.

"Too long."

"Well you might want to get on that. I haven't lived with you for the last two years, so what's the problem?"

"Work."

"That's a dumb excuse." Beth groaned.

Sandy shot her look. "Hey, who asked you?" She smiled.

"I thought I was family now."

"You are, Beth. I'm just a little sensitive when it comes to my love life. Right, Franki?" Sandy gave her one of her don't-push-it looks, but as usual, Franki never paid any attention.

"Okay, sensitive Susie, time for a little advice. You need a life. Stop working so much and find a guy to date. The crazies at the Edge won't even know you're gone. Someone else can hand out pills and wipe drool off their cheeks. C'mon. Life is too short."

"Thank you, psychiatrist Franki Martin. I didn't realize you were an expert on my love life. And I do more than push pills and wipe drool."

"Lack of love life."

"No, really, Sandy, my sister has a point. You have so much to offer someone. And I have only known you for a few hours. That says something about your character."

"I'll date when Franki hooks me up with someone that looks like Detective Gorgeous."

"What about online dating." Beth took a pull of her beer.

"No way! I'll take my chances with someone I can see face to face. Not over some site where I don't know anything about the person but what they lie to me about. Christ I could end up going out with Jack the Ripper, ladies. Please!" She shook her head. "I'm not looking to date anyone. If it happens, great. If not, my life will still stay on a good route. I know you don't believe me, but I am happy without a man. Look at this daughter of mine. I have you, and you are a handful." Sandy smirked across the room at Franki. "I have Ellen, and now I have a new friend, Beth. What else could a woman want?"

"Whatever!" Franki was not buying into the martyr crap. Sandy was a beautiful woman inside and out that deserved someone who would treat her as she treated others—awesome. "You still need a man in your life."

"More unsolicited advice." Sandy finished her beer. "Anyone want another?"

"You finished already?" Franki scolded.

"In case you haven't noticed, I've had a very stressful day, to say the least. And your unsolicited advice is not helping me. Now let me relax my way."

"Drink all you want. We can always dial a bottle if we run out." Franki laughed.

Upon her return, Sandy danced her way across the floor to the stereo. I think we should boogie." She cranked up the volume.

Franki and Beth joined Sandy, and all three danced to Michael Jackson's song, "Beat It," as it boomed loudly from the speakers suspended from all corners of the loft.

Meanwhile, back at Ellen's place, the trio assembled around the dining room table, chatting up a storm. Jack told the story about the time Tom tried to fly. He was seven at the time. He'd made himself wings out of a Canadian flag and jumped off the roof of their garage. Unfortunately, he didn't become the Wright brothers and landed like a rock, breaking his ankle. Ellen laughed; she could see Tom attempting a crazy stunt like flying. That's what she loved about Tom, his fearlessness. He wasn't afraid to try new things no matter what the risk was. *He married me, didn't he?* she thought.

Ellen could see Dorthy getting more fidgety by the minute, until she finally put her drink down, turned, and said, "I have an announcement." Then she picked her glass back up off the table.

"Go ahead, Dorthy," Ellen said.

"I'm considering leaving the convent." She waited for a wisecrack to come from her brother.

Although Jack was itching to say something, he didn't dare. This was a moment too good to be true.

"Oh! This is a surprise," said Ellen.

No shit, Jack thought and took a swig of his brandy.

"I understand. I don't feel it's my vocation any longer. I haven't announced my decision to Mother Superior yet."

"What's her number? I'll do the honors." Jack just couldn't help himself.

"And you wonder why I don't confide in you."

"I'm happy for you. What can I say?"

"This is my decision and mine alone, Jack. I have listened to your negative opinions, but what I need right now is support. You've made it very clear that you don't like my dress or my lifestyle. I appreciate support because down the road I'll need it more than ever. It will be quite a transitioning process after years of living with nothing. I mean, my needs are taken care of by God and the Sisters. I need for nothing living in Africa."

"Dorthy, you're a beautiful woman—for a sister, I mean." He winked. "I think it's a good thing to help the little orphans in Africa, but you matter too, sis. You've been away a long time, and well ... I've missed you. Tom missed you. It's not like I could just call and say, 'Hey want to come for dinner?' I respect the lifestyle, but what about your own family. I think we should matter too."

"I'm sorry, Jack. I was so busy. I never thought you guys were even missed me."

"Well, we did."

"Dorthy, what brought on this decision?" Ellen asked.

"I have given the better part of my life to serving the mission, and now I feel I need more. Jack's right. I've missed spending time with family, and now my older brother is gone. I can't get those missed years back. Tom's death has made me realize what I'm missing," Dorthy stated.

"Sounds sensible to me." Jack stood, heading to the kitchen for a refill of brandy.

"Taking care of yourself is not being selfish. I consider it healthy," Ellen said.

"I'd listen to Ellen, Dorthy. After all, she's the one with brain certificates on the wall, which gives her the knowledge and know-how about this feeling stuff." Jack rattled ice cubes and went out to the patio to have a smoke.

"Never mind him." Ellen patted Dorthy's hand and smiled.

"I would like to be someone's wife," Dorthy said, blushing. "Wear normal clothes that enhance my girlish figure, find romance. Live in normal conditions, have running water and indoor plumbing. Go out for a bite to eat with friends." She waved her hands in the air. "Who knows? Maybe the good Lord will bless me with marriage and a child one day. I want a love like you and my brother had. Jack and Mary have. I want a life filled with wonderful memories rather than a mind filled with misery. Watching children die every single day isn't easy. The world has more than enough provisions to feed everyone on our planet, and yet innocent children are still starving to death. One person can only do so much. It's soul-wrenching. My brother's death has made me realize just how precious my life is—and how short."

"I have never regretted one moment with Tom. We loved, we laughed, we argued, but most importantly, we lived every single day. My heart aches for his physical presence, but our memories will stay with me for a lifetime. Follow your heart, Dorthy."

"My only dilemma is the children."

"Dorthy, you are replaceable. I left my position at River Edge and was substituted by another great doctor that will dedicate himself to helping the mentally sick as I had. It's only my ego that believes I'm the only one who can help. Maybe God is telling you it's time to let someone else help those kids."

"I never looked at it like that, Ellen. Thank you."

Jack came back in after finishing his smoke on the patio.

"Well put, Ellen." Jack tipped his hat.

"If you need a place to stay, my home is always open," Ellen said to Dorthy.

"I don't want to burden you."

"If not Ellen's place, then mine," Jack piped up.

"Thanks, Jack, but you already have a full house. I think I'll take Ellen up on her offer. I promise we won't be strangers."

"I'm holding you to it. I just want you to be happy, sis. That's all I've ever wanted. I know … I come across as insensitive at times, but my intention is always good."

"I know that. Jack. I love you for it."

Dorthy and Jack finally embraced each other.

"Welcome home," he whispered in her ear.

The three of them stayed up chatting till midnight. Dorthy's decision was made. She was leaving Africa to start a new life.

Chapter Fifteen

A round ten thirty the next morning, all three women made it to Ellen's place carrying their clothes for the funeral. It was Franki's idea to get dressed there rather than having to drive back to the loft to change and then drive out to Ross's cemetery. Sandy and Beth agreed.

"Anyone home?" Ellen heard a familiar voice coming from inside the house.

"We're out here, honey," Ellen said.

One by one, the women wandered out onto the patio trying to hide their hangovers. Ellen spied their misery right away. The trio looked like something Muggins the cat dragged in and forgot to drag back out. All three were pasty with bloodshot eyes.

"What did you three get into last night?" Ellen winked at Dorthy and Jack, who were sitting around the patio table, enjoying the summer breeze.

"Does it show that much?" Sandy asked, feeling brutal.

"I know it's not the flu now, is it?" Ellen challenged.

"Nothing gets by you, Doc," Franki said, smoothing her dry tongue around her lips in search of moisture.

Jack couldn't help laughing at the misery on their faces. "Had a bit of a celebration, did you, ladies?"

"Yeah, too much obviously. I can't remember being this damn hung over though." Franki puckered a brow.

"You do remember—"

Franki interrupted, "Remember Magic Johnson. I'm just as healthy as he is. Live forever."

"Not if you keep over indulging, you won't." Ellen peered over her glasses at Franki.

"Okay! Relax. Party mode is over."

"Franki."

"Yes, Doc?"

"Are you going to introduce your sister to us?"

"Shit—sorry, Beth. Beth, I'd like you to meet Ellen Smith." The two women shook hands.

"You'll have to excuse my little sister; she's always been rude," Beth said.

"Ouch!" Jack snickered.

"I'm hung over!"

"And whose fault is that?" Beth folded her arms across her chest.

"Don't start," Franki said with a smile. "If my numb mind serves me correctly, it was you we had to coax to bed. What—four this morning, Miss Holier-Than-Thou?" Franki peered at her sister over the top of her sunglasses. "Isn't that right, Sandy?"

"No comment," Sandy said.

"Traitor."

"Beth, I'd like you to meet my sister-in-law, Dorthy, and my brother-in-law, Jack," Ellen said.

"Pleased to meet you." Beth shook hands with everyone. "I'm so sorry for your loss."

"Thank you," Tom's family echoed.

"Ellen, we put our stuff in the spare room. We're going to get changed here for the funeral. Hope you don't mind." Sandy announced.

"Not at all." Ellen sipped her coffee.

"Anyone have a good remedy for a hangover?" Franki begged, sprawled out on the lawn chair.

"Yeah, I do." Jack raised her hand.

"Mind sharing?"

"Don't drink so much next time." He laughed.

"Thanks, Jack, but a little late for that cure, don't you think?" Franki growled, sticking her tongue out.

"There is Alka-Seltzer in the bathroom cabinet. Go and get three tablets, Franki. It will ease the headache and anything else that's going on." Doc Smith prescribed.

"Why am I the elected gopher?" she said.

"Because you asked for the cure," Sandy explained.

"Fine. At least Doc loves me." Franki pushed herself up and out of the chair.

"Ellen, is there cold water in the fridge?" Franki asked.

"Should be. If not, there's fresh orange juice."

"Anything wet will work." Sandy stood up, holding her head, feeling like she was going to hurl.

"Beth, minus the hangover, I hope the visit is going well?" Ellen queried.

"Perfect, thank you. It's like we've never been apart, as you can probably tell." She smiled. "By reuniting us you made a dream come true for us, and we will always be indebted to you, Ellen."

"I am just so happy to see you girls together again. I'm sorry the system that was supposed to protect you both failed miserably," Ellen replied.

"It did, and Franki paid the price." Beth blinked back her tears.

"Beth, none of this is your fault. I'm glad you were placed in a wonderful foster home, but more importantly, so is Franki. Franki doesn't carry any resentment at how your life turned out. Her only dream was that one day she would get to see you again. And you know what?" Ellen reached up, touching the side of Beth's face.

"I know but—"

"But nothing. Live for today and cherish every second."

"Thank you." Beth wiped her tears.

Franki waltzed back out onto the patio carrying two tablets and two glasses of orange juice.

"Where's Sandy's?" Beth asked before taking a glass.

"She's bringing her own."

"You guys must be hungry," Jack said, leaving his chair to start the barbecue.

Franki winced, eyes speaking volumes of the nausea swirling around inside her stomach, not to mention the jackhammering going on within her skull.

"Eat something. It will make you feel better," Jack promised.

"He's right," Dorthy agreed.

"No offense"—Franki looked Dorthy up and down—"but how would you know anything about a hangover?"

"I wasn't always a nun, Franki." Dorthy winked.

"Guess you just got told, Miss Know-It-All." Ellen poured more coffee into her mug.

Franki laughed, blushing at her own ignorance. "Oh, I get it." She dropped the Alka-Seltzer tablet into her orange juice, watching it fizz before guzzling it down her throat. Next it was Beth's turn.

Finally Franki forced herself to walk across the patio to give Ellen a hug.

"Forgive me, Doc. How are you doing today?"

"At this moment, I'm good. Ask me again after the funeral." She patted Franki on the arm.

"I think that's why I got so drunk last night. I hope you're not too pissed at me."

"Give it up, Franki." Beth spun her gold bangles around her wrist.

"I think you should eat something." Jack advised.

The smell of bacon danced on the wings of the fresh morning breeze, tantalizing her taste buds. Franki's mouth began to water. *I guess a BLT would do the trick,* she thought, leaning back against the chair, praying her suffering wouldn't last too much longer.

Franki could hear happy chatter coming from Doc and her sister. Beth was busy telling Ellen about her life back in Ottawa. She was a stay-at-home mom, married to a really nice guy named Alex, who worked at the airport as an aircraft structure technician. She had two beautiful kids, a boy named Austin and a girl name Alexis. One was in preschool, and the other senior kindergarten. Beth had the life Franki always dreamed of. She wasn't jealous of Beth; if anything, she was happy that one of them was living their childhood dream.

Franki's life just took a different course. And for the most part, Franki knew how to cope with the ups and downs of her life. When horrible memories would rise from the darkness and try to drag her back to the dungeon of brutality, she'd talk to Doc right away. Sandy was always there to hug her until she felt safe again. Franki now had other avenues to take rather than the self-destructive road of drug abuse. She no longer let it rule her life. So, for the most part, Franki was okay.

After brunch and the table had been cleared, Beth peered over the patio rail. "Splendid yard you have, Ellen."

"My husband designed it."

"It's wonderful."

"Tom spent hours and hours out here."

"It shows. Is that a pond?"

"Yes, with goldfish. Go take a look for yourself."

"I'll do just that."

"Don't puke in the pond." Franki groaned, wishing she hadn't eaten her BLT.

"Yeah, like I would, spaz. In case you're all wondering, Franki was like this as a kid. She's changed a little—grumpier with age."

"Ah, now the truth comes out." Jack took a smoke from his pack.

"You can say that again," Sandy announced.

"Don't listen to her," Franki said, eyes still hidden behind her Ray-Ban sunglasses.

Sandy kicked Franki's chair. "What's wrong, wuss? Can't handle the big league?"

"Nope, can't argue with that statement."

"Franki, why don't you go and take a nap?" Ellen kindly suggested.

"No way!" Sandy objected. "No, the princess can stay awake. Look at Beth; she's no wuss, down in the garden enjoying the surroundings. Not like princess here, sniveling about a little hangover."

Franki cracked up, knowing Sandy was right.

"I know; she's making me look bad."

Franki sat up and watched her sister. Beth stopped to admire every flower in the garden. It reminded Franki of River Edge. How she liked to stop and smell and touch each of the petals. Years later, Beth was doing the exact same thing. She noticed a softness of awe on her sister's face.

"I think I'll join Beth." Franki rose from her seat.

"Good idea, kiddo." Sandy smiled.

"I think I'll go and take my shower now." Jack put out his smoke and entered through the patio screen door.

Ellen couldn't resist and rushed in behind Jack to retrieve her camera. Sandy stood taking shots with her cell phone. Everyone agreed; the two sisters looked like little girls, laughing and sharing secrets. Ellen captured the ladies' treasured innocence on film that would last a lifetime. A pristine moment, frozen in time for them to have as a treasured keepsake. It was as if they had never been apart.

Tom is smiling down from heaven, she thought, clicking a few more photographs.

Chapter Sixteen

fter the memorial service at Ross's cemetery, guests were invited back to Ellen's house for a bite to eat and to celebrate a man's wonderful life. Tom had touched many hearts with his warm smile and giving heart. He always had a project on the go, whether it was serving up soup at a local soup kitchen or mentoring young boys from broken homes. He could always be counted on when needed. The name Tom Smith sat sweetly on everyone's tongue. The emotional stress from the last few days was beginning to show beneath Ellen's eyes. Dark circles hung like half-moons, and her color was beginning to drain. Ellen stared around the room and sighed heavily. She had had enough condolences, company, and the idle chitchat about nothing. If she had it her way, she'd send them all home. Instead she sat trapped on the leather sofa with Martha Syns, a neighbor that lived across the street. On a normal day, Ellen would have enjoyed Martha's company, but not today.

"The young lady over there." Martha pointed at Franki standing a distance away, comfortably talking with Jack, her new adopted uncle. "The poem she read at the service was very touching."

"Yes it was, wasn't it?" Ellen smiled.

"I assume she picked it out of a poetry book."

Ellen rolled her eyes. "No, it's one of her originals. Franki Martin is very talented."

"She really should do something with a gift like that."

"She already has, Martha." Ellen glowed with pride.

"Oh."

"Franki is a published author."

"Well now, where can I buy a copy of this poetry book?"

"In any of our local bookstores."

"I'm going to Writeman's first thing tomorrow morning."

"I'm sure you'll enjoy Franki's creative work."

"How did you meet Miss Martin?"

"Oh we crossed paths a while ago."

Ellen eyed Sandy coming toward her, phone in hand. Ellen welcomed the interruption.

"Excuse me, Ellen, it's for you." Sandy handed Ellen the phone.

"Thank you, Sandy. Martha, please excuse me." Ellen rose up off the couch.

"You might want to take it in the bedroom. It's pretty noisy out here," Sandy said.

"I'll do just that. Who is it?" Ellen asked, covering the receiver.

"Said it was important." Sandy shrugged.

Ellen walked off to the bedroom, closing out the noise behind her.

"Hello." Ellen sat on the bed, finally having the liberty of kicking off her heels.

"Hi, kid. It's Bill, remember your long time buddy. I apologize for the interruption."

"I should be thanking you for the break."

"Tired of the company?"

"They mean well, but yes. What's on your mind, my friend?"

"I have a favor to ask, and trust me when I say it couldn't have come at a worse time."

"You have my complete attention."

"Your expertise is gravely needed."

"To do?" Ellen already knew the answer.

"Roger Taut."

"I gathered as much. I heard he's escaped from River Edge."

"The police need a new profile. Fresh eyes, so to speak. Captain Barlow believes Taut may be responsible for the murder on the west side."

"And the police have no other suspects."

"No. Captain Barlow knows you are the only one who has been able to interview him."

"Lucky me!"

"The captain is eager to hear what you have to say about this killer. If this is even Taut's kill. He's hoping you can add some insight before anyone else ends of dead."

"I won't speculate without first seeing the autopsy report and photographs. Bill, does Captain Barlow want me to give him a ring?"

"Yes. When you're feeling up to it. He feels awful, Ellen, for dragging you into this ill-timed ugly matter, so soon after—"

"Bill, Tom is gone," Ellen interrupted with a snap.

"I understand, but—"

"But nothing, my dear. I'm fine. Do you have John's number?"

Bill freely volunteered the captain's number. He knew there was no point in arguing with Ellen. She was strong willed.

"Okay, honey bunch, if you need anything, don't hesitate to call me."

"I won't. And, Bill, thanks for the distraction. It couldn't have come at a better time, really."

"Don't thank me yet."

Ellen laughed and hit the off button as a surge of adrenaline whisked through her veins. She felt alive and needed again. Without hesitation, Ellen keyed in the numbers to Captain Barlow's office.

Ellen meandered back into the living room, her expression fresh and confident like she'd just stepped out of cool morning spell of rain. The lines of fatigue were gone. Sandy stopped talking to Dorthy when she noticed the sudden change in Ellen's features.

"Business or pleasure?" Sandy asked.

"Bit of both. I've been asked to work on the Roger Taut case with Captain Barlow and his team."

"Please don't tell me you said yes." Sandy felt her stomach knot.

"I did." Ellen nodded.

"What about getting some well-deserved rest?" Sandy argued.

"I'll sleep when I'm dead."

"Keep pushing yourself thin, and it'll come sooner than later."

"My friend, you worry way too much."

"Well, someone has to," she barked louder than intended.

Franki, overhearing the bark, excused herself from Jack and joined the heated debate on the other side of the living room.

"Hey, is everything all right?"

"Ask Ellen." Sandy pouted, folding her arms across her chest, all of her motherly instincts visible.

"Doc, what's up?"

"I've been called back to work," she stated with a gleam in her eye.

"What kind of work?"

"The Roger Taut case." _____

"I knew it! I knew it wouldn't be long."

"The police need me. The detectives working this investigation need to understand how Roger's mind works if they are going to catch him. And who better to inform them than the one that knows him best. Me!" Ellen sounded just a tad bit too excited.

"Write a damn report, will you," Sandy protested.

"What about some well-deserved rest, Doc? You must be exhausted."

"I'm going to tell you the same thing I told Sandy. I'll sleep when I'm dead." She narrowed her eyes.

"I think this is ludicrous and perilous," Sandy remarked.

"It will be more dangerous for women if I don't help. Thank you for all the care and concern, but really, I'm fine. Tom would not want me sitting around feeling sorry for myself. He'd want me out there helping the police. We all know it."

"Sorry, Sandy, Ellen has a good point," Franki said.

"Please, Franki, don't encourage her. This is not okay in my books."

"Listen, Florence Nightingale, Doc is right about this. She knows this psychopath better than anyone. Besides, the police won't let anything happen to Ellen."

"So you approve of her jumping back into the saddle?"

"Yeah." Franki laughed.

"I think the two of you are insane."

Ellen and Franki glanced at each other. "We know." They snickered like defiant teenagers.

Franki nestled her head on Sandy's shoulder, "Lighten up. Doc will be just fine."

"Sandy, no one knows Roger the way I do. Trust me, not one woman will be safe until he's captured and placed back inside River Edge under lock and key."

"Okay, you win." She put her hands in the air. "Who will you be working with?"

"Captain John Barlow and Detectives Dan Kape and Jim Masker."

"Those guys came to my place the other night after someone tried to break in. The young detective is hot for Franki," Sandy said.

"Wants to have dinner, nothing major," Franki said.

"He's gorgeous, Ellen," Sandy said.

"Franki?" Ellen looked over the top of her spectacles.

"He'll do." She shrugged.

"To be young again." Ellen patted the top of Franki's head. "I think it's time we started saying good-bye to our guests." Ellen looked around at the gathering of people.

"Say no more." Franki went about politely letting the group know it was time to leave. Ellen was tired and needed some peace before her big day tomorrow.

Chapter Seventeen

Seven-thirty the next morning, the detectives were looking more than a little haggard. Jim's reason for lack of sleep was stupidity. He let his date keep him up half the night. Dan, on the other hand, was burning the midnight oil on the Roger Taut case. Since Roger's escape, the guy seemed to have vanished in thin air. The pressure to solve the murder on the west side began weighing heavily on Dan's shoulders. It wouldn't be long before the media mutts would be camped out in front of the building, looking for the latest scoop. The lack of information from the forensic lab only added fuel to Dan's frustration. Detective Kape sat hunched over his desk, carefully scanning Sarah Mile's old case file, looking for some hidden word that could link the old crimes to the recent one. Across from the desk, his partner scanned the computer data in search of friends and neighbors of Roger Taut, hoping to find some thread of evidence that could lead them to his whereabouts. As of right now, Roger Taut, the escapee, was the only person in question for the brutal murder of Josey Moran. Dan racked his brain trying to figure out why a young woman new to the city of Victoria would open her door to a total stranger. There were no signs of forced entry. What kind of ruse was Roger using these days? Could he have posed as a delivery guy or was he just that slick that the victim trusted him at a glance? Or was this perpetrator Roger Taut at all?

Jim rose from his chair, giving his body a worthy stretch. "When's the shrink showing up?" He glanced at his watch.

"Sometime this morning." Dan looked up, annoyance cascading in his bloodshot eyes.

"Rumor has it she just retired."

"Apparently not." Dan turned a page in the folder.

"Are we supposed to pick her up?"

"Nope. Arriving on her own."

"I hear she's a feisty old gal."

"How would I know?" Dan barked.

"Jesus, someone's grouchy." Jim sipped his coffee.

Dan stopped what he was doing; maybe it was time to take a break. He'd been at this since five this morning and was no further ahead than when he'd started.

"Why are you so grumpy this morning?" Jim asked.

"Unlike you, Mr. Social Life, I was here late last night working, and I came in at five this morning."

"All work is not good for you."

"Some of us don't have that luxury. Where were you last night?"

"Had an appointment."

"With who, a bimbo on a pole?"

"My doctor. I had no idea she made house calls." He gave a whistle.

Dan shook his head. "You don't look sick to me."

"She cured me, buddy." Jim laughed.

"So while you were home getting screwed, I was getting screwed out of sleep. Focus on the case, Romeo."

"You need to get laid. Rid your body of all that pent-up tension."

"The only tension I'm feeling right now is coming from you."

"Want a refill?" He pointed to Dan's empty mug.

"Why not." He handed over his cup and strolled to the bathroom to take a leak.

When he returned, a full steaming cup of coffee sat on his desk. He took a sip, trying not to scald his tongue. "Thanks."

"Welcome. Doctor Smith—why this case in particular?" Jim was relentless with his questions about Ellen Smith.

"She interviewed the nut." Dan replied.

"This doctor must know more than us." Jim said.

"It's not rocket science. He's a creep that gets his jollies murdering young women." Dan rolled his eyes.

"I mean his mental prognosis," said Jim.

"That is his mental prognosis. This animal needs to be locked behind bars, not some cushy mental facility."

"Personally, I don't care if Captain Barlow hires Humpty Dumpty to work with us, as long as it helps get this creep off the street. You've been here half the night and we're still in the dark."

"I don't know how she can help. I bet she hasn't opened his file in years."

"This morning, we will know the answer," Jim said confidently, returning to his chair.

"Enough about the old woman. Shouldn't you be reading notes, making calls, tracking down a lead, or something that will be useful to this case?" Dan growled.

Jim went back to staring at the information on the screen. A second or two later, he popped his head around the computer. "Why her?"

"Why who?" Dan dropped his pen onto his pile of papers.

"The doctor." He arched his brows. "Are you not listening to me?"

"I'm trying not to."

"Oh look." He pointed. "I think that's her."

Ellen had a presence about her when she entered any room. Dan strained his neck as he watched an elderly lady cross the room and approach the front desk, carrying a brown leather briefcase. It was the old-fashioned kind with the metal buckle at the front, like a doctor's bag.

The sergeant stopped clacking the computer keys. "Can I help you?"

"Good morning. I'm here to meet with John Barlow."

"Is he expecting you, Mrs. …?"

"That's Doctor. Smith. And yes he is."

The sergeant glanced around to see if the captain was floating about before picking up the phone.

Ellen took a seat in one of the lime-green vinyl chairs, leaning against the gray brick wall. There were stacks of self-help pamphlets on everything from rehab facilities to getting tested for hepatitis. The man sitting next to Ellen in his early thirties appeared nervous. His right leg never stopped bouncing up and down the entire time. Ellen smiled when their eyes connected, but it was clear the guy was in no mood for pleasantries. *Ah, it takes all kinds to make the world go around*, she thought.

Captain Barlow hurried across the room to his awaiting guest at the front counter. He opened the gate that separated the public from the detectives.

"Ellen." The captain greeted her with a kiss on the cheek.

"John. How are you?"

"I'm no worse for wear. Please come in." He motioned to his office. "We can talk privately in my office." Ellen trailed John.

The unit was a busy place. Uniformed men and women were putting in their long hours of service trying to keep the citizens of Victoria safe. Keys on the computers clicked and clanked, phones were ringing, copier machines were spitting out pages of information, and coffee machines gurgled nonstop. Voices softened to whispers as the two headed across the room. Captain Barlow closed the door. Ellen set her briefcase down and took a seat facing John.

"Ellen, you look wonderful. It's certainly been way too long."

She graciously accepted the compliment from the six-foot African American, a good-looking man with the build of a football player. Captain John Barlow, the best in the business.

"Can I get you anything?"

"No, I'm fine thank you."

"Ellen before we get started, I want to offer my condolences. I am so sorry to hear about Tom. He was a good man. And I can't thank you enough for coming on board at a time like this."

"Thank you, John."

"What the hell happened?"

"Tom had a massive heart attack. He died the day I retired."

"I'm so sorry. That had to come as a shock."

"You could say that. I had a surprise vacation planned for us, but it never happened."

"Were you aware he had heart trouble?"

"No. This is one of those medical mysteries."

"I hope you know I agonized over inviting you to join our team."

"As far as I'm concerned, the timing is perfect. I dreaded the long hours with nothing to do. Right now I need to feel useful."

"No one could keep you down, could they?"

"Afraid not." She smiled.

The captain opened the off-white folder in front of him.

"This murder on the west side, you believe there's a connection to the murders seven years ago?" Ellen asked.

"Yes, I do, or this perpetrator is one hell of a copycat."

"Before I form my opinion, I'll have to study the forensic report, victimology, and photographs. I must agree with you; it seems quite the coincidence. Roger escapes, and already a dead woman turns up in less than a week."

"Shame we don't have everything back from the forensic lab as of yet."

"I'll need to start with what you have so far. John, if your gut is correct and the man you're looking for is in fact Roger Taut, I don't have to tell you what kind of carnage he'll leash on Victoria."

"He's a sick one."

"The worst."

"Shit. I was hoping you weren't going to tell me that." John gave a pained expression.

"Do you have the autopsy report?"

"The detectives have all the reports. Dan was here half the night going over the data. I must warn you, they're not impressed that I called you in."

Ellen laughed. "A little too much testosterone."

"Ego. If you don't mind, I'll have them join us."

"Be my guest."

The captain stepped out of his office and released a loud whistle across the room, signaling to the detectives. In cooperation, the detectives grabbed what they needed and hustled to the captain's office. The two entered, and Ellen stood and shook their hands. "Good morning, gentlemen."

"Morning." Dan nodded.

John stood behind his desk. "It's a little crowded in my cubby hole they call an office. I think we'll move this meeting to the conference room." All three followed the captain down a maze of white corridors.

The captain unlocked the door and pushed it open. Ellen walked in first, feeling the cool air on her skin, and the detectives followed. The captain seemed surprised as he looked around.

"I pulled a late night," Dan said, feeling proud of his accomplishment. He'd spent part of the night getting the conference room equipped for the investigation of Josey Moran's murder.

"Good job," the captain said with a smile.

"Thanks."

"Brownnoser," Jim whispered.

Ellen stopped, taking in the view. Along the north wall were rows of crime-scene photographs of Roger's earlier victims, Sarah Miles, Clara Howard, and Tyra Field. Below each picture were hand-printed facts. Where they were found, when, and the cause of death. With the old crime-scene photographs tacked to the wall was a photo of who the police believe to be his latest victim, Josey Moran. Along the south wall was a city map marked with colored tacks at the locations where the bodies had been found. Ellen's gaze went to the photo of the latest victim, Josey Moran. If Roger was responsible, Ellen knew there would be many more snap shops tacked beside his latest victim. The detectives would have to work diligently in order to apprehend a slayer of such caliber. Each person understood the long hours that would be required sitting around the long, oval, cherry wood table, viewing and reviewing every piece of information they had. Eight chairs surrounded the table in case they needed reinforcements. Dark blue carpeting supported the importance of the room. The only picture on the wall was of Queen Elizabeth.

Ellen set her briefcase on the carpet beside her chair, taking a seat next to John. Dan and Jim sat across the table from Ellen.

"This is Dr. Ellen smith, the young lady you'll be working with. I'd like you to welcome her to our team." John winked at Ellen, but the room remained somber.

"Thanks for the compliment, John, but as you all have sight, I'm far from young."

"Why are you here, Ellen?" Dan didn't hesitate, firing out his disapproval.

"Two reason, Detective. One: the big guy upstairs doesn't believe I should retire." All three chuckled. "Second: I have knowledge that no one else has of the suspect you may be dealing with. I want what you guys want, and that is to catch Roger sooner than later."

"Taut is only a suspect," Jim announced.

"This is why I'm here this morning. I need to assess all the data collected on past kills and the most resent. After I have reviewed all the evidence, then and only then will I be able to give you my professional opinion as to whether or not I think you should look elsewhere. Roger may not be the man responsible for the west side killing, but I won't know until I've read all the facts."

"No offense, but I think this guy is just a fuck up who gets his kicks murdering vulnerable women. We don't need a degree to figure that one out," Jim said, fixing the cuffs on his shirt.

"Au contraire. Roger has great survival skills. It took a year to track him down seven years ago. He will be even harder to apprehend this time. He knows his freedom is at stake."

"How can your expertise help us catch this guy?" Dan asked, rolling his head side to side.

Ellen retrieved three thick manila folders from her briefcase and tossed each one on the table.

"Detectives, I'm not here to win a popularity contest with you two. I am very confident in the field of criminal insanity, or criminal behavior if you wish. In those folders is Roger Taut's life. I suggest you read over them. I know him better than you guys do. One woman will not satisfy his delusion for revenge, especially if he's come off his medication. If you are questioning my credentials, let me put you at ease. I have a doctorate in psychiatry and master degrees in criminology and forensics. I've also studied this man for two years. I have documented hours and hours of data that will be imperative to this investigation. His pattern of behavior from arousal to aggression. I have interviewed family, neighbors, teachers, friends, and anyone related to Roger. What do you guys have other than forensic facts?" Ellen nodded. "I also taught forensic psychology to many a man like you, in rooms like this all over the world. Roger Taut is not the first criminal mind I've studied throughout my career. He's slick and very dangerous.

"Now on a personal note, if you have a problem with me being here, too fucking bad."

Jim cracked up laughing, and Dan's bloodshot eyes bulged in their sockets. It was evident they weren't expecting to get their asses handed to them by a senior citizen with a whole lot of gumption.

"I'm here to stay or until we know for certain that the man you're looking for is Roger Taut. So with the time we do have, I suggest we team up and figure out a way to apprehend him before he has a chance to kill—and trust me, gentlemen, he will. It's in his nature."

"Why did he select you to interview him?" Dan asked.

"I guess he likes me. During his incarceration, I was asked by his lawyer to evaluate him. Roger must have taken a shine to me. I believe at the time of the murders, Roger Taut was clinically insane, and my diagnosis has not changed. Roger murdered those women during a complete murderous frenzy. A blackout caused by years of physical, emotional, and mental torture. Roger is guilty of the crimes committed, but none of his kills were premeditated. He is killing from a fantasy, not reality. Roger didn't murder Sarah Miles, Tyra Field, or Clara Howard."

"That's not what those pictures on the wall say." Dan swallowed a lump of anger. "Who did he kill then?"

"His mother. My recommendation to the court was that he not serve out his sentence in prison because I knew one day, they would have to release him back into society. The board of trustees at River Edge never had any intention of setting Roger loose. There are different guidelines for different institutions."

"Then how in the hell did he get out?" Jim finished the last of his coffee.

"I'm afraid I don't have the answer. The fourth floor is secured as a maximum security prison."

"This case is just getting started, and already it's getting more baffling by the minute," Dan complained.

"There you have it, gentlemen. Now you understand why I've called Dr. Smith in on this case." Captain Barlow tucked his hands into his front pockets. "And one more thing. Ellen is to be addressed as Dr. Smith. Is that clear?" His eyes leveled on Dan.

"As a team, we stand a chance of finding Roger. If we start bickering amongst ourselves because of personal prejudice, trust me, Detectives, many women will die in the process." Ellen commented.

"Sorry we judged you, Dr. Smith," Jim said.

"Yeah. Me too," Dan said.

"Apologies accepted. Now let's get down to business. Dan, get on the phone and call forensics. Tell them to send over whatever is available. Jim, I suggest you grab one of the folders on the table and start learning everything you can about Roger Taut. You'll need it."

"Oh, Derk is going to be pissed," Dan stated with a grin.

"Yeah. Well tell him to get over it." Ellen nodded, taking the lead.

Everyone had a task to do.

Chapter Eighteen

arly the next morning, all four trained specialists gathered inside
the conference room for a session of brainstorming. Derk, the
forensic lab technician, had faxed what little information the
tech had analyzed, and it wasn't much. It wasn't like on television
where forensics collected evidence from a crime scene, and the results
were back within an hour. The techs were still working on the data
collected in Josey's bedroom. Hair, fingernail clippings, fibers found
on the floor and bedspread. DNA samples were being compared
to other samples found in the apartment. Everyone knew that the
chance of finding Roger's DNA was slim to none. This man spent
years perfecting how not to get caught again. All the prints found in
Josey's bedroom so far were hers. The blood spatters on the wall, hers.
The partial print found on the lead pipe came back inconclusive. No
match could be found.

Ellen and the others sipped coffee, eyes glued on the reports in
front of them on the table. Captain Barlow began strategically placing
each photo, one by one, across the table to be studied. There were
similarities and differences between the old murders and the most
recent murder. Roger never sexually assaulted his earlier victims with a
weapon. *His brutality is escalating*, Ellen thought. The gruesome crime-

scene photographs were hard on the stomach. Josey's once beautiful face was now unrecognizable because of this man's murderous rage. An uncomfortable somberness loomed thick in the air as their eyes glossed over the handiwork of this psychopath.

Dan reached across the table, taking one of the pictures. He held it close to his face and studied, as if something profound was going to jump out from the picture and tell them what road to take in order to find whoever did this.

"Doctor Smith, what's your professional opinion? Is this the work of Roger Taut?" Dan asked, feeling as if all the air had just been sucked out of the room.

"I'm undecided. There are indeed similarities, but there is one difference."

"Is there a slim chance it could be him?" Jim injected.

"Without a doubt. The laceration to the victim's neck, the contusions, and the way the body was positioned on the bed tell the same story. But ..."

"But what?" Jim spun his pen around his fingers.

"Roger never raped the other three victims with a foreign object."

"Could his rage be escalating?" Captain Barlow asked.

"Sure. Especially now that he isn't getting his Decanoate."

"What the hell is that?" Dan asked, wrinkles forming above his brows.

"It's a psychiatric medication to treat delusions. The drug works to block receptors for the chemical dopamine in his brain. Its power is to decrease the release of hormones from the hypothalamus and depress the area of the brain known as the reticular activating system. Without this drug, Roger will stay in permanent delusion. He's still able to function, don't get me wrong. We won't catch him out on the street naked, babbling, or drooling."

"Can he get this drug on his own?" the captain inquired.

"He could buy something analogous on the street, like Fentanyl, known as Apache. Or a methamphetamine."

"Known as blue devils," Dan said.

"This is not good news. So the longer he's off his medication, the crazier this freak will get?" Jim said, taking a gulp of tepid coffee.

"Yes."

Dan held out the photograph of Josey Moran without a face. "This murder is premeditated. Whoever did this went to Josey's apartment with the lead pipe, intending to do some ruthless damage."

"I can't say yes for certain, Dan." Ellen's eyes connected to Dan across the table.

"Why not? What would a young woman be doing with a lead pipe in her bedroom? I think whoever did this meant for us to find the weapon."

"That's the question we need to find an answer to."

"The blood!" Jim remarked dourly. "Man, it's too early in the morning to be agonizing over this kind of gore." He shook his head in protest.

"Doctor Smith, I know your reasoning for having him committed at River Edge, but damn it. I think he should have been locked away where he'd have had to fight for his survival. You know, eat or be eaten. And now this animal is out to kill again." Dan stood up, shoving his hands deep into his front pockets, which he did when he didn't know what else to do.

"Dan," Ellen said, "have you heard about the Galvanic Skin Response test?"

"Can't say that I have, Doctor." Dan stood at the counter, refilling his cup.

"I performed the GSP on Roger about six years ago. The patient sits in a chair while I attach dummy magnetic electrodes to his arms, chest, and legs. Then he is told that within the next ten minutes a jolt of electricity will course into his body, causing him great pain. To a normal person, their immediate reaction would be stress and panic. After strapping a heart monitor to his chest and another around the skull to monitor brainwave readings, we were ready. In a normal patient, there would be fluctuations. A large clock stood directly in view, so Roger would know precisely when the voltage would pass through his body. He showed absolutely no change in either heart rate or brain wave."

"Did he get shocked?" Jim leaned on his elbows, eyes gleaming in hope.

"In Canada, it is illegal to torture someone. Gentlemen, only psychopaths will demonstrate zero response. To place Roger in a prison where he is free to roam would only put lives in danger, and that includes guards."

"Give me the damn electrodes. I'll give the bastard a shock he'd not soon forget." A frustrated Dan replied.

"Are you saying this test proved he's insane?" Captain Barlow asked.

"No, it showed us that Roger Taut is devoid of any emotion. I believe that seven years ago Roger was acting out of a fantasy place. Wavering between reality and fantasy is not easy for Roger, and that is part of my reasoning for my insanity defense. Today could be a totally different scenario. And, gentlemen, let's not forget, Roger could be working alongside his accomplice."

You could almost see the wheels in the captain's head turning with the word accomplice. Yet he remained quiet.

"Doctor Smith, lots of children are abused each year, but they don't go around killing and raping with a lead pipe." Dan stated the obvious.

"True enough."

"I got a few well-deserved smacks growing up. You don't see me hurting women for shits and kicks." Dan pulled his chair out and sat down.

"It's a psychosis, gentlemen. Please remember, we are not dealing with an ordinary mind. During these murderous rages, he is killing his mother. In one of my many interviews with Roger, he told me that after he murdered Tyra Field, believing her to be his parent, he stayed behind to admire his work. Once the psychosis subsided, he truly didn't know what or how it had happened. The last thing he remembered was Tyra leading him to her bedroom."

"Then why didn't he turn himself in?" Captain Barlow asked.

"Why would he? At that time, he was insane. Again, remember he is devoid of any emotion. What seems normal to us is not to him. We have a built-in conscience. Roger was predisposed to become a monster by the abuse he suffered growing up. It's a small part of this puzzle, but we can't forget the pieces are essential."

"All this scientific bullshit is great on paper, but if this guy is so crazy and intelligent, how are we going to find him?" Jim asked, walking across the room to the map on the wall.

"Good question." Dan nodded. "We know the why to his pathetic sob story. So in reality, who we're dealing with is a psychopath with delusional problems. Meaning the fucking creep doesn't even know he's a psycho with delusional problems. That's right up there with the strange and completely fucked section. And right now, we don't have one goddamn lead to his whereabouts. How can that be? He didn't just vanish into thin air, or is that one more of his strange psychotic delusions?" Dan leaned back, forking his hands behind his head.

"Ellen, could he have left Victoria?" Captain Barlow asked.

"I doubt it. Victoria is all he knows."

"More like Judas Playing Field, if you ask me." Dan shook his head.

"This just keeps getting better and better." Jim threw one of the photographs back onto the table.

"Roger is a good-looking man. He's very charismatic, manipulative, funny, and smooth as silk. Ladies find him intoxicating. The boy next door every girl wants to take home to meet the parents. He has no problem getting women to take a second glance. His appearance is trusting, far from a deranged monster women see in nightmares. His victims find out what really lies beneath his alluring façade when it's too late. They're dead."

"What's his trigger?" Dan questioned.

"Sexual advances. A naked body. Taut was raped and beaten repeatedly by his mother and boyfriend."

"I don't give two flying fucks what happened to him as a kid. There is no excuse in my book for this viciousness." Dan banged his thick finger along each lined photograph."

The captain stood, reaching his arms toward the ceiling. "Everyone, take fifteen and meet back here."

"Great idea, I've got to take a leak."

"Thanks for sharing, Dan." Ellen rolled her eyes.

His face flushed. "Sorry, Doctor. I'm use to hanging out with these guys." He opened the door and went into the hallway.

Fifteen minutes later, all convened back in the conference room, cigarette smoke clinging to Dan's clothing like bad-smelling body mist.

"Why hasn't the media reported any connection between the murder on the west side and Roger's escape from River Edge?" Ellen inquired. "Have they not put two and two together?"

"Well, they know only what they've been told." John cleared his throat.

"I believe its time they knew the truth," Ellen said. "The last thing this investigation needs is for the reporters to be printing sensational shit. Not to mention, sending out a warning to women."

"Ellen, the mayor says—"

"Ah, to hell with the mayor, John. The public has a right to know what they're dealing with so they can be on watch. Roger Taut is not just an average escapee from River Edge. This man is a convicted murderer. And I'm not going to sit around with my thumb up my ass waiting for more women to die, for the sake of his shiny reputation."

"Doctor Smith, you're my kind of gal." Dan clapped, cheering her on.

Ellen smiled, taking a bow.

"Tomus Cleaver will not put the city on fear." John shook his head.

"You kick his ass, Doctor Smith." Jim agreed with Ellen.

"Leave the mayor to me, John," she said, shoving folders into her briefcase.

"Ellen, I'm telling you, forget Cleaver. You are wasting your time.

There is no way he's going to allow you to post pictures of Taut on the front page with a headline like Murderer—Women Beware."

"The headline doesn't have to read murderer; prime suspect looks damn good to me. How about this. *If you've seen this man, contact police immediately.* We need the public's help if we're going to locate him and soon. May I use someone's phone?"

Dan was delighted to hand Ellen his cell. Tomus Cleaver was nothing but a pompous ass. This so-called act of defiance on Ellen's part would make their job a little easier. They would no longer have to work behind a blanket of deception. The public had a right to know that they had a dangerous predator in the mist. Roger Taut was not a nice guy, and women needed to be warned.

The captain sat back, rubbing his throbbing temples, admiring Ellen's balls of steel.

"Tomus Cleaver here."

"Tomus, Ellen Smith. It's been a long time."

"It certainly has. I'm sorry to hear about Tom. How are you?"

"I'm well, thank you."

"Did you get the flowers I sent?"

"Yes, Tomus. The bouquet is beautiful." Ellen rolled her eyes. "Tomus, have you an hour to spare for an old and dear friend?" Ellen grinned at the guys.

"I have a few minutes, yes. How can I help?"

"It concerns the Roger Taut investigation."

"I wasn't aware it had become an investigation. John hasn't informed me of any investigation."

"Well, I'm informing you now, Tomus."

"So when would you like to get together?" Ellen could hear the hesitation in his voice.

"I'll be there within the next twenty minutes or so." Her tone was as flat as stone.

"Sounds urgent."

"I'll discuss the matter when I get there."

"Well … okay," Tomus stammered.

Ellen slapped shut the cell phone and handed it back to its rightful owner.

"He didn't put you off," John said, smiling.

Ellen laughed. "He knows better."

"Glad to have you on board."

"My pleasure."

Ellen retrieved her purse and snapped shut her briefcase. *You never know when you'll need back up*, she thought.

Chapter Nineteen

Franki and her sister had just returned to the loft after a full morning of sightseeing. Franki gave Beth the grand tour of Victoria. Their first stop of the morning was the wax museum and then the underwater garden. They were in awe as they gazed from wooden benches at Cecile, the octopus in a large glass tank. Although Cecile's long tentacles moved effortlessly throughout the tank, Beth thought it was the most hideous underwater creature she'd ever seen. She hadn't seen the eels yet. Once the underwater tour had finished, they took a walk through the downtown core, stopping at each of the stores to browse. Beth bought souvenirs for her family. Then they took a two-block stroll back to the waterfront. Beth could hear music down by the harbor and just had to check it out. Hand in hand, like old times, Franki led the way. The sisters took in the juggler show sipping iced coffee. Franki threw a ten-dollar bill into a half-empty guitar case and stood listening to the musician play a Stevie Ray Van riff. Beth smiled the entire time. After the show, Franki suggested they have their picture drawn by a local artist. Beth and Franki were like little girls again, posing for the artist. Franki asked her sister if she wanted to go whale watching, but Beth declined. She was getting hot and tired and hungry. Franki took her over to the Irish Pub, located on First Street, for the best clam chowder in town. Franki could not let her sister leave Victoria without having a piece of chocolate mocha cheesecake.

Tired from their morning adventure, they sat in an air-conditioned loft and lazed around. Franki launched into the story that Beth had been begging to hear. It was obvious the girls had totally different childhoods. Franki told Beth stories about what it was like to be put into the foster care system without her and how lonely she felt. The houses looked warm and inviting from the outside, but they were everything but that. Each assigned room had three tiny cots, stainless steel dressers, and one closet to share amongst two other girls. Franki was completely out of her realm. Bullies picked on her constantly, called her names, took her things, and threatened to beat the hell out of her if she told. One time a girl named Natoe peed in her bed and then told the hen mother it was Franki, knowing Franki would receive the punishment. The boys tried to touch her in places she didn't want to be touched, and the horror went on. Then came the day when Franki thought she'd been saved.

A family wanted her to come live with them. During the interview, the Wilkens really seemed to want Franki. Unbeknownst to naive Franki, she was about to walk into yet another nightmare. The emotional cruelty, sexual abuse, and physical violence bestowed on her were nothing short of unimaginable suffering. But after arriving at River Edge and telling Doc the horrible tale of what went on inside the Wilkins's house, the matter was quickly dealt with. With a little persuasion, Franki ended up going to court. Judge Denac gave Gary and Susan Wilkins eight years, but knowing how the system worked, they'd probably be out in four. The good news was no more children would have to suffer at the hands of the Wilkins. At long last, Franki finally had vindication.

Beth was flabbergasted. How could an organization presumed to protect children fail so miserably and allow such atrocities to happen to her baby sister? The idea of Franki being so brutally beaten for running away to find her only made Beth's heart ache that much more. Beth needed to know why Franki had been committed to River Edge Mental Institution. Franki went on to tell her final tale.

"It had been raining for the past four days. I was cold, wet, and hungry. I was absolutely miserable. It all got to be too much, fighting off johns and thieves. I hated sleeping on the ground night after night. I had given up. All my dreams had faded away, and now it was just about continued existence. Although my friend Sparkie did the best she could to protect me, it wasn't enough anymore. I walked to the corner store and stole a package of razors. Lady Bick, if you can imagine. I ducked out into the alley behind Fong's Restaurant. So here I am crouched down beside the dumpster. I tore open the bag of razors; this was it. I didn't want to live anymore, like some piece of nothing. I mean it's not like I could use a bathroom when I needed to or even take a shower. My life sucked! I broke apart the plastic. I took the blade and cut across each wrist several times." Beth winced, grabbing her own wrist. "I could feel the warm blood trickle out of the veins, running down my hands. I lay back and waited to die. It was strange because for the first time in a very long time, I felt calm. I was going to be safe with Mom and Dad." Tears slid down Beth's cheeks. The despair and desperation Franki felt was enormous, and she wasn't there to shield her little sister. "Then before I blacked out, I remembered a dude on a cell phone. Then I was taken to Morial Hospital by ambulance, so I was told. The dude with the cell phone had called 911. When I woke up, I had two surgical bandages around my wrists. I was pissed. I didn't want to be alive. I didn't want this life of pain anymore. Surviving street life had crippled my soul, or so I thought. You know, men using me for sex, eating out of dumpsters. My world had become cold and ugly. That's why I tried to kill myself. I was kept in the hospital for a week and then transferred to River Edge, where I was imprisoned for a considerable amount of time. Lucky for me, Sandy saw right through that toughness and befriended me anyway. In spite of myself, I got the professional help I needed and became a better person for it. Sandy adopted me so I would have a loving home. One filled with love, laughter, and room to grow into the person I wanted to be. I love Sandy. And now, we are reunited again. I imagined this moment for years. I have to say, this is nothing short of a miracle." Franki's lip began to quiver. "Oh hell." She wiped away her tears. "I'm done talking about me. I want to hear about your life."

Now it was Beth's turn to get Franki up to speed on her life.

"So, what are your adoptive parents like?" Franki inquired.

"Grace and Lionel are absolutely wonderful to me." She spoke with admiration in her eyes.

"They did adopt you, right?"

"Yes, but they let me decide whether I wanted to use their last name, Beshure, or keep Martin."

"What did you decide?"

"I kept Martin."

"I was hoping you'd say that." Franki breathed a sigh of relief.

"I'd love for you to meet them one day. They were so happy I was coming to see you finally."

"I'd like that."

"I feel guilty talking about how good I had it, knowing how awful you did."

"Guilt is a useless emotion." Franki confirmed. "So, do tell. What was growing up like for you?"

"Grace and Lionel treated me as if I were their own child. They were strict but fair. You know, good grades in school, equal privileges. We went to Florida and Hawaii. I played volleyball after school. You know, regular stuff."

"How do your parents make a living?"

"Grace is a school teacher, and Lionel is an architect. I had a bulldog named Barney. He was the best. They felt it was good therapy for me to have something of my own to love, and they were right. I want you to understand, Franki, although I had a good upbringing, I still carried a huge void in my heart. There wasn't a day that I didn't think about you. I used Barney as my therapist. I used to tell the dog what you were like and how much I loved and missed you. Barney would look at me with sympathy in his big, old, brown eyes like he understood what I was saying. Crazy as it sounds, I think he did." The memory of her nestled on the couch with Barney flashed across her mind.

"I bet you were popular in school."

"Average. I wasn't the ugly duckling, but I wasn't queen of the popularity circle either. Did you finish school, Franki?" Beth changed the subject.

"As a matter of fact, I did." Franki beamed proudly.

"What school?"

"River Edge nut house."

"How?" Beth looked confused.

"Correspondence courses. Sandy didn't trust me to go to a regular school on my own. You know the saying—can't play well with others. It applied to me." Franki laughed.

"Wow! That takes a lot of commitment on your part."

"I'd say more like desperation with Sandy and Doc standing over my shoulder. I don't think I had any choice but to do well."

"And now look at you, Miss Author of the number-one best seller. Who taught you how to write?"

"Credit goes to Sandy Miller. I had a lot of pain inside. Sandy suggested if I couldn't talk about it, maybe writing it down would lessen the pent-up anger I'd been carting around. So I started telling stories about street life, and wham, I discovered I had the talent. Sandy helped me with grammar and punctuation. It was her idea to send my stories to publishing houses."

"Writing is an isolating business, is it not?"

"I guess." Franki shrugged.

"Who taught you how to paint?"

"Me."

"Dad use to paint. Do you remember?"

"No." Franki had a pained look in her eyes. "One day I picked up a brush and canvas and voila."

"It's in the genes."

"Nice to know. Hey, want to see my first painting?" she asked, leaping out of the recliner. She strolled across the loft to her collection of canvases leaning against the south wall. Franki loved how the streamers of sunlight made the dust particles dance. Thumbing through her art, she came across the first creative piece she'd painted, back in the hours at River Edge.

"What do you think?" She held up the colorful canvas.

"Holy moly, sis. That is your first painting?" Beth's eyes lit up.

"This maple tree represents my life. During my stay at Hotel Crazy, I'd sit on this wooden bench here"—she pointed—"under this maple tree and read and write for hours."

"The sacred maple. You always were a little strange."

"Thanks, sis." Franki rolled her eyes.

"Franki, why do you call it Hotel Crazy?"

"That's how I feel. You wouldn't be asking me that question if you were committed to one." She took a drink of her beer.

"Franki, are you dying?"

"We're all going to die one day, Beth."

"No. I mean because of HIV?" Beth swallowed her lump of dread.

"Yes, but I try to live each day as best I can. Worrying about tomorrow is useless."

"You tested positive for the virus after being raped by that horrible bastard, Doctor Blake?"

"Let me go grab a couple cold beers, and I'll tell you the whole story." Franki winked.

"Liquid courage?" Beth's eyebrows rose to a V shape.

"Whatever it takes." Franki laughed nervously.

It was a story Beth would never forget.

Chapter Twenty

octor Ellen Smith hadn't left the parking garage when Captain Barlow's phone rang. He answered on the second ring.

"Captain Barlow speaking."

The detectives sat frozen in their chairs trying to read between the lines of the captain's conversation. It wouldn't be long before they knew the exact nature of the call. A minute later, at most maybe two, the captain slapped shut his phone and stood to his six-three frame, staring down the length of the elongated table.

"Captain?" Jim's voice heightened with concern.

"Another body was discovered on the west side."

"Who found the victim?"

"A friend. Apparently the ladies had a shopping engagement. The girlfriend showed up and knocked. When the friend didn't answer the door, she let herself in with a spare key."

"And found the body." Dan sighed.

"Address is 2161 Trenor Street. Let's go before the evidence isn't evidence anymore."

"Can't forget the media dogs." Jim groaned, although he had to admit he did like seeing his face on television. All three hustled out to the elevator and down to the parking garage below.

Minutes after receiving the call, the detectives and Captain Barlow arrived on the scene. They were fortunate; the street was still fairly quiet. They understood all too well it would only be a matter of time before spectators would begin showing up, including the media. Captain Barlow was the first out of his vehicle. He crossed over to one of the officers standing guard on the lawn of a run-down little shack. The front veranda and siding were falling apart. There were Barbie toys out on the front lawn. It was obvious the victim had a young child. The captain prayed to God that the child hadn't witnessed the murder.

The two men shook hands. "So what do you have, Gill?" the captain asked.

"A young woman, twenty-five years old. Shelby Port. The child wasn't in the house at the time. I doubled searched the entire house, making sure the child wasn't hiding under the bed or in a closet. I was very careful not to contaminate anything."

"What's the damage?"

"Looks like the victim was murdered in the kitchen."

"Her friend found her there in the kitchen?"

"Yes. Friend's name is Anna Kellis. She's waiting in her truck. She's pretty messed up."

"Gill, tape off this area. No one goes in or out without a badge."

"Yes, sir!" Gill crossed the sidewalk to the cruiser and unlocked the trunk to retrieve the yellow crime tape to cordon off the assigned area.

By this time, the detectives had caught up to their captain.

"Jim, find out all you can from the friend. Who the victim knew. Next of kin. Recent boyfriends and enemies. Anything you can find."

"On it, sir." Jim made his way to the old brown pickup truck with pink primer on the tailgate parked at the curbside in front of the house.

"Dan, you come with me."

When the two men reached the porch, Captain Barlow and Dan pulled on gloves and rubber booties. The wooden door opened with a loud creaking sound. The house was old, but the victim kept it spotless. In the corner of the living room next to a television set sat a toy box filled with girl toys and puzzles. The furniture had seen better days. Captain Barlow and Dan followed the trail of blood droplets leading into the kitchen where the victim was found. Dishes sat drying in the rack. A tipped over mug lay on the counter. Dan spotted the body sprawled on the floor, next to the patio window. Her face had been beaten. Her blonde hair matted with congealed blood. The blood splatter across the floor and up the patio window appeared to be from blunt-force trauma to the skull." They'd have more information after the autopsy.

"I don't see a weapon anywhere." Dan scanned the kitchen.

"He's getting smarter and takes the weapon with him." The captain rolled his eyes.

Captain Barlow leaned over the body, gently pulling up the victim's bloodstained shirt. She had several long puncture wounds to her torso and upper chest. Her peach shorts had been yanked to her ankles, indicating sexual assault. No ligature marks; maybe he ran out of time. Maybe a knock on the door or a phone ringing spooked him. This was the work of forensics to figure out.

"This young woman didn't stand a chance; she was obviously struck from behind." Dan observed.

"My guess is she didn't see it coming. He surprised her right here in the kitchen. The blood droplets in the hallway must have dripped off his knife. It appears he knocked her unconscious and then finished the job." Dan gave a loud whistle, and he stood up. They both turned away from the body, hearing a rapping sound in the doorway. It was Derk from forensics, carrying his black-and-silver case.

"Hey, guys."

"Hey," Dan answered.

"This victim isn't as ugly as the last one," Captain Barlow replied.

"Good to hear. I'm still playing catch-up from the last one." He leaned over and checked the victim's pulse before moving on to document the time on a paper clipped to a wooden clipboard. Then he went straight to work, snapping photographs with his standard 35 mm digital camera, from the four corners of the kitchen, before zooming in on the body.

"How long do you think she's been dead?" Dan stared down at the dead body.

"By the muscle rigidity, I'd say no more than twelve hours." The whir of the clicking camera continued.

"Murdered last night in the safety of her own home. Scary shit." Dan shook his head.

Jim entered the kitchen with his notebook opened.

"The girlfriend of this victim will need some therapy."

"What do you have?" The captain wasted no time.

"The victim's name is Shelby Port. She is twenty-five years old. Her little girl, Annabel, had a sleep over at her grandma's house last night. Shelby Port was a nice girl. She'd been attending college, trying to make a better life for her and her daughter. No current boyfriend. Father of the child is non-existent. Shelby Port is a bit of a loner."

"So she's not a bar girl?" Dan asked.

"Not according to Arial Cure." Jim glanced at his notebook. "The two had a lazy night last night. They chilled and watched *The Devil Wears Prada*. Arial was bagged and went home. They were supposed to go shopping this afternoon for her little girl's third birthday, next week."

Dan shook his head, ripping the gloves off his hands. "Some birthday that kid's going to get."

"You two find the address of grandma's house and drive over there and deliver the bad news. And then find out what kind of past Shelby Port had. Maybe she has secrets."

"On it, Captain." Jim and Dan started walking away.

"Meet back in the conference room at six o'clock sharp. We need to stay tight on this one."

"One more thing, Captain. There are reporters across the street." Jim stated.

"Tell them nothing."

"Not a problem."

The wooden door creaked closed.

The captain turned his attention back to Derk.

"Captain, I'll have the results faxed to you as fast as I can."

"Thanks, Derk."

"The body will be going to the cooler. Then she will have to be identified by the next of kin."

"Grandma." The captain's stomach rolled at the thought of another mother having to see her daughter on a steel slab because of some mental defect that enjoyed murdering women. "When will you be finished up here?"

"I should be finished here around five. I'm afraid the viewing will have to be this evening some time. I'll let you know when the body is ready to be identified."

"No problem." Captain Barlow watched his step as he moved down the hallway. He stopped at the wall and stared at the picture of a smiling mom, holding her precious baby girl. It reminded him of his wife and daughters. At times like these, Captain Barlow hated this job.

He stepped out into the warm sunlight as the wooden door creaked closed behind him. He pulled off his gloves and booties before heading down the steps.

"Gill, I want you and couple of others to survey this area. Time to start knocking on doors and find out who heard what last night and what time. Give me a report at the end of your shift. And have someone safeguard this house until Derk is finished collecting evidence and the body is transported to the morgue."

"Roger that, Captain Barlow." He gave a loud whistle to a couple of the uniforms standing around getting a tan. He'd give them something to do, all right. Gill watched Captain Barlow get in his vehicle and drive away.

Chapter Twenty-One

Ellen drove into the parking garage of the municipal building on Second Street. All the ammo she needed was hidden inside her worn-out attaché case. This was one mission she intended to win. Lives were at stake. The bell rang, and the elevator doors opened. She stepped inside the mirrored box and pushed number three on the brass-plated numeral panel. During the ascent to the third floor, Ellen had time to fix her hair, add a light coat of lipstick, and straighten her collar before the steel doors slid open. *Not bad for an old gal*, she thought. She smiled, giving herself an approving wink prior to stepping out. She took a deep breath, having no qualms about what she was up against when it came to Mayor Cleaver's obduracy.

Ellen eyed Cleaver's bombshell of a secretary with her low-cut white blouse and silicon breasts. This beauty had curves in all the right places. Ellen wasted no time, making her way to the counter.

"May I help you?" Cleaver's secretary asked with a veneer white smile.

"Doctor Smith to see Mayor Cleaver." Ellen leaned on the polished counter and waited patiently. She had learned a long time ago that if she put doctor in front of her name, it commanded faster service most of the time. A form of manipulation she didn't mind throwing around.

The secretary placed the receiver back in its cradle and politely said, "The mayor is expecting you. Please go right in."

"Thank you." Ellen moved along the super-soft red carpet that led to a corner office just down the hall. She was surprised to find the door ajar. She knocked a couple of times. "Anyone in?" She poked her head inside the opening.

"Ellen!" Tomus smiled, coming away from his cushy black leather chair to greet her. "You look as lovely as ever."

"Who are you trying to kid?" She gave him the look, letting him know she wasn't buying his bullshit.

"Can I get you something?"

"Water will be fine, thank you." Ellen took a seat in one of the leather, black chairs positioned in front of Cleaver's desk.

Mayor Cleaver's secretary appeared in the doorway.

"Mr. Cleaver, is there anything you need?"

"Ice water for Doctor Smith."

"Right away." She wiggled out the door, her plaid mini-skirt showing the long legs of a super model.

Cleaver let out a sigh. "My condolences, I am so sorry to hear about Tom." Ellen could almost see a hint of feeling in his eyes.

"Thank you, Tomus."

Tomus rounded his desk, returning to his chair behind his desk.

The secretary returned to the office, carrying a silver tray, holding a crystal canter filled with ice water and two crystal glasses. She set the tray down on the corner of the desk and again gave her boss her best flirtatious smile.

"Is there anything else, Mayor Cleaver?"

"Hold my calls," Cleaver said, "and close the door on the way out, please, Lily."

"Yes, Mayor Cleaver." She silently exited the room.

"Mayor Cleaver, well now," Ellen teased, making a point to look over her shoulder at the closed door.

"Great manners." His face flushed.

"That's not all she has, is it?"

"Are you implying there's more to this professional relationship?"

"No. No implying. Just hope she can type for your sake," Ellen said, gesturing a surrender motion by putting up her hands.

"You are so bad, Ellen." Tomus smiled, shaking a finger at her.

"Sweet old ladies can get away with being flip now and again."

"Old, my ass. You have double the vigor of anyone I know, including Miss Wiggle."

"So you have noticed."

"I'd have to be dead not to."

Ellen raised her glass before taking a long sip to quench her thirst. Tomus moved his chair in closer to his desk, getting comfortable.

"Our conversation earlier sounded important. I mean, you are not the kind of lady that makes office calls without a motive. What is it I can do for you?"

"You would be correct; this is not a social call. I wish it were."

"So?"

"I'm here about the Roger Taut investigation."

"The media is having a field day with this lunatic's escape."

"Tomus, I want the truth printed."

"Truth? I believe that is exactly what the media is printing."

"Tomus, seven years ago, three women were brutally murdered by Roger Taut. I know what he did to these women and what he is still capable of doing. A young woman was found murdered in her west side apartment. I think it's the same MO."

"Ellen, I know where this is leading. But you have to be 100 percent sure. This guy Taut is probably long gone by now."

"Tomus, let me remind you, I interviewed this deranged psychopath. I've seen crime-scene photographs, and it makes the hair on the back of my neck stand up and pay attention. The murder on the west side is him."

"Where is the forensic evidence to back up your theory? I need physical evidence, Ellen. You know, blood, hair, a fiber, something that can tie him to the crime. I can't order the press to release information based on a theory and lack of proof. It will become a witch-hunt for the guy. Not that he doesn't deserve to be back in lock up, it's just …"

"Then call it my proficiency, if you will. Tomus, I have devoted most of my life studying minds of the mentally sick. I believe I have the credentials to back up what you call just a theory."

"And what if you're wrong?"

"What if I'm right?" She let the thought hang in the air for a moment.

"You can't accuse a man of slaughtering some woman because he's escaped from River Edge. I agree it's impeccable timing, but it's not bulletproof. Like I said earlier, he's long gone."

"Right now he's our number-one suspect."

"Yes, suspect."

Ellen could feel the warmth creeping its way up her chest like a thick spider web, spreading across her neck. It wasn't a hot flash; she was way beyond menopause.

"Captain Barlow personally invited me on board this investigation because of my extensive research and knowledge of this known offender. We are not dealing with a normal mind here. Roger taut is a delusional psychopath with underlining issues, which makes him far more dangerous and harder to catch. The trail of devastation he will leave in the wake of this city will be unfathomable."

"What is it you want from me?" Tomus asked regretfully.

"I need your permission to place a front-page article warning women that Roger Taut is dangerous. To immediately call police if anyone has seen him."

"I will not put this city in a panic on a bloody whim or instinct. Whatever the hell you want to call it." He leaped out from behind his desk and paced back and forth in front of the window. "How can you ask me to push a panic button without the evidence to back it up?"

"If you don't, the body count will rise well into the double digits. Trust me, seven years ago, Roger Taut was just getting started. At least in River Edge we were able to keep him medicated, but now that he's loose, it will be one big Judas Playing Field to him. And when more women end up dead and the families find out that I came to you for help and you turned me down, you won't win the next election—guaranteed."

His thoughts were spinning like a gerbil in a wheel, round and round.

"Oh Christ! How did this son of a bitch escape from a secure, locked-down mental facility?"

"I can't give you the answer to how he escaped, but I promise I intend to find out."

Cleaver wiped the edgy sweat from his brow. "I should have said I was too busy to see you. Goddamn it, Ellen!"

"You could have, but you didn't. The fact still remains. This city has a serial killer at large, and it's your duty and responsibility to keep these women safe. You took an oath, remember?"

"I want to say yes go ahead, but I'm afraid I can't. I need concrete evidence linking him to the murder on the west side."

"You would risk one more life for the sake of your precious reputation?" Ellen glared across the desk, leveling Cleaver with her hard eyes. He tried to look away, but she had him in her sights.

"My reputation? The media will hang me out to dry if you're wrong and Roger isn't the one responsible for the west side slaying."

"Damn it!" She slammed her hands down on the arms of her chair. "I have never in my career accused anyone of something so horrendous as murder. If Roger keeps killing these women, and he will, you won't have a goddamn reputation to worry about. And don't think I won't go tell the media I warned you that women will die." Her nostril flared.

Cleaver put his head down momentarily. Ellen thought, *Finally, he's come to his senses.* His head snapped back up.

"Listen to me for a moment. I am not undermining your professional integrity or the years of knowledge and training. But before we go scaring the hell out of this city, how can you know it's him for certain?" Cleaver asked.

"This is how!" She nodded, opening her briefcase.

One by one, she spread the gruesome crime-scene photographs across his uncluttered desk. Sarah Miles, Tyra Field, Clara Howard, and last, Josey Moran.

"What the hell are these?" He tried to look away from the grizzly sight.

"These are Roger's victims!" She pointed at each picture. "You still want more proof?"

The color suddenly drained from his face; he felt sick to his stomach. "Christ have mercy!" he exclaimed, fear protruding from his eyes.

"Satisfied?" Ellen barked. "Now try to imagine the horrible suffering these women must have felt while Roger went to work on them. Try to visualize the suffering and fear women must have felt when they knew they were going to die. And this lead pipe here"—she pointed to the blood-splattered piece of pipe—"was the weapon used to rape Josey Moran. One of these images could be your wife."

Ellen looked up from the desk. Cleaver's pale complexion turned a yellowish green. Tomus dashed from the office—she assumed to go to the men's room and puke. A few minutes went by before Tomus returned. He was noticeably sallow. The morbid display still stretched out across his desk.

Ellen turned from the window, hearing him reenter. "You okay?"

"What do you think?" He wiped his mouth with his silk hanky.

"Think about the families who have lost these loved ones. They will never be the same, but you have the power to caution other unsuspecting victims."

"Okay, Ellen. You've made your point," he declared, taking a sip of ice water, trying to cool down the burning in the back of his throat.

The doctor slowly collected each individual photograph and slid them back into their assigned files.

"You win! Warn the public."

"We all win if we catch him. Thank you. I won't take up any more of your time." She clicked her briefcase closed.

The mayor cordially escorted Ellen to the door, placing his hand on her shoulder. "Catch this bastard."

"Count on it!" She nodded and walked out the door and down the hall to the elevator. *Mission accomplished*, she thought and pushed the button.

Chapter Twenty-Two

The next morning, Franki woke up, sunlight pouring in through the cracks of her shutters that she'd forgotten to close the night before. The clock on the nightstand read 8:09. She threw back the sheets and rolled out of bed. The loft was unusually quiet since Beth had gone back to her family in Ottawa, and Sandy was at work. Franki shuffled to the bathroom to take a pee; against her better judgment, she decided to forgo brushing her teeth. It wasn't like she had anyone to talk to; her morning breath mattered only to her. *What's wrong with being lazy once in a while?* she thought as she walked down the hall.

Franki stood at the counter, taking a mug down from the glass cupboard. Her usual tantalizing waft of fresh brew smelt burnt. It had been sitting on the burner for who knew how long. She shrugged; the stronger the better. Moving over to the sink, she filled her glass with cold water and began gobbling down her daily supply of vitamins and medication. Pills that kept her alive, thanks to the late Dr. Blake.

Franki yawned, headed down the stairs, opened the door, and retrieved the morning paper. Making herself comfortable on the kitchen stool, she laid the paper out flat on the black marble counter and began to read. Roger Taut's picture was splattered across the front page with the headline; Women Beware. Convicted Murderer Escapes

River Edge. Considered To Be Very Dangerous. *This will certainly put women on alert*, thought Franki. Dr. Ellen Smith, head of psychiatry, sends warning to women of Victoria. "Roger Taut, convicted felon, is wanted for questioning in the death of Josey Moran. Women are to please be vigilant of your surroundings. Use the buddy system if you have to be out. If anyone has seen Roger Taut, please contact the police immediately."

Franki rubbed the nape of her neck. "Way to kick some political ass, Doc!" When Dr. Smith set her mind to something, there was no hurdle too big to leap. She was a tough, old bird. Franki stared at the photograph, mesmerized by Roger's chiseled features. But it was his vacant eyes. The eyes of someone so evil that it sent cold chills racing up her spine, covering her entire body with goose bumps. Her body shivered at the vacant orbs of blackness. This man had no soul. Empty. Dark. Evil. She wrapped her arms tightly around herself, trying to rid the memory of her own encounter with eyes as cold and evil as Roger's. She shook the dread off and finished reading the rest of the paper. Then she dropped it into the blue recycling box where it belonged. Franki had given all the attention she was going give those psychopaths. It was time to get on with her day.

After a hardy breakfast of bacon and eggs, she quickly made herself presentable for the day ahead before settling down at her desk to complete a day of writing. Her new book was scheduled for release next year. She of all people knew how fast time could fly by and began clicking keys as fast as the story unraveled in her mind.

Chapter Twenty-Three

Sandy arrived around seventy twenty at River Edge for her morning shift. The weather was beautiful, the sun was glowing, and a light breeze caressed her face as she walked across the parking lot. The weather did not reflect the pandemonium outside of River Edge. The place was swarming with added security. The media had entered the parking lot—how, she had no idea. No one was supposed to get beyond the gate without a pass. Luckily for her, she'd already been alerted as to what to expect. Her only hope was that inside the building was calmer than outside. This kind of unwarranted hullabaloo could certainly throw a few of her patients into a mental spin. With all of Helen Strat's phobias of the outside world, this would surely have her running for cover under her bed. And it would take a fair amount of negotiating to get her to come out. Before Sandy even stepped foot inside the facility, she sensed it was going to be one hell of a day.

The corridors were overflowing with loud chatter about the escapee. Security marched the hallways and guarded the exits, as if by some miracle Roger would appear out of thin air. *Nice try*, she thought. Nurses, doctors, and orderlies bragged at how they could do a better job finding Taut than the police department. *Everyone's a hero in someone else's field of expertise*, she thought, making her way along the corridor to the staff area. Opinions were like asses, and everyone had one. Sandy placed her belongings inside her locker and headed straight to the second-floor nurses' station. She said her good mornings and proceeded to view the five charts hanging on the wall peg. The nurse scanned the medical data, looking for any changes that might have transpired throughout the night before heading across the hall to check in on Gloria Shelby.

Sandy opened the door and stepped inside. Gloria was lying underneath her covers, staring up at the ceiling, waiting for breakfast to arrive.

"Good morning, Gloria. I see someone is feeling better." Sandy smiled, stepping up to the bed.

"No tubes." Gloria pointed to her face.

"How do you feel?"

"Tired."

Sandy took off her stethoscope from around her neck to examine Gloria's vitals. Blood pressure one-twenty over seventy-one. Sandy could no longer hear the rub in her lungs caused by pneumonia. And Gloria's pulse was sixty-six beats per minute. Perfect range. Sandy charted the findings, pleased that Gloria was well on her way to recovering again.

"Are you tired?"

Gloria shook her head. "No." She sighed.

"Do you hurt anywhere?"

"No." She remained staring up at the ceiling.

"Remember, you still need rest and don't forget to take your Tenofovir. You know the bright blue pill. It will help block the HIV from going into your healthy cells, okay?"

She nodded. "No do that again."

"Learned your lesson, did you?"

"Stupid virus make me real sick."

"Bad virus is right. That's why it's so important you take your pills."

"Bad cough." Gloria put her hand on her chest to show Sandy where it hurt.

"Within a couple more days of rest, you'll be feeling as good as new." Sandy smiled, stroking Gloria's red hair.

"Franki come today?" Gloria threw back the covers and waited for an answer.

"I don't know, sweetheart. Franki has been very busy. She had to go to a funeral."

"My daddy die."

"I know."

"Franki tell me Da … ddy go to heaven." She pointed to the ceiling.

"Yes, heaven."

"Can't see him no more." She shook her head back and forth. "Where Franki?"

"I think she's at home."

"My friend Franki." An expression of sadness washed over her features.

"I'll tell her that you miss her."

"I have present." She pointed to the colorful picture on the nightstand. "I give it to her."

Sandy picked up the colored picture of a princess and prince sitting alongside a brook with bunnies and butterflies.

"Are you going to wrap this pretty picture?"

"No paper." She shrugged.

"There's paper in the craft room. You could paint a nice design and then wrap the picture inside the paper. This way Franki won't know what it is."

Gloria's eyes lit up. Suddenly she was out of bed, housecoat half slung over one shoulder, marching her way to the door.

"Hey! Where are you going?"

"Art room."

"The art room is closed."

"When?" She placed a hand on her slender hip.

"After lunch. I'll come and get you."

"Promise?"

"I promise." Sandy smiled.

"Tell Franki—present for her." Gloria was now struggling to catch her breath. She wasn't as healthy as she thought she was.

Gloria walked back to her night table and held up a book. *Love You Forever* by Robert Munch.

"And she has to finish reading you the story. Gotcha." Sandy made an accurate guess.

Gloria came around the foot of the bed and plunked down on the side of it.

"I hear breakfast," Sandy sang, cupping the outside part of her ear.

"Hungry." Gloria patted her empty belly.

"I'll get breakfast right now."

Gloria let out a dramatic, "Please," like she hadn't eaten in a month.

A moment later, Sandy returned carrying Gloria's morning feast. She set the tray down on the table and rolled it next to the bed. "Anything else, my dear?"

"Nope." She quickly removed the lid.

"I'll come after lunch and take you to the art room."

"Art room." She nodded, taking a bite of her toast.

"Have a nice morning." Sandy stepped into the hallway, leaving Gloria to her breakfast.

By late afternoon, Sandy was due to take her last break. She was just passing by Ellen's old office when the door swung open, scaring her half to death. She jumped. Then grabbing her chest a second later, she was able to take a breath. Dr. Sutherland had walked out into the corridor.

He snickered. "Sorry. I didn't mean to startle you."

"I'll live." Sandy flushed a scarlet red.

Maybe all this talk about Roger Taut was really getting to her. Plus the fact that someone had tried to break into her home had left her a bit unsettled.

"I was just coming to find you. Do you have a minute?" The doctor smiled.

With the day from hell she'd been having, what was one more interruption? "Sure, why not."

"Please come in."

Sandy entered his office, closing the door behind her. "How may I be of service, Dr. Sutherland?"

"Please call me Mark. Sutherland sounds so formal."

"Okay." Sandy could feel a tiny pool of sweat forming on her palms. This guy was absolutely gorgeous.

"I wanted to try that new restaurant on Lemix Road, the Quill. I was hoping you would accompany me? That is, if don't have other plans."

Sandy's stomach plummeted like a falling elevator. This dating thing was not her field of expertise. It was obvious how uncomfortable this felt to her by the web of red capillaries slowly creeping up her neck. Her last relationship with her best friend, Peter, hadn't ended so well. Their friendship broke up, leaving her wounded and afraid to take another chance on love.

"Pardon?" There seemed to be a loud ringing in her ears, never heard before.

"I said—"

"I heard you," she interrupted. "I mean, why … me?"

"One: I'd like to get to know you better. Two: I thought it might be fun."

"Mark, there are gorgeous, single nurses that would trade their grannies to have dinner with you."

"I'm looking at a gorgeous woman, and you are single, right?" He smiled at her shyness.

"Yeah, I'm certainly single."

"And you do like to eat, right?" He began stepping closer.

"Of course."

"Good. Then it's a date, Saturday night. I'll pick you up around seven."

"Seven … a date." She nervously laughed. *He could have any single lady he wanted at River Edge, and he picked me,* she thought.

"Can I have your address and telephone number?"

"Sure."

Mark picked up his cell phone and keyed in the information Sandy was giving. Just like that, she had a date with Mr. Drop-Dead Dazzling.

Mark dropped his cell back into his white jacket pocket and moved across to his desk. He leaned over, picking up a manila folder file.

"There is a second reason why I need to see you."

"And?"

"Her name is Sofia Orella."

"Admitted a week ago. She's still on the third floor."

"Can you have her brought down?"

"I can, but she's not stable."

"Meaning?"

"We've had to sedate her the past couple of days. Doesn't believe she belongs in a place like this. Everyone else is responsible for her problems. Wants to get out and back to her life of prescription medication. And she's upset to say the least."

"So there's been no diagnosis yet?"

"I'm afraid not."

I'll make the trip to the third floor."

"Bring reinforcements."

Mark smiled at Sandy's warning, but then again, he hadn't experienced Sofia Orella's wrath."

"Coming along?" He opened the door.

"Sorry, I'm on break." She looked at her watch. "You might want to take John in with you. She seems to respond better when he's standing at the door."

"Then John it is." He locked his door. "Enjoy your break, Sandy."

"I will. Thanks." She hurried to the staff room with only eight minutes left. She had just enough time to eat her granola bar.

Chapter Twenty-Four

llen drove straight to River Edge after completing her mission at the mayor's office. The news vans had finally been ordered to the outside gate. They waited impatiently to be fed scraps of juicy details, like a bunch of vultures on fresh road kill.

Ellen parked in the underground garage and rode the elevator to the first floor. It was a sneaky way to avoid being bombarded with questions from the media. How could Roger escape the fourth floor without anyone knowing? Preoccupied in thought, she stepped out of the steel trap and headed toward the receiving station. Hearing a familiar voice trailing footsteps behind her, Ellen stopped to look behind.

"Well, look who it is."

Ellen smiled. "And a hello to you too."

"Here on business as usual?"

"Fourth-floor business."

"I take it retirement is cancelled."

"Oh, Sandy, I'd be bored to tears sitting at home. You've made it quite clear how you feel about me working with the police since Tom's death. But truly, it is helping me."

"I think it's only prolonging the inevitable grief you're trying to run from. You taught me that, Doctor." Sandy wiggled her brows.

"Stop listening to me."

"Yeah, like that will ever happen. So any new developments?"

"Trying to find answers to insanity." Ellen laughed.

"Playing detective, are we?"

"I know what questions to ask." She winked. "Are you still at Franki's place?"

"I'm going home soon. I hope."

"You stay put until your house is safe again!" Ellen ordered.

"Hey, no one is giving you trouble about being home alone. If my memory serves me correctly, Jack and Dorthy have gone back home, right?"

"Indeed they have. One: I'm certainly not Taut's type. Two: my place wasn't broken into." Ellen continued to count fingers. "And three: I'm hardly ever home."

"That sounds like a pot of justification if I ever stirred some. But to ease your mind a little, I will stay with Franki until my house is secured again. The guys from Homing Security are coming Thursday evening to put an alarm system in, and Home Depot is replacing my old door with a new one tomorrow night. By Friday, I should be back home safe and sound."

"Good to hear." Ellen nodded.

"I have good news. Want to hear?"

"I'd welcome it!"

"I have a date Saturday night."

"With whom?"

"Dr. Mark Sutherland." Sandy giggled.

"He's a real cutie, that one," Ellen said.

"He's taking me to dinner at the Quill. The new place over on Lemix."

"I'm impressed."

"Following the teasing I received from you and the brat the other day, you guys left me no choice but to prove both of you wrong. I'm not afraid of dating."

"That's the spirit. Congratulations."

"Thank you." Sandy took a bow.

"Why don't you give me a call this evening?" Ellen asked.

"No promises. I'm planning a nice long nap after I leave here. This place has been pretty crazy, if you know what I mean."

"No pressure."

"Try to stay out of trouble." Sandy shook her head.

"That's like telling a cow not to milk." Ellen gave a wave and headed in the opposite direction.

"Try not to burn out, old woman!" Sandy yelled over her shoulder.

On the fourth floor, Ellen approached the enclosed station with two official release documents for Taut's medical records. The signatures were from Bill Cobie, president of River Edge, and Judge Susan Denac. Ellen no longer had the authority to view patient medical records without proper authorization, since her retirement. Ellen was looking for some kind of interruption in Roger's day-to-day routine that could show her a sign to the event leading up to his escape. Even one little inconsistency might shine some light on how he fled to freedom.

The head nurse on duty, Cathy Kale, smiled as Ellen walked toward her.

"Well, well. I can only guess why you've come to visit."

Ellen smiled and handed Cathy the appropriate papers. "I need to have a look in Taut's quarters please. And all of his medical files."

"Sure thing. I knew it had something to do with Mr. Taut and not because you've missed this place." Cathy took a set of keys out of a locked drawer and handed the ring to Ellen through a window hole in the Plexiglas bubble. "You need company?"

"I'll be fine."

"The files will be ready for pick up upon your return. How's that for service?"

"I could always count on you." Ellen winked and walked across to the huge iron door that was designed to keep men like Roger Taut inside.

Ellen first made her inquires of the two security guards. Disappointed by their lack of information, she stuck the key into the deadbolt lock and clicked it open. The guard to the left pulled the door open so Ellen could enter. The familiar tortured moans and screams filled the corridor as she made her way along the passage to room 411. She stopped, taking a breath before stepping inside the madman's quarters. At first glance, everything within appeared ordinary.

Ellen began her search by first flipping the mattress, checking for small cuts or tears in the fabric where paraphernalia could be hidden. Nothing. She opened the nightstand drawer. Inside she found a romance novel and a stack of cards and letters. Ellen sat on the bed, flipping through the pages of the novel. Nothing. Then she began scanning the contents of the letters. One letter was from a woman, Ivy Strom, claiming she cured him of bad thoughts by sending him her uncontaminated vibrational energy from across the city. Another one declared her love for him. Apparently it happened the morning of his trial. The second was from Deni Race; she fell in love the second she laid eyes on Roger. Her heart told her they would be together, if not in this life, then the next. *Fan mail,* Ellen thought, shaking her head. A couple of photographs fell out, fluttering onto the bed. Ellen studied these photographs for a period of time, trying to get some sense as to why good-looking, well-educated women such as these two would risk writing to a man of this caliber. What could be missing in their lives that they felt the need to touch the fires of diabolical nefariousness? "Misery loves company," she said.

Ellen tucked them into an empty file folder. Now these love-stricken women would need police protection if Roger decided he needed a place to stay. Ellen sighed. She'd so desperately wanted to find a cryptic note, a map, a lead of some kind that could tell her where Roger was. The window was sealed shut. The screen and bars were still intact. It was clear he didn't go out the window. His clothes were in orderly piles on shelves in his closet. No coat hangers allowed. Ellen came to the conclusion Roger had to have had an accomplice. The son of a bitch didn't walk out of there on his own. He had help, but who? More importantly, why? Her mind fogged up, trying to conjure up a motive. Why would someone be so foolish as to set a dangerous psychopath free? The answer was not in this room. She stomped out to the hall and slammed the door behind her. The loud bang reverberated down the corridor like a loud explosion. Ellen didn't bother locking the door behind her.

Cathy had Roger's medical documentation sitting on the counter, as promised. The nurse came out of her protective barrier and handed Ellen her package.

"Cathy, I'll need collect surveillance tapes as soon as possible."

"Sorry, no can do. A big glitch in the security computer. The security company has been working diligently around the clock to reboot the system. All tapes for the last week have turned to snow."

"How convenient."

"Our computer tech doesn't understand. The system seems to be running fine, yet our tapes are still snow. And get this, the system goes down, what, a week—"

"I know, I know, right around the time Roger decides to take a hike out of here. I'll give the report to Captain Barlow."

"So how is that retirement working?" Cathy placed her hands on her extra-large hips.

"Me retire?" Ellen chortled.

"Not that it's any of my business, but you really should be home resting, instead of getting involved with this nightmare. Bloody hell, Ellen, Tom just passed away. I bet you haven't had the chance to even grieve yet."

"Don't worry. I'm just fine." Ellen patted Cathy on the shoulder. "Staying busy is good for me."

"Busy? Sounds like you're on the front line. I read the article."

"Then I don't have to warn you to be extra careful."

"Can I be frank?" Cathy didn't wait for Ellen's response. "There is no way Roger just strolled out of here. This is not the Holiday Inn. We maintain our strict protocol when handling patients from this area. This is a secured ward."

"I hear you. But something went wrong for Roger to go missing. And everyone working on this floor will be questioned."

"We were wondering when the police would get around to us."

"Within the next day or two."

"Since that warning to women came out in the paper, Dick is driving me everywhere, including the grocery store. And he hates grocery shopping. He'd rather have crows pick out his eyes, if you get my meaning, kinda hate." Cathy gave a hardy laugh.

"He wants to keep you safe."

"Yeah, must be love." She rolled her eyes. "All 203 pounds of me."

"Never mind. Be careful."

"I will. Oh, Ellen—"

"Yes?"

"Never mind. You take care, you hear?"

"I will." Ellen adjusted the files under her arm. "Thanks again." She held up the files and sauntered across the black-and-white checker tiled floor to the elevator. The guards said their mannerly good-byes as Ellen stepped into the steel lift that would take her to the underground parking garage.

Chapter Twenty-Five

Throughout the day, Franki periodically stepped away from her desk to take breaks from working on her newest novel, *Beyond the Fear*. Aimlessly, she roamed around the loft, twiddling her pencil around her long manicured fingers. Images of her sister's pretty face flashed across her mind. The shopping trip, museum, and underwater sea garden, all fond memories tugging at her heartstrings. Feelings of abandonment threatened to flood away a week of amazing memories. She would not let the darkness of her past life flood into her future. She'd already torn down those insecurities brick by brick, vowing to never build the wall again. Yet she couldn't help feeling like something good had been ripped away from her life, leaving her empty. She hated that Beth had to return home to her family. Tears sprang to her eyes. She wanted and needed a family too. Her mind swirled in a maze of jumbled, negative emotions, like usual. Franki felt selfish for even having those thoughts. Sandy and Doc were her family. It was just that she wanted to be close to Beth again. Close enough to look in her eyes, hear her laugh, feel the warmth of her hugs. It was hard to say good-bye to Beth. At least she had phone calls and text messaging to rely on. She would still be a part of her sister's life.

Franki wiped at her tears with the back of her hand. *Okay*, she thought, *enough acting like a spoiled brat. I can handle Beth being there and me here. It's not forever. Besides I have work to finish.* Franki had a sudden huge urge to drive to the airport, buy a ticket, and board the next flight leaving for Ottawa. Just to make sure her time spent with Beth was real and that her mind was not playing evil tricks on her. Franki plunked down in the old recliner to think this impulsive thought through. She knew Beth was real. What they shared in that week of being together was authentic and non-fictional. She chalked it up to having one of her moments, a moment of sadness that would pass like all the rest. Franki closed her eyes and began slow breathing until the turmoil inside subsided. She would not allow herself to call Doc or Sandy every time she had a little emotional disturbance. Although she was told to call anytime. Franki wanted to remain independent.

Franki was on her way to the kitchen when the phone rang, scaring the crap out of her. Taking a breath, she answered, "Hello."

"Hello, Miss Franki. How are you on this wonderful sunny day?" Asked her agent Salley.

"I'm good. And you?" She added cream and sugar to her steaming brew.

"Can't complain."

"So … what's up, Salley?"

"I'm having a get together at my place this evening. I was hoping to entice you away from work for a little while. I'm sure you could use a break."

"Yeah, no. Maybe so. Anything special going on?"

"Dinner with friends."

"Up to anything I should know about?"

"Like?"

"Trying to set me up on a pity date again."

"Wouldn't dream of it, dear." Salley giggled. "Besides, you work too hard."

"Not that hard." Franki winced, feeling a twinge of guilt while looking at the clock on her stove.

"Will you come?"

"What time?"

"Six-thirtyish."

"Can I bring something?"

"Just your pretty little self."

"Now I know I'm being set up." Franki laughed.

"Friends only. Promise."

"And besides, I have a—"

"Do I know him?"

"Nope, and I ain't telling."

"Now, now, I'm hearing terrible grammar."

"Oh piss off. How's that for grammar." Franki groaned, setting the dirty spoon in the sink.

"So will you join our little assemblage?"

"I'll be there."

"Can't wait. Kiss, kiss."

"Thank you for the invite."

Salley disconnected. The phone call from Salley was exactly what Franki needed to lift her spirits. She went back and finished the chapter she'd been struggling with. Her aim was to have another bestseller.

The next time Franki looked up from her laptop, Sandy was slowly making her way up the stairs. Franki's hard work had paid off. Day was now fading into late afternoon.

"Hey, Mama. How was your day?" Franki greeted Sandy with a hug.

"Long and tiring." She dropped her purse onto the floor.

"That bad? I heard it was a zoo over there. The press was ordered to stay behind the gate. Security? What the hell, the maniac is gone. He has no intention of returning. What are these people on? Glue?"

"Scavengers, my honey. Something tragic, they'll print it. Guy helps an elderly woman cross the street. That story doesn't see the light of day. Serial slayer. Now that sells papers, especially a murderer that escapes a mental facility."

"I know. I watched the news. This guy is a wackjob for sure. What I don't get is why all the security at the Edge. I mean, the guy is gone, and he isn't going back there. Like he wants to get himself arrested," Franki said.

"No clue." Sandy shrugged.

"Well until this psycho wackjob is captured, you can stay with me. I'll protect you." Franki winked.

"Hey, speaking of protection, I have good news. My new alarm system will be installed tomorrow, and Friday I'll have my new door put back on. And you, my dear, will have privacy again."

"Privacy?" Franki curled her lip. "You make a point of knowing my business." Franki felt a sharp stab of rejection.

"Hey. You know I love you. I just want to sleep in my own bed. I know you understand what I'm saying."

"Yeah, I do." Sandy held Franki in her arms and kissed the top of her head.

"It's just …"

"A little lonely since Beth went home?"

"How did you know? I miss her."

"I know you, sweetheart. I have a feeling you'll be seeing Beth soon. Why don't you call her and make arrangements to visit. It's not like you don't have the money. You can always take your work with you."

"Franki inhaled deeply. "I'll think about it."

"Okay now?" Sandy smoothed Franki's long blonde hair.

"Yes. Thanks." Franki sniffed and stepped back so Sandy could see she was fine again. "Okay, back to the wackjob. How did this guy get out of a locked-down prisonlike facility?"

"River Edge is not a prison."

"Could have fooled me. Remember, I lived inside that place," Franki said.

Sandy sighed. "Anyway, you and thousands of others are asking the same question. How did Roger get out of a locked-down facility? The answer is I don't know." Sandy rubbed her tense, sore neck.

"Other than Crazy Ville, how was your day?"

"Oh I almost forgot. Remember when you and Ellen were teasing me about dating? Well today, I've proven you both wrong. I am not afraid to date. In fact, Missy Miss, I have a date this Saturday night with Dr. Mark Sutherland."

"Why does that name sound familiar?" Franki tapped her finger against her bottom lip.

"He took over for Ellen."

"That dude is hot for his age! Way to go."

"Thank you. I think."

The two gave each other a high five.

Sandy plunked down on the leather sofa. "Before I forget, I have one more message for you."

"Shit! Gloria, I completely forgot."

"She really misses you. And you have a book to finish reading to her."

"*Love You Forever.*" Franki smiled fondly. "I'll stop by first thing tomorrow morning. Does she need anything?"

"Company. Her pneumonia is cleared, and her lungs are empty of fluid. She is happy to be rid of the oxygen tube. She's still tired, so don't do too much with her tomorrow."

"That's like saying, 'No, Franki, don't do that.' And guess what I'll do? The very thing I was told not to. Gloria's a lot like me, you know."

"Two little attitude peas in a one pod." Sandy shook her head.

"Do you have plans this evening?"

"Bed. I'm exhausted, honey. If I wake up later, I'll give Ellen a shout. What about you?"

"I should get over and see her too."

"Good luck with that. You want her, you'll find her at the police station."

Franki cracked up. "At least one of us has an exciting life. I came home thinking I'd have lots of time to play catch-up with missed family, friends, calls, and dates. Life of a writer is very time consuming."

"Anytime you want to trade glamour for bedpans, I'll go gladly to sign books and meet fans."

"Yeah right, Florence. You wouldn't last a day. You need people to need you. But to answer your earlier question, I'm having dinner at Salley's place."

"Please be very careful. Don't do anything that could put you in jeopardy, Franki. And don't roll your eyes at me. I mean it! Taut is a very dangerous individual."

"Chill, Mama. I got this. Now go to bed. I'll lock up when I leave."

"I'm serious, but I'm going." Sandy struggled onto her tired feet and shuffled down the hall to the spare bedroom.

She changed out of her nurse's uniform and into a cotton nightshirt. Then she slipped between the scented sheets. It had been a very long day; she sighed. She closed her heavy eyelids and fell into a deep slumber, hoping for sweet dreams of Mark Sutherland.

Chapter Twenty-Six

Detective Jim Masker had just finished confirming his date with Franki Martin for Saturday night. Dan sat opposite his partner, arms folded across his chest, hoping she'd turned Jim down. When he ever-so-confidently placed the receiver in its cradle, Dan knew without a doubt that his sleaze-bag partner had scored.

"So, tramp, what'd she say?"

"What do you think, big guy?" He grinned, snapping his mint-green gum.

"How do these nice women fall for the likes of you?"

"Irresistible charm, my man."

"Whatever happened to that Rosa? You know, the model you professed to have feelings for."

"Too serious. Started talking about moving in together."

"The city hooker is too serious for the likes of you."

"You should think about dating again. Get rid of some of that negative tension you have." Jim laughed.

"Yeah right." Dan picked up the report and began reading.

The captain popped his head out of his office and yelled at the detectives across the station. "Hey. You two!"

Simultaneously, they turned, eyeing the huge frame standing in the opening across the room.

"Yeah. I'm talking to you two. Get in here," he ordered.

They knew better than to keep the captain waiting. The two hustled from their desks.

"What's up, Captain?" Dan asked, standing just outside the door.

"Here's the medical report on Taut. All his comings and goings for the last week. And here is the research report on him, done by our genius Doctor Smith, here. I want both of you to read these reports. Find me a clue on how he got out."

Dan poked his head inside the office door.

"Hi, Doctor."

Ellen smiled. "Hello, Dan."

"Can I ask you a question?" The captain moved aside so Dan and his partner could enter.

"Hope I can help." She took a sip of her iced coffee.

"Is it possible Taut's gotten out of the city?"

"I don't believe so. Remember Josey?"

"And you think he'll kill again?"

"He already has, gentlemen."

"Your spider sense wouldn't happen to know who and where the body will be found, does it?" Dan rolled his eyes.

"Kape, cut the smartass crap," Captain Barlow said.

"Sorry, ma'am, no disrespect intended. But how can you be so sure it's him? There's been no report of a body turning up since Shelby Port, and we have nothing back from Derk saying it was the escapee. And as far as evidence found at the crime of Josey Moran, it was a partial print, which can't be identified as Roger. I think we should be looking at other unlawful perverts who don't like women, instead of tunnel visioning this lunatic."

"You can look elsewhere if you like, but I'm telling you it's a waste of time. I know Roger's behavior better than anyone. Trust me when I say he is responsible for the murder of Josey Moran and the Port woman and many more women to come if we don't catch him." Ellen swirled the ice around the tan liquid.

The captain walked around his desk and gathered up some loose papers and placed them back in the folder.

"It's a little cramped in here. Why don't we take this little meeting of the minds to the conference room."

"Good, 'cause I have more questions for Doctor Smith."

Ellen picked up her briefcase off the floor.

Immediately, all three followed Captain Barlow down a set of corridors until they reached the big wooden door marked Conference. The captain clicked the door open with a key and pushed it ajar. Once inside, each took a chair around the table. One by one, each person got comfortable, with the information needed in front. Ellen waited. Dan took a swig of his now tepid coffee and cleared his throat.

"Ask away, Dan." Ellen leaned her elbows on the table.

"Okay. I understand you studied this guy, but this is a high-profile case. Have you ever been wrong in a case like this one?"

"Yes, I've been wrong, but it was earlier in my career."

"And how were you wrong?"

"The case wasn't a high-profile one. It was a young mother who threatened to kill her children and herself. She was admitted to River Edge after her neighbor learned what she was going to do. She was assessed and incarcerated for a month, meaning she could not sign herself out. After a period of counseling, she seemed to be making progress. This woman no longer wanted to murder her children. I placed her on antipsychotic medication and signed her release. She was no longer a supposed threat. Three days after her release, she drowned her two kids in the bathtub. I should have trusted my gut and kept her incarcerated until I was 100 percent positive, but I went with patient trust. As much as we would love to, we don't have the funding to keep patients forever. I should have trusted my instincts and followed up, and I didn't. And two children are dead because of my oversight. I learned that it takes more than medical knowledge to make an accurate diagnosis. Today I use both, just like you, Detective."

"Ellen, I remember that case. You weren't the only one responsible for those children. If CAS had kept those babies safe like they were supposed to, those kids might be alive today. So you can't shoulder the entire burden," Captain Barlow said.

"Thanks, John, but it doesn't bring the babies back."

"I'm sorry, Doctor Smith. I didn't know." Dan straightened the papers in front of him. "Back to this case. Before Roger was committed to River Edge, where did he live? How far away did he live from his victims? Does he pick these women at random or is there a certain characteristic he looks for? I feel like I'm fumbling around in the dark here. Hands stretched out, but I can't feel squat. Know what I'm saying?" He raked his fat fingers through his already messy hair.

Ellen smiled. "First question first. Roger lived at 2127 Bodus Lane." Ellen pushed her chair back and moved across the room to the taped map on the wall. "All three ladies were murdered in this vicinity." She circled the location with a marker. "All three lived three or four blocks from Roger's apartment."

"Did he stalk these victims?"

"According to Roger, no. He'd met them at Legends, a nightclub on the main street. Again, let me say, these murders were not premeditated kills. It was an instant flash of rage brought on by a delusional psychotic breakdown owed to his tortured past. Now whether he's escalated into a monster, I have no way of knowing until he kills again. I'm sure after he's reinstated back to River Edge, the last thing he'll want are doctors picking his brain for answers like a lab rat. Although some people will disagree with me." She smiled across the table at Dan. "As far as fumbling in the dark, Dan, the documentation in the reports should shed light on the man this team is looking for." She sat back down, satisfied.

"Fuck, are we supposed to feel sorry for this guy or arrest his ass?" Jim flailed his hands in the air.

"Captain, what about the tips coming in? Who's handling them?" Dan asked, tossing his pen on the table.

"Constables Waun Firy, Sam King, and Lacy Hagen are manning the phones, while Detectives Matt Cure and Michael Lissner are out combing through every lead. So far, Roger's been seen at the grocery store, walking his dog, jogging through the goose trail. Every lead has been followed up with a big fat nothing, but the day is just getting started."

Dan leaned over the table, aggressively grabbed one of the many files on the table, and began carefully examining the information on each page. Seconds later, his partner joined the task. The room became quiet as each member of the team tried to figure out what Roger's next move would be and which part of the city the body would be found.

A couple of hours passed. Dan stood up to stretch his now aching back. Jim decided it was time to break for coffee. It was going to be another long day and a longer night if Captain Barlow had anything to do with it.

Chapter Twenty-Seven

Down in the vault at headquarters, Detective Masker was just opening the driver's door when his partner's cell phone rang. Dan flipped it open and leaned against the side of the Camaro. "Kape here ... When? ... Where?" He flipped his notepad open and jotted down the address while trying to balance his cell phone on his shoulder. "Fifteen minutes tops ... Yeah, secure the area, and no one goes in or out. Got me?" Dan didn't wait for a reply before sliding his bulk into the front seat and shutting off his cell phone.

"What's up?" Jim asked, already knowing the answer.

"River Edge will have to wait. A body found at 1616 Braze Road."

"I think you should notify the captain." Jim roared the engine to life.

"I'm already on it." The detective began keying the numbers to the captain's cell phone.

Jim backed out of his parking space, heading onto Mow Street. He listened to Dan giving the captain details of what little he knew. "Yeah ... yeah ... I'll know more when we get to Braze, sir. See you there." Dan placed his cell phone back in the case. "He'll meet us there."

"That much I figured. This prick better not interrupt my date with

Franki Saturday evening or I'll be pissed." Jim turned south onto Lower Street, a block and a half from the crime.

"Don't get too excited about your date, Romeo. If Doctor Smith is right about this guy, the only woman you'll be spending time with is one on a cold metal table in the morgue. At least she'll be naked, buddy, just the way you like them."

"There you go breathing out all that negativity. And just to let you know, buddy, my date with Franki will go forward. I don't care how many bodies show up. It's not like the dead are going anywhere."

Dan chuckled. He loved getting a rise out of his partner. It was one of the highlights of his day.

"C'mon, get real. The only fragrance you'll be sniffing is decomposing flesh at the morgue. There will be no bedding down the good author for you. You'll see a naked body all right—"

"I'm not listening." Jim put his hand up.

"Karma is a wonderful thing." Dan smirked, leaning his head against the headrest.

As the detectives pulled up to the curb, the entire front yard at 1616 Braze had been secured with bright yellow crime tape. At the end of the street, a cruiser was parked, blocking all access. A gaggle of concerned faces had already begun gathering across the street. Detective Kape was the first out of the car. He looked back and saw his partner doing some male grooming. "Hey, it's not like the corpse will be impressed there, lover boy."

"You should take lessons on appearances." Jim popped a breath mint in his mouth and smirked at his partner. "You never know when you'll find your photograph on the front page."

"Get out of the damn car, will you. We have work to do." He raised his brow and walked over to Officer Terry Levine.

"Hey, Terry."

"Hi, Dan. How is it going?"

"If we could catch this prick, the sun will shine again."

"I hear down at the station there are no leads."

"Oh there are leads … from every nut job in the city. So what do we have, Terry?"

"Got a call from the neighbor, Barb Push. Said she hadn't seen the victim, Diane Gibber, in a couple of days. The car hadn't moved in a couple of days, which meant the victim obviously hadn't been to work. She called over to see if she was okay. When Gibber didn't answer her phone, Mrs. Push decided to make a house call. No one answered the front door, so she went around to the back and found the patio door unlocked. She let herself in. Found the victim in her bedroom."

"Dead!"

"You guessed it. Called 911, which was dispatched to me. And here we are."

"Terry, get a statement from the Push woman and tell the other officers to scout the neighborhood to see if anyone saw something— starting with the people across the street. We need to know if this woman's murderer is the perp we're looking for."

"No problem. I'll have a full report for you by the end of the night."

"And, Terry, find out the names of the victim's family. Tell the captain when you do."

"Right away."

Dan watched Terry make his way to the woman standing near the yellow fire hydrant, her face drained of color. She had to be the neighbor who found the victim. The finders always had the look of incredulousness and shock.

Detective Masker stood by the car, taking snapshots of the crowd across the street when Dan yelled out his name. Together they made their way up the driveway and entered the home of 1616 Braze Road. The house had been airtight for at least two days. Dan and Jim stepped inside the door, and the stench of death hit their senses like a wet wool blanket. Jim gasped, covering his face with his arm.

"Aren't you glad you combed your hair and ate a breath mint?" Dan winked, covering his mouth and nose with a handkerchief.

"Jesus Christ!" Jim coughed into his sleeve. "Where's the body?"

"Upstairs bedroom. Follow the scent, you wuss." Dan led. He made a right turn on the landing, eyeing the officer standing in the open doorway. He looked like he was fighting back the bile rising up in suds in the back of his throat.

"Take a break. We got this." Dan patted the officer's shoulder.

"Thank you, sir." He took off running, taking the stairs three at a time. Dan heard the door slam shut seconds later.

"Saved his ass," Jim grumbled, trying not to gag.

The detectives pulled on latex booties and gloves before entering, making sure they contaminated nothing at the crime scene. In the master bedroom, Diane Gibbers' naked body was positioned in an X. Her ankles and wrists were tied to the bed with rope. Dan stepped over to the bed, noticing her wrists and ankles were lacerated from the struggle. There were signs of sexual assault, but they would know for certain once the deoxyribonucleic acid results came back. There were hesitation cuts on her throat, meaning this could not be the work of Roger Taut. Arterial spray danced up the headboard. Everything in the bedroom looked to be in order. Could Diane have known her attacker? Or was this some random kill done by a stranger looking to prove something? Dan stared into Diane's milky eyes, seeing the last moments of her life. She knew she was going to die.

There was a knock on the door. Jim and Dan turned in the direction of the sound. Captain Barlow and Doctor Smith stood in the opening, suiting up to enter. The two stepped up to where the detectives were standing. Ellen slowly moved around the bed to the other side, not saying a word.

"What do we have?" the captain asked.

"The victim's name is Diane Gibber. Her throat has been slashed; she bled out quickly, by the arterial spray. She appears to have been sexually assaulted, and as you can see, she was tied to her bed during the attack."

Ellen shook her head, deeper wrinkles furrowing between her brows. She leaned down for a closer inspection. She too noticed the hesitation cuts on the victim's throat. The victim's blonde hair had been brushed, fanning out on her bloodstained pillow. She looked across at the guys and cleared her throat. "This is not one of Roger's victims."

"Ellen?" The captain eyed his trusted companion. "Are you sure?"

"One: There are indecision marks on the throat. Roger would not vacillate. Two: Roger makes his victims suffer for as long as possible. This murder was made to look like Roger did it." Ellen turned and walked out of the bedroom, leaving the captain and his detectives in awe.

"I'll go find out what that was all about. Jim, get on the phone and tell Derk I want this entire room scanned and dusted for prints. Leave nothing unturned. And tell him I want all reports back on my desk like yesterday. This case is his number-one priority."

"Oh he's going to love hearing this." Jim began to dial Derk's number.

"I don't give a shit!" Captain Barlow stripped off his gloves and rubber booties.

"C'mon, Captain, give the forensic geek a break. He's still trying to play catch-up with the last murder," Jim said.

"And I still don't give a shit. We need to know if this city has two psychopaths on the loose. Hear me?" He yelled from the hall.

"I hear you!" Jim yelled back. "Loud and clear." He groaned.

Detective Kape stepped outside, inhaling a couple deep breaths. The fresh air couldn't cleanse the layer of decomposition from his lungs. Instead, he walked to the bullpen and lit a smoke. He looked out, eyeing Jim chirping on his cell phone. A few feet away, Captain Barlow and Doctor Smith were in what looked to be a pretty heavy discussion. Cops were across the street questioning the concerned neighbors and taking notes. Blue and red lights flashed against the backdrop of twilight that was slowly pushing out the daylight. Dan inhaled another lungful of poison, taking in a minute's peace before this insanity would start all over. When he was finished, he crushed out his smoke and tucked the filter back in his pack. He wasn't one for littering. Dan started for the car when Jim came rushing up beside him.

"I talked to Derk, and he is pissed."

"Hey, we all have a job to do."

"Yeah, but the guy has been on his own for over a week. The rest of his team is out on holiday."

"Not for much longer if the captain has anything to do with it."

Dan leaned against the passenger door, hands hidden in his jean pockets.

"You know, I don't get it. One minute, the doctor says bodies will turn up in the double digits. And then, when a body is found, the old woman recants, saying it's not the freak from Crazy Ville. I mean, Jesus H. Christ, make up your mind. I don't know why she's here in the first place. What does she know about police work?" Frustration strained Jim's larynx to the point where his voice cracked.

"Captain called it. All we can do is wait on forensic." Dan spat.

"Don't you agree? She's a shrink, not a cop. I don't understand why the old woman was asked to join us in the first place. As far as I'm concerned, all she's given us are her damn files. What we need to be doing is chasing down leads with Cure and Lissner, not reading some damn reports."

"At least now we know more about our suspect. Her profile is accurate and insightful."

"So what! We could learn just as much from reading forensic reports. We've caught bad guys before without her expertise."

A few minutes later, the detectives watched Derk get out of the black van, open the rear doors, and take out his matching black box. Suited in his magnolia latex attire, he gave a wave. Then without warning, a beautiful blonde opened the passenger door and slid out, dressed in a pair of skinny jeans that fit to perfection and a long-sleeve T-shirt that clung in all the right places. Her long blonde hair hung almost to her waist. Jim's mouth gaped opened.

"Well, well. Looks like Derk isn't working alone."

She smiled at the detectives and walked to the back of the vehicle.

"Close your mouth before you get your shirt all wet from the drool you're about to spill," Dan said to Jim.

"She's hot."

"That's what you said about Franki Martin. You do remember the date. Saturday night?"

"I have a date. I'm not dead."

"You are such a womanizing dog." Dan walked over to the van.

"Hi, Dan, I'd like you to meet my life saver and best friend since high school. Brook Margin, meet Detective Dan Kape. The best in the business."

"Please to meet you, Brook." Dan shook hands.

"Brook has offered her services. Lucky for me she's a crime-scene photographer and on holiday. Two of my guys are out sick, and Ivy is taking a week that's been owed to her."

"Lucky for you. I hear you're backlogged."

"You could say that. Pretty soon I won't be able to find my desk for paperwork."

"I feel your pain, my friend." Dan placed a hand on Derk's shoulder.

"You guys any closer to catching this nutcase?"

"I'm afraid—"

"Not at this point," Jim interrupted. "So you're not alone?" He smiled his pearly white smile.

"Brook, this is Detective Masker. Dan's partner in crime."

"Have we met before?" Jim turned on his charm.

"I'm afraid not." Brook continued to suit up before rummaging in the back of the van for her digital equipment, avoiding any physical contact with the stud, including a courteous handshake. It was obvious she'd been warned.

"Sorry to cut this little social short, boys, but death awaits. Do me a favor and tell Captain Slave Driver over there that I'm doing the best I can."

"Tell him yourself," Dan teased.

"Funny, Danny boy. One body?"

"Tied and throat slit. Yup."

"Messy?"

"A little arterial spray, but you've seen worse."

"Brook, I'm not trying to tell you how to do your job—"

"So don't," she snapped and walked toward the house.

Derk laughed. "I'll collect whatever evidence is there and get it to you as soon as I can."

"You're a good man, Derk."

"Tell that to the boss." He picked up his black box.

Dan saw the offended scowl on his partner's face. "What?"

"Who pissed on her rose bush?"

"Maybe you should learn to keep your opinions to yourself. Thanks."

"Anytime." Dan shrugged his shoulders.

Dan left his conversation with Jim to talked to Captain Barlow "Sorry for the disruption, sir. Just wanted to let you know I'm stopping for a bite to eat first. Want anything?"

"Lost my appetite."

"Doctor?"

"No thank you."

"I want the ex-husband brought in for questioning. I hear he's not too fond of his ex." Captain Barlow ordered.

"I'll pick him up once I've had something to eat, sir. Man cannot live on death alone. Text me the address when you have it."

"Ellen and I will be heading across town to the victim's brother's place."

The detectives sped down the road to Burger King, and Ellen and Captain Barlow to their first stop, the home of Manuel Gibber, brother of Diane Gibber, deceased.

Chapter Twenty-Eight

After returning from 1616 Braze Road, Ellen and John sat enveloped in the quietness of the conference room, collecting their thoughts. Captain Barlow had his head leaning against the back of his chair, eyes closed. The murders were getting to him. Ellen busied herself with the crime-scene photos of Sarah, Tyra, and Clara, and the recent one of Josey Moran. Her mind kept flashing back to the latest victim, Diane Gibber. Her lying on the bed didn't add up to the others. She was 100 percent certain that the death of Diane Gibber had nothing to do with Roger Taut. The cut across the victim's throat was not nearly as vicious, and the hesitation marks—someone was trying to make it look like the work of Roger Taut but had trouble going through with it.

Captain Barlow opened his eyes and gave a loud sigh into the still air. Ellen turned. "C'mon, out with it." She broke the silence.

"We don't have one solid lead. Roger hasn't vanished into thin air. Where could he be hiding? Detective Mike Lissner and Matt Cure have followed every lead. They've checked all of Roger's friends and acquaintances. The entire police force is out on foot patrol looking for this guy. Every area of this city is being patrolled, and still nothing."

"If you're asking me if he's left the city, I'm telling you no."

"How can you know this for certain?" He fingered the knot of his tie.

"To know and understand the mind of a dangerous man is to identify the design of behavior. Roger will not deviate from his pattern. Most perilous killers have a set design. Roger was apprehended once; he'll be apprehended again."

"Yes, and how many other women will lose their lives in the process?"

"I can't answer that."

John rubbed the stubble on his face.

"My wife is terrified."

"And so are a lot of other women. John, you must believe you're doing the best you can. The pressure is enormous; I get it. But you will catch him."

"I understand the whole abused psyche thing, but I've known lots of children that come from horrible backgrounds, and they've gone on to live productive, humanitarian lives. Predators like Taut make it hard to have compassion for their abusive childhoods."

"The horrible atrocities Roger suffered growing up literally changed the trajectory of his life. I'm not asking you to feel sorry for him. Some time ago, Roger had no choice but to shut the pain down in order to survive. It was as if his personality split into two parts. One part of him remained the defenseless child boy that was forced to endure unfathomable cruelties, while the other became the vengeful, narcissistic psychopath. That part of him feels nothing for anyone."

"What will happen when he's detained?"

"He will be taken back to the asylum and placed under heavy security. He will be watched twenty-four/seven until his trial date."

"Then what?" John slammed his hand down on the table. Ellen watched as papers fluttered off the table, landing onto the carpet.

"Feel better?" She bent down, retrieving the pages. "I can promise you this time, John, he will not finish out his sentence at River Edge. This time Roger will go to prison. I'll make sure of it."

"In the meantime, the son of a bitch will be lying around in his pajamas, lost in his own little land of delusion. What about the families of the deceased? Each day for them is another day spent in hell. They don't get to escape the pain and grief. Josey's mother fell apart at the news of her daughter's death. And this morning, I got a call from Tyra's mother, begging me to catch him before he comes to claim another daughter. No matter how long I've been with homicide, this job never gets any easier."

Ellen got up from her chair. "I have an idea, my friend," she said, smiling.

"What's that?"

"You're taking me to Woody's for a drink."

"Now?"

"Yes now. Get up, let's go."

"In case you've forgotten, there is an ongoing investigation to be solved."

"I know, and if we're not too drunk when we get back, we just might solve it."

"You're serious." His jaw tightened.

"Damn straight. Now move your ass."

"I'm beginning to wonder who the crazy one is here."

"Besides, a change of environment will help clear out the cobwebs. Being stuck in this room is not moving this investigation along any faster. Agree?"

"Agree. But—"

"But nothing." Ellen cocked an eyebrow and held open the door.

At the door, John shook his head. Maybe Ellen was right; they could use a change of scenery. Together they exited the conference room.

Chapter Twenty-Nine

Franki's date with Detective Gorgeous was fast approaching. One hour to go. She stood staring at her reflection in the mirror, clad in a Simon Chung floral print dress that angled from knee to ankle, hanging by spaghetti straps. A chiffon shawl made by Badgley Mischka would keep her shoulders warm, come evening. She was flowing with elegance. A far cry from street life she'd once known. Her outward appearance was self-assured, a complete contradiction to how she was feeling within. Why had she agreed to a date with Jim Masker? Franki hated the dating scene. It always felt awkward and superficial. It wasn't as if she was desperate for male companionship. If anything, her life was exciting and uncomplicated. Just the way she liked it. Now because she said yes to this stupid date with Detective Gorgeous, her life had climaxed in a direction she didn't trust.

Franki rushed out to the fridge, cracked open a cold berry cooler, and guzzled down three quarters of its sweet nectar. She licked her lips. *That should do the trick*, she thought, hoping it would stop her trembling hand long enough to apply a layer of mascara to her lashes without poking an eye out.

Earlier that day, Sparkie called Franki to make plans to go clubbing on Broad Street and to let her know she hadn't done anything stupid since the episode with Mr. Can't Get His Dick Up. Her face had healed—no more shiner. This was Sparkie's inconspicuous way of seeking her friend's approval. If Franki could get her life together, there was still hope for her. Both women had at one time walked the same journey of prostitution, drugs, violence, and all the rest of the depredation that went with street life. Franki had become the driving force behind all the good changes in Sparkie's life. With the mental hell Franki had gone through at River Edge, contracting the HIV virus from the late Dr. Blake, there wasn't an excuse in the world she could use for sliding back into the dark life again.

Franki could hear the disappointment in Sparkie's voice when she told her she couldn't make it to the club. Although Sparkie masked her vulnerability, Franki was fully aware of her friend's disappointment. Before hanging up, Franki promised to go clubbing the following weekend. Sparkie wasn't all that happy, but she agreed. Franki said her good-bye and went to get ready for the big date.

Franki took one last glance in the mirror, giving her mirror image a wink of approval. Then she entered the kitchen. She took a seat at the counter and finished her berry cooler. The more she thought about her conversation with Sparkie, the more uneasy she became. Fear rose in her like an empty jug filling with toxic waste. Something just didn't sit right. As streetwise as the two women were, Sparkie should not be going out to any bar alone, especially knowing a psychopath was on the hunt in their city. She reached her cell on the counter and dialed Sparkie's number. It rang four times before the recording kicked in. Franki left a message. "Hey, it's me. I've had a change of heart. I'll meet up with you at the Legends after my dinner date. I'll call before I leave." Franki hit the off button, feeling better.

Meanwhile, across the city at Sandy's place, she was in a total state of panic, running around her bedroom like a certified lunatic searching for something nice to wear with time running out. The bedroom looked as if a tornado had touched down. Clothes and shoes were strewn in every direction. Sandy couldn't count how many outfits she'd tried on, but as far as she was concerned, everything looked terrible. One looked too small, one made her look like a cow, another hung on her, and so on and so on. After much frustration and time about to expire, she finally settled on a double-breasted cotton poplin coat, silk pencil skirt with a light peach trim, and leather toe pumps made by Narciso Rodriguez. Sandy had just enough time to gloss her lips before the doorbell rang. Her date had arrived.

Sandy's trepidation hammered against her ribs as she swung open the front door. There he stood, her knight in shining armor with a bouquet of roses and bottle of wine.

Mark handed Sandy the flowers. "Hello, beautiful."

What a wonderful way to begin a first date, she thought and invited Mark in for a drink.

Chapter Thirty

B y the time dinner time rolled around late Saturday afternoon, Captain Barlow had finally convinced Ellen to go home. She'd been at the station since five thirty that morning, viewing and reviewing files, checking on leads, and calling homeless shelters to see if anyone had seen the notorious monster. There wasn't any more she could do. John noticed the dark circles bagging beneath Ellen's eyes, indicating she hadn't slept much since the death of her husband. And this investigation wasn't helping.

Ellen felt in some small way responsible for Roger's escape. Hindsight is twenty-twenty, and maybe she should have had him incarcerated in a prison cell rather than the fourth floor of River Edge. Perhaps that was the reason she worked incessantly. Getting her to go home definitely took some prodding. The captain also knew he'd be seeing her first thing the following morning. Tired or not, she'd be in the conference room, combing through every lead that had come in the previous night. This woman was committed to catching the serial killer she once had committed indefinitely to River Edge.

Franki looked at her watch; Jim would be arriving any second. She stopped wiping the already sparkling marble countertop when she heard the doorbell. She gently slid her hands along the front of her dress, as if ironing out imaginary wrinkles. Taking a deep breath, she opened the door.

"Hi." She stood in the opening, smiling.

Franki had forgotten how attractive Jim Masker truly was as butterflies circled her stomach.

"Hi. These are for you." He handed over a bouquet of yellow roses.

"They're beautiful."

"Almost as beautiful as you."

"Come in, come in." She motioned with her hand. "Would you care for a glass of white wine?"

"If you're having one."

"I will. Let me put these roses in water, and then I'll get to pouring us a glass." She escorted Jim into the kitchen. She took down a vase from the cupboard and began filling it with water. Then she placed the roses in the crystal vase. The fresh scent was stimulating.

"Now the wine." She took two glasses out of the cupboard, placing them on the countertop.

"Allow me." She handed Jim a bottle of Kooyong Chardonnay.

He popped the wooden cork, and out came the rippling vapor, followed by the enticing scent. Jim poured, each taking a polite sip. Jim's eyes roamed around at the expanse of the loft. "Franki, this place is spectacular. Wow!"

"I fell in love with it the minute I walked in. It had the feel of home. So I bought it."

His close proximity gave Franki a sudden jolt of heat, making her more than a little self-conscious. His cologne made her want to wrap her arms around him and get lost in his aroma.

"Jim, may I say something before this evening begins?"

"Okay." Jim's smiling expression went to a swift *oh shit*.

"I am not one for dating much. So if I seem a little off center, I apologize."

He had a look of relief that the awkwardness was out. "Really, I hadn't noticed." He smirked playfully. "It's not every day I get to date a beautiful and intelligent woman like yourself. It's usually one or the other, but not both at the same time."

Franki laughed. "Whatever, but thank you for trying to make me feel at ease."

"It's the truth. I swear." He laughed.

Glass in hand, Jim made his way across the loft to where Franki's paintings were drying on three separate easels.

"Wow! These are exceptional."

The first painting: colorful fruit positioned beside a fruit basket lying on white linen. The second one: a man falling into a dark hole with black branches all around. The third: three large, naked women lounging on violet overstuffed furniture, drinking tea from refined cups.

"A hobby of mine." She shrugged off the compliment.

"Tell me, Miss Martin, is there anything you can't do?"

"Skate." She laughed.

"I'll teach you how to skate. If you teach me the art of painting."

"Have you used color before?"

"Grade one." Jim relaxed. "Does that count?"

"Grade one, you say?" Franki tapped a finger to her lip.

"And it might have been finger painting for all I know," he said, making her laugh.

"I don't think painting is for you." She sipped her wine.

"So much for Michelangelo; better stick with being a detective. Oh, we now have a mutual friend."

Franki smirked, knowing this mutual friend that Jim was referring to. "Dr. Ellen Smith?"

"Good guess." He raised his glass.

"She is the warmest, most thoughtful person I know. Next to my adopted mother, Sandy Miller."

"Sorry, didn't get quite that impression of Dr. Smith." He rolled his eyes.

"Did you do something to displease our mutual friend?" Franki laughed, knowing Doc had zero tolerance for self-absorbed idiots.

"We didn't start out on the right foot; let's put it that way." He played with his pinky ring. "All her degrees, a little intimidating to say the least."

"She is sixty-five, and there is no stopping her."

"I found it odd that she'd want to get involved in Taut's case so close after the death of her husband."

"Tom was an awesome man. He would do anything for anyone. It's hard on her, but she'll be fine."

"I think it was inconsiderate of Captain Barlow to ask her to join our team; the woman hasn't had time to grieve yet."

"She didn't think so. In fact, she welcomed the idea of being busy. Helps take her mind off being lonely."

"She's unquestionably spunky."

"Plus some."

"She warned me to be the perfect gentleman this evening."

Franki burst out laughing. "My bodyguard."

"Seems to me you can hold your own." He checked his watch. "We should leave, Franki. Our dinner reservation is in twenty minutes."

"I'll get my purse." She swallowed the last of her wine and set the empty glass in the sink.

In the short time they had spent together, Jim was impressed by Franki's refreshing honesty and realism. When the two arrived at Montgomery's, the maître d' was waiting to escort them to their table. Soft candles flickered on the tables in the low light of the exquisite crystal chandeliers. Jim pulled out her chair before the maître d' had the chance, proving he was the perfect date. Franki sat on the plush chair, letting her shawl slip from her shoulders. She wanted proof that Jim could be a man of his word. It quickly became evident that he would have banged her right there on the white linen tablecloth given the chance. Perhaps it was the leering in his baby-blue eyes that gave him away.

In the comforts of home, Ellen sat on the leather sofa going over the files she'd snuck off the table from the conference room. She began comparing the forensic evidence on Josey Moran to the two latest victims, Shelby Porter and Diane Gibber. She scrutinized each page, line by line. Roger was owner of two deaths, but not three. He was not responsible for the murder of the Gibber woman. Her head snapped up, startled by the noise of the ringing phone. Ellen tossed the file beside her and reached for the receiver on the glass end table.

"Hello."

"Hi, doll. How are you?"

"Just reviewing a case file. And you?"

"I'm on my way over to rescue you from your workaholic self," Bill scolded. "I'm taking you out for ice cream and a walk along the beach. You could probably use some fresh air, being cooped up in the police building all day and half the night."

"Sounds too tempting to pass up."

"You know I won't let you. I've heard you've been going at it full throttle."

It was Ellen's turn to laugh. "The usual pace."

"Christ, you don't know how to stop. Do you?" Bill lectured. "May I remind you that you were only to give your expert opinion and get the hell out of there? Not take over the damn investigation."

"Disturbed minds are my expertise, Bill. And until Roger is captured, I will remain there to give my expert recommendation. Your concern is not necessary, my friend."

"You are a stubborn old fool. I'll be at the house in ten minutes. Be ready."

"Yes, boss." She laughed, placing the receiver onto its cradle, and walked back to the couch. She put the forensic evidence back in its rightful place. Then she made her way to the bathroom for a quick appearance check. She touched up her lips with a light shade of pink lipstick and was satisfied with her result.

Chapter Thirty-One

During dinner, Mark had a way of making Sandy feel comfortable and safe, like they had been dating for months. He ever-so-gently asked how she got the scar on her face. Without reservation, Sandy began telling her story. Mark hung onto her every word, wincing at the mere thought of boiling coffee being splashed in Sandy's face. He reached across the table, placing her hand in his. Layer by layer, the facial skin had blistered, destroying any chance of rejuvenation to the cells. When she finished, Mark leaned across the table, softly caressing the scars left behind with his fingertips. Goose flesh rose up on her arms at the sense of his tender touch. "I think you are breathtaking, Sandy Miller." His alluring smile melted away any insecurity she had left.

At the other end of the city, Franki was becoming reasonably amused with her date. Jim asked her numerous questions about her upbringing and parents. Had she brothers and sisters? What she was like as a teenager? And of course, Franki being Franki, she answered the surface jargon but refused to go any deeper. She didn't trust Jim enough to get personal yet. Street life and foster homes weren't one of her favorite subjects, not to mention how—*Oh, I tested HIV positive after being raped at the loony bin by Dr. James Blake. You might have heard about the case. The slime bag hung himself in jail before he could stand trial.* That conversation could really get a second date—not.

As a teenager, Jim had been the average, good-looking jock that all the girls wanted. And he wasn't ashamed to say he'd obliged as many as he could.

"Why haven't you married?" Franki asked.

"Haven't met the right one."

"Give me a description of the right woman for you."

"Would you give me points if I said you?"

"No." She shook her head. "I'd say you're full of it. And a coward's way out of telling me the truth." She put a forkful of salad into her mouth and smirked.

"Dr. Smith has nothing to fear."

"No she doesn't."

"I'll make sure to tell her." He shook his head.

Jim felt a little off kilter; he was use to dating attractive women with meager brainpower, unlike Franki Martin, who was beautiful, strong, and powered with intelligence. He was not going to be able to sway her easily.

"You still haven't answered me about this perfect woman."

"She hasn't come along yet." Jim could feel the pressure of his bachelor ways spreading like a web of silk up the collar of his neck.

"Okay, if you had to choose between beauty or brains, which would it be?"

"Oh that's a loaded question."

"Shall I get the gun?"

"I have the bullets. You, Miss Martin, are relentless."

"Haven't been with too many intelligent women, I'm assuming?" Franki placed her fork down.

Before Jim had a chance to stick his foot in his mouth, the waitress came to their table, carrying dinner. Franki had ordered the lobster dish, and Jim the eight-ounce sirloin steak medium-rare with all the trimmings.

"Will there be anything else?" the server asked with more than a twinkle in her eye.

"No that will be all. Thank you." Jim smiled at the stunning brunette.

"You like her?" Franki watched her strut away.

"No!" Jim crinkled his face into a red knot. *Busted.*

"Then you're a big flirt."

"I am so pleading the fifth." He held up both hands.

"Okay, change of subject. I promised a friend of mine we would stop in for a drink at Legends. To be honest, it was my way of an excuse in case I didn't like you." Franki laughed, taking a sip of her water.

"What's the verdict?" Jim picked up his steak knife.

"Ah, you're not such a bad boy. A little flirtatious but seriously harmless."

"I am going to have to take a rain check on the club this evening. I'm afraid I'm still on the clock. Captain gave me a small reprieve from the case so I could take you to dinner."

"This may be the shortest date you've had in history."

He shook his head. "Meaning what?"

"Oh I think you know, player." Half a smirk unfurled around her mouth.

"C'mon, I'm a nice guy."

"I bet you haven't read one of my books."

"I am so offended."

"Then I apologize."

"Thank you." *Whew, that was close*, he thought.

"This case must be pretty draining."

"You can say that." Jim was grateful for the subject change. "I'm married to my career, and my partner is as close to a wife as I have right now."

"I never thought of it like that, but … yes, that must be true."

"I spend more time with Dan than anyone else."

"Does he know?"

"Change of subject." He winked. "So tell me, Franki, how did you get started in the field of writing?"

Now this topic Franki was willing to discuss in depth.

Chapter Thirty-Two

After a delicious banana split, fresh air, and good conversation with her friend Bill Cobie, Ellen was back at home poring over the case files on Josey Moran and Shelby Porter's life. Victimology profile. Ellen was looking for verification as to how Josey must have encountered Roger. There was no forced entry, meaning she opened the door and allowed him inside her apartment. The same for Shelby Porter. They were young, beautiful, and living alone. Josey had moved to Victory two months prior to attend college, and Shelby was a single mom, raising her three-year-old daughter. Shelby wasn't into the party scene. Both women were every parent's dream daughter. Josey volunteered her time at the local hospital in Victoria. Shelby worked full-time days at a local Tim Horton's so she could be with her daughter at night. Their high-quality caring characteristics might have been their downfall.

Ellen took out the forensic pictures and scanned the carnage carefully. The lead pipe caught her attention. What was a nice girl like Josey Moran doing with a lead pipe in her apartment? She leaned over, retrieving the phone from the table, and dialed Captain Barlow's number.

"Captain Barlow speaking."

"John, it's Ellen. The lead pipe, do we know the owner? I mean, who did the pipe belong to—Josey or Roger?"

"Only the partial was found. Josey's prints weren't found on it. Why?"

"Roger uses knives. He lives to carve. So the pipe had to have been left behind by another tenant."

"Ellen, that is a possibility."

"Ask the landlord."

"Okay, okay."

"I just want to make sure his psychosis isn't growing into something more deadly." Ellen rubbed her stiff neck, trying to prevent the tension from turning into lactic acid buildup.

"Ellen, take tomorrow off—and that's an order. We'll find him, but you need to get some rest," he said, smiling, knowing he was blowing smoke up his own ass. She wasn't going to listen.

"Yeah, yeah," she snickered. "Goodnight, John."

"See you in the morning, my dear."

Ellen placed the phone on the coffee table and looked around her house. The pictures of Tom made her feel even lonelier. She missed him terribly. Her heart had a physical ache that wouldn't go away no matter how busy she got. She sighed and placed all the evidence back in the folders. She walked out to the kitchen and poured a full tumbler of bourbon and headed down to the bathroom off the master bedroom. Time to take a swim in the tub.

Around eleven that evening, she climbed into bed. The same sadness swept over her again, bringing on another wave of tears. She was so lost without the security of Tom lying next to her. If she could, she'd never go to bed again, but she only had enough energy for one day. Hers was now used up. She curled up with Tom's pillow and prayed for sleep.

Chapter Thirty-Three

Once their plates were cleared, Franki excused herself from the table to go powder her nose. A polite way of saying, "Excuse me, I have to take a lady's leak." Halfway through dinner, Franki realized she liked Jim but only as a friend. He would not be a good boyfriend. With his flirtatious way, he'd be too much of a player for her. At this time in her life with friends, family, and career, dating Jim would be a bad decision.

Jim watched her weave in and out of tables like an angel until she evaporated around the corner. He sat drinking his club soda, really feeling good about Franki. This beautiful woman could be the one for him.

On her way out of the ladies' room, Franki noticed the strap on her handbag had come apart. Preoccupied with fixing it, she didn't notice the man coming toward her until it was too late. She collided right into him, knocking the purse out of her hand. She watched in utter horror as the contents spilled onto the floor, revealing her time of the month. Flustered with embarrassment, Frank quickly began gathering her things. He didn't seem to notice her tampons or didn't care. Either way, she was grateful. He picked up her lipstick and compact, handing the items over to her. When she looked up to thank him, their eyes suddenly locked for a brief awkward moment.

"I'm sorry, Miss, have we met?"

"Do you read?" she mumbled nervously.

"Pardon?"

"I mean no disrespect. I'm a writer, and when readers read my material and see my picture … ah, forget I said anything." Her face flushed.

"No, I don't believe that's it." He shook his head. "But I do read." He handed her a tube of lipstick.

"Thank you. And sorry for being such a klutz."

A wave of memory suddenly surged through her body like an electrical storm brewing on the horizon. No matter how many years passed, Franki couldn't forget this man's face.

"I'm Steve." He put out his hand.

"Franki." The two shook.

"I met a Franki once, a long time ago. Pretty name."

"Well, I must be getting back to my date. Nice meeting you, Steve." Franki quickly made her exit.

Franki sat down at her table, still reeling from the raw eruption of emotions.

"Are you feeling okay? Your cheeks are flushed."

"I'm fine."

Jim was just about to ask if she would like to see the dessert menu when his cell phone rang.

He looked at the number. "Shit!"

"Better take that call." Franki glanced around the restaurant, trying not to eavesdrop on Jim's conversation.

"Jim here … When? … Are you sure? I'm on my way … Yep! I said I'm on my way, partner."

"Was that the better half of your perfect relationship?" Franki teased.

"Yeah." Jim pushed back his chair. "I'm sorry, Franki."

This date was officially over. He leaned down and kissed her on the cheek. "Forgive me. I'd like a rain check on the next date. Get home safe, okay?"

"I'll be fine. Go!" She motioned for him to leave and watched him wind in and out of tables and then disappear out the glass front door. Leaving her to pay for dinner. *Some date he is*, she thought. Lucky she had her credit card on her or she'd be in the kitchen cleaning pots and pans to pay for their delicious meal.

Franki was about to leave when Steve snuck up beside her.

"Franki Martin, don't you dare run away again." She was busted. "I knew you remembered me."

"It's been a long time."

"Way too long. Have coffee with me tonight."

"Don't you think it would be just a little rude to leave your date at the table?" She tilted her head in that direction.

"Her?" He pointed. "That's my sister."

"Whoops. My mistake."

Franki felt paralyzed, completely unable to resist the flame of Steve's affection.

"I'll meet you at Starbucks on Douglas." Franki flirted.

"Nice try."

"What about your—"

"My sister came with her own ride."

"Okay, you win!" Franki put up her hands. "But before we go for coffee, I promised a friend I'd stop by Legends for a drink."

"No problemo. You are of age, right?"

Franki slapped him on the arm and shook her head. "Ah yeah."

Steve laughed. "I'm just so damn happy to see you again. We have some catching up to do, and I can't wait. I want to hear everything."

Franki waited by the door while Steve went back to his table to tell his sister, he was leaving with Franki. Franki took a seat on the bench, reminiscing about the one and only night she and Steve spent together. How he rescued her from the storm, made dinner, bought her a new coat, allowed her to open up to him around a fire place, drinking hot cocoa. It seemed like a lifetime ago.

The two made their way across the illuminated parking lot where Steve had parked his Jeep.

"I bought a Jeep. A black one."

"Why?"

"Just because." She laughed. Steve opened the door, and Franki hopped into his Cherokee. Happily, they drove off to the club to meet Sparkie. *She is not going to believe this*, Frankie thought and almost giggled out loud.

Chapter Thirty-Four

As evening approached, dusk began settling; the detectives raced across the city. They arrived at the crime scene only seconds apart from each other. Outside the apartment complex, squad cars parked with flashing lights, bright enough to illuminate half a city block. Mr. Comp, the coroner, waited good-naturedly for the authorization to take the corpse to the morgue. He was waiting on Derk to finish processing the murdered victim. ABC, CBS, and FOX were all competing for the sensational story that just might buy a reporter one more rung on the golden ladder to stardom.

Taut stood on the sidewalk with the rest of the nervous, nosey parkers. His face was hidden by a black hoodie he wore. His eyes glistened with excitement as he looked around at the nervous expressions and heard fear in the voices up and down the street. Police officers were pushing people back. The doctor's worst prediction had come true. His murdering sprees were no longer about slaying his mother; this was pure appetite for torture. The volume of worried chatter began to take on a life of its own. Women were hugging their babies and crying as they tried to convince each other the world would be a safe place to live again. This gave Roger immense gratification. He looked over at the news vans anticipating what tomorrow's paper would say about this grisly slaying. *The slut deserved to die*, he thought, plunging his hands inside his pockets.

The detectives met just inside the apartment lobby. They rode the elevator to the third floor.

"This scumbag is on a roll now," Dan said.

"Looks like the doctor is right," Jim added. "Any details from the captain?"

"Just that he messed this one up big time."

"What exactly are we walking into here?"

"He wouldn't elaborate," Dan said.

The entrance to 311, the victim's apartment, was sealed off with yellow crime tape. There were police officers guarding each end of the corridor, allowing only authorized personnel onto the floor. Dan was the first to enter the apartment, his eyes moving around the devastation. The apartment had been ransacked, furniture turned on its side. Dirt was spread across the floor from the plants that were knocked over. Shards of glass littered the hardwood floor. The television, stereo, and everything else had been destroyed. This scene was minor compared to what awaited them down the hall.

"Where is the victim?" Dan questioned the first officer at the door.

"The primary is in the bedroom." His eyes held the detective's. "I'm warning you, it's really, really bad, man."

The detectives were nearing the bedroom door when Captain Barlow came out holding a handkerchief over his mouth. His eyes expressed an uncertainty neither detective had seen before—a cold, deep fear. He peeled his bloodstained slippers and gloves and tossed them into a white plastic container outside the door.

"How bad?" Dan asked.

"I've never come across anything this vicious in all my time on the force."

The captain made a gagging reflex like he was about to puke.

"That evil?" Jim said above a whisper.

"He tortured her almost to death."

"She's alive?" Dan asked.

"No! She died a few minutes ago. No one could have survived such savagery."

"I'm going in," Jim announced bravely, slipping a pair of rubber slippers over his Italian leather shoes and latex gloves over his manicured hands.

Dan hung back to talk to Captain Barlow.

"You know, sir, I've been on the force for twenty plus years now, and I will never understand how a man can deliberately kill a woman. After I caught Shelia with her boy toy"—Dan shook his head at the memory—"I admit I thought about punching her in the face, but I couldn't hurt her."

"That's what makes us different from this sociopath."

"That he is."

"Trained, specialized professionals like Doctor Smith who have the guts to study these monsters help us to understand their behavior in order to catch them. We have to try to understand what's inside their mind. You know, like what makes them tick. She makes our job much easier."

"If it was up to me, I'd say shoot the bastards. And quit trying to fix what can't be fixed. He is a psychopath that pulled the wool over the doctor's eyes with his poor, deranged childhood bullshit. Taut was just waiting for the opportunity to escape. He's mentally sick, my ass. He is a monster that preys on the vulnerable," Dan said.

"I'm not so sure Ellen would agree with you, Detective. We know more about him now than we ever did, thanks to Ellen. And speaking of, I have to call her."

Captain Barlow walked away to a quiet area down the hall, leaving Dan to sneak out the front door, down the hall, and out back of the apartment building to have a quick smoke.

The victim was a bloodied, discarded figure lying on the bed, naked from the waist down, looking like something out of a horror film. She'd been bound with rope and horribly disfigured. Her face was unrecognizable. The killer had shoved a pair of white cotton panties into her mouth to silence her screams. A tiny piece of her panties, barely noticeable, hung out the side of her mouth, stained red. Approximately thirty stab wounds ran the length of her body. The blood had sprayed the floor, wall, and ceiling. Her pink hair was torn from the scalp and littered across the bedroom floor like clumps of dust. Jim scanned the bedroom. Dresser drawers were pulled out, but the contents were untouched. The gag used had to have come from the lingerie drawer. The closet appeared untouched. There was one framed photograph sitting next to a jewelry box on top of the dresser. Jim stepped up for a closer inspection. Blood smeared the surface of the glass, hiding the faces behind the glass.

Jim glanced across the room at Derk, who was bagging and tagging evidence in plastic bags and then sealing them with red tape.

"Hey, Derk, can I remove this photo from its frame?"

"No. It's evidence."

"There are two women in this photograph."

"That's nice. The answer is still no."

"Put this frame on top priority. I'm guessing our next victim is in the photograph. And you might find the killer's print on the glass."

"You guys know how to say please?"

"Sorry. I'm a little stressed."

"Get in line. By the time this case is over, we'll all need therapy at Hotel Wacko!"

Derk went back to cutting the ropes from the victim and placing them in evidence bags. Then he placed the victim's hands in paper bags to preserve any trace evidence collected under her fingernails during the struggle. "She's almost ready." Derk took a few more close-up shots of the victim's battered and bloodied body.

Jim had seen enough. His partner was coming back from his usual before-entering-a-crime-scene smoke.

"Guess I'm up." Dan shrugged.

"Good timing. Derk is almost finished processing the body. And they weren't kidding when they said it's bad," Jim warned.

"This is what we get paid to do." Dan slipped on the latex and ducked under the tape, entering. The scent of coppery blood seeped in through his protective mask. This victim would be forever etched in his mind, and Dan had seen his share of death from car accidents to murder. But nothing could prepare him for this. His palms began to sweat inside his latex gloves as his heart banged with fury against the wall of his chest. He momentarily struggled for air.

"What the hell!" he shouted, feeling every ounce of rage wash over him like a tidal wave. He could not believe the carnage done to this woman, someone's daughter. This act of violence was the labor of pure evil.

"I warned you!" his partner yelled from the doorway.

Dan would work day and night to catch this sadistic bastard. Whatever it took to catch this monster, he was prepared to do. He didn't need to stay any longer; he'd seen enough. He walked out, throwing his gloves and booties in the basket.

Jim touched his partner's shoulder. "You okay?"

"No, and inside that room is not okay. Another woman was tortured to death because we can't find this prick." He rubbed his unshaven face. "We're running out of time."

"We'll catch him. We always get the bad guy."

"When?" Dan yelled, alarming the cops and forensic guys around him. "Hey, what are you staring at?" He eyed the officer in the kitchen.

"Chill out!"

"Okay—when, one, two, three more women turn up tortured to death. When?"

Beads of perspiration began forming on his upper lip.

"He'll make a mistake. They all do," Jim guaranteed.

"Yeah, well right now he's giving us the big jerk around. This animal is like fucking bin Laden hiding in some cave somewhere laughing his ass off. While we run around like chickens with our fucking heads cut off, knowing nothing and finding bodies." Dan pointed down the hall at his superior. "What's that all about?"

"Dr. Smith."

"She's right. This maniac is a savage. There is human skin on the wall like some brilliant piece of artwork. Jesus Christ." Dan shoved his hands into the front pockets of his jeans.

Captain Barlow called them from the living room.

"What did the doctor say?" Jim questioned.

"She's baffled at the condition of the body, at the grave level of hostility. And not surprised that Roger's violent tendencies are escalating. She did, however, ask how we were doing."

Dan pointed sharply to the bedroom behind him. "How in the hell are we supposed to be after exiting that display of gore? Captain, we need a lead. We can't let this animal do this to one more woman."

"Come on, guys. Ellen has tea on." The captain motioned toward the door.

"Tea?" Dan's lip curled.

"Are you kidding me? Tea now?" Jim brows raised into a high arc.

"Don't you think we should be hunting with the same aggression he's killing?" Dan glared around at the trashed apartment.

"Listen, Derk is taking care of forensics here. Mr. Comp is on his way up to take the body to the morgue. We'll know more when the autopsy is finished. I have a group of officers walking around this complex and beyond, gathering information. So unless you feel like going door to door, I suggest we get going." Captain knotted his tie.

"Captain, who are we kidding? Derk isn't going to have any results for at least three weeks. It's going to take Derk at least two days to process the bedroom alone. In the meantime, we're going to a damn tea party." Detective Kape shrugged.

"Take it easy, Dan. Breathe," Jim strongly suggested.

"Don't tell me what to do. That son of a bitch is still free to kill again," Dan argued with gritted teeth.

The captain patted Dan's shoulder. "Let's get out of here now—and that's an order."

"I can't believe we're going for tea." Dan groaned.

"At least your date wasn't canceled," Jim said.

"Poor baby. I'd like to feel sorry for you, but I was trying to track down a serial killer while you were busy wooing Miss Martin."

Jim laughed. "I think she likes me. C'mon, you're wound tighter than a virgin."

"Not the time for cracks, Jim. Not now." Dan stormed out of the apartment, taking the stairs two at a time. He needed time to clear his head and process the reality of what his eyes tried to deny. Another vicious slaughter.

Chapter Thirty-Five

Ellen stood at the kitchen counter pouring boiling water from the kettle into a ceramic teapot she'd made back when she and Tom were first married. She finished pouring and placed the lid on so the tea could steep. The doorbell rang. Dressed in a jogging suit and slippers, she hurried down the stairs to open the door. Jim was the first to arrive, shoulders slumped and head down. He looked up when Ellen opened the door. He tried to cover his consternation with a fake smile.

"Come in. Come in."

He stepped just inside the foyer, eyes locked on hers, searching for comfort. He needed answers and assurance that everything would be okay again. Soon.

He broke the silence. "He's not human, Doctor Smith."

Ellen gestured him to the living room. Jim had no problem making himself comfortable on the couch. He leaned his head against the back of the couch, taking slow, deep breaths, trying to liberate the tension.

"The violence, I mean the …" He paused, trying to comprehend what his eyes witnessed an hour ago. "Christ, Doctor."

"I'm afraid it's going to get worse."

"I don't know how he can top that horror show."

"You thought I was wrong about Taut?"

"Wishful thinking on my part." He tried to smile.

"How are the rest of the guys doing?"

"Dan wants to put a bullet in Taut's brain. And Captain Barlow, well ... calm on the exterior, worried as hell on the inside. The magnitude of violence hasn't yet sunk in for any of us."

"Roger's work will be unforgettable, I assure you. Somehow, someway you are going to have to detach, knowing that you guys are doing everything in your power to catch him."

"If you saw the brutality we had tonight, detachment is a big word. This was a savage kill. I'll let the captain fill you in. Right now I need to think about something else."

Ellen placed the folder on the coffee table. "How did your date go with Franki?"

"Short. Oh shit!" Jim sat straight up.

"Something I said?"

"When I received the call, I rushed out of the restaurant and left Franki to pay the bill."

Ellen burst out laughing. "Franki will understand. You hope?"

"So much for a second date." He threw his hands into the air.

"Other than running out on the bill, do you like her?"

"Franki is an amazing woman. Her smile and intelligence are so refreshing. And she doesn't need any protection from you. Trust me. That woman can hold her own against anyone."

"Sounds to me like you guys hit it off."

"I'll call her tomorrow and apologize."

"Let's not forget restitution."

"Yeah, that too." He gave a little smirk. "I never thought about marriage, but I could see myself being married to Franki."

"I'm not so sure Franki is the marrying kind. Besides, you've only been out on one date. How can you know Franki is the one for you?"

"I think I could convince her to fall madly in love with me. Doctor Smith, we clicked. And she knows how to challenge me without any reservation."

"Pretty self-assured after only one short date."

"Franki is into me."

"Okay, Romeo."

After a few knocks, the front door opened. "Hello!" Captain Barlow yelled from the bottom of the stairs.

"We're in the living room." Ellen heard footsteps coming up the stairs.

Their eyes spoke volumes of unspeakable dread as they crossed the carpet into the living room. Jolly old Dan wasn't so jolly. He plopped his heavy frame down on the white leather loveseat, dropping his head into his hands.

Ellen walked in from the kitchen, carrying a silver tray with a teapot, cups, cream, and spoons and set it down in the middle of the glass table.

"No, thank you." Jim shook his head.

"None for me," Dan said, rubbing his bloodshot eyes.

"Ellen, do you have anything stronger?" John asked, needing a drink.

"As a matter of fact, I do," she said, picking up the silver tray, unaffected by the change in plan. "I have beer, wine, rum, and our good pal Jack. What will it be?"

The three decided on Jack Daniels.

"You are truly an angel. I swear," Dan said.

Minutes later, she returned a second time from the kitchen with the same silver tray. This time it held the bottle of Jack Daniels and four crystal tumblers with ice. Muggins the white Persian strutted into the living room as if woken from a deep sleep. She stretched and flopped over at Jim's feet, meowing for attention. Jim took a swig, allowing its smooth flavor to tantalize his palate before swallowing. Then he leaned down to pet Muggins. Although he would have preferred caressing Franki's soft skin, Muggins would have to do.

Ellen took a drink. "Anyone want to start?"

"There are no words to describe that butchery. The psychopath punished that poor woman mercilessly," Dan stated, feeling the bile rise up in his throat.

"Can I hear the details?" Ellen braced herself for the impact of Roger's carnage.

"This victim suffered. He restrained her with ropes and then stabbed her over thirty times, so Derk is guessing. There could be more. She had a gag hanging out of her mouth coated in blood."

"Can't forget the artwork on the wall," Dan interrupted.

"Artwork?" Ellen took a drink.

"Yeah. The bastard took pieces of her skin and displayed them on the wall, like some kind of masterpiece." Jim rubbed him palms together.

Ellen's expression changed, but she said nothing. "Avulsion," she whispered.

"We'll know more after she's been washed at the morgue. Not that anyone will be able to recognize her. He cut up her face pretty good," Dan said, helping himself to another drink.

"Roger is no longer killing the image of his mother. I'm afraid he's crossed over, and without his medication, these murders will continue."

"No shit, Sherlock. But crossed over to what? The fucker is already insane. Isn't that what you labeled him? You're the one that kept him from going to prison," Dan said trying to hold back his disdain. "Now he's free to torture and murder again." Dan slapped his legs.

"I get it—you're pissed off at me. I understand. This is not about you or me right now. You and I can deal with our issue later." She winked. "But what you've just described doesn't sound like Roger's kill. I mean … hear me out. Yes, with Roger off his medication, he will murder again and again. He slices and dices. The skin on the wall does not fit his profile."

"Are you saying we could have a copycat on our hands?" John swiveled the ice around in his glass.

"To be honest with you, I'm not sure. Which body parts were avulsed?"

"Ellen, there was too much blood to pinpoint the exact locations." Dan remarked.

"Her bedroom looked like a slaughter house," Jim added.

"Roger's first crime spree started out with reenacting his childhood rage. He was so powerless as a child, but then as he grew, so did his power for vengeance, amplify into something he could no longer control. His first three victims were demeaned, degraded, and then murdered. Josey Moran's murder was slightly more aggressive. Roger beat Josey with the lead pipe."

"Let's not forget he stabbed her," Dan said.

"The first three victims seven years ago were all murdered by knife and strangulation. Josey Moran and Porter had knife wounds."

"Porter was killed by blunt-force trauma to the back of her head, fracturing her skull. This caused cerebral contusions and hemorrhaging, causing her to bleed to death. And the Gibber woman was most definitely not one of Roger's victims. Now his appetite for violence will be on a grander scale, but not flaying his victims." Doctor smith reported.

"Okay, simple stabbing isn't enough for delusional boy. Now he's got to go and rip the hair from the victim's scalp. In chunks, I might add." Jim felt his stomach swirl at the memory on the bedroom floor.

"It's called delusional agitation. Roger no longer has any form of control."

"That's nice to know." Dan rolled his eyes.

"Any identification on the victim?"

"There was a picture frame on the dresser. We couldn't identify the faces because the animal took the victim's blood and smeared it across the glass. Good news—Derk believes he'll be able to lift a print off the glass," Jim said.

"Ellen, is there a possibility he's working with a partner?" John asked.

"To my knowledge, no."

"Who in their right mind would help a madman escape, knowing his past? We have more questions than answers." Dan jiggled the ice cubes around in his glass.

"Any of the love letters hold a clue?"

"Nope. Jim and I interviewed all the crazies on his list. Nothing."

"Okay, the guy murders three women, goes to Crazy Ville for a little treatment like he broke his pinky finger or something. These so-called fans know what he did, and yet these lonely hearts write to him, spewing lines of I love you. Let me fix you bullshit. And I mean these ladies are beautiful women—houses, jobs, nice jobs, except the elevator doesn't go all the way to the penthouse. I mean, who would have thunk it." Dan pressed his plump lips into a skeletal line.

"Did you guys find anything at River Edge?" Ellen asked.

Dan jotted the request in his notebook. "Too busy going from one crime scene to another. I'll get on it first thing tomorrow morning."

"Ellen, if I may, how did you know that Roger didn't murder the Gibber woman?" Jim inquired.

"It was obvious. She had hesitation marks on her throat, for one. Roger doesn't hesitate. Secondly, she was tied to make it look like he was going to brutalize her but ran out of time."

"You're right; he didn't." Dan said.

"Was it the ex-husband?" Jim asked.

"Give this woman a gold star. He rolled over like a tire the minute we started to interrogate his ass. I mean, the classic offender, sniveling, 'I'm so sorry, I didn't mean to hurt her. I loved her.'" Dan frowned.

Dan shook his head at the madness. "And that's why you tied her up and slit her throat, buddy—because you loved her so much."

"Loved her to death. Pardon the pun," Jim said.

"Good one. Mystery solved," said Captain Barlow.

Dan rose to his feet. "Ellen, I need to use the bathroom."

"Down the hall, first door on your left."

"Thanks." Dan left the room.

"Refills, anyone?" Ellen lifted the bottle of Jack off the table.

"I'm good." John looked at his glass. "What baffles me is with all the media coverage, why in the world would any woman open their door, not knowing who is on the other side?"

"And again, more questions than answers, Captain," Dan said, returning to the living room.

"Roger is an exceptionally charming fellow," Ellen stated for good measure.

"Yeah, and so is Jim, but he's had a couple doors closed on him." Dan tried to lift the gloom in the air. "On that note, I think I'll head back and start digging for answers to all these questions."

"I would suggest getting some sleep, Dan. You can start digging first thing in the morning." Ellen glanced over top of her eyeglasses.

"I'll take a vacation after this creep is behind bars." Dan rose from the loveseat, cracking the tightness out of his neck. "Thanks for the drink, Doctor."

"You're welcome."

"I think I'll join you. Thanks again for the drink," Jim said.

"Welcome."

Outside under the stars, the detectives stood leaning against the side of Dan's Dodge Ram. Jokes here and there were thrown between the two detectives in an attempt to take the edge off the night. The lightheartedness would be shortly lived.

"So how was the date of all dates with Franki Yum-Yum Martin?" Dan took a drag off his smoke.

"Man, the woman is unbelievable. I'm not sure she will ever speak to me again, though."

"What did you do this time?"

"I left without paying the bill."

Dan cracked up. "You stuck her with the dinner bill, numb nuts? You are right; she's never going to speak to you again. Way to go, Romeo." Dan slapped his partner on the back. "And you thought she'd sleep with you."

"Thanks for the support."

"I mean … the bill. I bet she thinks you're one big loser, man."

"I blew it!"

"No shit. Maybe a woman like Franki with style and class isn't in the cards for you. But don't worry. I bet there's a bimbo on a pole this second just waiting for a stud like you. As you say, women are like buses; miss one another one will come in its place."

"Shut up. I really like Franki." Jim sulked, wiping a speck of dust off his leather shoe.

"Man, you fall in lust more times in one week than I change my frigen undies."

"Too much information."

Dan crushed his cigarette out in the driveway. This time he didn't pick it up.

Inside Ellen's place, Captain Barlow was getting ready to leave and go home. He missed his wife and daughters.

"Ellen, why don't you come and stay a few nights at my place? Bella would love the company, and I'd feel better about not leaving you here alone."

"Thanks for the offer, John, but really I'm safe. My alarm system works. No need to worry about me."

"If you change your mind ..."

"I know who to call. Time for you, young man, to get home and get some sleep."

"I am." John lifted his large frame off the couch, and his cell phone rang. He took it out of the case and glanced at the number. "Shit!"

"So much for sleep?" Ellen groaned.

He put the phone to his ear. "Barlow speaking ... "When? ... What's the damn address? ... Got it." He closed the phone and sighed.

"Let me guess."

"It's going to be another long night. Another victim." Captain Barlow called Detective Kape.

Dan answered on the second ring. "Yeah, Kape here."

"Where's your location?"

"The doctor's driveway, sir. What's up?"

"Another DBF."

"Busy bastard. Where, sir?"

"Southside. Fifteen Alexander Drive."

"Jim and I are on it." Dan hit the off button and opened his driver's door.

"No way!" Jim stood, arms folded across his chest.

"No sleeping tonight. We have a call at 15 Alexander Drive. Meet me there."

"Shit!" Jim jumped into his Camaro and followed Dan out of the driveway. The detectives were gone into the night before Captain Barlow came out of Ellen's house.

Chapter Thirty-Six

Strangely enough, considering he was the last to leave, Captain Barlow was the first to arrive at 15 Alexander Drive. The moment John's feet hit the pavement, he could instantly smell the mortal terror lingering on the night's chill. He shuttered, looking up at the opaque clouds rushing to shadow the half-moon's glow. In one long breath, the two detectives squealed to a stop behind the captain's Nissan Altima. Three uniformed police officers were busy patrolling the street, keeping the nosey parkers from getting in the way. It was fortunate for the team that the press hadn't gotten wind of another homicide yet. This would give the task force enough time to secure and begin investigating the scene without having to respond to questions for which they had no answers. Everyone on the force felt the raw edge of knowing it would only be a matter of time before reporters were breathing down their necks demanding they work around the clock to catch this homicidal maniac. All felt the immense pressures of solving these brutal murders.

There were two more officers posted outside the front door while Officer Tani McCloud kept busy securing the outside perimeter of the yard. The somber expressions of the two officers guarding the door weighed heavily on the captain's heart. He saw the fear and felt the weight as if a boulder were set on top of his chest, crushing his organs beneath. Slowly the life was being sucked out of this case, leaving everything barren in its wake.

The captain walked up the three steps to the landing.

"Evening, sir," Tommy, the big burly officer spoke first.

"Hey, Tommy." The captain lit up his watch. It was 1:37. John's body ached right into the marrow of his bones. The effects of exhaustion were wearing him down. He'd been at work since five o'clock this morning. His body screamed for rest, but his mind raced with adrenaline.

Team leader, Captain Barlow, braced himself and stepped over the threshold. The stink of blood and decomposing organs rushed at him like an angry wind, wrapping itself around his five senses. A pool of congealed blood lay next to a pool of vomit. Not every cop had the stomach for the grizzly sight of a murder. To the left of the tiny foyer was a spacious living room fully furnished in a country décor. Strangely, everything seemed in place, unlike the last crime scene.

The captain took out a handkerchief from his breast pocket of his suit jacket to cover his mouth and carefully stepped further inside, wearing his customary latex apparel. Derk was busy measuring blood spatters and snapping photographs. Talk about multitasking. The other forensic gal was busy lifting prints.

"Do we have identification?" Captain Barlow started with the questions.

"Julie Saunders. He seems to be killing outside his comfort zone."

"Meaning?"

"Alexander Drive is a little upscale to the west side of the city."

"Sure." Captain Barlow frowned. "Any information on this victim?"

"Apparently the victim was a church goer. Husband died a year ago. Quiet girl; went to work and home. Nothing electrifying."

"Who called this one in?"

"Anonymous. Got a 911 report on a dead body at Alexander. Tani was the first officer to arrive, found the front door half ajar. Came in to check. That's her stomach contents, by the way."

"And how do you know all of this?"

"People tell me things, sir." He pushed his glasses up on his nose.

Derk walked around the living room, discussing the details and snapping more photographs.

"Do you know if she had enemies?"

"Not to my knowledge."

The continuous whir of the camera penetrated the eerie darkness of death.

"What do we have?"

"Exactly what's in front of you."

"Derk, stop with the games! I'm too tired for this vague bullshit."

"Hey, don't bark at me. I've had five hours of sleep in three days." Derk stood toe to toe with the big African American. "So please back off. I just get the evidence bagged and tagged, and I'm called to another slaughter scene. The prick is killing faster than I can collect the damn evidence. I need my team here if this case is going to be solved."

"Where are they?"

"Gile and Cross are at the lab, trying to provide you guys essential data that could help find this guy and put him away for a very long time. And Ivy Frost is out on an overdue sabbatical."

"Not anymore. I'll get them here."

"They're going to be pissed."

"Don't care. You need them here. The faster this data is collected, the quicker it can be analyzed in the lab."

"Captain Barlow, even if we work through the night, don't expect to have any results by tomorrow. It ain't going to happen."

"True enough."

The captain hurried outside and handed Tommy a piece of paper with the numbers on it. "What's this?"

"Call these forensic guys and get them over here, including Frost. No excuses."

"Right away, sir." Tommy opened his cell phone and began dialing.

The detectives finally entered the premises, eyeing the pool of blood and someone's regurgitated dinner. Jim wretched like a pregnant woman with morning sickness. He retreated out the front door faster than he entered.

"Where in hell is he going?" Captain Barlow barked.

"Out to toss his cookies. He's green around the gills, remember?" Dan teased, trying to ignore his own roiling stomach.

"Hey, where's the body?" Dan asked, looking around the living room.

Before the captain had a chance to respond, Derk interjected.

"In the bedroom."

"He likes that room, don't he!" Disgust twisted at the corner of Dan's mouth. "What's the damage this time?"

"With one mean swipe of his blade, he almost decapitated her, except for the epidermis on the back of her neck. The killer sliced right through the epiglottis."

The captain gave him a look.

"The cartilage flap that covers the larynx. This guy is letting us know he's in control of this sick and twisted little game."

"Anything else?" Dan asked.

"The usual, Danny boy." Derk took another snapshot. "He likes to make them suffer, and then when he's good and satisfied, he ends it. He is the one calling the shots."

The captain inhaled a small breath of death air. "Go and get your partner back in here."

The detective carefully stepped over the puddles on his way out.

"Hey, wuss, the captain wants you in here pronto!" Dan shouted across the yard at Jim who was leaning against the redwood tree, sipping on a bottle of water.

"I'll puke if I go inside there."

"And you'll find your ass standing in the unemployment line if you don't." Laughter echoed in the night. "Get in here. We got work to do!" Dan ignored the snickering and slammed the front door.

Before stepping inside the house of horror, Jim took out two Vic's nasal capsules and placed them into his nostrils. This helped ease the foul stench of vital fluids and slow decomposing parts.

All three moved methodically from room to room, taking it all in. Each room was immaculate, as if this victim surrendered without a fight. Almost like she knew her fate. Victim number five lay underneath the wine-colored top sheet. Her head was disconnected from her neck. Congealed blood pooled on the floor beside the bed. Dan scribbled line after line in his notebook. Not that anything he saw could be erased from memory. Questions to be answered at a later date. Dan began checking the closets, under the bed, in search of the weapon that was used to murder this victim. Jim suddenly yelped and fell back into the wall, catching his partner's attention.

"What is your problem tonight?" Dan asked, rubbing his double chin.

"Ummm … you might want to have a look at this." He pointed to the sheet.

"You know, we really don't have time for this bullshit." Dan made his way back to the bed. "What is it?"

"Her private part. He took her privates. He cut it out!" Jim yelled, hands flailing in the air.

Dan slowly lifted the sheet from the victim's body. Then he quickly turned away. "Jesus H. Christ!"

"I'll go get the captain."

"Good fucking idea. Bring that geek in rubber back with you. He might want to take a picture or two." Dan let out a loud breath.

The detective could no longer stand next to the bloodied corpse and moved to the doorway and waited. Thoughts of what this serial killer would do to his next victim swirled like a drowning man trapped in a current. Roger Taut was not going to quit killing until he was stopped.

Dan turned, hearing footsteps coming toward him. The captain was the first to enter, followed by Derk and Jim.

"I've seen a lot of shit in my day, but this … this is the stuff you see in nightmares." Jim's head began to swim.

"He's one sick fuck. I'll give him that." Dan added shaking his head.

Derk immediately began snapping pictures from the four corners of the room before taking close-ups of the corpse. "He started his murderous ritual in the living room, with I'm guessing a few punches to the face to keep her in line. At least that's what the large droplets of blood are showing throughout the carpet. I'm assuming he dragged the victim half-unconscious in here to finish her off," Derk began, the whir of the camera amplifying three-fold inside the bedroom.

"Just for shits and kicks, anyone want to tell me where her ... a ..."

"Spit it out Jim," Captain Barlow snapped.

"Private part, sir. Where is it?"

"Looks to me like he cut it out," Derk announced with a level of detachment.

"Ah, no shit. Go to university for that." Jim teased.

"Hey, you asked." Derk smirked beneath his mask.

"Well ..."

"If you're asking if her genitalia has been found? The answer is no." The forensic expert, Derk informed.

"Captain, is that our job?" Jim made a sour face.

"Search the entire house."

"One day detectives, and the next we're organ finders. Fuck!" Dan rubbed his bloodshot eyes. "Let's go, partner." He smacked Jim on the back and moved out of the bedroom and down the hall.

Once the detectives were out of sight, John turned to Derk.

"I need to know, was this victim alive when he cut her open?"

"I'll know more once we get her on a steel slab, but I'm guessing yes. Dead people don't bleed out from an open wound, Captain." He lifted the sheet, showing the gaped open incision. "I'm afraid her heart was still beating, but not for long."

"This case is insane. Now he's changed from stabbing to removing vaginal organs. I have a call to make."

"If it's the same perpetrator," Derk said and went back to doing what he did best—finding clues to help the police catch a madman.

Chapter Thirty-Seven

Ellen had just gotten back to sleep from another nightmare when the phone ringing jolted her awake.

"Hello?"

"I'm so sorry to have had to wake you out of a sound sleep, but we need you."

"Who is this?"

"It's John. John Barlow."

Ellen sprang upward, the dawn's light stealing away the darkness from inside her bedroom. "John. Sorry, I was—"

"Asleep, like we all should be."

"Yeah." She leaned over and turned on the side lamp.

"Ellen, has Roger ever had fantasies about collecting human body parts? Private body parts."

"No. Why do you ask?"

"Guess what's missing on this victim?"

"John, do you have the name of this victim?"

"Julie Saunders."

"Julie Saunders. Julie Saunders," she repeated.

"Does the name ring a bell?"

"Yes. She was a patient of mine last year. She came to see me for counseling after her husband died."

John smiled. "Ellen, I think we just found our connection to these murders. I'm going to ask you to get a list of all the patients you've counseled over the last five years. And then cross-reference the recent murdered victims to your list of patients. I don't believe Roger is picking these women at random."

"It will take me some time to go through the boxes in the basement in order to find the list going back five years."

"If you need a hand, let me know. But do what you need to do and then meet me in the conference room. I can finally see light at the end of this long, dark tunnel." He breathed a sigh of relief.

"Okay then. I'll see you as soon as I'm finished at River Edge." Ellen hit the off button.

Captain Barlow placed his cell phone back in its case that was clipped to his belt and walked across the street to give instructions to the other two officers.

Meanwhile, the detectives were still roaming the house, room by room, in search of the murder weapon used to mutilate Julie Saunders's body. And if they were really lucky, they wouldn't come across the grotesque trophy. As they searched the inside property, Dan continued his angry rant. "You know what I think?" He stopped mid-step and looked at his partner with fierce determination on his pudgy face.

"No, but I have a feeling you're going to tell me." Jim closed the closet door of the spare bedroom.

"We've been looking for a motive, right? I think this bastard's connection to these murders is the nuthouse. You know the big 'fuck you' to the funny farm for keeping him locked up for the last seven years."

"Revenge?"

"Exactly! Why else would someone escape the funny farm and not get lost? I mean, the guy's hanging around Vic killing these women for a reason. And as soon as we find the correlation between these murders and River Edge, then and only then will we be one step closer to catching this sexual deviant. I mean, we have interviewed every one of his friends, family, and acquaintances and have come up with zip, zero, zilch. Like some dog chasing its tail, all he does is get dizzy. Cure and Lissner have squat, and they've put just as many man hours into this investigation as we have."

"Okay, say you're right. But why would Taut want to raise hell against River Edge? That place kept him from going to prison for life."

"If I had all the missing pieces to this insanity, we wouldn't be standing in this house looking for body parts, now would we?" The detective grunted.

"I think the answer is going to come from our good buddy."

Dan rolled his eyes. "Let me guess, Doctor Smith. Give me a break. The old woman doesn't know any more than we do. The only thing that's going to catch this maniac is good old-fashioned police work. Not some shrink that gets inside minds of depraved and downtrodden. Believe what you want."

"You"—Jim shook his head—"need to get laid."

"Thanks to Mr. Serial Boy we're chasing down, it leaves no time. I don't have time for a hooker's hand job let alone some warm fuzzy sex. Can you kindly get off the sex train and back into the case?"

The detectives walked the wooden steps down into the basement. The wheels in Dan's head were spinning like a hamster wheel. Dan was the first to spot the cubed freezer in the corner by the washer and hurried across the cement floor, anxiety building inside his chest. He winced and with one swift motion yanked opened the lid on the white box. Taking in a breath, he glanced inside. Whew, frozen meats only.

"No organs?" Jim asked, looking away.

"No organs."

With no success under their belt and another night gone by, the detectives strolled outside to take a break. Dan lit a smoke, staring up at the gray sky frittering away to early morning and the sun lazily coming to life.

"Man, I'm beat," Jim whined.

"I can't remember the last time I slept other than a catnap at my desk." Dan blew a cloud of poison from his lungs before taking a couple of steps down and plunking himself on the last step. Jim walked down the driveway, heading toward his Camaro.

"Hey, pretty boy, where you going?"

"To get coffee. Want one?"

"Sure, if you're buying." Dan watched as his partner drove away down Alexander Drive.

Seconds later, the captain stepped outside for some fresh air. He stripped down to his suit before walking down the steps. He stopped in front of his detective.

"Hey, you okay?" Captain Barlow asked, looking down.

"I'd be better if we could catch this prick," Dan said.

"Me and you both." John rubbed his face. "Find anything?"

"Nada. This guy is too smart to leave any clues behind. How are you holding up, sir?"

"Tired and miss my family. I can't remember the last time I spooned with my wife."

"Hey, that's privileged information, sir." Dan held up a hand, laughing.

"Okay, enough said." John shook his head and smirked.

"I keep the mantra operating that we'll catch him, but with each passing hour, my optimism turns to skepticism. Know what I'm saying, sir?"

"I believe there could be a connection between our latest victim and Roger Taut. Julie Saunders was a patient of Dr. Smith's last year. Ellen is on her way to River Edge to retrieve records of all her patients counseled, going back five years. We may have a lead, I hope." The captain tried to appear sanguine.

"Sir, I told Jim the exact same thing just a little while ago. We need to find the association between these murdered women and the nuthouse. Who knows, maybe the numb nuts thinks he's doing these depressed women a favor by taking them out of their misery. Like a mercy killing and having his sick fantasy party at the same time."

"I hear you." Just then the captain's cell phone rang. In one quick motion, he swiped it off his belt and checked the number. He smiled. "It's Isabella."

"Guess the wife misses you as much as you miss her, sir."

"Guess so." He walked out of earshot, leaving Dan secretly wishing he had a special someone.

Dan looked out toward Alexander, hearing the roar of the Camaro come to a stop. Jim got out, carrying two large Tim Horton coffees. He handed Dan a cup of fuel.

"Anything new?" Jim asked, tucking in his white dress shirt.

"As a matter of fact, partner, there is. Remember me saying earlier that I thought there was a connection between these killings and that haven for the extreme crazies?"

"Yeah." Jim rolled his eyes.

"Well, the captain agrees with me. Julie Saunders use to be a patient of Doctor S. And now Ellen is on a mission this morning. The doctor is heading over there to grab patient files for everyone she's counseled in the last five years. Hope there's a connection. That's all I can say."

"So these murders are well-calculated kills. Not some random acts of homicide?" Jim kicked a stone with the toe of his leather shoe.

The captain joined his detectives. "Hey, guys, I'm leaving." He jingled his car keys.

"Where you going, sir?" Dan asked, taking another smoke from his pack.

"Home for a couple hours. I thought you were going to quit?" Barlow scolded.

"As soon as we catch this prick, sir."

"Or he ends up with lung cancer," Jim said.

"I'd rather have a lung disease than my dick fall off from some STD, Romeo."

"My dick is fine, buddy, but thanks for caring."

Dan chuckled. "You, my friend, are hopeless."

Captain Barlow shook his head and laughed. The one characteristic he admired about his detectives was no matter how horrific a case, those two always managed to keep it together with humor.

"Sir, I thought I'd hang around and do some door-to-door canvassing."

"That won't be necessary. We have uniforms to do that task. Matt Cure and Lissner are setting up interviews with workers from River Edge. I strongly suggest you two go home and get some rest. We'll meet back in the conference room when I know something."

"I'm bagged," Dan said.

"No argument from me," Jim agreed.

All three jumped into their means of transportation and headed home.

Chapter Thirty-Eight

Across the city, Ellen was driving into the parking garage of River Edge to begin her dreaded task of the day. She managed to find a parking spot without too much trouble. She exited her white Lexus and rode the elevator up to the sixth floor, Bill Cobie's floor. Ellen hadn't had the time to warn him of her visit. She stepped out of the elevator at the same time Bill was coming down the hallway. The two stopped, eyeing each other in surprise.

"Good morning." He smiled. "Did I forget a meeting?"

"No. Sorry for showing up unannounced."

"Good, for a moment I thought I'd forgotten we had an appointment." He kissed her on the cheek.

"I'm sorry to barge in on you like this, but I need a favor."

"Let's talk in my office, shall we." Ellen wrapped her arm in the crook of Bill's arm, and the two sauntered down the plush carpeted corridor to Bill's office.

"Please have a seat. Coffee?"

"Yes, please."

Bill poured steaming liquid gold into Ellen's mug from the carafe sitting on the corner of his desk.

"Milk, sugar?"

"Black is fine. I need all the fuel I can get."

Bill walked around the desk and took his seat. "First up, you look like hell, but what do I know, right." He took off his glasses, placing them on his desk. "You won't listen to any advice given, so I'll save my breath with the lecture. I know you didn't stop by to have coffee with me. How can I be of service?"

"Bill, I need permission to take the files of all patients I've counseled over the last five years."

"You serious?" His brows furrowed.

"Yes. And I need them like yesterday."

"I gather it has to do with the investigation?" He took a sip of his morning brew, looking at Ellen from across the desk.

"Yes. The woman that was murdered last night, I counseled a year ago. And now I need to go to the basement and recover the boxes. Next I have to go through each of the files to see if there are any other matches to the already deceased victims. The captain believes these killings may be revenge motivated. He also thinks there is a possible connection between Roger Taut and the murdered women."

"In that case let's go to the record's storage room and retrieve what you need. Where are these boxes being taken?"

"Squad room over on Chanex."

The two stepped into the elevator and rode to the basement.

"Take as many boxes as you can, and I'll have the rest delivered sometime this morning."

"Bill, have I told you lately how wonderful you are?"

"When this investigation is over, and Roger is back here under lock and key, what do you say you and I go out for a nice sit-down dinner together." Bill didn't give Ellen a chance to answer. "And if there is anything else I can do, give me a ring. I'll help if I can." He opened the door to the storage room. Inside were shelves and shelves of boxed-up files.

"Thanks. Bill. And I'll put dinner on my calendar."

He smiled, leaned over, and kissed the side of her cheek. "Okay, let's get busy. You've got a pile of work ahead of you. I hope Captain Barlow knows how lucky he is to have you on his team."

"Flattery will get you everything." Ellen laughed and started pulling boxes off the shelves. An hour later, the two began loading up the Lexus with white sealed cardboard boxes. Afterward, Bill stood at the elevator and waved as she drove out of the parking garage. Once she was out of sight, he took the elevator back up to his office.

Chapter Thirty-Nine

Later that afternoon after a couple hours of tossing and turning, Dan gave up on sleep and jumped in the shower. He let the cool spray wake him back to life before stepping out of the tub. He toweled himself dry, brushed his teeth, and applied a little pit stick under his arms. He stepped back into his bedroom to dress. He tossed on a wrinkled blue shirt and a wrinkled pair of beige pants. He didn't give a shit about appearances. He grabbed a smoke, lit it, ran his fingers through his thick mane, and sauntered out to his tiny kitchen. There was enough coffee in the stained pot for one mug. How old, again he didn't give a shit. He placed the mug in the microwave and hit sixty seconds. Steeping cup of thick, black gold. He took a sip and then poured the rest into his traveling mug to take with him. He swiped his keys off the counter and headed back to Alexander Drive. The forensics team would still be there collecting samples of blood, guts, and gore. The body would now be in the cooler at the morgue waiting to be autopsied. At the rate Roger was killing, she'd have to wait her turn to get on the table. Dan lifted his heavy frame onto the front seat of his Dodge Ram pickup truck and roared down the city streets until he came to the upper side of the city. He pulled alongside the curb and jumped out. The street was quiet, a good sign.

He walked up to the front door and knocked before entering.

"Anyone home?" he yelled, stepping inside.

Before anyone had a chance to answer, another knock came at the screen door. Dan turned around, surprised by the figure coming in. Jim had changed his wrinkly suit clothes from the night before, but the rest of him looked like Dan felt.

Suddenly like an apparition, Ivy appeared in the doorway to the living room. Dan gave a little wave, which was reciprocated back with a warm smile. Jim's "hello," on the other hand, was coldly ignored. Instead she stuck up her middle finger and flipped him the bird before she walked away.

"She hates you, dude." Dan could not hold back a smirk.

"That's Ivy. One big walking resentment." Jim tried to make light of her snub.

"What did you do to piss her off?"

"Nothing."

"Her giving you the bird looked like something to me."

"She's pissed because I broke it off with her."

"Ivy is more than pissed, man. She hates your guts." Dan laughed, getting his latex booties on over his running shoes.

"She'll get over it."

"That's it, lover boy, show your sensitive side."

"What ever happened to one-night stands?"

"Gone!" Dan frowned. "You keep discarding women the way you do, and you'll find yourself gone. There is nothing like a woman's scorn. Got it?"

Jim popped a breath mint into his yap and started further in. Dan went in the direction of Ivy.

Ivy Frost, a beautiful woman with looks of a glam model and body perfect. She was indeed intelligent and a very punctual forensic scientist who cared about the secrets of the dead. She was warm-hearted and obviously naïve when it came to men. She did date Detective Jim Masker, didn't she? All the same, Dan loved her spirit.

"Good afternoon, doll."

"And the same to you."

"Anything?"

"The usual. Keith is in the bedroom collecting fibers off the bed sheets with his trendy little vacuum. Adam, as you can see by the black smudging on every surface, is collecting prints. Speaking of prints, we ran the print through the database from a prior homicide over on the west side. I believe it was apartment 3. Although a foreign print was identified through AFIS, we still don't know whom the print belongs to. Either way, this person was in the room at the time the young victim was brutally murdered."

"Are you saying we're hunting two serial killers?" Dan's face drained.

"Not sure. I'll find the clues, Dan, and you solve the murders."

"I hope you're wrong. Christ, we can't catch this prick."

"And maybe there is a reason why."

"Please, Ivy, don't even go there." He shook his head. "Since we're heading down the slope of disaster, might as well ask, did any of you forensic experts happen to come across her missing private parts?" Dan looked away for a moment, not wanting to hear the answer.

"Yes, as a matter of fact, I have. The grisly discovery was found in the fridge's freezer, hidden inside a popsicle box."

Just then Derk half-staggered into the living room. "Hey, what are you doing here?"

"Can't sleep." Dan groaned. "Where's Jim?"

"Talking with Adam."

All three turned, eyeing Keith as he blew by, heading toward the front door, arms loaded with evidence bags.

"If that's not our cue to get back to the lab and start processing, I don't know what is." Ivy shrugged. "Hey, Keith, wait a second. I'll give you a hand." She followed Keith out to his Suburban.

Jim came in the room.

"I have new information that might put a different spin on the investigation Dan," Derk said.

"What now?" Dan gave a sigh.

"I swabbed the victim's breast this time. Why, you ask? I'll tell you. As I was getting the victim ready to be transported to the morgue, I could smell this faint scent of mint around the chest area. I moved in closer, and sure enough I was correct. I swabbed the area and then checked the bathroom cabinet and cupboards to see what perfumes Mrs. Saunders wore. Lavender and Puma do not fit the scent. So if my spiny senses are correct, the perp was chewing mint gum at the time he gave Julie a lick job. So maybe this prick isn't so smart after all." Derk smiled, removing his Tyvek suit."

"Let me know as soon as you hear something." Dan patted Derk on the back. "Time for beddy-bye, little man."

"My thoughts exactly. The crew can handle the rest."

By the time the detectives and forensic team stepped outside, the afternoon heat was like a sauna. All that was left of Julie Saunders's vibrant life was yellow crime tape sealing off the premises.

Chapter Forty

The next morning in the conference room, three out of four looked as if they'd been side swiped by a front-end loader. Pale faces, bloodshot eyes, and the inability to sit still from the gallons of coffee coursing through their veins. Jim was the only one looking bright eyed and bushy tailed, like he'd slept all night instead of a few hours.

Ellen started the meeting of minds. "Some of you guys look like you've been beat up and left out to dry. No offense."

"It shows, does it?" Captain Barlow asked, rubbing his tired eyes.

"How many hours now?"

"Stopped counting," Jim said.

"I'm guessing too many," Ellen acknowledged, checking her watch. She'd been at the station since five this morning, thanks to Captain Barlow's late-evening wakeup call. It was now quarter to ten.

"What's the saying, Doctor? You can sleep when you're dead," Dan said.

"Quit learning my bad habits, Dan."

Dan smirked, taking a swig of black coffee.

"Give me the run down on Julie Saunders." Ellen inquired looking over her glasses.

"Practically cut her damn head clear off. And gutted out her private parts and hid them inside an empty Popsicle box." Dan answered.

"The knife used, anyone know the brand name?" Doctor Smith asked.

"Derk thinks it was a bone knife," Captain Barlow said. "Ellen, was this guy ever employed as a farmer or butcher?"

"Not to my knowledge. Why?"

"He's got some power behind him, I'll give him that. This is the second victim that he slit right through the sternocleidomastoid. I mean holy shit," Jim stated.

"Tell me something I don't know." Dan went to reach across the table to retrieve a paper when he accidentally hit his mug, spilling his coffee. Lucky for him, he jumped out of the way before the hot liquid splashed on his crotch. "Fuck!" He flew out of the room to the men's room down the hall for paper towels. He returned shortly in the same frustrated mood as when he bolted out the door.

"Ellen, do you think there is a connection between Julie Saunders and River Edge? I have a hunch this sick retard thinks he's doing these women a favor by murdering them," Dan said, throwing the paper towels in the garbage. "I respect patient privacy and all, but at this point in the investigation, we need a connection or more women will die. And I'm getting the feeling that he ain't working alone anymore."

"I think you might be on to something. This morning I retrieved all of my patients' files that I've worked with for the last five years. I've only worked with two of the victims. One being Julie Saunders and the second being Diane Gibber. I've counseled many patients over the course of my career, gentlemen, so I still have more files to go through before we can make an accurate conclusion, so to speak."

"Please don't take too long, Doctor. Lives are depending on you." Dan kept his voice level. "Another couple of hours, and we'll be meeting like this again."

"Thanks, no pressure, right?" She winked. "What about forensics?"

"I called in the rest of Derk's team last night," the captain said. "We should have something this afternoon. In the meantime ..." The captain checked his watch. "Dan, Jim, go downstairs and begin the interviews with staff from River Edge. They're sitting in the waiting area."

"Got you, boss." Dan grabbed the file in front of him and rose out of his chair with his partner in tow.

Ellen leisurely walked around the room, stopping to look at each dead woman's photograph tacked onto the wall. She hesitated, turning around. "Has Julie Saunders's family been notified?"

"Shit!" John yelled.

"You need to speak with them before the press does."

"I know. I know," he snapped, feeling the crinkles around his face tighten from the pressure of this investigation. Since John had become captain, sure he saw victims and deaths due to violence, but nothing of this magnitude. Every day there seemed to be a new body turning up and more brutalized than the last. This guy was a damn killing machine.

"C'mon, pull yourself together. This isn't your first kick at the can." Ellen smiled and went back to poring over boxes of files.

Within seconds, the captain was on his way to 69 Governor Road to deliver news that would change some people's lives forever.

The captain slowly made his way toward the brick walkway and up three steps to the front door. He knocked three times. A gray-haired man about sixty answered. He was dressed casually, beige shorts and a golf short-sleeve shirt. There was no mistaking that Julie was his child. They were spitting images of each other. He was clean-shaven with sparkling blue eyes like his daughter and full lips.

"Yes?"

"Are you Allan Saunders?"

"Yes, I am. What can I do for you?"

"Mr. Saunders, I'm Captain John Barlow. May I come in?" the captain asked, flashing his badge.

The brightness in his eyes suddenly paled.

"Why?" Fear began rising up in his throat.

"I would rather not discuss it out here, sir."

"Who is at the door, dear?" Helen came and stood next to her husband.

"What's this all about?" Allan persisted.

"It's about your daughter, Julie Saunders. I'm afraid I have bad news."

Helen looked at her husband. A fear beamed from her eyes into his.

"What's this all about?" Her voice became heightened.

"It's about your daughter, ma'am. I'm afraid I have bad news," Captain Barlow replied gently.

"What's wrong? Did something happen to Julie? Is she okay?"

The captain had seen this apprehensive expression many times before. It was a brief moment of clarity as to why he was there.

"Please, may I come inside?" Captain Barlow gently asked once more.

Allan suddenly froze, forcing Helen to push him out of the way so that the captain could enter. Helen pointed to a spacious living room decorated in glass and leather. A round Chinese rug accented the velour drapes, exquisitely comforting to the eye. Allan took his place next to his wife on the overstuffed leather couch, holding her hand.

"I'm afraid I have horrible news to tell you." Captain Barlow broke the mounting silence.

"What is it?" Allan asked.

"Julie was murdered last night," Captain Barlow answered softly.

The room suddenly shrieked with the sound of pain, loss, and disbelief.

"Not my Julie. My baby. Tell him it's not true, Allan!" Helen screamed, shaking her husband's hand violently.

"We found her identification in her purse." Captain Barlow handed over Julie's driver license.

"This is my daughter, Julie." Allan dropped his head into his hands, fighting hard not to break down. "Who murdered my baby?"

"We suspect it's—"

John never got the opportunity to finish his sentence.

"It's that son of a bitch that escaped, isn't it?"

"He is our number-one suspect at this time."

"Where's my daughter? I need to see my daughter," Helen sobbed.

"I'm afraid that request is not possible," Captain Barlow said.

"Why not?" Anger rose up in Allan's throat.

It was tough enough to tell these loving parents that their daughter was dead. And now they wanted to know how she died.

"Your daughter was found decapitated." The captain decided to leave out the other gory detail. The expression of absolute horror on the faces of Allan and Helen would remain in John's mind for a lifetime. It took every ounce of strength for John not to get swallowed up in emotions.

Captain Barlow could feel his blood boil as he watched these parents fall apart in front of his eyes. Here he was, again, telling another family their child was never coming home. No more birthdays, anniversaries, celebrations of any kind. It was all over. And he felt responsible for Julie's death because this serial madman once again outsmarted his team.

The captain convinced Allan to call his family physician. Helen would need to take a sedative to calm her. Her entire body was vibrating. She was not taking the news very well.

Before getting into his vehicle, John briefly glanced up the walkway, eyeing Allan Saunders staring at him with a cold, murderous look in his eyes. John's only hope was for his team to find Taut before Saunders did, or they would be facing a whole different set of circumstances. It gave John a sudden chill.

Chapter Forty-One

Mid-Sunday morning, Sandy awoke. She smiled, feeling eyes and hands roaming all over her. Although she might have slept an hour total, she felt revitalized like never before.

"Do I detect eyes on the back of my head?" She laughed, rolling over to face her lover.

"Good morning, beautiful." He lightly covered her mouth with his.

"How can you say I'm beautiful? My hair looks like a chia pet. My breath smells like … never mind. And you—this has to be a dream I don't want to wake from. Pinch me just to make sure this isn't a joke."

"I assure being with you is no joke." He pinched her butt.

"Ouch!" she yelled, rubbing her bare backside.

"You told me to pinch you." He laughed playfully.

"I didn't think you would." She sulked.

Mark smothered her mouth with kisses.

"I could get used to this sinful attention."

"Glad to hear."

Sandy and Mark made love once more before finally dragging their bedraggled selves out of bed for a well-deserved breakfast. The first thing Sandy went for was cold orange juice from the fridge, downing half a glass in two gulps.

"Thirsty?"

"Dehydrated. Pardon my manners. Want some?"

"Please." Sandy poured juice into the same glass she'd only seconds ago drank from. It was evident how hung over she was.

"How much did I drink last night?"

"More than enough to take the edge off a first date."

She handed him her glass.

"Thanks." He rolled his eyes and hydrated his parched throat.

"Hungry?" She asked, intending to go out for breakfast.

"Starved. I'll make breakfast if you show me around the kitchen."

"I thought we'd go out. Save us the trouble of making a mess."

"Than that thought would be wrong. Another one of my passions is cooking."

Mark, with his masculine frame and washboard stomach, moved around Sandy's kitchen like he truly belonged. He got out the ingredients to make omelets and proceeded to cook up a breakfast feast.

"Coffee?" he asked.

"Canister." She pointed to the ceramic jar with the letter C scripted on the front. He shoveled five heaping spoonfuls into the filter with a few sprinkles of cinnamon for flavor. A half an hour later, breakfast for his queen was prepared.

After breakfast, Sandy went to the front door to retrieve the morning paper. She glanced at the front page, shocked.

"Oh my god."

"What's wrong?"

"It looks like our escapee found another victim to slay, according to the *Post*."

"Where was this victim found?"

"West side of the city." Sandy took a drink of coffee. "This is getting very scary."

"Don't worry. I'll protect you."

"Good to hear. Mark, I don't understand how he was able to get free in the first place, especially the fourth floor. It makes no sense."

"And all the cameras going down at the time of his breakout.

His breakout was planned; that's for sure. But if it's okay with you, I'd rather not spend my Sunday morning talking about him," Mark said.

"You're right. He's not worth it."

He lifted her up onto the counter, squeezing between her legs. "I have better things we can do."

"I bet you do." She giggled, leaning down to kiss him playfully.

"I think we should become an item."

"I don't know," she teased, hugging him tight.

"I know what we can do today since we're both off work."

"What's that?"

"Take a nice drive in the country. Park under a shady tree and have a picnic of fresh fruits, salad, and cold chicken with a nice bottle of Dom Perignon. Then afterward we can cuddle while you share some of that talent you have. It's not every day I get to sleep with a poet."

"The first part sounds romantic. But the poetry part … well, I think you're full of it."

"I want to know everything about you."

"Now I know I'm dreaming."

He tucked his two fingers under her chin, lifting her head up so there eyes locked. "I think I'm falling in love with you, Sandy Miller."

"I believe you're delusional with hangover syndrome." She tried to play it cool.

Mark was taken aback by her lack of faith in his proposal of love. "Okay then." He shook his head. "What do you say we wash up this mess and get on with our planned day?" He quickly changed the subject.

"You wash. I'll dry." She leaped off the countertop.

"Deal. Maybe we can slide a cool bubble bath into our plans, because after all, it is a hot day." He gave a sly wink.

"You have the best ideas, Doctor."

At home, Franki was growing frantic as she tried to get a hold of Sparkie. She'd left three messages, and still no return phone call. This wasn't like Sparkie to leave Franki dangling with worry. Franki thought, *If she's hiding because she got high on cocaine last night, I'm going to be pissed off at her.* She put the phone down. *I'll try again after my shower.*

An hour later, and still no Sparkie closure, Franki started feeling claustrophobic and needed to get out of the loft for a while. She decided to hit the streets to search for her friend. The drug-infested hideaways of Victoria were still very familiar to Franki. One was not privy to forgetting such a debilitating life style. If Franki failed to find Sparkie, then she'd stop by Sandy's place for an unexpected visit. Sandy was always there when she needed her. Franki couldn't shake the dread in the pit of her stomach. Dressed and almost out the door, she stopped at the sound of the phone ringing. She bolted back up the stairs and answered.

"Hello."

"Hi, Franki, it's Steve. I hope I'm not disturbing you?"

"No," she lied. "How are you?" Her heart smiled at the sound of his voice.

"Never better, and you?"

"Feeling is mutual."

"Umm, are you tired?"

"A little." She laughed. "But I'll live."

"Sorry for keeping you out so late. Franki, will you have dinner with me this evening? I apologize about the short notice."

"Can I let you know later? The reason I can't commit to you now is because the friend I was supposed to meet last night is still missing. I've been trying her cell phone all morning, and nothing. I'm going to look for her, and I don't know how long it will take."

"If you need my help, I'd be happy to join the search."

"Well that's very kind of you. Thanks."

"I'm holding you up. Call me if you need me."

"I'll talk to you soon." She smiled before disconnecting.

Franki's mind wandered back to her and Steve cuddling on the porch swing under the twinkling stars. It was so romantic and perfect it gave her shivers. They talked and kissed into the wee hours of the morning, sharing their hopes and dreams of tomorrow. The evening was unequivocally faultless.

Chapter Forty-Two

Mark and Sandy were getting undressed for their romantic bubble bath when they heard the doorbell.

"Expecting company?" he asked.

"No," she replied, flustered and wrapping a robe around her body.

Sandy almost made it to the front door before Franki came barging in wearing a big grin. Sandy had forgotten to lock the door after grabbing the morning paper.

"Afternoon, Mary Sunshine. Whose car is that?"

"Afternoon to you too."

The two gave each other a hug.

"Hey, you look like the cat that just ate the canary. Whose car?"

Just then Mark came into the living room wearing a huge smirk. Franki didn't have to ask a third time who the car belonged to.

"Hi, I'm Mark. The Grand Am is mine." They shook hands cordially.

"Franki. Am I interrupting?" She blushed a little.

Sandy was busted.

"Would it make a difference?"

"No." Franki laughed. "Doc told me you had a date last night."

"Good news travels fast."

"I came to see for myself. I didn't really believe this shut-in had a date."

"You're a brat."

"I know. Coffee on?"

Franki couldn't help noticing Mark's washboard abs. This guy was definitely on the hottie list.

"So you're the famous Franki Martin Sandy's been raving about."

"Don't believe a word she tells you."

The trio laughed.

"How did your date go with that handsome detective?" Sandy asked.

"Not as well as yours obviously." Franki arched one eyebrow up and down naughtily. "Jim is a self-centered ass."

"Loves himself, does he?"

"To the extreme. The guy had the audacity to flirt with our server right in front of me."

"Really."

"No shit."

"I guess no second date for that moron."

"No way. I should go."

"Stay and visit, Franki," Mark said.

Sandy gave her new lover the sideways look.

"We can play in the bubbles another time, honey," he teased.

"I'm holding you to it."

Franki made her way to the kitchen, making herself at home. She didn't need to be waited on. After all, she practically grew up in this house. After leaving River Edge, Franki came and lived with Mama Sandy for six years before going out on her own. She smiled at the lovebirds whispering sweet nothings in each other's ears from the living room.

"I'll be back later, promise." He kissed her good-bye.

"You better," she ordered, not wanting him to leave.

"Promise, baby. Enjoy your visit with Franki."

"I'm killing her after you leave," she growled.

"Hey! I heard that." She laughed. "Can't you just feel the love?"

Mark popped his head around the kitchen corner. "It's a pleasure, Miss Martin."

"Miss Martin, oh please." Sandy snorted playfully. "Call me Franki."

"Good-bye, Franki."

Moments later, the front door closed.

Sandy sprang up the stairs and into the kitchen as Franki handed her a cup of coffee.

"Let's go sit on the deck. It's beautiful outside," Franki suggested.

"We have catching up to do," Sandy said.

"You're not going to believe what happened to me last night."

"With your lifestyle, anything is possible."

They sat comfortably across the table from each other.

"My date started out pretty good," Franki said. "We had a glass of wine at my place before leaving for the restaurant. He inspected my paintings, nice icebreaker. We're now at the restaurant doing that phony, idle crap that I hate. When the server comes to our table to take our order, my wonderful date, who obviously can't help himself, starts flirting with her. I mean right in front of me. The jerk has zero class. I knew it was all downhill from there. So I drilled him a bit as to why he wasn't married. Don't need to be a rocket scientist to figure out why. On a date with one woman, flirting with another is not cool. That's not the worst part." Franki paused to take a drink of her coffee. "I got stuck with the dinner bill because he got called away. I'm getting ahead of myself here. After we ate, I went to powder my nose. Now here comes the good part. I was coming out of the bathroom and banged right into Steve Michaels." Franki beamed.

"The Steve Michaels from long ago?"

"In the flesh. My stomach turned to butterflies instantly, palms sweating. The whole nine yards. He's like a fine wine; he gets better looking with age. Long story short, Jim got called away, and Steve and I spent the rest of the evening at his place. I got home around five this morning. And he's invited me to dinner at his place, and, baby, I'm there."

"Bye, bye, Jim." Sandy waved.

"A guy like that wouldn't stick by me."

"Trust your guts, honey."

"Steve loves me. I can see it in his eyes."

"I can see it in yours." Sandy smiled warmly.

"Sandy, I'm afraid he'll walk when he finds out I'm HIV positive."

"I think your wrong, kiddo. I take it your health didn't enter into the conversation?"

"Nope."

"You have to trust that he's back in your life after all these years for a reason. Give him a chance before you decide to sabotage."

"I just dread telling him the truth."

"The truth will set you free, my dear."

"Exactly what I'm afraid of." Franki frowned, taking a sip from her mug. "Enough about me. Mark is gorgeous—and those abs. You got it going on, Sandy."

"It was the most amazing night of my life. That man is everything I've ever dreamed about. He's perfect, charming, funny, and great in bed I might add."

"You are glowing."

"I know!" Sandy giggled like a schoolgirl.

"Here's to happy endings." They dinged their cups together.

"Where'd he go?"

"Home to shower and change. We're going on a picnic in the country."

"Sounds romantic." Franki leaped out of her chair, giving her foster mom a big hug. "I should go so you can get ready."

"What are you up to now?"

"I'm on my way to find Sparkie. We were supposed to get together last night, and she was a no show. Not to show up at a bar is not like her. I'm heading over to her place to see what's up. Go and get ready for your picnic."

"Yes, boss." Sandy beamed with joy.

"Love you." Franki hugged Sandy one more time and headed out the door.

Chapter Forty-Three

At noon, Captain Barlow rejoined Ellen back in the conference room. He'd just left Mr. and Mrs. Saunders' home. He had a pain in his heart he couldn't get rid of. He plunked himself down and dropped his head into his hands.

"Went that well?"

"The grief. Such gut-level grief."

Ellen placed her glasses on the table and took a seat next to John. "You are really going to have to get a handle on this. The only way you are going to catch this monster is if you detach. Do you hear me?"

"How? How can I?"

"To know that these crimes are not your fault. You are following every lead that comes into this station. Visiting every autopsy, going over every file I hand you. You are doing everything, including canvassing the areas, which I might add is not in your job description."

"Thank you for being such a good friend. Have you found any more links?"

"I'm afraid not. I've gone through every box I have. Nothing."

Scribbled beneath each of the photographs were the victims' names, possible motive, and how each body was found. Susan Dutch and Julie Saunders were new addition to the list. Ellen and John sat in silence, staring at the wall of gruesome photos exhibiting the last minutes of life each victim had to endure before death. The city map began to look like pin the tail on the donkey game. The different colored tacks showed the different locations. Taut was messing with the task force; he wanted the police to find these women. The handiwork of a serial madman on display for a selective few to view. Stacks of evidence sat on the table to be examined and reexamined again. The team was anxiously waiting on any forensic they could get their hands on.

Captain Barlow sat, his eyes glued to the photographs of last night's crime scene while Ellen continued her search for clues to back up Dan's hunch. There was no parallel; Julie Saunders and Diane Gibber were the only two victims who sought help at River Edge, according to what she'd discovered in her files thus far. Josey Moran never saw the inside of the institution. Susan Dutch had minor offences with police for prostitution. Something didn't add up; even the kills were becoming a bit inconsistent with the modus operandi. Indeed Roger Taut was a cold-blooded murderer, but he was no sadistic butcher. And from the crime scene photographs of Julie Saunders, this was not the work of Roger Taut.

The door opened, and in stepped the detectives, taking a break from interviews. Ellen politely informed Dan that she didn't think his theory about revenge killings were correct. He began combing his hands through his hair, almost desperate.

"Jesus, what is it were missing if it's not revenge?"

"Something so goddamn obvious that we can't see it." Ellen stretched her tired body. "The proof is here. Josie Moran, Shelby Porter, Susan Dutch aren't in any way connected to River Edge, and yet they wound up dead."

"I thought for sure there was a connection."

"Sorry, Detective."

Upon hearing a surprised knock, all four faced the door. Derk entered, looking like the rest of the bedraggled crew.

"Afternoon, gentlemen. Doctor Smith."

"Afternoon," they echoed in unison.

"Tell me you have something." Captain Barlow put his hands together.

"You guys decide. I'm just the messenger."

"Start singing," Dan declared.

Derk laughed at the detective's joviality in the face of adversity.

The forensic specialist strolled across the blue carpet to the table, spreading out more data.

"The prints found in Julie Saunders's bedroom don't match Roger Taut's, just like the ones found in Josey Moran's bedroom."

All four gasped with disbelief.

"Say what?" Dan rubbed his face, trying to comprehend.

"We ran the prints through AFIS, and no match. This means whoever is assisting your psycho doesn't have a record."

"This investigation is going nowhere," Jim said.

Derk opened the file and pointed to the new photo. "Remember the frame on the dresser covered in the victim's blood? Well this is the woman."

"It's Franki Martin." Jim's eyes went wide.

"Calm down. It's probably a fan. The photograph could have been taken during one of her book signings." Ellen wiped the nervous sweat from her brow.

"Ellen, we need to know," Captain Barlow said.

"I'm calling her," Ellen grabbed her cell.

"Pay close attention. There's more," Derk said.

"Do we want to know?" Dan looked bewildered.

"Look closely at the footprints on the floor by the east wall. What do you see?"

All four hunched in for a closer inspection.

"There are two sets of footprints." Derk pointed with his pen. "This shoe print is a size nine, and this special one here is a size seven and half."

"Maybe it's the victim?" Dan shrugged.

"Impossible, my man. The dead woman wears a six."

"So someone else was in the bedroom watching the killer torture this nice woman with the pink hair?" Jim asked, alarm bells going off in his head.

"Or participating."

"Now it's starting to make sense. Whoever is hiding him is also helping him to commit these heinous acts of butchery," Dan concluded.

"Got to love science. It's never wrong." Derk showed off his pearly whites.

"Shit, now we're hunting two sick freaks. This is a serial nightmare that just keeps gaining momentum by the second." Dan shoved his hands into his jean pockets.

"Break time is over, boys. If those employees know anything, we need to know," Captain Barlow ordered.

"The ones I've interrogated know nothing. They're more curious as to what we're doing to catch this prick," Jim responded, rising from his seat.

"Then move onto the next person until you find something."

"Sir, we're going to need reinforcements here," Jim complained.

"Yeah. It will take forever to interview everyone on the list. We may need to track down a few MIAs, if you know what I mean. And we don't have the time to chase ghosts," Dan said.

"He's right, John," Ellen agreed.

"I'll order up another team," Captain Barlow said and quickly exited the room.

Derk pulled up a chair. "My team is working on lifting the latent shoe print, which will lead to the make of the shoe and the company that sells its type."

"Way to go, man. How long will that take?" Dan slapped Derk on the shoulder.

"I'm a forensic guy, not David Copperfield. I want you guys to catch this maniac so we can all get a decent night's sleep."

"Don't even go there, buddy." Dan rubbed his eyes. "I'll get the prick."

"AFIS offered nothing on this mystery person?" Ellen spoke more to herself then the others.

"None found, Doctor Smith," Derk said apologetically.

"At least we know for certain he's not working alone. Doesn't make this investigation any easier, but it's a lead," Jim announced, trying to sound optimistic.

The captain returned to the conference room. "We have a second team."

"Who?" Jim asked.

"Officers Trex, Bruse, Fritz, Gail, and Thea."

"I hope they're ready to work long hours," Dan retorted.

"In the meantime, Jim, Dan, I have a new assignment for you two."

"What, sir?"

"Head back to the Royal Deal complex and start demanding answers from the tenants. Threaten jail if you have to, but find something. Someone saw or heard something that night. Jog their memories."

"Yes, sir." Dan was biting at the bit for a smoke.

"We're gone!" The detectives gave a wave before closing the door.

"I'm out of here too." Derk pulled himself to his feet and disappeared out the door and back to the lab.

The room fell mute.

"Want a coffee?" John asked, breaking the uncomfortable silence.

"Love one," Ellen said.

A minute or so later, John arrived carrying two steaming cups. They sat at the table, quietly praying for answers.

"Did you finally get some sleep this morning?" she asked.

"No. Every time I closed my eyes, my mind flashed to dead women with the missing genitalia, the parents, and this whole ugly investigation. I have an idea, Ellen. Let's get out of here and grab a decent lunch. And on the way, you can call Franki."

It didn't take long to comply. In seconds, the two joined arms and meandered out the door and down a maze of corridors.

Chapter Forty-Four

The detectives drove onto the Royal Deal parking lot in Jim's shiny corvette, relieved not to find a frenzy of spectators sniffing around. The detectives quickly hustled up to the main entrance. Dan leaned on the buzzer to the manager's apartment. She refused to unlock the door but said through the intercom she'd be right out. They held their badges against the glass door. A serial killer had entered the apartment building a couple nights ago, and she wasn't taking any chances. Dan guessed the manager was scared to death.

The landlady was not a beautiful woman of poise and elegance. If anything, she was the opposite. This dame was a skinny, old woman with a gray mullet and yellowing teeth. Her dress code could use a makeover. The deep wrinkles etched on her face illustrated life hadn't been too kind to her.

"No one's getting in this building without authorization, including cops," she snarled.

"I can appreciate that, Miss …" Jim glanced at his notepad. "Miss Joyce."

The detectives stepped inside the lobby, noticing handmade flyers tacked on the walls warning tenants not to allow anyone into the building they didn't recognize.

"Why are you here?" Miss Joyce asked.

"To question your tenants," the detective answered.

"I'm not promising they'll answer. Half the people in here don't like cops, and the other half have given their notice to vacate. Not that I blame them."

"Did you see or hear anything the night before last?"

"No," she said flatly.

"How well did you know Susan Dutch?"

"We didn't have tea if that's what you're asking." She rolled her eyes.

"Good tenant?" Dan pressed on.

"Paid her rent on time. You cops better find this animal."

"We're doing our best, ma'am." *We got a piece of work here*, Jim thought.

"I can't believe the damage in that apartment."

"The wreckage is the least of your concerns," Dan snapped.

"Well ... excuse me."

"Lady, what is your malfunction here?" Jim questioned sternly.

"My problem is one of my apartments looks like a cyclone hit it, and I'm the cleanup guy."

"Hire a crew," Dan said.

"How? Tenants here are on welfare. I have to fight every month to get rent. I don't have extras to pay for a cleaning crew."

"The ways of the world," Jim said without pity.

"Yeah right." Her jaw tightened a little more.

"I need a list of all tenants living in this building," Dan ordered.

"Why?"

This lady was pushing Dan's patience to the edge.

"We need it, that's why. So stop wasting my time, lady, or I'll throw the cuffs on and have you jailed for not cooperating with an investigation!" he said, raising his voice.

"Give me a few minutes I have to print it from the computer."

"Now was that so hard?" Dan shook his head. "We're going to start on the ground floor. When you have the list, come and find us." The detectives stormed away. "The nerve, worried about a cleaning bill when there's a maniac out there hungry to kill again."

"She should be worried about her life," Jim added.

"People's priorities are to be desired."

The manager found the detectives on the second floor. Taking the list, Dan thanked her and began checking off the names of the tenants they'd already interviewed.

Finally the detectives came to the last door on the right, number 515. Detective Jim Masker rapped his knuckles against the grain and waited. Moments later, a little, old woman peeked out through the crack in the door. The door was still secured by the cheap chain.

"Yes, can I help you?"

"I'm Detective Masker, and this is my partner Detective Kape. May we come in and ask you a couple of questions regarding the murder of Susan Dutch?"

"How do I know you're real police officers?"

Dan smirked, happy she didn't just open her door like a few of the other tenants. The detectives held up their badges. The door closed. She slid the chain, and the door opened.

Dan checked the sheet. "Mrs. Twillie."

"Please call me Ethal. Come in. Come in. You are making me nervous."

The detectives followed her into the kitchen/dining area.

"Okay, Ethal." Dan smirked at Jim. "On Saturday night did you see anyone in this building that you hadn't seen before?"

"I was bringing my groceries in. I usually do my shopping in the evenings because there aren't so many senior citizens clotting up the aisles."

Dan gave a chuckle; this eighty-two-year-old, Mrs. Twillie, didn't consider herself old.

"Did you see anyone at the front door you didn't recognize?" Dan brought the conversation back to point.

"Now that you mention it, a woman. She said she was waiting for someone. I'm not sure if she looked suspicious or not."

"Tell us what happened, Ethal," Jim probed patiently.

"The cab drivers these days don't bother to help you with your parcels." She shook her head. "The world is going to hell in a hand basked." She sighed. "I fumbled for my darn keys at the bottom of my purse. My daughter is always giving me hell, saying I should have them ready before I reach the door."

The partners grinned.

"Ethal, you were fumbling to find your keys and …" Jim asked.

"Yes, yes. After I unlocked the door, the woman waiting outside came to my aide and helped me carry my parcels to the elevator. I asked her if she was coming on, but she said she liked to stay in shape by taking the stairs. No offense—she was a little hefty and needed to take the stairs. I never asked her whom she was visiting. You can't be too nosey these days."

"Can you tell us more about her appearance?" Dan inquired.

"Big lady wasn't very attractive, that's for sure."

"Her face, Ethal, what did she look like? Was her face round, narrow, big nose? Anything odd about her?" Dan sounded desperate for information.

"She's um … let me think now. What did she look like exactly?" She drummed her two fingers along her thin bottom lip. "She was older. Did I say that already?"

"No, but go on," Jim answered.

"Oh, she wore glasses and had bright red hair. I thought it was a wig. But dear me, I didn't have the heart to ask." She smirked shyly.

"This woman was overweight with glasses. How tall was she?" Jim asked.

"Taller than me. I'm shrinking with each birthday. Can I offer you a piece of apple pie?"

"No, thank you." Jim spoke for them both before Dan had the chance to indulge.

"Did you catch that awful man I read about in the newspaper?"

"Not yet. That's why we're here, ma'am." Dan smiled.

"Thank you for your time, Ethal. If you think of anything, give us a call." Jim handed Ethal his card.

"Sorry I don't know more."

"You've been a big help. Thank you." Dan politely shook her fragile hand and walked out into the hallway. "Lock your door and don't open to anyone you don't know," Dan advised.

"My daughter says the same thing."

"You have a wise daughter," Jim said, walking toward the elevator.

The evidence Derk presented earlier may have had more merit than the team anticipated. The important question now was who was the woman that entered Royal Deal apartment wearing glasses and a red wig the night Susan Dutch was viciously murdered?

Chapter Forty-Five

Ellen reached Franki on her cell, a block away from Sparkie's place.

"Franki here."

"Hi, Franki. It's Doc."

"Doc. Sorry, didn't recognize the number."

"Where are you?"

"I'm heading to Sparkie's place, and later I have a dinner date. Why? What's up?"

"Can you come to the station?"

"Need a ride?"

"No. I need you to look at a photograph."

"Of who?"

"One of the victims, Franki."

"Holy shit. Why me?"

"Because you are standing beside our victim, Franki. Don't panic; she could be a fan. We need to know."

"I'll be right over."

"Thank you, sweetheart."

Franki cranked up Keith Urban and made an illegal U-turn back toward the station.

Doc was waiting at the front counter for Franki to arrive. They hugged, and Ellen led the way to Captain Barlow's office. Franki looked in awe at all the chaos going on around her. Printers spitting out pages, phones ringing nonstop, keys clacking, and voices echoing throughout the room. *I could not handle this noise every day all day long*, she thought, smiling at a female officer with her arms loaded with file folders.

"Have a seat." Ellen pointed to the chair in front of the desk.

"This sounds serious, Doc."

"Franki, do you know a Susan Dutch? She was murdered Saturday night. In her bedroom apartment, forensics found a photograph of you and Susan. We want to know if she's a friend or fan."

Franki ran the name through her memory bank. It didn't take long before recognition sprang in her eyes. "Yes. I know Susan." Her lip began to quiver.

Doc opened a folder, handing Franki the picture in the sealed evidence bag. She stared at her best friend, tears dripping down her cheeks.

"Where did you get this?" A darkened fog rolled into the room, adding a slight chill to the room's atmosphere.

"The victim's bedroom."

"Where was she found?"

"In her apartment at the Royal Deal."

Ellen handed Franki a tissue to wipe her eyes. "I'm terribly sorry, honey."

"She's really dead?"

"Yes," Captain Barlow answered.

"How?"

"I can't give out that information."

"Sparkie was one of my best friends. I have a right to know how she died."

Franki stood up, walked over to the open door, and with all her might slammed it shut. "Fuck!" she screamed, falling to the floor where she wept. Doc got down on the tiled floor next to her and held her until the heavy sobs subsided into tiny, painful moans. Franki had lost so much in her young life. She didn't need to feel one more ounce of grief. But life was not fair, and pain was a reality to endure.

When the door slammed, the detectives outside the office jumped, automatically grabbed for their weapons. It sounded like a gun had gone off. Everyone looked around, as if to say *what the fuck was that.*

Captain Barlow quickly opened the door to ensure that everything was fine. "Back to work, people. Thank you!" he yelled at the frozen faces staring at him with doubt in their eyes. No one slammed the captain's door without getting tossed out on their ass. What made this woman so special?

The captain helped Ellen get Franki back into a chair. "She was the toughest chick I know. Christ, she grew up on the streets, and now she's dead." Franki wiped her eyes, trying to prevent the torrent of emotions from erupting again.

Unexpectedly, the detectives barged in without knocking. They stopped as soon as they saw Franki. She struggled to pull herself together.

Jim didn't miss a beat. He walked over to where Franki sat and placed her hand in his and stared into her tear-filled eyes. "I promise we'll get this bastard and put him away so he never sees the light of day again."

"Kill him. That thing doesn't deserve to live." Her pain was raw and visible.

"Does Susan Doe have relatives living here?" Dan said.

"Sparkie has an older sister."

"Do you have an address?"

"Sorry."

"Last name?" Dan questioned.

"Charlotte Postibil."

"Weird name; shouldn't be hard to locate her."

"Detectives, you know what to do."

"We're on it, sir. Miss Martin, I'm very sorry for your loss," Dan said, patting her on the shoulder.

"Thank you, Detective." The two closed the door.

For twenty-five minutes, Franki talked about how Sparkie cleaned up her life. Stopped hooking, started college, worked as a waitress part-time at a burger joint down on Miller Road. Once in a while, she'd get wigged out with normal life and have to create some shit to feel better, but most of the time she was on the mark.

Captain Barlow whispered a prayer. "God, if you're listening, we need help down here."

Ellen didn't tell Franki the gory details of her friend's death, but she did tell her that Sparkie put up one hell of a good fight; their belief was she couldn't win against psychotic strength no matter how street-tough she was.

"Thank you. I should really get going."

"You okay to drive?" Ellen asked, concerned.

"Doc, I'm good. My meltdown is over."

"Be careful out there, Miss Martin."

"Catch this bastard." She gently closed the door behind her and rushed out of the building before anyone saw her break down again.

Chapter Forty-Six

The detectives parked along the curb in front of an old debilitated house. The tar shingles were breaking off, littering the front patches of yellowed grass.

"So this is 506 Timer Road?" Jim said.

"Let's get this over with." Dan groaned.

The detectives were approaching the old metal gate when a woman wearing a waitress uniform came out. The detectives flashed their badges.

"What do you two want?" Charlotte quipped.

"Are you Charlotte Postobil-Dutch?"

"Dutch is my maiden name. What do you want?"

"I'm Detective Kape, and this is my partner Detective Masker. We would like to talk to you."

"If this is about Susan, I don't want to hear it. I'm tired of bailing her out of trouble. I haven't seen my sister for a long time, and I like it that way."

"I'm sorry, ma'am, we have bad news."

"Say what you need to say right there."

"I'm afraid Susan was murdered Saturday night," Dan began.

"Is this some kind of joke?" Charlotte's face crinkled into a mask of anger.

"I'm afraid not, ma'am. May we come inside?"

"Hurry up. I have to go to work."

"We'll make this as quick as possible," Jim said without expression, walking inside the front door.

Charlotte made the detectives stand just inside the doorway. Jim was grateful she did after he glanced around the living room. Hardwood flooring littered with books, clothes, dirt, and dust. Dried food stuck to plates that sat on an old metal TV tray. The stench of stale cigarette smoke burned the inside of Jim's nostrils. It was apparent the place hadn't been cleaned in some time.

"You're positive it's my sister?"

She lit a smoke, throwing the lighter on the dust-covered coffee table in the hallway.

"Franki Martin just identified your sister as Susan Dutch."

She inhaled a big puff of smoke before slowly releasing a blue cloud of toxic chemicals into the air. The poison hung thick in the streaks of sunlight coming in from the broken blind hanging on the door window.

"Good. She saved me a trip to the morgue."

"Yes, ma'am."

"All that's left to do now is bury her. I don't have the money," Charlotte said frowning.

"Try the ministry of health; they will assist you financially. Susan is at the city morgue. You'll be notified when her body is ready for the funeral home."

"You said she was killed. It was probably one of her johns." Charlotte smashed her butt out in the overfilled ashtray, spilling more ashes onto the table. She didn't seem too concerned, which made Jim cringe, being a clean freak himself.

"How'd she die?"

"She was bludgeoned and then stabbed to death. I'm sorry." Detective Kape answered.

The detectives decided it was in Charlotte's best interest that she not know all of the gruesome details of Susan's death. Charlotte didn't need to know that Susan's pink hair had been ripped from her scalp in clumps and that her eyes were no longer in their sockets because they had been burnt out with the end of a curling iron.

"Truth be told, fellas, was it a john or that psycho in the papers?"

"All our evidence points to Roger Taut."

"What did he want with my sister? She didn't have anything of value."

Tears sprang to her eyes as she fought hard to conceal her pain.

"We're very sorry. Is there anyone we can contact for you before we leave?" Dan asked, trying to be helpful.

"I'll be fine."

"If there's anything we can do, please give the station a call."

"She's better off. The streets gobbled her up a long time ago. And she was never the same Susan I knew growing up." Her voice cracked.

Dan thought it was a shame that Charlotte was so in the dark about how well her sister was doing in life since meeting Franki Martin. Jim was never so happy to get out of the place. He wanted to drive home to his condo, have a shower, and change his clothes.

Charlotte stood at the door, glaring out as the detectives drove away. That's when the tears gushed like a waterfall.

Chapter Forty-Seven

The next afternoon, John and Ellen got comfortable in the war room, looking better than they had since this investigation started. It was amazing how a full night's rest could rejuvenate both mind and body. Pop, chips, and chocolate bar wrappers littered the tabletop. There shoeless feet rested on chairs in front of them.

"Ellen, give me everything you know on our suspect."

"When Roger was first arrested, he truly didn't believe he was responsible for murdering three women. He came walking into the interview room, cuffed of course. He looked frightened. It took him awhile to warm up. Now keep in mind he's a charming psychopath. The first two weeks or so, he kept that pity-me persona. Perfect I'm-not-a-guilty-inmate routine. When he realized he might go to prison for the rest of his natural life, he began coughing out information about his life. The abuse he suffered as a child is almost unfathomable to comprehend. I believe the abuse he endured set the stage for what he has become today. Nature versus nurture. John, psychiatry has been probing patients like Roger for centuries, and there is no proof of what actually makes a serial killer. Since Roger was a young boy, he'd been physically attacked, sexually exposed, mentally broken, and emotionally scarred. I mean, his first memory of sexual abuse is being forced to rape his mother, at age five, while his stepfather cheered him on. This was to teach him how to please a whore. He's got scars from the physical beatings given by his stepfather for stepping out of line. There were no boundary lines to gauge from because there were no boundaries. Especially given the circumstances of how he was brought up—having sex with your mother is okay, but taking a cookie from the cookie jar without asking deserved a beating with the belt. The young boy existed in a world of confusion. He didn't have a clue between right and wrong."

"Why does he kill women instead of men like his stepfather?"

"His mother was the one who was supposed to protect him, and she didn't. I believe she had been beaten, demoralized so badly that she'd just given up. The father was the role model in Roger's day-to-day life. His stepfather was the aggressor, and his mother submissive. Over time, his subdued anger grew into a rage boiling beneath the surface like hot lava. And the trigger is a naked woman. John, Roger wants to see women as protective, loving, nurturing. That's why the beginning of his relationship is fine, and no one suspects his dark secret—until the relationship progresses to a sexual level. He's very organized because he's had to be in order to survive. He also has this charming quality to his personality. Inside his mind, the evil one waits to strike. Guys like Taut stamped criminally insane, you won't see them running down the road naked and crazy eyed. He's managed to fit into society well. That was until he murdered three women, seven years ago. Intimacy sparks episodes of delusion, and he revisits the scenes with his mother."

"Are these planned kills?"

"No. It's psychological defense of projection, which is a painful rage that wells up inside of him during any act of sex. Blames the victims for his impulses and guilt for getting aroused. He has an overpowering impulse to destroy what hurts him the most, his mother. Major reason I stamped him insane."

"How does he choose his victims?"

"To him, they aren't victims; they're potential mates for life. Roger appears normal in every way, except what sets him off. A naked body, the guilt of an erection, and the emotional pain he can't escape."

"He's far from normal," John countered.

"Roger suffers aggression, expressed in polar attributes; under the surface lays a powerful destructiveness. It's an aggression that moves like lightning. These acts of brutal aggression are all unconscious. He doesn't have the ability to separate mother from date. In my opinion, Roger is personification of created evil. If we examine how his victims suffered before death, the facts will confirm how disturbed Roger is."

"He's one tall drink of sociopath."

"I agree, and that's why he needs to go back to the asylum."

"And you really believe he's still insane?" John shook his head in disbelief.

"Yes, John, I do."

"I hear what you're saying, but try selling that psychobabble theory to the victims' families. You said he's likeable?"

"Charming, actually. At the time of his trial, Roger's neighbors thought of him as the boy next door. They couldn't believe he was responsible for committing such heinous crimes. I mean, he'd go out of his way to help old ladies with their parcels. He took care of his neighbors' pets while they went away on vacation. Now that does not fit the code of behavior of a psychopath, does it?" She wiped the dirt off her glasses.

"How is he getting around the city undetected? We've checked out rental companies, family, friends, and everyone but you seems to think he's fled."

"Because Roger is still in Victoria. Whoever helped him to freedom is hiding him. Why? That's the answer I wish I had."

"Ellen, I've investigated a few homicides in my career, but this one has me completely baffled."

"Once we find the why, then we'll find the who." Ellen crinkled the empty chip bag, tossing it onto the table. "I don't know about you, but I could use some decent food."

"Later. Break is over," John asserted his authority. "Let's review the autopsy reports again. The photographs have silent answers. What about victimology? Susan Dutch was a party girl, and Diane Saunders was a churchgoer. What did these two women have in common, because if what you say is true, something sure doesn't add up. And let's find these answers today."

"May the voices of the dead speak." Ellen sighed.

"Well, they better yell pretty damn loud. Time is running out," he said, reaching across the table to retrieve a forensic folder.

Chapter Forty-Eight

ranki was on her way back from a long drive in the country. She thought about Sparkie as she drove. The two shared a bond that only street people understood. An unspoken language of willingness to survive the misery day in and day out. She struggled to comprehend how someone as tough as Sparkie could be taken out the way she was. Where was the justice for Sparkie?

Images flashed in her mind to their first encounter. It was the middle of September, and the nights were growing colder by the day. The half-moon was casting creepy shadows that weren't there. Scared and alone, Franki walked the alley, searching for a place to curl up, sheltered from the cold and wind. The stars appeared a zillion miles away. The night emerged darker than usual. She came upon the doorway of Molly's clothing store. Feeling sheltered from the wind, she pulled a wool sweater from her pack-sack for added warmth. She crouched into a ball, listening to the screams of hunger coming from the deep, hollow space of her stomach. It was going on day two since she had had anything to eat. Franki vowed she'd never eat from a garbage bin, no matter how starved she was. Little did she know what it would take for her to survive. She wrapped her arms around her legs, fighting off the cold from creeping into her tired bones. Just as she dozed off, a stranger's yell startled her awake. Franki jumped.

"Who the fuck are you?" the stranger shouted.

"Franki. Why?"

"What are you doing here?"

"None of your business." She tried to sound tough.

"This is my alley. And you're here uninvited. Dig?"

"Dig what?" Franki growled back.

Without warning, the stranger stopped yelling and sat down next to her. She sensed he could smell her intimidation from a mile away. She wanted to tell this loser to get lost, but the words got stuck in her throat.

"How'd a nice girl like you end up here?" He put his arm around her neck, pulling her in closer.

"I ran away."

"Girl, where you running to?"

"I haven't figured that out yet."

"Are you hungry?"

"Starved. Why? Do you have something to eat?"

"Come to my place. I'll find you something to eat."

"I don't think that's a good idea."

"Why not?"

"I don't know you." Franki could feel his grip around her neck getting stronger.

"I know exactly what you need."

"I don't want to go." Franki struggled to loosen his grip.

"No one tells Ace no." The foul smell of his breath made her gag. Then he grabbed her by the hair and jerked her head back. He slapped her hard across the face. The sudden fear replaced the sting.

"I tell you you're coming, bitch, you're coming. Got it!"

"No!" Franki yelled back, trying to fight him off.

In one swift motion, Franki was on the ground with Ace on top of her. He thrashed about, trying to unzip her jeans, but Franki hung on. In the midst of the assault, Franki heard a guardian angel.

"What the hell you think you're doing, Ace?" She stood over him.

"What does it look like, bitch?"

"Get off her," the angel declared.

"Go to hell or you'll be next."

"Is that right?" She laughed.

Then Franki heard it. It sounded like a loud thud, like when a basketball is thrown hard to the ground. Sparkie had booted Ace right in the head. He rolled off, holding his head and swearing. Franki leaped to her feet, getting away from him as fast as she could. He staggered a couple of steps, hands frantically searching his head for blood.

"Fucking bitch. I'll get you for this." Ace groaned.

To keep him from chasing them, Sparkie gave him another good boot. This time it connected to his nuts. He went down like a sack of potatoes. She was making sure he stayed down. "I'll get you." He moaned, rolling back and forth.

"I don't think so ... bitch." Sparkie laughed at Ace.

"If I ... get uh ..."

Franki watched Sparkie's boot connect to his face one last time. This time he fell back and didn't move.

"Holy shit, is he dead?" Franki asked, slowly backing away from the lifeless body on the ground.

"No, but he's missing a few teeth."

"How can I ever thank you?"

"What the hell are you doing out here anyway?"

"I ran away."

"I figured that much. Are you hungry?"

"I have no money."

"That's clear. Come on, I'll show you where you can dine for free," she said with a laugh.

"How?"

"How did I know you're broke? People with money don't hang around back alleys, kid."

Sparkie led the way out of the alley. Two blocks south to Bolder and back into another dark alleyway. Partway down the lane, Sparkie stopped in front of a gigantic garbage bin, lighting her lighter.

"I'm not eating garbage," Franki stated, repulsed.

"Fine. Starve." Sparkie reached in, pulling out a white dinner roll with a couple of bites taken out of it.

"Hey, today's lunch special."

"How long have you been out here?" Franki asked, appalled.

"Long enough to know how to stay alive. Here, have a bite, princess. It won't kill you."

Franki grudgingly accepted the ration of food.

"You get used to it."

"Never."

"You can always go back to where you came from."

"Screw that!" Franki wolfed down the rest of the dinner roll and waited for something else. Sparkie smirked, handing Franki chicken balls, and laughed when she gobbled them down like they were fresh from Grandma's kitchen.

"Stick with me, kid. I'll teach you how to stay alive." Sparkie kept her word.

Back in the city, Frank drove over to where she knew she would feel loved and safe.

Chapter Forty-Nine

arly evening, the captain's phone rang, sounding another familiar warning. He looked directly at Ellen, defeat written on his face. "Captain Barlow," he answered.

"Sir, we have another 187 over here on Blane," Dan said.

"This guy doesn't quit."

"No shit! He's just warming up, sir."

"Address?"

"Fourteen Blane Road."

"I'll be there shortly."

The captain tucked his phone back in its case and rose up out of his chair.

"Where?" Ellen inquired with a red tack in her hand.

"Fourteen Blane."

"Ready?" Ellen finished pinning the tack on the map and was strolling toward the door with fierce determination.

"Where do you think you're going?"

"With you."

"No way! You are going home. Find a friend, go for coffee, do something ... but you are not hanging around here."

"And you listen to me, John Barlow—"

"Sorry, my friend. Time to go home."

"Fine!" Ellen scowled, not accustomed to being told what to do. "If you need me—"

"I have your number, sweetie." John walked to her and held her in his arms.

"Okay, goodnight then." The doctor gathered her things and hesitantly walked out the door.

Captain Barlow rushed out of the conference room and into the bullpen. He spotted Boss, Kife, and Barkley sitting at their desks clacking keys and filing their day's events into computers.

"Hey, fellows, come with me," he ordered. "Barkley, you ride with me. Boss, Kife, meet us at 14 Blane Road."

"What's up, Captain Barlow?" Kife asked, already on his feet.

"I need you guys to keep order. The forensic team is already there. And the meat wagon is waiting to take the body to the morgue. Lookers are already gathering. So, Boss, here's the camera. Start snapping the crowd as soon as you arrive. Do it inconspicuously."

They all dashed out of the building and drove across the city, lights flashing and sirens blaring. Boss and Kife were feeling competent and important to be a part of such a high-profile case.

The captain pulled up to the crime scene, and after taking a deep breath, he and Barkley climbed out of his vehicle.

His loyal detectives walked down the driveway to meet him before he entered the home of Constance Veil.

"What do we have?"

"She's dead; that's for sure," Dan announced.

"Forensics team is inside," Jim said.

Captain Barlow suited up before entering. He looked around at the carnage. This victim had been tortured before being killed.

"Sir, you have got to catch this guy." Derk pleaded.

"Her name is Constance Veil," Ivy replied from behind. "Sir, there is a name scripted on the wall in blood. We're assuming it's the victim's." Ivy led the captain to the wall. John knew the name. He grabbed his cell phone and began dialing.

"Hello."

"Ellen, it's John."

"Oh, so you do miss me?" She laughed.

"Don't you have a friend named Sandy?"

"Yes, why?"

"Written on the wall in our victim's blood is the name Sandy. Now I'm not trying to scare you—"

"What else does it say, John?"

"Is next."

"I have to make a call," she stated. A cold chill clawed its way up her spine.

"Are you trusting what I'm trusting?"

"The motives have always been about revenge."

"Ellen, I'll order round-the-clock surveillance at Sandy's place. I'll need her full name and address. I'll make sure these psychos don't get within a hundred yards of your friend."

"Don't make promises you can't keep, John. Remember, Taut is evil, and whoever is working alongside must be the epitome of depraved."

"Do what you have to do. I'll call you later with an update. Make sure Sandy isn't alone."

"Thanks for calling me." Ellen hung up so she could warn Sandy.

Keith Gile was busy taking snapshots of the body with his high-powered lens while Ivy and Adam were scanning for trace, blood splatter patterns, semen, and fibers. All had to be bagged and sealed for evidence. Each member worked diligently, trying to find the smoking gun that could end this madness. Before leaving, the captain urged the forensic team to produce whatever evidence they could as soon as possible. Not that they didn't already know that.

Once outside, he motioned the detectives to head back to the station. And then he gave orders to Boss, Kife, and Barkley. Boss and Barkley were ordered to canvass the area. Kife was to stand guard at the house until the body was taken to the morgue.

The captain needed an update regarding where they were with the interviews. He felt those interviews held the golden ticket to solving the case.

Chapter Fifty

Early the next morning, Mr. Withers was brought in for questioning. Officers Trex and Fritz got down to business. These guys were hungry for answers.

"Where in the hell have you been?" Officer Trex demanded.

"Holidays man, holidays." Mr. Withers looked up at the big bald cop.

"You work up on the fourth floor of River Edge?" Trex began.

"Yeah, between three and four."

"You were working the night Roger Taut disappeared. Did you see anyone suspicious?"

"I saw a nurse escorting him to the elevator."

"Why didn't you come forward with this information?"

"I didn't think it was that important." He shrugged his shoulders.

"There is a guy out there killing women, and you didn't think it was that important. And why is that?" Trex yelled.

"Cause she's a nurse, man. A lot of activity goes on in a place like River Edge. Chaos, screaming fits. You get deaf to it after a while."

"Is it protocol for a nurse to be leading a patient to the elevator in the evening?"

"I guess."

"You guess?"

"No, not at that time of night."

"What time did you see this nurse with Roger Taut?" Fritz jumped in.

By this time, Captain Barlow and Ellen were standing behind a two-way mirror, listening in.

"Let's go back to the nurse in question," Trex said. "Give us something here. We got all night."

"It was around ten thirty. I was coming back from the bathroom. That's when I saw her leading Taut."

"What did she look like?"

"Big and ugly. Oh and she wore wire-frame glasses. I didn't know she was helping the nut escape—honest."

The officers were interrupted by a knock at the door. "Don't go anywhere." Fritz went to the door, stepping into the corridor.

"Problem?"

"Ask him again if she was the only one leading Taut."

"Okay, Doctor Smith," Fritz replied with a warm smile.

He turned back, closing the door.

"Mr. Withers, was there anyone else with Roger Taut and this so-called ugly nurse?"

"No. And there was no one around either. No guard, no one. It was creepy, man."

"Describe this woman in length."

"She was old and ugly. What can I say?"

"How old?" Fritz broke in.

"About fifty."

"Her face, what did her face look like? Moles? What?"

"Wrinkled. She was ugly in more ways than one."

"Elaborate."

"She looked like she belonged in the psycho ward."

"What else?"

"She's big. Manly big."

"Fat, tall, muscular? What?"

"Big. She looked like she could handle Mr. Taut." He shook his head.

"Hair color?"

"Blonde."

"You sure?"

"Positive. Most blondes are attractive. She was the ugliest blonde I've ever laid eyes on." He made a face.

"Okay, hang tight, Mr. Whithers," Fritz ordered.

The two officers strolled out into the corridor, meeting Captain Barlow and Ellen.

"I'll call our forensic sketch artist, Kadus Payley," Captain Barlow said.

"I think he can give a pretty good description."

"I'm surprised he can find his way home," Trex said, not assured.

A few minutes later, Ellen glanced down the corridor, eyeing John, Jim, and Dan.

"Did you reach her?" Ellen asked.

"She'll be here in twenty minutes."

"Which artist?" Jim asked cautiously.

"Kadus Payley."

"Shit."

"Don't tell me you dated her too?" Ellen asked.

"Yeah you could say that."

"You'll never learn."

He rolled his eyes.

Dan slowly stepped past carrying a cup of coffee for Mr. Withers.

"Is it Kadus?" he asked with a smirk.

"Sure is."

"You're in the doghouse, eh, partner?" He laughed.

"Hey, you two on holidays? If not, get your asses back and interview the next staff member," Captain Barlow demanded.

"I'm going." Jim turned in time to see Dan howling at his misfortune. He quickly flipped him the bird. He knew why Dan was poking fun. The last time he encountered Kadus, she smacked him across the face in front of Dan for cheating on her. Jim dreaded seeing her again.

Jim entered the second interrogation room. "Have a seat please."

Doris sat like she was asked.

"Do you know why you're here, Doris Webble?" Jim asked, glancing at the sheet, making sure he got the name correct.

"It's about the serial killer."

"Tell me anything you know about the night Roger Taut escaped River Edge. The smallest details count."

Doris folded her hands, placing them on top of the table, unperturbed. "What do you want to know?"

"Anything at this point." The detective sat across the table, enjoying her Western drawl.

"I was with Roger Taut the night he was taken out of River Edge."

"What? You alone?" Jim shouted.

"No, not alone. I was coming back from a pee break when the elevator door opened on the second floor. A nurse with blonde hair and wearing wire-frame glasses was exiting the elevator with a patient. I didn't know who he was until the next day."

"What did you do?"

"I got in the elevator of course. Detective, no one person is permitted to be with patients alone. Especially a woman with a man. That's how people get hurt, you know. It's in case a patient becomes uncontrollable."

"Where did you take Roger?"

"Morial Hospital. Migraines."

"Can you give us a complete description of what this person looks like?"

"Oh yes, Detective. That fake pale hair didn't fool me one little bit. It was the nurse that was fired from the second floor some years back. Sorry, I can't remember her name."

Jim leaped out of the chair with a rush of excitement.

"Don't you leave. I'll be right back."

"Something wrong?"

"No everything is right." Jim kissed Doris on the cheek and rushed out the door. Moments later, he returned with the team in tow. Doris told her story again.

Chapter Fifty-One

In spite of the possible threat on her life, Sandy was in good spirits. The next day, she went to work as usual. There was no way she was allowing Taut to interrupt her life. Mark was by her side, making sure she was safe. The two had been inseparable since their first date. This was a love she couldn't get enough of. Mark made her feel beautiful and loved.

Tonight they were having a barbecue, but first Mark had to swing by his place to retrieve more clothing. He had no idea how long he'd be staying at Sandy's place. So after work, Sandy convinced him that she'd be fine while he scooted to his place to get what he needed. She reminded him that not only did she have a police escort, but that this officer would be parked out front for her protection. Grudgingly, he went back to his place without her.

Back at home, Sandy decided to take a shower before Mark arrived. She had sweet sexual plans for her new lover this evening. Dressed in a lovely cotton, yellow sundress, she was standing at the kitchen counter preparing her specialty salad when the phone rang. She danced her way to turn down the stereo prior to answering.

"Hello." No answer on the other line.

"Hello," she repeated. Dead air gripped the line.

"Mark, quit fooling around."

"You're next, bitch."

Sandy screamed, dropping the phone. Her blood ran cold inside her veins. Suddenly she felt like throwing up. She rushed to the front window, making sure the cop was still there. She was relieved to see Officer Mavis still sitting in his car. Her mouth was as dry as cotton. She hurried to the kitchen and gulped down half a glass of water. The cold water couldn't quench the thirst of the demonic voice that echoed in her ears, "You're next, bitch." Sandy had to report this; now she was scared. Entering the living room, she retrieved the phone off the floor and began dialing.

An officer knocked on the interrogation door. Jim answered with reservation, expecting Kadus Payley.

"Sorry to interrupt, Doctor Smith. You have an urgent phone call."

"Thank you." She hurried to the phone. "Hello."

"Ellen, it's Sandy. I just got a call … It was … I think … I'm not sure—it could be a prank," she stammered.

"Sandy, what did the person say?"

"*You're next, bitch.* What do I do?" She was almost brought to tears.

"Did you notify the police officer out front?"

"No. I called you."

"Okay, this is what I want you to do. Go out and tell Officer Mavis so he can report it and get a tap put on the phone. Where's Mark?"

"He went to get some things from his place."

"Tell the officer, Sandy, and then wait for Mark. Whatever you do, do not go anywhere by yourself. You hear me?"

"No worry there. Ellen, is it … you know?"

"Yes there's a good possibility."

"Why me?" Sandy asked.

"That we don't know yet." She hated not being able to answer. "Sandy, you'll be okay. I promise."

"I hope so."

Suddenly the doorbell rang. Sandy jumped almost out of her skin.

"Ellen, I have to go. Mark is here."

"I'll call you later."

"Okay, bye." Ellen hung up, fearing for her friend's life.

At first glance, Mark knew something terrible had happened. Sandy's complexion was as white as Casper the ghost. She sat him down and explained everything, and then the two went out to talk with Officer Mavis. Sandy invited the officer inside for a bite to eat, and he was more than happy to oblige. During dinner, Mark decided it wasn't safe for them to be staying at her place. He said they should go back to his condo where there was more security to the building. Sandy agreed without argument. It was her life that was at stake here.

While she and Mark cleaned up, Officer Mavis made a call to headquarters. A few minutes later, he returned to the kitchen, saying that the new plan was in flight. Whenever they were ready to leave, they were to let him know. Before exiting the house, he thanked them both for their wonderful hospitality.

In the meantime, back at the station, Officer Boss requested to see Captain Barlow immediately. He'd received a manila envelope containing photographs of Constance Veil being tortured and murdered. Step by step. Ellen was just coming back from her telephone call with Sandy.

"Sandy just received a call from a man I believe was Roger Taut."

"I know. I got word from Mavis she's moving to a new location."

"Where?"

"Her boyfriend's condo."

"What about protection?" Ellen asked.

"I've posted an officer right outside his door. No one is getting within five feet of that door unless he wants to get shot."

For the first time since she joined this team, relief washed over her. "What do you have there?" she asked, staring at the manila envelope.

"Step-by-step photographs of Constance Veil's murder."

"That name rings a bell."

"Ellen, these aren't from the lab."

"What?" she asked, apprehensive.

"Whoever took these participated in the crime."

"Hand them over." Ellen held out her hand. She gasped, scanning each snapshot carefully. Her mind exploded with rage. This was something you watched on a fictional horror flick if you had the stomach for it. "Once this animal is caught, I'll be dammed if he's going back to River Edge. He belongs in a cage, and so does his partner in crime," she said breathlessly.

"Who is Constance Veil?" Dan inquired.

"She was a patient of mine years back."

"See, I told you guys there's a connection between the nut house and nut case," Dan sang confidently. "No one can convince me otherwise now."

"We'll know after the composite sketch is finished," Ellen announced, seeing Kadus coming down the corridor.

Kadus stopped, staring into each of their tormented eyes. "In here?" She pointed to the closed door in front of her.

"Thanks for coming on such short notice. Go on in," Captain Barlow said with sigh.

"I'll find you when I'm finished." She opened the door, eyeballing Jim.

He said, "Hello," and then quickly bolted to freedom. He wasn't about to risk another slap in the face.

Back in the war room, all four scrutinized the photos, one by one. The son of a bitch made sure each photograph depicted the victim's pain as he plunged the knife into her naked body.

"This is too sick for words," Dan stated, puffing his cheeks up like balloons.

"Ellen, how many victims did you know?"

"Three."

"Susan Dutch was a friend of Franki, who is a friend of yours, correct?"

"Correct."

"And now another friend of yours is threatened. This investigation leads somehow to you. We need to know why."

"Let's not get ahead of ourselves here. There are few victims I didn't know."

"But you said in the beginning he could be just warming up." Dan pressed his lips into a skeletal line.

The sergeant knocked before entering. "Sir, reporters are camped out front demanding answers."

"Tell them I'm waiting on a sketch of the mystery nurse last seen taking our suspect out of the institution."

"Yes, sir." The sergeant closed the door behind him.

"That bitch is totally responsible for this mayhem." Dan pointed to the array of dead women on the wall. "She's going to a nice steel cage where she can live out her day with the rest of misfits."

"If anyone needs a ten-minute break, now is the time."

Dan went for a smoke, Jim for a coffee, and Ellen to the ladies' room. The captain slouched in a chair, praying they'd catch these animals before they could strike again.

Chapter Fifty-Two

All four walked briskly down the corridor toward the exit door, to the awaiting media out front.

"Captain Barlow, do you have any new information regarding the whereabouts of Roger Taut?" The first question was fired.

"Not at this time."

"We've heard you have a drawing of the person responsible for Roger Taut's escape? Is that true?" The second question was fired.

"Yes. Here is a drawing of Gertrude Caller." He held up the sketch so the reporters could take snapshots. "This is the woman we suspect is accountable for taking our suspect out of the institution."

"Are you certain she's the person responsible?"

"Yes. A staff member from River Edge gave a good description to Kadus Payley earlier on."

"Doctor Smith, do you know this Gertrude Caller?"

"Yes. She was fired six years ago for choking a patient while in our care."

"What can you tell women of Victoria?"

"Lock your doors and stay as safe as possible."

"What do you believe her motive is?"

"I'm not sure at this time."

"Are these slayings revenge related?"

"I can't answer at this time until we know more."

"What are the detectives doing to catch these two supposed monsters?"

"They are following up on every lead. That's all I can say," Captain Barlow said.

"Do you think these two fugitives can be apprehended?" A blonde reporter in the front row asked.

"Yes."

"How many more women will have to die before that happens, Captain Barlow?" She plunged right in.

John ignored the question. He held up the drawing of Gertrude Caller once again. "If anyone has seen this woman, please contact the police immediately. She is considered very dangerous. So don't try and take the law into your own hands. We don't want dead heroes. Call the police."

"Captain Barlow—"

"No further questions at this time. Thank you for coming down."

All four turned and walked back in the building.

Chapter Fifty-Three

That evening, Franki and Steve returned to her loft after their stroll through the inner harbor. Getting out of the Jeep, the two happily approached the front door.

"Expecting mail?" he asked suspiciously.

"Nope." Franki yanked the yellow envelope off her door.

"May I?"

"Fan mail," she said playfully.

"You sure it's not a love letter from a boyfriend?" he teased, opening the envelope. Suddenly his facial expression changed to absolute horror.

"Holy Mother Mary of Christ!" he uttered, clenching his stomach.

"What? What's wrong, Steve?"

He was speechless as bile rose in his throat.

"What's in the damn envelope?" Franki demanded, frightened.

"Please don't look inside," he warned, trying to hide it behind his back.

"Steve, you're scaring me."

"They're photographs."

"Of who?" Franki tore the envelope from his hand. She hadn't noticed her hands trembling until she peeked inside. First: a photograph of Salley Whitewall strapped to a chair. Second: blindfolded and gagged. Third: her clothes being cut off with a knife. Fourth: a masked man holding the blade to Salley's throat. The fear in Salley's eyes couldn't portray the terror she was feeling. Fifth: the blade cutting deep across her throat as the blood sprayed from her throat. Sixth: her head had fallen foreword. Seventh: the killer's hand yanking his victim's head back by her hair, like a trophy. Franki unintentionally just witnessed the brutal murder of her agent and good friend, Salley Whitewall. She let out a primal scream that she herself didn't recognize.

Steve grabbed her before she hit the ground. When she finally became stable enough, Steve helped her inside. He planted her down on the kitchen stool and grabbed two beers from the fridge. Franki was traumatized, tears streaming down her face at the horrific recollections. Franki took a swig, feeling her stomach swirl. She flew to the bathroom. A few minutes later, Steve found her kneeling in front of the toilet bowl puking up the horror. He knelt down next to her, softly sponging her face with a cold washcloth. Unexpectedly, she fell against his chest, weeping like a child. Two people she loved and admired were now dead.

"I'm sorry." She looked at Steve, so vulnerable.

"Come on, honey, we have to call the police."

"I know. I know." She sniffed back a few more tears. "I need a stiff drink."

Steve poured her a shot of bourbon and then called the police.

"Sergeant McCalley speaking."

"My name is Steve Michaels. I want to report a murder."

"You want to do what, sir?"

"Photographs of a woman being murdered were delivered to my girlfriend's place a few minutes ago."

"Where did you find these pictures, sir?"

"They were in an envelope taped to the front door. The murdered woman is Salley Whitewall."

"Mr. Michaels, I need the address."

"What is Salley's address?" he asked Franki.

"No, your address, sir!" the Sergeant shouted.

"Oh sorry, 10 Princess Street. Please hurry.

"Stay put. We're on our way."

"Thank you." Steve hung up and waited.

Chapter Fifty-Four

Officer Boss and Kife were already in the assigned squad car when Sergeant McCalley came running out to the parking lot. The two sped out of the parking garage on their way to Franki's place. On the drive over, McCalley grabbed his cell phone, thumbing numbers as he drove. He hated to do it, but Captain Barlow needed to be alerted of another possible slaying. Isabella, the captain's wife, answered the call.

"Hello."

"Isabella, it's David McCalley. Is John home?"

"He's asleep, and I'm not waking him."

Isabella didn't have a chance to say anymore. She turned, hearing her husband's voice behind her.

"Who is it, baby?"

"It's David. What are you doing out of bed?"

"Can I have the phone?"

"You should be sleeping," she scolded.

"Isabella, please," he begged, holding out his hand.

"Here." She threw the cordless at him and stormed away, mumbling something under her breath.

"David." John cleared his throat.

"Sorry, sir. She's right; you should be sleeping."

"She's just overprotective."

"Someone needs to monitor you."

"It's nice to be loved. What's up, David?"

"I'm on my way to 10 Princess Street. A Steve Michaels just called in a murder. He said his girlfriend received photographs of a woman being murdered. I thought you should know, sir. Heavy-duty shit, if you ask me."

"Come again?" His voice escalated with frustration. "Who's the girlfriend?"

"Don't know."

"Give me the address."

"I got this; go back to bed."

"Address!" he demanded.

"Ten Princess Street," the sergeant repeated. "See you shortly."

"Isabella is going to hang me," David complained.

"You won't be alone, buddy."

Isabella didn't have to say a word; the worried glare in her coffee eyes was enough. Her husband hunted dangerous, deranged psychopaths for a living. And she didn't like it one little bit.

"Sorry, baby, it's my job."

"Isn't there anyone else? You haven't slept properly since this nut case escaped."

"Baby, please, help me find my damn pants."

Isabella marched over to the overstuffed cherry antique chair and plucked them up, reluctantly handing them to John.

"When this is all over, I promise more family time."

"This isn't about me, John. I'm worried about you. You couldn't even find your pants you're so tired."

"It's because I just woke up. I'm fine. Is the coffee made?"

"Yes. I shouldn't be helping you." She stomped out of the bedroom.

"Isabella!" he yelled. She stopped at the door and turned around.

"What, John?"

"I love you."

"I love you too. Lord knows why, but I do." She threw her hands up, smiling her way to the kitchen.

John quickly threw cold water on his face, brushed his teeth, and dressed for another long night of blood, guts, and gore. By the time he made it down the stairs, Isabella was standing in the doorway, holding hot coffee in one hand and a granola bar in the other. He kissed her good-bye.

John managed to drive, drink his hot coffee, eat half his granola bar, and talk on his cell phone all at the same time.

"Ellen, hi."

"John, how are you?"

"Bitter, tired, and could be divorced by the time we catch this bastard, but I don't need a therapy session right now. I'm on my way to 10 Princess Street."

"Repeat that again?"

"Bitter, tired—"

"The address?" Ellen interrupted.

"Ten Princess Street," he repeated.

"That's Franki Martin's address. What's going on, John? Is Franki okay?" Ellen could feel her heart banging hard inside her chest.

"She's fine, I think. An envelope was sent to her with photos of another murder. I'm on my way over to check out the story."

"John, I'll meet you there." Ellen hung up, prepared to give up another night's sleep.

Steve invited Sergeant McCalley and two officers inside. The three men sat in the spacious living room to discuss what they found taped to the door. A few minutes later, all five turned, hearing the knock. Steve invited Captain Barlow in.

"Captain Barlow," he introduced himself.

The two men shook hands. "Steve." Steve showed the captain to the living room.

"Hi, Franki. We meet again."

"Hello."

"Do you know the woman in the photographs?"

"Yes. Salley Whitewall is my literary agent."

"I'm sorry. Ellen is on her way."

"You and the officers take a drive over to Miss. Whitewall's address and have a look around."

"We're on it, sir."

The three men walked out.

"Franki, you mind if I ask you a few questions?"

"Go ahead."

"Where did you find the envelope?"

"Taped to my door."

"When?"

"An hour ago."

"Have you received any strange calls, messages? Anyone following you?"

"No weird phone calls. And I haven't noticed anyone."

"Phone number listed or unlisted?"

"Unlisted. Why, Captain Barlow?"

"If your number is unlisted, I'm guessing you were followed home."

"Great—this freak knows where I live."

"I'm guessing he does."

"How is this guy getting around undetected?" Steve asked, concerned.

"I don't have the answer."

"What is he, a fucking ghost?"

"No, a genius."

"Is Franki in danger?"

"Yes."

Franki's eyes grew large at the answer she wasn't expecting.

"Sir, this serial killer is murdering people I love. And the threat against Sandy's life? What's going on?"

"Franki, did you know Josey Moran, Julie Saunders, or Constance Veil?"

"They could have been fans."

The captain wrote in his black book to check if any of the victims were big fans of Franki's work.

"I believe there's a link between the killings, me, Ellen, and River Edge. In spite of what the evidence says," Franki voiced strongly.

"I'm not ruling anything out right now."

Ellen rushed into the loft. "Franki!" she yelled from the stairs.

"Right here." Ellen rushed over, giving her a huge hug. Ellen saw the fear bleeding out through that tough mask.

"I'm fine really."

"Don't be tough with me, girl. It's written all over your face. You're afraid and you should be."

"Doc, this is Steve Michaels."

"Please to meet you, Mrs. Smith."

"Call me Ellen. The woman in the pictures?"

"It's Salley. He killed her and took snapshots as he did it."

Ellen tried to hide her shock.

"Somehow these crimes are linked to me. Why else would he tape photos to my door?"

"Don't go blaming yourself, sweetheart."

"Sparkie, Salley, and now Sandy. You can't convince me that there isn't some kind of correlation between me and him."

"Franki, you didn't know the other victims."

"True."

"Did you watch the news?"

"No why?"

"The woman believed to be responsible for Roger's escape is Gertrude Caller. Remember her?"

Franki's hand flew to her mouth, ice running through her veins.

"She did it? She's the one that helped that psycho get out. What the fuck!"

"Yes."

"There's the motive, Doc, Captain Barlow."

"We're looking into it."

"I swear they slaughter one more person I love, I will personally find a means to hunt them down and kill him and her myself."

"Franki, remember she's one sick woman."

"Yeah and I'm one pissed-off friend."

"Look, the police have enough to take care of without you messing in this investigation. Franki, you have no idea what kind of monsters we're dealing with."

"I don't care, Doc." Franki took a sip of her bourbon.

"What's that you're drinking?" Ellen pointed to the almost empty glass.

"Bourbon. Want some?"

"No. Okay, maybe one sip," Doc said.

"Christ, by the time this investigation is over, we'll all be attending AA," Franki retorted.

"Why don't you come and stay with me for a while?" Ellen said. Franki looked at Steve. "He's welcome too," Ellen added.

Steve's perfect smile lit up his entire face. "Thank you."

"Steve, why don't you help Franki pack a bag."

"Not a problem." Steve helped Franki out of the chair.

Ellen walked out to the kitchen for a drink of water. When she returned to the living room, she held out her hand. "Can I see the photos?"

John handed her the manila package. Ellen's eyes cautiously roamed over each photograph.

"She wasn't butchered like the other women. Something about this murder seems wrong, John. Whoever murdered Salley was in a hurry or took pity. Roger is not one to take pity on his victims."

"Jesus, what are you saying? We have a copycat?"

"No. Maybe the phone rang, and it spooked them."

"How do you know this?"

"He kills with intense rage, remember. I know the pictures are of him with the victim, but trust me, this isn't his kill; she was dead before these shots were taken. Roger forces his victims to suffer."

"Oh, that's comforting." John rolled his eyes.

John's phone buzzed on his belt. "Excuse me."

Ellen examined the photographs one more time before placing them back inside the envelope.

"That was David. We need forensic and the freaking coroner over at Salley Whitfield's house. These pictures are real." John dialed it in and then wrote the address, 1614 Taffey Avenue.

"If you don't want me to come, I'll head back home."

"Best thing you've said since this evening. One less thing I have to worry about," he teased Ellen. "You want an escort home?"

"Are you kidding?" She gave John an odd stare.

"Why not?"

"Because I'm sixty-five years old and not Taut's type."

"Don't forget stubborn old women."

"Be careful who you're calling old." She winked. "I'm out of here."

"You do that."

The captain shook his head at the relentless strength and courage of this woman. In mind and body, she was no way near her age. The way she was going, she'd live forever.

Chapter Fifty-Five

Meanwhile back at Ellen's place, Franki used her spare key to unlock the door and stepped inside. Franki and Steve got set up in one of the spare rooms while they waited for Ellen to arrive. An hour later when she hadn't come home, they assumed she stopped off at police headquarters. To know Ellen was to understand how stubborn she could be. When she got something in her head, the last thing that stopped her was time.

Around midnight and still no Ellen, Franki decided to call before trotting off to bed. Her phone went right to voicemail, meaning Ellen had her cell off.

The next morning, Franki woke up before Steve. She quietly got out of bed and tiptoed across the hall to Ellen's bedroom. Her bed hadn't been slept in. Franki instantly felt a strange fear creep into the very fiber of her core. Something was wrong.

Ellen was sprawled out on a musty, tattered mattress, trying to recover from her injuries. She'd been beaten up and blindfolded with her hands tied behind her back. She could faintly hear voices outside her door. Her nerves were electrifying with anticipation of what was to come. She didn't have to wait long to find out. Abruptly, two hands clamped onto her shoulders, and she was manhandled into an upright position. This time she didn't resist.

"I'm going to remove the duct tape. If you scream, I'll slit your throat." Roger swiftly ripped the tape off in one motion. Her bottom lip burst open as the blood trickled down her chin. *So much for waxing my mustache*, she thought. The tape did the manicuring for her. She started wiggling her lips, forcing the circulation to move around.

"Aren't you going to slit my throat anyway?" She coughed the words from way down her dry air tube.

That one act of defiance cost her a punch in the face, knocking her sideways. She was sure Roger fractured her cheekbone from the searing pain that shot up into her eyeball.

"Shut your mouth." He jerked Ellen back up by her shirt and backhanded.

"Planning to beat me to death?" She spitefully spat a gob of blood onto the floor.

Roger threw her across the room. She landed hard against the dresser and dropped to the floor, smacking her head against the dirt-covered floor. She gagged on the bitterness of her own blood.

"That's it," she gasped, slowly getting up. "Beat up an old lady." Ellen fell against the wall, trying to breathe, but at least she was standing.

"Shut the fuck up before I silence you permanently."

"You're the man, Roger. Must make you feel good"—she took a small breath—"to pound on an old woman that can't defend herself. You low-life piece of shit." Ellen gasped for air.

Once again, she found herself sailing to the other side of the room. This time her chest slammed against the wooden rocking chair. She collapsed on the floor. It was excruciating to take the tiniest breaths. She was sure her ribs were broken.

"Have you had enough, you old fool?" Roger screamed in her face.

Ellen held her tongue.

Roger picked her up off the dirty wooden floor and tossed her back onto bed.

"Welcome to the party, Doctor Smith." He walked out, slamming the door. Seconds later, she heard the click; she was trapped.

Ellen, exhausted, bleeding, and feeling pain she never felt before, started silently sobbing. Deep inside the crevices of her mind, a voice told her to fight if she was going to make it out of this alive.

Chapter Fifty-Six

Around three o'clock the night before, Captain Barlow sent his detectives home to get some sleep, unaware that his good friend and colleague was missing. They were all dog-tired from the late-night, early-morning shift.

Jim walked into his apartment and straight to his bedroom. He never bothered changing out of his clothes. The second his head hit the pillow, he was out like a light.

Dan, on the other hand, wasn't as fortunate. He went home and collapsed in his old recliner. Grabbing the remote off the coffee table, he began surfing channels. He was trying desperately to escape the gory images of the murdered women in his mind's eye. His body and mind were beyond exhaustion, yet he couldn't sleep. Bored at gazing into the screen without sound, he finally dozed off, only to awaken a few minutes later with a stiff neck. He pulled himself out of the chair and stumbled off to bed to get what was left of a night's sleep.

The next morning, Dan walked in the war room, eyeing his partner tacking pictures of the latest victim to the wall. Shortly after that, the captain entered.

"You guys seen Ellen?" The captain wore his usual serious, no-bullshit face.

"No," Jim replied.

"Nope. I thought you had given her the day off," Dan said, chewing on his stir stick.

"I was hoping one of us was home in bed doing what normal people do—sleep," Jim concurred.

"Give me your phone." A raw sickness began reaching its way into the core of his guts. Something was wrong. Ellen was too punctual to be late. The captain moved around the room in circles. "Damn it! I knew I shouldn't have listened to that old fool and made her take an officer with her last night." He began quickly punching numbers.

"Hello." Franki answered on the second ring.

"Franki, it's Captain Barlow. Is Ellen at home?"

"Captain, I was just about to call you."

"Shit! Did she come home last night?"

"Her bed has not been slept in."

"Jesus."

Dan and Jim looked at each other with depending doom.

"Okay, Franki, call me back if you hear anything." The captain hung up.

John was mad at Ellen for not taking an escort, but madder at himself for not insisting she do so. He knew how dangerously close she was to this case. He began punching her number into his cell phone. No answer. He left a message telling her to get in touch immediately.

The detectives were staring at him with concern.

"No one has seen her at River Edge," Jim said, throwing his phone on the table.

"I should have never let her go off alone. Jesus, she's so damn stubborn."

"She's a tough, old bird. That girl gets something in her mind, you have to perform a lobotomy to remove it," Dan added, bending down to retie his shoe.

"Four feet nothing and thinks she's six feet tall and bulletproof," Jim said.

"That describes the old fool perfectly," Captain Barlow said sharply. "We know she left Franki's place heading for home. I know the route she takes, so I'm going to send out a search for her car. I'll be right back." The captain was on a mission.

Even though the detectives wanted to pursue Ellen's disappearance, they still had to focus on the task at hand, which was the murder of Salley Whitfield. If something came up, the captain would let them know what to do.

"It's strange why these snapshots were taped to Franki's door, don't you think?" Jim asked.

"Nothing surprises me at this point. These murders are linked to that goddamn nut house."

"Yeah, well, what about Josie and Constance? Those girls had nothing to do with the pill farm. I mean, how can you prove your theory?"

"I can't. That's what's pissing me off. We have deliberate kills by two people affiliated with the Edge, and the rest …" Dan sighed. "Who the hell knows. I'm going for a refill." He held up his cup. "Want one?"

"Sure, why not. I have a feeling we're in for a very long day."

"The captain won't rest until he finds Ellen."

Dan went to get coffee and then returned. A short time later, Captain Barlow came back.

"Sir, you know if we don't find her within the next twelve hours, he'll kill her," Dan proclaimed sadly.

"You think I don't know that, Detective?" Captain Barlow shouted across the room.

"What do you want us to do, sir?"

"Keep digging. The damn answers are in the files. Find them."

"Sir, wouldn't it be better if we were out there looking?" Jim said, tossing a folder on the table.

"I agree, Captain. Where is the search being done?"

"Ten Princess Street spread out in a ten-mile radius."

"Better pray they come up with something," Dan said, trying not to sound pessimistic.

"They better." They all went back to the paperwork.

It was coming on lunch when a call came in for Captain Barlow. It was Franki checking on news of Ellen.

"Anything, sir?"

"I'm afraid not. I have a search team out looking for her and her car. I'm now scheduling a press conference in a half hour."

"I'd like to be there, sir."

"No problem." He hung up.

"You believe Taut has Ellen, don't you?" Jim asked.

"I believe so."

"What I'd like to know is how?" Jim asked.

"That prick is as slick and slime—that's how," the captain said.

"She's alive, and we're going to find her," Dan stated, keeping the faith.

The only sound in the war room was the rustling of papers.

Franki walked into Steve's open arms. "We'll find her."

"I hope so," she said, fighting back the tears.

Captain Barlow had made the arrangements to meet the press out in front of the station within the hour. Franki was right; he needed to make this public if they were going to get Ellen back. Alive.

The reporters went crazy with questions. When they weren't getting the answers they wanted from Barlow, they quickly turned to Franki Martin, who had a plan of her own. Without any notice, she challenged Taut to come for her. The captain quickly jumped in before she could do any more harm. There was already enough chaos to this investigation without Miss Martin's suicide operation.

Chapter Fifty-Seven

By the time Gladis and Gus unpacked from their trip, it was six o'clock. The weather was sweltering. Gus and Gladis wanted to retire inside their air-conditioned house. The two sat in their living room to watch a little television. As Bob Barker from *The Price Is Right* entered the stage, an important news story flashed across the screen. They'd heard what was happening from the newspapers but didn't understand the full implication of the horror until now. They had a suspicion this broadcast was going to be about the escapee. Gladis clasped her hands tightly together and said a silent prayer of mercy. Not so long ago, Gus and Gladis remembered how Victoria was beautiful, peaceful, and safe. Now their city was blanketed in dark shadows of evil waiting to strike the innocent.

Gus had become very protective of Gladis these days, not letting her out of his sight. Even before the killings started, he'd accompany her to the grocery store. Sometimes she wished he'd stay in the car because of his complaining. Prices were too high. She took too long, or she bought too much. When she got really fed up, she'd just shut her hearing aids off so she wouldn't have to listen to him bitch and chew.

Five minutes into the broadcast, Doctor Smith's photograph flashed on the screen. The anchorwoman reported Doctor Ellen Smith missing.

Next came a sketch of the woman responsible for setting the serial killer free. Gladis nearly fell out of her chair. "Gus, Gus, look! Look!" she hollered, pointing frantically at the television.

"Be quiet so we can hear what the cops are saying."

Gus strained to hear Captain Barlow pleading to the public for information regarding both of these women.

His old arthritis didn't seem to be bothering Gus by the way he leaped out of his recliner like a sixteen-year-old and dialed 911.

"Detective Masker speaking."

"Let me speak with your captain. It's important."

"How can I help you?"

"I just told you!" Gus yelled in Jim's ear.

"What is this about, sir?" he asked, remaining calm, drumming his fingers on his desk.

"It's about the woman you flashed on television. Now get me the captain."

The captain was just passing by his desk when Jim waved him over.

"What's up?"

"This guy wants to speak to you directly."

Captain Barlow rolled his eyes, hoping it wasn't another crackpot with a false lead.

"Captain Barlow speaking."

"It's about that woman."

"You are going to have to be more specific than that, sir?"

"The nurse."

"Who is this?"

"It's Gus Wagnall over on Sower Road. I know who that woman is. I mean, she lives right beside the Mrs. and me."

This call was like a gift from God. The detectives had checked out two of her former addresses and came up with nothing. At this point, Gertrude Caller had no fixed address—that was until ten seconds ago. Another lead.

"We've been neighbors for twelve, thirteen years I'd say. The Mrs.

used to go to bingo every Saturday night up until about five years ago. She just plumb stopped. Wanted nothin' to do with no one no more."

"Sir, is she there now?" the captain asked, trying to control his excitement.

"Afraid not. She packed up, said she was afraid of that serial killer stuff. Not that I blame her much. The Mrs. here is pretty scared too."

"Did she tell you where she was going?" Captain Barlow crossed his fingers.

"Didn't ask; figured it was her business."

"Was she with anyone?"

"No."

"How did she seem to you?"

"Really tense-like and in a hurry."

"Is it okay if I send my detectives over to get a statement?"

"Sure—111Sower Road. I hope I've helped."

"Yes, you certainly have. Thank you."

"Are the detectives coming now?"

"Yes, is there a problem?"

"No. I have to get the Mrs. out of her nice fancy nightclothes is all. Wouldn't want her scaring off the men in suits. You know what I'm sayin'?"

Captain Barlow smiled on his end. "Thanks again, Mr. Wagnall."

The captain gave Jim back his phone and slapped his hands together in victory.

"I want you two to hustle over to 111 Sower Road and get a statement. Then check out Gertrude's existing home," he ordered.

"What about a search warrant?"

"I'll handle the warrant on this end. She isn't there, left in a hurry."

"We're on it!" Jim slammed his hand down on the desk, happy to have a lead.

"Find something that will lead us to Ellen. Go, go!"

The detectives raced out of the precinct like their pants were on fire.

Chapter Fifty-Eight

The following night, Taut stood outside the home of Rachelle Baum with an evil twinkle in his eyes. An insatiable hunger clawed at his soul for the taste of her electrifying fear. He watched Rachelle from the shadow of the elm tree.

The stereo played at full volume as she went about cleaning her home. Singing and dancing, Rachelle made housework effortless and enjoyable. The three antique vases on the corner of the coffee table sparkled with shine. She smiled with pride, glancing around at a job well done.

Standing by the tree surrounded by the blackness of the night, sweat trickled down his back, making a dark stain on his gray T-shirt. The impulse to destroy was growing stronger and stronger with each passing second.

Without warning, a memory from deep within his memory pierced his soul like a dagger. A time when he was forced to have sex with his mother while his stepfather smacked his bare ass, cheering him on. The small, pleasuring moans from her lips still haunted him, as well as the helplessness in her eyes. He vacillated between sorrow and pain and dropped to his knees, clasping his hands tightly over his ears. His stepfather's words raged on—harder, faster—causing him physical pain.

By the time Roger turned eleven, he was having sex with his mother on a regular basis. One ghastly image after the next fell like snow in his psyche.

Then an evil sneer slowly crept across his face like a thick rolling fog. He felt the intense power in his groin. He was in control of someone else's destiny, destination to hell. He would be far more superior then his stepfather ever was. No longer the sex puppet, he had grown to be the master of the show. He covered his watch, hitting the glow light. It was 11:30. The lights finally went out. It wouldn't be long now before his bloodthirsty craving for the ultimate high would be rewarded.

Rachelle decided to take a hot bath before calling it a night. Grabbing her white silk robe from the back of the door, she sauntered to the bathroom. She lay back against the bath pillow, putting her headphones on. Closing her eyes, she relaxed to Mozart. Her hands softly caressed the top of the water, swirling the frothy bubbles around her body. She felt safe. All the windows and doors were locked.

Rachelle had had a rocky three last months as she recovered from a bike accident. The damage done to her cartilage and tendons from the tree she smashed into while riding the rough terrain had cost her a day's surgery. And if that wasn't bad enough, she said good-bye to her boyfriend of five years, Austin Silverspring. The harsh reality—no trust, no love. Austin begged and pleaded with her to take him back. To her, an affair was an act of unforgivable betrayal. At times she missed him terribly. But she couldn't love someone she didn't trust.

Rachelle was so engrossed in Mozart she didn't hear the glass shatter on the basement floor. The monster slid inside like a serpent slithering in the dark, hunting his prey. He quietly started up the steps, listening for voices. It was safe.

Feeling her body free of tension, she pulled the plug. Grabbing a light blue towel, she patted her skin dry. Afterward, she sat on the toilet applying aloe lotion on her copper skin. The summer sun had little mercy on her skin. She brushed her teeth, combed her hair, and hung up her towel.

She slipped out of her robe and climbed between the silk sheets, naked as a jaybird. The feeling of freedom helped her sleep better. She propped up her pillows for her half-hour reading ritual. Minutes later, her eyelids grew too heavy to read another sentence. She placed the bookmark on the page and closed the book. Snuggling as snug as a bug in a rug, she fell sound asleep.

Roger could hear faint little snores echoing throughout the bedroom. This was his cue. He carefully opened the door. The blade glittered against the moonlight peeking in through the cracks in the blinds. Rachelle didn't stir. In one swift movement, he pounced, pinning her underneath him. She instantly felt the cold steel pushing against her throat. Her body quickened to ice; heart began pounding hard against her ribs. She was so terrified she accidentally peed in the bed. Sheer terror swirling and swirling like she was caught in an ocean whirlpool cutting off her oxygen. He leaned down, smelling her freshly shampooed hair. The fresh scent of aloe wafted up his nostrils. It was his turn. The adrenaline gushed through his veins like a raging river. He licked her from chin to eyeball.

"Don't move, bitch, or I'll gut you like an animal."

"Please don't hurt me," she begged.

"You scream, and I'll punish you in ways unimaginable."

He turned on the lamp and then yanked her up by her wet hair, the blade still pressed against her throat. This was the first time since she was a little girl she wished she'd worn pajamas, a nightshirt, something to hide her vulnerability.

"Oh and what do we have here?" His mind flashed from his mother to Rachelle.

He methodically slid the knife slowly down, stopping at her breastbone, then moving the point across to the left nipple.

"Please don't hurt me." Rachelle winced. Her body trembled violently.

"Tell me why I should spare you," he whispered in her ear, lowering the weapon down along her stomach, stopping in between her legs.

"Please," she cried. "Take whatever you want. I promise I won't tell anyone you were here." Her eyes were two orbs of horror.

"I already have what I want."

She jumped, feeling a sharp sting between her legs. The torture had begun. He'd deliberately nicked her clitoris with the point of his knife. He grabbed a fistful of wet hair, yanking her head back as far as it would go. For the first time, Rachelle stared into the face of true evil. Oh how she wanted to look away from the devil. He unzipped his jeans, forcing her to perform oral sex. Afterward, he tied her hands behind her back. Rachelle struggled, but Roger managed to tie her hands with little problem. This animal didn't have a soul. He dragged the steel blade across her chest like a skilled surgeon; tiny dots of blood came to the surface. Her heightened adrenalin and endorphins coursed through her veins. Rachelle didn't cry out. This was an act of defiance that had to be dealt with. He waved the blade millimeters from her face, taunting.

"Please. I don't want to die." She struggled to move her face away from the knife. He squeezed her face like a vice.

Rachelle knew she was in serious trouble, another statistic on a wall of murdered women. Her life didn't mean anything to this guy. Roger struck her across the face so hard that she lost her balance. Suddenly he began dragging her across the hardwood floor by her hair. When he reached the hallway, he let go. The sadistic glare in the monster's eyes made her blood turn to ice in her veins. He wanted her to see what was coming next. With her hands tied behind her back, Rachelle had no way of protecting herself. She had just enough time to turn her head as his boot came down, crushing bones in her cheek. Her eyeball felt as if there were an explosion behind her eye. She spat blood and broken teeth out of her mouth. Again his boot stomped down, caving in the right side of her face. She knew she was going to die a horrible death this night.

At that moment, Rachelle had an out-of-body experience. She saw herself floating above her own body. She watched Roger unleash his fury but could not feel the pain of his blade. Finally she found her voice. "Why me?" she screamed. He stopped at the piercing shriek. Rachelle didn't recognize her own face. Her long, brown hair was matted with blood. Again he went untamed with the blade. Blood sprayed the walls and floor from each savage wound. She watched as he brutally plunged the knife into her chest over and over and over. *Is this what it feels like to be dead?* she wondered. The gurgling sound from inside her chest echoed loudly in her ears. And then everything went black.

Chapter Fifty-Nine

Bright and early the next morning, Austin showed up at Rachelle's place. He wanted to give back the things he accidentally packed, belonging to her. He rang the bell and waited. He looked at the driveway; her red Firebird was parked, so she had to be home. He rang the bell again. Still no answer, he decided to go around back to see if she was out there. Before opening the gate, he stopped; the basement window had been smashed in. Fear went off like bells ringing in a fire drill.

He opened the gate and tore around back. He bolted up the patio steps and started banging against the patio window. Then he stopped, noticing the blood smears. He jerked on the patio door, surprised to find it open. He cautiously stepped inside, yelling Rachelle's name. No reply. Why she hadn't answered him would soon be revealed. He yelled her name a few more times. Still no answer. From where he stood, everything was in its proper place, until he reached the hallway. His hand flew to his mouth, and a sudden scream escaped. Austin froze. "Oh my God!" he shrieked, eyeing Rachelle's bloodstained body on the floor.

He rushed to her aid, checking to see if she still had a pulse. He stared down at the grisly sight. Her beautiful face assaulted beyond recognition. There were too many stab wounds to count. He grabbed his cell, dialing 911. He stayed next to her, waiting for an operator to answer.

At last he heard a voice. "Emergency 911. Kathy speaking."

"I need an ambulance to 717. Oh my God!" He tried to breath. "I need an ambulance at 717 Planter Drive. Oh my God, she's bleeding. There's blood everywhere. Please someone help her!" he cried hysterically.

"What is your name?"

"Austin Silverspring."

"Austin, where is the victim bleeding from?"

"Jesus Christ, she's covered in blood. I just found her. Get someone here now!"

"The ambulance is on its way. Is she breathing, Austin?"

"I don't know." He shook his head.

"Put your hand to her mouth and feel if there is air coming out."

"I think she's dead! Somebody help her please!" he shrieked.

Austin tore the panties off her wrists so he could hold her. He ever so gently placed her battered face in the crook of his arm.

"Come on, baby, please don't die. Oh God!" He rocked her cold body back and forth, crying. "Where in the hell is the ambulance?" he screamed into the cell phone that was sitting in a small pool of congealed blood beside him on the floor. He was thankful to hear the loud noise of sirens barreling up the road. It was the cavalry—police cars, fire trucks, and ambulance. He softly placed Rachelle back on the floor while he ran to unlock the front door.

Two attendants rushed in with a stretcher.

"She's in the hall." Austin led the way.

The attendants moved Austin out of the way so they could evaluate Rachelle's condition. Austin was so preoccupied with what the attendants were doing, he didn't notice Officer's Sammy Smiles and Tony Buick behind him. Smiles gasped, eyeing the grotesque figure of the floor.

"God have mercy," declared Sammy.

"Oh Christ." Tony looked away.

The ambulance attendants worked quickly. Rachelle was in critical condition but alive. Her lungs were collapsed. They immediately started a tracheotomy. Multiple stab wounds throughout her head, torso, and legs. The right side of her face was caved inward.

Sammy touched Austin on the shoulder.

"What's your name, son?"

"Austin Silverspring, and that's Rachelle Baum."

"Why do you have blood on you?"

"I found her. I tried to help her." Austin had lost all color in his face.

"You are a boyfriend, friend, what?"

"Can we do this later? Can't you see she might die?"

"No, we'll need to do this now."

Austin kept an eye on the paramedics while he answered their questions.

"We're going to need your clothes," Tony said, pointing to Austin's soiled clothes.

"Fine. I have some clothes left here. You might want to check the smashed window in the basement," Austin spat sarcastically, eyes glued on what the attendants were still doing.

"She's critical. We have to move her now." In one quick motion, Rachelle was lifted onto the stretcher and rushed out to the awaiting ambulance.

Rachelle Baum had survived one of the most heinous acts of violence the paramedics had ever witnessed. They had been to head-on collisions that weren't this bad.

"Where are you taking her?" Austin asked wiping his tears.

"Morial hospital."

The two officers watched as they wheeled Rachelle out.

Austin came up from downstairs carrying his soiled clothes. He handed them to Sammy. "Can I go?"

"Don't leave town."

"I'll be at the hospital if you need me." Silverspring raced out to his Ford Escape and sped down the road, trying to catch up to the ambulance.

Officer Sammy Smile radioed the captain. Captain Barlow ordered the two to stay put; he would be there shortly. He ordered them to block off the area with tape. He hung up and called forensics.

Chapter Sixty

llen had no idea how long she'd been in and out of consciousness. Time seemed to stand still. The blindfold blocked out any sunlight coming through a window. Her head felt like it was about to burst open. Her eyes felt pressurized, caused from the tension of the blindfold. She was so thirsty she gagged every time she tried to swallow. Her arms were agonizingly numb and cold. Roger tried to steal her sense of worth when he threw her around the room like a ragdoll, but it would take a hell of lot more than a beating to make her fold. Ellen knew she had to stay positive. She refused to die like this—in some smelly, abandoned room, in the middle of god-knows-where. The warm keepsakes of Tom were keeping her fear at bay. She needed to focus on staying alive. The stale stench of cigarettes, mold, and dust was all she could smell.

Then it came, the click of the lock being opened. She wasn't strong enough to go another round. Beating up a sixty-five-year-old woman was one thing, but keeping her tied and sightless while he bashed her around was another. Ellen recognized both voices. A strong hand seized her by the shoulder, pulling her up.

"Are you going to behave, Doctor?" Roger spoke quietly.

Ellen nodded. She jumped, feeling the cold cloth touch her mouth.

Her lips were swollen and caked in dry blood. Roger gently washed away the dried blood from her face.

"Thank you," she whispered.

"It can't be pleasant not being able to move that mouth of yours." She tried to smirk, but it hurt too much.

At that moment, Ellen had no idea what came over her. An unexpected peace flowed into her like a warm summer breeze. If God wanted her, she was ready, smelly room and all. If she lived through this horrific ordeal, she was going on one hell of a vacation.

"What day is this?"

"Doesn't matter."

"Here to hurt me again?"

"Does that scare you?"

"Nope." Her lips hurt to move.

"You're pretty tough. I'll give you that." He laughed at her.

"You find me amusing?"

"A little."

"So what now?"

"Be quiet."

"Murdered anyone else?"

"Last warning."

"Did she beg for her life?"

He lunged out, grabbing her throat. "Shut up!"

She wheezed when he let go. "You win. Please untie me. I can't feel my hands."

"Why should I?" he taunted her.

"Because I asked nicely."

Roger's eyes roamed over her curiously, waiting for a reaction.

"Free my wrists," she demanded.

Roger grinned, striking her across the face. It sent bolts of searing pain through the side of her face.

"Bastard." She snarled through broken dentures. "Free me and see if you hit me like that again."

"You just don't give up do you?"

"Fuck you!" She spat blood out of the side of her mouth.

The doctor waited for the next blow but instead heard laughter echoing around the room. She seemed to be the only one brave enough to challenge him. At this point of captivity, Ellen didn't care. If she was going to die, it was going to be with dignity. She also knew if she showed fear, she'd be dead.

Roger rolled her on her side, cutting away the duct tape with his pocketknife. She clawed at the blindfold trying to free her eyes. Finally, she managed to slip the scarf down over her face. Her eyelids twitched from the light. At last she saw two shadows become visible. The two responsible for holding her against her will. Pins and needles prickled up and down her arms. A good sign she was regaining circulation back into her extremities.

"You despicable bitch," Ellen said, pulling at her hands.

"Who's in control now, Doctor Shrink?"

"Are you completely mad? You helped free a convicted murderer for what? Revenge?" Ellen shouted, forgetting her injuries.

"I warned you."

"These murders are because I fired your ass. What? Six years ago?"

"I told you I'd get you back."

"You set Roger free out of spite. Why?"

"You took James from me. It's my turn to make you pay. One by one, they will disappear from your life."

"James Blake raped and destroyed lives and then killed his sorry self. He never loved you, you idiot," Ellen roared.

"He did love me," Gertrude protested. "You had him arrested before he could say the words."

"So you hired *him*?" Ellen pointed at Roger. "A three-time convicted murderer to do your dirty work. You demented piece of wacko." Ellen was on her feet, screaming at Gertrude.

Roger leaned against the wall, enjoying the show.

"You're certified. At least Roger here has a bit of an excuse for what he does. How could you have done something so stupid? And Blake was nothing more than a sick rapist hiding behind a coat of ethics. Those principles were supposed to aid not destroy."

"You made him leave."

"The police will catch you. And when they do, I hope they lock you away forever. And you bet your evil ass I'll be in the wing watching you go down."

"Never happen. We have the control now."

"Oh yes it will."

"The almighty Doctor Smith isn't looking so almighty now, is she?" Gertrude danced around in circles. "All battered and bruised," Gertrude sang, laughing.

"This is only temporary, sweetheart," Ellen threatened.

"You'll beg me to take your life after I kill lovable Franki Martin and endearing Sandy Miller. Then it'll be my turn to see your pain. I was the one who ordered you here."

"Must be a very proud moment."

Roger laughed at Ellen's mockery. She was not backing down from Gertrude. "You are keeping me here while Roger kills the people I love because you want to see my reaction?"

Ellen thought she'd seen and heard it all, until now. *This psychopathic lunatic is seeking revenge for a fantasy lover that didn't love her back.*

"I'm going to bask in your grief."

"You belong in a steel cage. You're pathetic."

Ellen turned for a second, and Gertrude flew across the room, wrapping her hands around her neck and squeezing. Ellen clawed violently, trying to break the grip. She struggled, needing air. Roger watched the entertainment, amused. After a minute or two, he grew bored, stepping in to pull the tigress off its injured prey. Gertrude whirled around, eyes as black as coal. "You agreed she needs to suffer," Gertrude huffed as the bulging artery in her neck pulsed rapidly.

"She won't experience shit if she's dead."

Ellen coughed, trying to catch her breath. Looking up, she saw Roger wink.

"Are you hungry?"

"What?"

"Hungry? You know—food you eat?"

"Yes."

"Don't touch her again." He pointed his finger in Gertrude's face. "I'll be back in five."

Gertrude stalked Ellen as she paced the length of the bed.

"Trying to intimidate me?"

"Shut up."

Roger reentered as promised.

"Why are you feeding her?"

"She needs to eat," he declared calmly, like he had a guest for dinner.

"Like hell she does." Gertrude insolently blocked Roger's way.

"Excuse me."

On a peeling tin tray sat two pieces of toast smeared with margarine and a small glass of juice.

"Since you two insist on keeping me captive, coffee would be nice. And I will need to go to the bathroom, unless someone wants to clean up after me," Ellen said, injecting tension rising between the fugitives.

"You will get nothing." Gertrude swore, knocking the tray out of Roger's hand. He glanced from the floor to Gertrude. With lightning precision, he stuck her across the face, knocking her against the wall. The beasts were turning on each other.

He made Gertrude clean up the mess and then go to the kitchen and make Ellen a new breakfast, with coffee this time.

He walked over, holding out his hand. "Stand up?"

"Why?"

"Do you have to use the bathroom or don't you?"

Ellen clutched her side as she struggled to her feet. Roger had Ellen at the elbow, guiding her slowly down the hall. She cased the joint quickly in search of an exit.

"In there." He released her elbow. She turned to close the door, but he stuck his boot in side, blocking the entry. Ellen spotted blood on his boot. He had killed again.

"What—you want to watch?" She narrowed her eyes.

"Leave it open." Roger gave Ellen privacy by turning his back to the open entrance.

Ellen slowly made her way, each step excruciating. Bit by bit, she inched her pants down as the burning pain shot through her side like bullets from a gun. Any sudden movements made her want to scream, but there was no way she would give that maniac the satisfaction. She scanned the bathroom for a way out. The window above the tub was hopeless. The mirror over the sink had a long crack down the middle, caused by someone's anger. He'd know if she stole a piece of glass. She stopped to look in the mirror, absolutely shocked at her appearance. Her white hair was matted with dried blood. Her face had black-and-blue markings below her swollen-shut eye. Her lips protruded out an inch. Her once upon a time, nicely ironed white shirt was a wrinkled, bloodstained, dirty mess. She sat on the toilet, grateful to relieve the pressure in her bladder. It took her a few seconds longer to pull her pants up than it did to pull them down. The tub had a disgusting black ring around it, like it hadn't been washed in years. No liquid soap to cleanse the germs from her hands.

Back in the bedroom, the mess had been cleaned, and breakfast sat waiting at the foot of the bed.

"Enjoy," Roger said.

"Thank you."

"Don't do anything stupid."

"Like choking on my toast," she said, snarling.

He pointed to the dirty window hiding behind the ugly green sheer.

"Can't fly. Can't even walk fast, thanks to you."

"It had to be done."

"Why?" Ellen forced herself to sit.

"To make sure you understood who's in charge."

"Like I didn't already know."

"Had to be sure."

"Am I going to die?"

"Eat your breakfast."

"My last meal, you mean?"

Roger walked out, locking her in.

Ellen managed to pull the tray up to where she was sitting. She could only take small bites of her toast. There were large clumps of margarine that hadn't melted. She didn't care. She ever so delicately wrapped her swollen lips around the glass and slurped down the cold orange juice. It felt so good to finally drink something, and it was a good way to keep up her strength. Once she was finished, she lay back down and tried to get some sleep, confident her friends would find her.

Chapter Sixty-One

Officer's Sammy Smiles and Tony Buick had already blocked off the area with yellow crime tape when Captain Barlow drove up in his in black Nissan Altima. He got out and slipped under the tape, making his way up the stone pathway to the front entrance of the house. He gestured hello by a nod.

"How bad?"

"Nothing I've ever seen before," Sammy confessed.

"This guy is pure animal," Tony agreed.

"Who else has been in there?"

"The boyfriend and paramedics."

"Sammy?"

"She's gone," Sammy replied.

"Shit!"

"Captain, she's alive."

"She's alive?"

"She's at Morial fighting for her life."

"But she's alive?"

"Barely. The paramedics weren't too optimistic about her recovery."

"I mean, sir …" Buick could feel bile rising in the back of his throat. "He worked her over good. Half of her face was literally caved in."

"Murder weapon?"

"The condition she was in, I'd guess he used a knife."

"His weapon of choice."

"Sir, can I be blunt?"

"Go ahead, Sammy."

"He's giving the police a big fuck you. This prick is coming and going as he wishes without a care in the world of getting caught. It's like he's unstoppable."

"We'll get this cocky son of a bitch. Jim and Dan are collecting evidence at the second accomplice's place."

"They better come up with something and fast. We're seriously running out of time, and the body count is rising," Sammy complained.

"Tell me something I don't know."

All three looked out, eyeing the gaggle of spectators gathering on the sidewalk, eager to know what happened. Captain Barlow saw the nervousness in their eyes. Roger was in control of all their lives.

John picked lint off his pants and loosened his tie. The weather didn't help, being unbearably hot. Small beads of sweat slid down his face into the white collar of his shirt. He patted his face with a handkerchief.

"Another scorcher," Tony said.

"Got that right." Captain Barlow pulled at his collar.

"Any news on the missing doctor?" Sammy asked.

"We received a few calls about a maniac that apparently slammed on the breaks in the middle of Spelling Road last night. I have two officers over there now checking it out."

"Anything we can do to help?" Sammy volunteered.

"Right here is your mission."

"Roger that."

"Anyone know his point of entry?"

"The basement window is smashed in. I suspect that's how he got in."

"Why didn't she call the police, scream, when she heard glass breaking?" Captain Barlow probed.

"I saw her Discman lying on the side of the tub. If she was listening to tunes, she wouldn't have heard glass breaking," Tony answered.

"Damn things. Anything else?"

"We didn't go in any further, sir."

All three stopped, staring in the direction of roaring engines pulling to a stop in front of 717 Planter.

"Didn't take them long," Captain Barlow fumed

"Good news travels fast," Sammy barked derisively.

A barrage of reporters had arrived.

John ignored the journalists yelling questions from across the road.

"They want to make you a star, sir." Sammy smirked.

"Not today." The captain slipped on latex gloves and rubber booties before entering the crime scene. The copper smell of blood and torture rushed into his nasal passages like a cold, breathtaking wind. First stop the basement. The captain found the door leading to the basement and followed the steps down. The basement was in the process of being renovated. Sheets of drywall, paint, nails, rolls of plaster tape, and buckets of plaster lined the wall. Shards of splintered glass littered the floor. This house invasion had been well planned. It was certain Roger stalked this victim before entering. He knew exactly what window to target and the exact time to target it.

The scene down in the basement was meek compared to what was waiting for John in the upstairs hallway. He flicked the switch, closing the door behind him. The décor of upstairs was much richer. The living room was elegant and pure with a white leather sectional. A Wine Steward cocktail table was positioned diagonally in front of the sectional. The opposite side of the generous salon held a white leather tufted chaise. Nora nesting tables stood next to the arm of the leather couch. On top of the glass were three twelve-inch antique vases from Greece. A stylish flora arrangement gave the room a feminine glow. White silk drapes tied at the sides with beaded rope amid a glossy sheer added to its sophistication.

A Samsung forty-six-inch flat screen sat next to a smoky glass metal table, which held a five-speaker stereo system. Captain Barlow was very impressed at Rachelle's designer talent.

On his way to the kitchen, Captain Barlow heard Derk. The forensic crew had arrived.

"Captain, you in here?" Derk yelled from the doorway.

"In here."

Derk sauntered in, carrying his trendy medical kit.

"Hi. Where's the rest of your team?"

"Keith is on his way. Where's the body?" Derk asked.

"At Morial Hospital."

"That's great news."

"I called over. Rachelle Baum is in surgery."

"Captain, I hope she makes it."

"Me too! There's one hell of a mess in the hall. Sammy and Tony didn't go any further after catching a glimpse of the gore."

"Anyone else come through here?" Derk questioned.

"The boyfriend and paramedics. The paper bag contains the clothes he was wearing when he found her. Want to go take a look?"

The two stopped dead in their tracks, eyeing what looked like a massacre.

"You sure she's still alive?" Derk asked, dazed. He couldn't believe someone could survive such violence.

John pointed to the basement.

"Bring your Luminol and alternative light with you."

"Don't leave home without it." Derk held up his black leather bag.

"Good. Let's go to the basement."

"Why the basement?"

"Point of entry, my friend. Kicked clean. It's not the brightest down there."

"Everything we need is in here." He patted the bag.

Before Derk plugged in the Mag light, they put on their specialty glasses. The entire room lit blue. Derk followed the footprints from window to stairs.

"Now I know why you guys get called in." John grinned at the evidence.

Derk chuckled. "It's not our expertise. It's the equipment they let us play with."

"What you got, lad?"

"This is the same boot print from the last few crime scenes."

"Only one set of prints?"

"This time he was alone. It's hard to fathom how a person could become so violent."

"I'm starting to believe he isn't human."

Derk and the captain were climbing the steps when Keith opened the door.

"Where would you like me to start?"

"Hallway, and there's no body."

"Where's the body?" he asked, puzzled.

"The victim is at Morial. She's in surgery."

There was a slight flicker of hope in Keith's baby blues. Derk led Keith to the evidence.

"Holy shit!" He turned to Derk. "There is no reason why she should be alive."

"She must have had one hell of a will to live," Captain Barlow said.

"A miracle." Keith pointed to the spray of blood across the floor and wall. "What's her condition?"

"Critical."

"Holy Christmas." Keith shook his head at the carnage this animal left behind. He suited up, stepping over pools of congealed blood.

"How did the monster get in?" Keith asked Derk.

"Kicked in the downstairs window and climbed inside."

Keith picked up Rachelle's CD player from the side of the tub, holding it up for the guys to see.

"We know why she didn't hear him enter." He raised a brow. "These damn things get more women assaulted every day because they don't hear their attacker until it's too late." He placed it in a plastic evidence bag.

Derk set foot in the bedroom.

"This is good place to trap unseen fibers." He got out a specialty vacuum and began suctioning the bedding, trapping any trace evidence into the funnel. This machine could pick up microscopic fibers.

"I found what he used to tie her up." Keith held up blood-soaked panties and placed them in another evidence bag and sealed it closed with the date and a number.

"Put a rush on the bag, can you, Keith. Hopefully we'll find bodily fluids belonging to the killer. This way when we get to court, the DNA evidence will put him where he needs to go." Derk then moved onto into the hall to examine the blood spatter patterns on the wall and floor.

The captain patted Derk on the shoulder. "You guys have this under control?"

"Sure," Derk said.

"Yeah right." Keith laughed. "This is a nightmare. Hey, sir, any news on the doctor?"

"Nothing yet."

"I have faith you'll find her, sir."

"I hope alive. Need anything, Sammy and Tony are right out front." Captain Barlow gave a wave.

Chapter Sixty-Two

A s the days ticked on, the detectives were growing more and more discouraged about ever finding enough evidence to bring this second person to justice. Dan and Jim had been at Gertrude's place most of the night. Then they went home, caught two hours of sleep, and were back at Gertrude's place again. In the back of the bedroom closet, Dan found a running shoe. He turned it over. It had the same markings as the print found in Susan Dutch's bedroom. He bagged the runners to take to forensics. As he was headed outside for his smoke, his cell phone rang.

"Kape here."

"Danny boy. It's McCalley. Busy?"

"Up to my arse in nothing," Dan replied.

"You still on Sower?"

"Yep."

"Find anything interesting?"

"A shoe. What's up?"

"Captain's orders, get over to Serbet. They've found the doctor's car."

"Abandoned?"

"Believe so."

"We're on our way, buddy." Dan put his smoke back in his pack and ran into the house.

"They found Ellen's car."

"No shit! Where?"

"Serbet Road. Let's go."

Ten minutes later, Jim pulled off the road, parking in front of the police car. He was careful not to alter any evidence on the shoulder of the road, like a tire print that could be used later on in court.

"Here comes the hotshot now." A police officer pointed at Jim. The detective had made quite a name for himself as a player. It was painfully evident some cops didn't approve of his lifestyle on and off duty.

Jim and Dan stepped up to where the officers were standing.

"Morning, gentlemen," Dan greeted the boys in blue.

"Keys are in the ignition. Briefcase is on the passenger seat, along with her cell phone. And a manila envelope."

"Did you guys touch anything?" Jim said, adjusting his shirt.

"No, sir." Crotchety, old Jerry Bull, who should have retired a long time ago, saluted sarcastically.

"Good work." Jim snapped his gum.

"You might want to come and have a look back here!" Dan yelled at his partner.

"What's up?" Jim stepped up to where Dan was hunched over behind Ellen's car.

"Drag marks and a second set of footprints. She was forced into the car."

"Her phone is sitting on the passenger seat," Jim said, staring at the ground.

"Why would she get out of her car without her phone?" Dan asked. "Ellen was so much smarter that. Something happened to make her pull onto the shoulder of the road."

Dan glanced up, seeing Old Bull standing next to the trunk of Ellen's Lexus. "Hey, Einstein, did any of you think to pop the trunk and see if the doctor's body is inside?" Bull quipped.

Jim glanced at his partner, embarrassed.

"No fuck head. We're busy looking at the drag marks back here. But I'll open it now," Jim snapped.

Everyone breathed a sigh of relief, seeing a crowbar and a spare tire.

"Time to get a hold of Ivy," Dan suggested.

"We need to collect these prints before some jackass decides to park behind the car," Jim stated.

"Who's going to be the brave one?"

"I'll do the honors," Jim said, loving the challenge. Jim dialed as he walked.

"Ivy Frost here."

"Hey, baby, it's Jim. Where are you?"

"Don't call me baby," she demanded. "If it's any of your business, I'm on my way to Serbet Road. Why?"

"Good. We need a mold of the tire track and the car towed back to the lab."

"I know!"

"How?" Jim asked, puzzled.

"Physic."

"Hurry up then."

"Let's get the tape and seal off this area," Dan said to the officers. The officers and Dan worked with the loud roar of engines passing by. Afterward, Dan took a little stroll around the field beside the road in search of Ellen's body. He was thankful he found nothing. He was on his way back up the hill, huffing and puffing like an old man. He was tired, hot, and very out of shape.

Jim closed his cell wearing a Cheshire smile.

"Don't tell me, a date with Ivy?"

"Nope. You were right; she hates me." He laughed. "Good news and bad. Roger struck again, but this time his victim is still alive, buddy. Rachelle Baum survived the attack."

"Did you say Rachelle Baum over on Planter?" The redness in his puffy cheeks drained white.

"I see your hearing isn't failing," Jim joked.

"Are you sure?" Dan yelled.

"Yeah, why?" Jim furrowed his brow.

"That's my ex-wife's sister."

"Oh, shit, sorry, my friend. I didn't know."

"What's her condition?"

"Critical. But, Dan, she's alive."

"We've got to get over to the hospital," Dan said.

"Not until Ivy gets here."

Dan walked away, lighting a smoke, totally torn up inside.

"You and Rachelle close?" Jim came up behind him.

"We used to be. She didn't want me to divorce her sister. She thought I should give Shelia a second chance. You know … to redeem herself. That was the last time we had a serious conversation."

"Sorry, man." Jim patted Dan on the shoulder.

"When we find that ogre …"

"Don't go there," Jim strongly suggested.

"Women from the funny farm aren't his only targets."

"Rachelle's never been to River Edge?"

"No, man, she's pretty solid."

"What does she do for a living?"

"A real estate agent."

"We'll find this piece of shit, Dan."

"And send him straight to hell where he belongs." Dan threw his butt on the ground, squishing it under his powerful foot, like he would do to Roger's head given the occasion.

"Why did you break up with Miss Ivy?" Dan asked, changing the subject.

"Not my type," he answered, almost regretful.

"You dog. When did you date her?"

"A couple months back."

"So what's wrong with Miss Ivy? I mean she's beautiful, smart."

"No sex until marriage shit."

"All about you. Man, and you wonder why women like Miss Martin won't give you the time of day." Dan chuckled, lightening the burden in his heart.

"Her loss, not mine."

Dan shook his head. "Ivy really looks broken up about it too."

"It didn't work with Ivy, but I haven't given up on Franki," Jim admitted.

"Keep dreaming, shallow boy. This time karma's coming back to bite you in the ass. A nice, big chunk, buddy."

"If not Franki, then the right woman will come along."

"Not before Armageddon. There isn't a woman on this planet, a sane one, that would put up with your sleazy womanizing crap. And you know it!"

"I don't have time for complications," Jim rationalized.

"There's only one complication—you."

"I'm touched by your support."

"Stop being a hustler." Dan noticed Ivy's SUV at the stoplight a half a block away. "Here she is now."

Dan stood on the gravel directing her where to park. She turned down the radio, shutting off her engine. Dan walked up to the window.

"Hello, Detective Dan."

"Hi, beautiful." Dan opened her door like the perfect gentleman.

"Have I told you I think your ex-wife is a simpleton for letting a charmer like you go?"

"Roger's latest victim is my ex-wife's sister. At least she's alive."

"I'm sorry. I didn't mean to—"

"I know. Shelia and I didn't part on the best of terms." He quickly briefed her on what needed to be found.

"Tell the big stud over there I think he's an asshole."

Dan chuckled, walking back to the car.

"You need someone to talk to later, give me a call!" she yelled as Dan was climbing in Jim's car.

"Thank you, darlin'."

Jim pulled off the shoulder of the road, and curiosity got the better of him. He had to ask. "What was that all about?"

"She said she loves you." He laughed, doing up his seatbelt.

"You got a date with cold Ethal there?"

"Be nice," Dan warned. "I can have women friends, unlike you."

"I have women friends." He crinkled his face into a knot.

"Name one that you haven't tried to sleep with." After a long pause, Dan cracked up. "Just what I thought."

"Don't be a jerk."

"And you're still a dog." Dan sat in the passenger seat, asking God to please make Rachelle okay. The rest of the drive to the hospital was a quiet one.

Chapter Sixty-Three

After parking in the parking lot, the detectives hustled in through the glass doors of Morial Hospital and followed the red line to the information desk. They stopped and got directions to the intensive care unit. Then they hopped into the nearest elevator and rode to the third floor. Nervous sweat slid down Dan's temples. This was the first time he had seen or spoken to his ex-wife, Shelia, since their divorce. These were not the circumstances he had in mind. He hated her for cheating, but there was still love left. It's a very fine line between loving someone and hating someone. The crazy part was he blamed himself for the affair. By the time he realized Shelia was craving his affection, it was too late. He was born to catch bad guys, and there was nothing he could do to change that. The question now was could he comfort the woman he loved and lost?

The nurse's station was busier than a bus depot. Men and women dressed in green rushing in and out of different doors, looking serious. The detectives passed the station unannounced.

"Gentlemen, you are not permitted on the ward without authorization."

"Here's your authorization, lady," Dan countered, flashing his badge.

"Who are you here to see?" she asked cordially.

"Rachelle Baum," Jim answered.

"Captain Barlow is with her now. Only one person is permitted at a time."

"What's her prognosis?"

"She's lucky to be alive. If you need further information, I'm afraid you'll have to talk to her doctor. I can't give out the details."

"Is her family here?" Dan inquired, fingers tapping nervously against the desk.

"Yes, in the side room around the corner."

"Thank you." Dan nodded his head sadly.

Dan wiped the sweat from his hands onto his faded jeans and rounded the corner to the private waiting area.

Family and close friends filled the small room. Shelia was the first to notice the detectives in the doorway. His heart began pounding like a jackhammer inside his chest. Despite the pain she was going through, she still looked beautiful. Dan held her while she sobbed in his arms.

"We'll catch this guy, I promise."

"Thank you for coming." She held onto him like a drowning person would to a life preserver.

"I'm so sorry, Shelia." He wiped her tears with his thumb. "How is Rachelle?"

"Not good."

"What's not good?"

"If she makes it, she'll need reconstructive surgery to repair some of the bones crushed in her face. Apparently the boot print is still there from the force he used. A hundred some stitches in her face. He sliced her from lip to ear. She has multiple stab wounds from her chest to her pelvic area. Her right lung is punctured, so she's on a breathing respirator. A drainage tube inserted into her lungs is extracting the excess fluid so she doesn't drown. The surgeons lost count of the number of slashes and gashes up and down her arms and legs. Her right arm is broken at the elbow. The doctors can't tell how severe the head trauma is until she wakes up. If that is to happen at all. They had to induce her coma in hopes of lessening the swelling on her brain. I don't know how she's still here."

Tears began welling up in Dan's eyes. There were too many unexpected emotions escalating to the surface. "We'll find him."

"Promise me, Dan. Promise me you'll find this animal and kill him."

"Shelia, we'll get him."

"The doctors don't know if she'll make it through the next twenty-four hours."

"She's tough like someone else I know." He tried to smile. "Can I see her?"

"Yes."

"I'm so sorry, Shelia. Which room is she in?"

"Across the hall." Shelia watched her ex-husband waddle away; he had put on twenty pounds at least since their divorce.

"Why did he come?" she asked Jim.

"He cares, Shelia."

"It's not personal. I get it—once a good cop, always a good cop."

"You should know; you married him." Jim smiled.

"I have no regrets. Dan was the best thing that happened to me." Shelia put her head down in shame. "But I was too stupid to figure that out. And he was always working."

"He'll always love you."

"I know."

Jim spent a few minutes consoling Shelia before it was back to business. He could not discuss the details of the case. Jim turned and walked toward the man sitting alone in the corner with his eyes closed. Jim assumed it was Austin Silverspring.

"Austin Silverspring?"

His eyes sprang open. "Yeah! Yeah it's me." He sat up straight, rubbing his red eyes.

"I'm Detective Masker. I'm here to ask you a couple of questions. Would you mind?"

"I don't know what else I can tell you that I haven't already told Captain Barlow."

"Oh, he's already spoken to you?"

"I found Rachelle." His mind flashed to the blood-soaked broken body on the floor. "I could have never done that to Rachelle. That animal deserves to die."

"Sorry about Rachelle."

"Detective, find that bastard before I do."

"Austin, in the best interest of this investigation, don't go being a hero. You could jeopardize this entire investigation. Stay here with Rachelle and let us do our job. We'll find this guy and put him behind bars where he belongs."

"Find that son of a bitch." There was coldness in his eyes.

Captain Barlow was coming out as Dan was about to enter.

"Hey what are you doing here?"

"I want to see her, sir."

"Brace yourself. You'll see the ruins of what pure evil leaves behind."

"I'll meet up with you guys shortly."

"Don't take too long. We have a killer to catch."

Captain Barlow thought twice about letting Dan see Rachelle, but he also understood the reason he had to see her. Dan needed to see for himself the carnage Taut left behind. Now it was getting dangerously close to the guys working the case.

Dan pushed the door open. Myriad life-support machinery with flashes of light and beeping sounds filled the space. The room reeked of the aftermath of violence. It was painful to see Rachelle so powerless and battered. Her swollen face bandaged in white gauze. Spots of blood seeping through the white cloth where they had to stitch her face back together. The beast had slit her from mouth to ear. Her right arm placed in a cast. The swishing noise of the breathing apparatus engulfed the room. White bandages covered the stab wounds the surgeon had to stitch together. All he could see were eyelids peeking out from the white gauze. He took a deep breath, crossing the tiles to her bedside. Tears slid down his cheeks. He couldn't help noticing the needles and tubes running up and down her left arm. She was a ghastly sight he'd never forget. In all the years on the force, he'd never witnessed anyone survive a sadistic assault as this.

He angrily brushed the tears away with the back of his hand.

"Rachelle, it's Dan. I came to see you, honey. I'm so sorry. I swear I'll get the animal that did this to you. But you have to promise me that you'll keep fighting no matter what. Don't let this sick bastard win, Rachelle. Your sister needs you, and you need her. Austin found you. Did you know that? He loves you so much. Fight, Rach, fight for the right to be alive. Can you do that for me, sweetheart? Show all of us how strong you are." Tears fell from Dan eyes. "I love you, sweetheart." He slowly made it out of Rachelle's room, determined more than ever to catch this son of a bitch.

Captain Barlow met Dan in the corridor. "You okay?"

"I'm just going to say good-bye."

"I asked if you're okay."

"Let's get this bastard before he tortures one more woman."

"See you downstairs." The captain and Jim left.

Shelia hugged him warmly. "I know you have to go."

"Take care of yourself." Dan kissed her wet cheek, forcing himself to pull away. Just as he was leaving, Dan eyed a man standing in the doorway. This was the asshole that had no respect for his marriage.

Outside, Captain Barlow ordered the detectives back to the station. Ivy had new information.

Chapter Sixty-Four

Ellen sprang upward at the sound of angry voices screaming at each other from outside her door. An uninvited nervousness filled her veins. Something scary and unpredictable was brewing on the other side of the door. She moved slowly to the door, placing her ear against the wood.

"What in hell do you think you're doing?" Gertrude shrieked.

"I didn't know!" Roger yelled back.

"How could you not know she was alive? How can you be that stupid?"

Ellen smiled; a woman had survived Roger's vicious attack.

"I give the instructions, not you," Gertrude said.

"I take orders from no one."

"That was our deal, damn it."

"Deal, schmeal."

"I give the damn orders. I tell you who to eliminate; that's our agreement."

"Shut up. You're giving me a headache. Remember—I'm free now?"

"I could undo that in a nanosecond. No one knows I'm responsible for setting you free. I could go say you abducted me, and you'd be in jail. So you better start obeying me," Gertrude threatened.

"Obey? Obey you?" he shouted.

"Yes, obey. Don't know what the word means, stupid?"

"Don't call me stupid." His eyes jutted outward, his jaw locked.

"Stop acting retarded. You're going to get us caught. Do you hear me?"

"You're screaming an inch from my face! How can I not?"

"Our plan is for my revenge, not yours. What's wrong with you?"

"Lots." He smirked. "What's wrong with you?"

"Roger, you're seriously pissing me off."

"So." He shrugged his shoulders, flashing his malevolent smile.

"We have an arrangement," she whined.

"I've done everything you've wanted me to."

"Yes and satisfied your own hunger in the process. So don't lay pity in my lap."

"I want more." His voice began to calm.

"That's not possible." She shook her head adamantly.

"Yes it is."

"You're screwing with a good arrangement is what you're doing."

"You asked for the good doctor, and I delivered. You, my dear psychopath, had a hand in killing that agent. Oh … and what about the chick with the pink hair? Tell me you didn't enjoy burning her eyes out with the curling iron."

"The doctor is not going to undergo misery if you continue to kill strangers, will she? You have to murder the doctor's loved ones. I need her to suffer, damn it!"

"What do you want me to do?"

"Kill the nurse!" Gertrude's face twisted into an even uglier mask than her own face.

Ellen's legs suddenly went weak. She grabbed the door handle so she wouldn't fall to the floor. The nurse Gertrude planned to execute next was Sandy.

"I can't get within a hundred yards to her."

"Why not?"

"Because you decided to write her name in blood on the wall, remember? Now who's the idiot? The police take that as a threat. I'm not killing a cop for you."

Ellen could feel her pulse slow with relief and her legs getting stronger. Roger couldn't get to her.

"You'll do what I say."

"How then, genius?"

"Be quiet and let me think."

"Good plan, simpleton." Roger danced around, waving his hands in the air.

"I'm not an idiot. I set you free, didn't I?"

"I set you free, didn't I? Bitch," Roger taunted her.

"Don't you dare call me vulgar names! I demand respect."

"I should go in there right now and kill your beloved doctor. That will put you back in place, won't it?"

"We're supposed to be a team."

"You have what you want. I am Judas, and Victoria is my playing field." His words were haunting.

"For a madman," Gertrude scoffed.

"What did you say?" Roger suddenly clutched Gertrude around the neck with one hand, slapping her across the face repeatedly. Roger was teetering on the edge of rage. He didn't like taking orders from anyone.

"You lied to me." She choked out the words. "What will you do if that girl talks, you jackass?"

Roger broke out laughing.

"What's so amusing?" Gertrude demanded an answer.

"Trust me. She won't talk."

"How do you know for sure?"

"Fear, my dear. Fear."

"How scared will she be surrounded by half the police force twenty-four hours a day?"

"You didn't see what I did to her."

"Obviously not enough. She's alive."

"This one was so frightened she pissed on the floor like a beaten down dog." Roger laughed at the memory.

"Yeah, well you assumed she was dead too. It's all over the news, how she miraculously survived your attack. I'm on the news. You're on the news." Her hands flailed in the air like some kind of lunatic. "The missing doctor and her car are splattered across every magazine and newspaper across the countryside. Rachelle Baum wasn't in the plan!" she shouted again.

"Rachelle will die."

"What are you—psychic now?"

"Shut that mouth or you'll be next."

"Like hell. Have you forgotten you owe me your freedom, moron?"

Ellen had to stop the fighting from escalating further. If she didn't, Gertrude would depart this life permanently; she'd served out her purpose. She began pounding her fist against the door, crying out. The door flew open. "What?" Roger shouted. The mental illness blazed in his eyes.

"I have to use the bathroom."

The television was blaring with newscasters reporting they'd found her abandoned car on Serbet.

"This will make you even more famous, Doctor," he said.

"No thanks."

"Christ, now they know where I live," Gertrude bellowed from the living room.

"Did she think the police wouldn't find her house?" Ellen asked.

"Use the toilet and hurry up."

"Why are you so angry?"

"None of your business."

"Holding me hostage makes it my business."

"Finished with that psychobabble?"

This time Roger declined her privacy. He stood in the doorway, arms folded across his chest, glaring from eyes gone ice.

"Why are you two fighting?"

"We won't be too much longer if she doesn't shut that big mouth of hers!" he yelled down the hallway.

Gertrude came storming down the passage, ready for another round. Her fat lip wasn't enough of a deterrent.

"Is that so? Well if you weren't such a jerk-off, I wouldn't have to treat you like an idiot child, would I?"

"Fucking imbecile."

Common sense, if she had any, would've told her to back off. You don't go picking a fight with a man who loves to torture and kill.

"Gertrude, shut the hell up," Ellen ordered from the bathroom.

This brought both surprise and comfort to Roger.

"Watch it or I'll give you something to really complain about," Gertrude threatened.

"Bring it on, you ugly beast."

Roger cracked up laughing. Before Gertrude had the chance to get to Ellen, who was still seated on the throne, Roger reached out with brute strength, slamming Gertrude hard against the wall. Her head hit the wall with a loud thud.

Gertrude reached out to strike her partner in crime. In one swift motion, Roger grabbed her arm, and she screamed in pain. Ellen heard the sound of her bones snapping. Gertrude wailed on the floor, holding her disfigured arm.

"No one can hear you." He jerked her head back, forcing her to stare into his cold heartless eyes. Then he walked away. That's when Ellen knew she had to do something; she struggled to get down on the floor.

"He broke my arm," she wailed in pain.

"Be quiet and listen," Ellen whispered.

"You broke my arm, you stupid bastard!" she screamed, ignoring Ellen.

"Be quiet."

Gertrude swung out with her good arm, knocking Ellen flat on her back. She struggled a second time to her knees.

"He's going to kill you if don't shut up."

"Get away from me." Gertrude stumbled down the hall, heading into the lion's den. Within minutes, Gertrude Caller was dead.

Chapter Sixty-Five

Six o'clock the next morning, Sandy reached across sleeping Mark to shut off the alarm. Still half asleep, she staggered to the shower. Once dressed, she followed the scent of coffee brewing from the kitchen. She stood at the counter daydreaming about finding Ellen. Deep in thought, she didn't hear Mark sneaking up behind her until he wrapped his arms around her waist, scaring the hell out of her.

"Don't do that again," she snapped, grabbing her chest.

"Sorry." He raised his hands in the air.

"Fine. Don't do it again."

"And good morning to you, grouchy."

"I'm just stressed. Sleep well?" she asked, trying to change her attitude.

"Better than you. I woke a couple of times because you were yelling."

"You kidding?"

"Sounded like a nightmare."

"Don't remember."

"Lucky you don't."

"Sorry for waking you. Coffee?" she asked.

"Please."

She took a second mug out of the cupboard, filling the cup with black gold.

He glanced at his watch, grinning.

"What?"

"We have time for a quickie."

"Not in the mood."

"Are you okay?"

"Umm, not sure how to answer that, Mark. Let me think—no. Someone is trying to kill me, my best friend was abducted, and you're thinking about sex. C'mon, give me a break."

"Ellen can take care of herself."

"Get real. Ellen is sixty-five years old. Roger is fiercer, faster, and meaner."

"He doesn't have the one thing she does."

"What's that?" Sandy folded her arms across her chest.

"She knows him better then he knows her."

"I hope you're right. Coffee on the balcony?"

"Sure." She handed Mark his mug.

"I like you better without clothes," he tried to joke.

"Society has a different standard on nudity."

"Shame."

Sandy cracked a smile.

"You are the love of my life," he said, beaming.

"You are the love of mine."

It was hotter outside.

"Have you thought any more about my proposal?"

"To move in together?"

"That's the one."

"Yes and no. Yes, I would love to spend every waking moment with you. No, I'm not ready to sell my grandmother house to strangers."

"What about renting it out?"

"I'm not sure I'm ready to pack up and leave. I wish Ellen were here to give me sound advice."

"Babe, memories follow you wherever you go."

"Please don't pressure me," Sandy said flatly.

"Sorry, I want to be with the woman I love."

"These should be happy days; instead I'm congested with despair and worry. I warned her not to get involved in this damn case."

"She had to; it's who she is. It would be like me telling you not to work at River Edge. I promise there will be happy days for us in the future."

"How do you always know what to say to make me feel better? Let's put off moving in together for a while."

"Take all the time you need." He kissed her hand.

"Thank you. It means a lot."

Mark went to take a shower.

The television was on when he came out to the living room, handsome and smelling as good as ever.

"Time for work."

"I'm ready."

He clicked off the television. Sandy opened the door and handed the officer on duty a hot morning coffee. "Here you go, Officer Pick."

"You are a fine woman. Thank you. I hear you're off to work?"

"Yes, before I go crazy."

"Officer County is downstairs waiting to make sure you get to work safe and sound, Miss Miller."

"Appreciate it."

"I'll walk you down."

All three stepped into the elevator.

Chapter Sixty-Six

In spite of the emotional upheaval with Ellen gone, Franki awoke with a calming in her heart, still in the arms of the man she loved. She closed her eyes and prayed for Doc's safe return. Like Sandy, Franki needed to do something with her day. Although Steve had been her rock, stress of not knowing was taken its toll on him, too. Franki didn't disrupt his slumber as she quietly slid out from under the covers. Standing at the kitchen counter, a wave of happy memories washed over her. A lot of subjects were discussed around this very kitchen counter. And Franki longed to have more with Ellen in the future. She pressed the button on the coffee maker and went to the bathroom. She was disturbed by the reflection staring back in the mirror. Her complexion was white as powder with dark circles below her eyes. Her lips were dry and cracked. She applied Vaseline to her lips and ran a brush through her hair. *Not great, but it'll do*, she thought, spreading Crest along her toothbrush. Franki opened the door to see if Steve was awake. He smiled, holding his arms out for her to join him.

"Morning, beautiful."

"Morning, handsome." She smiled, thinking he needed glasses.

"Is that fresh coffee I smell?"

"It sure is." She slipped in beside him.

"How are you this morning?" he asked, squeezing her tight, like he was never going to let go.

"Grateful to have you here."

"No regrets about last night?"

"Not a single one." She beamed.

"Honey, I love you. Trust is a fantastic part of a relationship."

"Absolutely. You know what?"

"What?"

"I do trust you."

"Good."

She kissed his chest. "Feel like doing something today?" she asked.

"Bad news. I have to go into work. There are a couple of job sites I need to check. Make sure my loyal crew is on top of the game. Afterward, I'm free. Why?"

"Remember Gloria Shelby?"

"Need a ride to River Edge?"

"Want to meet her?"

"At the funny farm?" He made a droll face, sitting up on his elbow.

"Steve." She slapped his arm playfully.

"Of course I'll go. When?"

"This afternoon," she said.

"Settled. But we have plenty of time now."

"Plenty of time for what?"

He pulled at the tie of her silk robe, exposing her mouth-watering body. They made love one more time.

Chapter Sixty-Seven

John Barlow was lying in bed, looking deeply into Isabella's big brown eyes, regretting the fact he had to leave his beautiful wife to go to work. He would rather stay immersed in the passionate moment with his wife for the rest of the day. He and Isabella were interrupted by a faint knock at their bedroom door. "Come in!" John shouted. Two beautiful girls with dreadlocks opened the door, excited by the sound of their daddy's voice.

"Daddy, you're home!" Aaron yelled joyfully.

"Not for too much longer, girls. So you better come give Daddy a hug."

The two ran across the bedroom floor and jumped up on the bed.

"I miss you, Daddy." Alix frowned, snuggling in between her mother and father.

"I miss you too." John gave them both a long squeeze.

"Did you catch the bad man?" Aaron asked, sitting next to her father on the opposite side of her sister.

"Not yet, sweetheart."

"He's going to jail when Daddy catches him. Right, Daddy?" Alix confirmed innocently.

"He sure is."

"Okay, ladies, time to get ready for your summer trip," Isabella instructed.

"Where are you going today?"

"The petting zoo," Aaron complained.

"Can't we stay home today? It's not safe to go out—right, Daddy?" Alix said.

"Nice try. I'll drive you to the zoo and pick you up afterward. You two have nothing to worry about."

"Mommy won't let anything happen to you, ladies. Now go and get dressed."

He gently lifted each girl out of bed, making them giggle.

"I get the bathroom first." Alix raced out of the bedroom.

The meeting yesterday with the team and Ivy put a new spin on the investigation. The soil found in the grooves of the tires tracks found behind Ellen's car wasn't city soil. It was Brohduel dirt, found from in the farming district outside of the city. This investigation changed direction like wind. Ivy also informed the team that the car they were searching for was a 1999 Mazda.

During breakfast John looked around the table at his family. Isabella had a sparkle in her eye once more. The girls were as sweet as sugar pie as they mowed down blueberry pancakes, talking a mile a minute. It was nice to experience family life again, even if it was for a few minutes. This was the reason John worked long hours taking bad guys off the street, so his family would be safe.

Isabella felt a twinge of guilt for the way she'd treated her husband lately; she knew he was only doing his job. The few days since Roger escaped had taken their toll on their relationship. John never being home was a big one. She worried that John would burn out if he didn't take better care of himself.

He kissed his girls good-bye first and then his loving wife. All three were still in the doorway waving as John drove down the road.

Chapter Sixty-Eight

Franki sauntered around the house aimlessly, bored to tears, waiting for Steve to arrive. After her shower, she decided on a white, cotton short set with open-toe sandals. The weather was supposed to climb again today into the double digits. She hooked a white shell bracelet around her left ankle. Her toes were painted a pale pink. She felt pretty and vulnerable. She glanced in the mirror and laughed; gone were the days of wearing the same clothes for days. Things certainly had changed. She felt blessed to have everything she'd ever dreamed of and more.

Franki stepped out onto the patio and sat down in one of the patio chairs around the table. The hot sun beat down, warming her from the inside out with its light and beauty. After her smoke, which she did in stressful times only, she remembered the overgrown goldfish in the pond that needed feeding. Relieved to find none of them had gone belly up, Franki sprinkled a few flakes from the can and stood watching the fish surface for nibbles of food. She watered the flowers that needed watering and pulled out a couple of weeds. This nature shit sure wasn't for her, she thought. She headed back for the house. On her way up the stairs, she heard the phone ringing. "Damn." She rushed to answer it.

"Hello, my love," she said, thinking it was Steve.

"I didn't know you cared."

"I'm sorry. Who is this?" Franki's face flushed.

"Don't you read the papers? I would have thought you'd be more concerned with the current events in your city."

"Is this some kind of joke?"

"Here's a hint. I have something—or should I say someone—you want."

"Like what?" Franki played along.

"Isn't there a loved one missing?"

Franki froze, her brain catching up with her emotions. "You! You bastard. Where's Ellen?" Franki shouted, quickly regaining control. Her heart thundered angrily as she gripped the phone tighter. "Listen, you maggot, where is she?"

"That's not very nice." Roger laughed. "I'm hurt that you would speak to me like this."

"Let me talk to Ellen," Franki demanded.

"I can't do that."

"Quit playing games. What do you want?"

"I already have what I want."

"Stop! I want you to give Ellen back."

"I'll say when the game is over." His voice sent chills down her spine.

"Is Ellen alive?"

"In time, you'll know the answer, sweet Franki. And how is poor Captain Barlow and his two bumbling detectives? They can't seem to find their way out of the dark with a flashlight. They've been working endlessly trying to find their lost teammate," he said, snickering.

"Stop fucking around and tell me where she is, you piece of shit."

"Shame on you. I was going to give you a hint ... but since you've been so disrespectful, I've changed my mind."

"I'm sorry. Ellen needs to come home, Roger," Franki pleaded.

"Next time you'll be nicer to me. That is, if you want your precious doctor back. Alive."

"Is Ellen alive?" Franki screamed into the receiver. Dead air swept across the phone line.

A minute after she hung up, the phone rang again.

"Roger, I'm sorry."

"Who is Roger?" Steve asked, wondering if he dialed the right number.

"Steve. Oh my god, he just called. Roger called here. He knew who I was!" she cried, running out of breath.

"When?"

"A minute ago—if that."

"Call Captain Barlow Franki and tell him. I'm ten minutes away."

"Okay." She could feel her voice shaking.

Franki's hands trembled as she keyed in the numbers to the police station. The officer on duty connected her to Captain Barlow's cell.

"Captain Barlow speaking."

"Captain, it's Franki Martin. I just spoke to Roger Taut. He called the house phone."

"What? When?"

"Not even five minutes ago." She looked at her watch.

"Did he say if Ellen's alive?"

"He wouldn't say."

"Okay. Franki, where did he phone from?"

"I don't know. Ellen doesn't have caller ID."

"Hang up and check with 411 and call me right back."

"Okay, sir." She did what Captain Barlow asked and called him back immediately.

"Sir, the number is 555-9090."

"Just a second." He took the phone away from his ear. "Dan, write this number and find its location now. Roger called Ellen's place five minutes ago."

"On it." Dan dashed out of the conference room.

"Franki, stay put. I'm sending Barry Lundman and Chris Beach over; they're recording experts. I'll get them to put a trace on the line in case he calls again."

"Sir, he wouldn't tell me anything."

"He's a cocky bastard, Franki."

"Do you think he'll call back?"

"Let's hope so."

"Stay put. The detectives should be there shortly."

"Sir, by him not telling me …"

"Don't even entertain that thought. Ellen is alive, and we are going to get her back."

Franki smiled. "Thank you, sir."

An hour later, Dan returned.

"What did you find?"

"He called Franki from the pay phone across the street, sir."

"You're kidding."

"He just gave us the big fuck you, sir."

The captain threw his pen across the room, pissed. "Goddamn it!"

"Balls of steal or he wants to get caught."

"Not likely, Dan. Any news from Jim?"

Jim was out driving around the countryside searching for a Mazda.

"Nothing yet." Dan took a sip of his ice tea.

The captain's phone rang, sending his heart into a spasm. "Barlow."

"John, it's Tomus Cleaver."

"Good day."

"I don't know how to say this easily, so I'm just going to say it."

The captain braced himself for impact. "Give it to me."

"You have twenty-four hours to catch these killers before the FBI steps in."

"Serious?"

"Afraid so. Here's the bad news. You are to hand over everything you have. You and your team will no longer be needed."

"Like hell we will. Why?"

"Ellen's disappearance has brought national media attention, John. And now our newest victim, Rachelle Baum. They have concerns about you and Detective Kape. And the body count is still increasing. The public doesn't like being afraid, John."

"And whose damn fault is that? You were the one who wouldn't allow us to warn the public. Maybe if we had, we might have found the guy. Instead, you made us work under the blanket of deception. And now the FBI wants to come into my jurisdiction and take over my investigation." John shook his head. "Why the concern about Dan?"

Dan shoved his hands into his pockets, giving a curious stare at his superior.

"He's a relative of the surviving victim, John."

"Sister of his ex-wife. So what?"

"The Federal Bureau of Investigation feels you guys are too close to this case now to make any headway."

"Dan's judgment is just as good now as it was in the beginning. He's an excellent cop, and you know it. How can we not be emotional? Jesus, you haven't witnessed the damage this monster leaves in his wake. We're willing to work alongside the FBI, but I'll be damned if you think we're walking away from this investigation."

"John."

"Give the uppity ups a message."

"What's that?"

"Tell them to go to go hell for starters." The captain could feel his blood pressure boiling in his veins. "We'll find the serial killer, so tell them not to pack."

"Don't let pride get in the way of a good administrative decision."

"This administrative decision is bullshit, and you know it. The autopsies we've attended, not to mention the grief and sorrow on the faces of the parents we've had to tell. Don't tell us how we should feel."

"Twenty-four hours, John."

"Oh and by the way, Tomus … fuck you!" He threw his cell phone on the desk.

Dan stood, waiting to be filled in. "Sir?"

"We're off the case in twenty-four hours if we don't catch Gertrude and Taut."

"Reason?" Dan asked, shocked.

"For me, it's Ellen, for you, it's the latest victim, Rachelle. According to the FBI, our emotions could compromise this investigation."

"Bullshit. Where did this lovely order come from?"

"Quantico—the top of the heap."

"I'm not going anywhere," Dan stated flatly.

"Me either."

"They'll have to drag me to jail if they want to get rid of me."

"I'll be right with you." Captain Barlow looked like he'd had enough.

"What now, sir?"

"Get out there and follow up on these leads." He handed Dan a piece of paper.

Dan was fuming as he walked out to his car. There was no way in hell these pompous assholes were going to push him aside. He promised Rachelle he'd find the animal that did that to her, and he intended to keep that promise.

Chapter Sixty-Nine

Dan didn't get very far before he was radioed back to headquarters. He rushed down the corridor, eyeing his superior. Dan didn't have to ask; he already understood why he got called back

"Captain?"

"Homicide, 224 Bees Road."

"How old, sir?"

"Nineteen, twenty tops."

"Same style?"

"Didn't ask."

"I'll ride with you, sir."

The two hurried out to the black Nissan Altima. Dan blew out a gust of pent-up air.

"Twenty-three hours and forty-two minutes left."

"Not a lot of time."

"No shit, sir. Can those pricks really kick us off this investigation?"

"Yes, but were not supposed to take it personally."

"How the fuck not! It's just our friends and careers."

"That's the problem; we're too close to the case. Emotions are overriding our intelligence," John said, hostility flaring out his nostrils.

"That's such a load of crap. You already know my opinion on Tomus asshole Cleaver."

"Politics, my Danny boy."

"So we have to find this mother like yesterday. How? Who the fuck knows." Dan was talking more to himself than to Captain Barlow.

Captain Barlow could feel the muscles tense as they approached Bees Road. The captain parked in front of a four-plex. Not a bad neighborhood; he looked around. Two cruisers and an ambulance with its lights flashing and its siren quiet waited for the command to take the body to the morgue. A slew of vultures with microphones and cameras stood on the other side of the road, yelling questions at Captain Barlow as he exited the car. A few concerned neighbors stood holding hands. Dan watched his boss struggle for composure.

"Pretty bad when everyone not involved gets here before us," Dan complained.

"Dial the crime lab," John ordered.

"Right away, sir." Dan began keying in the numbers, eyeing a frenzy of reporters.

"What's up, my friend?" Derk asked, almost happy.

"Your services are needed."

"How bad?"

"Don't know. Just arrived—224 Bees Road."

"Give me ten. Got to round up my crew. They're all hiding in the lab somewhere."

"Don't blame them."

"Yeah really. Chow."

Dan slipped under the crime tape and over to Captain Barlow. "Forensics is on their way."

Dan nodded to Sammy, who was coming toward them. Trex and Fritz were moving spectators back from the yellow line.

"What's the damage?"

"The victim is dead. Her parents are standing right there." Sammy pointed to the distraught couple inside the tape.

"Lucky parents to discover their daughter's body." Sammy winced, shaking his head.

Captain Barlow vacillated between anger and pity.

"The victim was scheduled for a family reunion. When she didn't show up, the mom and dad drove over. Using his spare key, he let himself in."

"What a thing to see," Dan replied.

"There's vomit on the floor belonging to the father."

"You need more than a strong stomach to embrace what that monster leaves behind," Dan said, flashing a look of anger.

Dan lit a smoke, watching Captain Barlow make his way to the grieving parents. Loud sobs of unbearable anguish echoed above the noise of the nervous crowd.

"Excuse me, I'm Captain Barlow. I'm very sorry for your loss."

"Henry Baston, my wife, Kaylie."

Kaylie remained hidden against her husband's chest, obviously in shock.

"Mr. Baston, you were the first to find your daughter?"

"Yes, I found my Sadie. When she didn't come to the family reunion, I came over. She had plans with her friends last night, so I assumed she slept in. I called, but there was no answer. She likes to sleep late after a night of fun with her friends."

"Most young adults do." Captain gave a sympathetic smile.

"My baby's been murdered," he murmured.

"I might need to ask you more questions later."

"I'm going to take my wife home now."

"The officer will escort you to your car. We'll be in touch."

"I have nothing else to tell you, Captain Barlow."

"Did you touch anything inside the house, Mr. Baston?"

"My daughter. I didn't know she was dead until I saw the blood. Oh my God!" Mr. Baston rambled.

"If you wouldn't mind, Mr. Baston, could you write a list of Sadie's friends? I'd like to talk with them."

"Sure. I'll find out who she chummed around with last night."

"That would be a great help. Thank you. Sammy!" Captain Barlow shouted.

The officer ran over to his superior. "Yes, sir."

"Escort Mr. and Mrs. Baston to their car safely."

"No problem."

Henry held his wife close, protecting her from the gaggle of reporters.

The captain felt his chest constricting, fighting for breath. The young victim was spread eagle on the bed, saturated in her own blood. One horrific image a father should never have had to witness. Her body temperature indicated she was murdered sometime after midnight. Her right arm was broken at the elbow. She was naked from the waist down. Sadie had defensive wounds running up and down both her arms. The dark bruising around her inner thighs indicated that she'd been brutally raped—with what? Only an autopsy would tell. Her left arm was still tied to the rail of the headboard. The ligature burns around her ankles showed he had freed her after the assault. Sadie looked like a discarded mannequin. This time the killer didn't disfigure the victim's face. He had changed his modus operandi. Pretty girl, sky-blue eyes, full lips, and bleached blonde hair with funky streaks of orange.

The captain thought about his two little girls. Henry Baston's life would be forever altered. A wave of relief almost made him choke up, knowing his family was safe.

Dan viewed the young victim, feeling his own pains of sadness. Sadie didn't deserve to die like this; she had her whole life ahead of her.

"Dan, we need to know where this victim went last night. I want you to trace her every step. I don't care if she talked to a corner store clerk, document it."

"Can I grab Sammy?"

"Sure. And if there are officers out there with their thumbs up their ass, recruit and brief them. Go!"

"No problem," Dan said, relieved to be out of the bedroom.

Dan ordered two spare officers to start questioning people within a two-mile radius. Dan started knocking on doors as he made his way down the block. Three quarters of an hour later, he returned frustrated as hell. As long as he lived on this planet, he would never understand the human race. How could anyone not hear the screams of someone being murdered? Were they deaf and blind? Turning to go back toward the four-plex, he saw a commotion on the lawn.

"Take it easy, Miss."

Officer Trex struggled with the young woman.

Dan jumped in to help. "Calm down, Miss. This is a secured area. What do you want?"

"Is it Sadie? Tell me my friend isn't dead!" Black tears streaked down her face.

"What's your name?"

"Jill Callwell. I'm a friend. Can I see Sadie?" she begged, wiping her eyes with the back of her hand. "Is Sadie okay?"

"When did you see her last?"

"Last night. We went to Slammers."

"Were you with her all night?"

"Almost."

"Almost. What does that mean?" Dan led Jill away from the noise.

"Tell me everything, Jill."

"We went to Slammers around ten to party. And we did. It was around eleven thirty when I decided to leave. There wasn't enough action for me."

"Action?"

"Not enough men to go around, Detective. Sadie didn't want to leave. The party is never over for Sadie. She lived in the moment. I had to remind her about the family reunion this morning. That convinced her she should go home but not before her last beer was empty. When she was halfway done, the waitress brought another round to our table, telling us it was from the blond at the bar. Free beers—why not." She tried to smile. "Later on, he walked over to our table, introducing himself."

"His name?"

"Todd Lynex. Sadie invited him to join us. He seemed real nice and very intelligent. This guy was into her. I felt like the third man out and decided to head home."

"Was she upset?"

"She was the fun girl. I told her the bus was leaving. That's when Todd jumped in. He said he'd make sure she got home safe. To my surprise, when I was ready to go, so were they."

"Describe Todd."

"Good looking, well built, wore wire-frame glasses. I answered your questions, now where is Sadie?"

"I'm sorry, Jill. Sadie is dead. Did she have an ex, an enemy?"

Jill's hand flew to her mouth, muffling her cries. Her hazel eyes darkened with pain.

"Jenson, Jenson Shake was her last flame."

"Got an address?"

"Twelve Porter Lane. He lives with his parents."

"Was this Jenson a jealous fellow?"

"No. But he was at Slammers last night."

"Did he leave the same time you did?"

"No. He usually closes a bar. That's why they broke up."

"You said she likes to party too?"

"Not as much as him. Oh my God, she's really dead," she whispered, the reality slowly sinking in. "I should have driven her home."

"Ever see this Todd before?"

"First time. He seemed so nice."

"Remember anything about the vehicle he drove?"

"It was a Mazda, dark color, could have been blue or black. I'm not sure; Slammers' parking lot isn't the brightest at night." She rummaged in her backpack.

"Shit—where are they?" Jill shook her pack fiercely.

"What are you looking for?"

"A damn smoke."

"Have one of mine." Dan handed her one.

"A real lung bleeder." Jill plopped down on the grass, inhaling one deep cloud of smoke after the other.

"Do you want someone to drive you home?"

"I'll be okay. I just need a couple of minutes." Her bottom lip began quivering as she closed her eyes, trying to fight back the sadness.

Dan rushed back inside, informing everyone that it was a blue or black Mazda they were looking for.

Chapter Seventy

Ellen had no idea how long Roger intended to keep her alive. She knew the only power she wielded over him was not to show fear. And so far she managed to accomplish just that. In every inch of her body, she felt pain. She drifted in and out of slumber, waiting for Roger to come back. Gertrude's corpse was sprawled on the dust-covered wooden floor a few feet from her door. The foul odor of decomposing flesh seeped its way into her room under the door. With the house locked up and no air circulating, it wouldn't take long for a corpse to quickly decay. The stench would be intolerable. She struggled to sit up, hearing the doorknob wiggle. Roger entered. The rotten stench assaulted her senses like a hot flame. She gasped, putting her hand over her mouth. The pent-up aggression in his eyes was gone; he'd killed again.

"Hello, Doctor," he said cheerily.

"Hi."

"Hungry?"

"Hungry, thirsty, and want my freedom."

"Which one?" he teased.

"Thirsty."

He brought his hand from behind his back, holding up bottled water. "Ask me nicely."

"I'm in no mood for your childish games."

"Guess you're not thirsty."

"Please. May I have the water, Roger?" She choked on her humility.

"Okay." He threw the plastic bottle on the bed. Ellen twisted the top off and downed half the bottle in one gulp.

"You were thirsty," he proclaimed, surprised.

"Leave anyone in these horrible conditions, and they're bound to dry up."

"It is warm in here." He was acting like everything was right with the world. And in his demented thought process, it was.

"Where've you been?"

"Out playing."

"With who?"

"You know, Doctor, women are so gullible. Especially the one last night. Young, dumb, and full of cum."

"I assume she's dead?"

"Than a doornail."

"What was her name?"

"Sammy, Salley, Sadie." He paused for a second. "That's it—Sadie."

"How old?"

"Young enough to know better."

"You murdered a child, you mean."

"She was no child, I assure you. A little whore that I had to put down. Trust me; I did the tramp a favor."

"A favor?" Ellen shouted. "Am I a whore, Roger?"

"No, Doctor."

"What makes me different?"

"Morals, values, old age." He laughed, taking a seat in the rocking chair next to the bed. "And you were a faithful wife."

"You never gave Sadie a chance to find true love and be faithful. How do you know she wouldn't have turned out like me? You're playing God."

"I administer punishment on filth."

"Punishment? Try saying what it really is—murder. You're no better than the pig farmer, Paul Bernardo, and the rest of the sick pricks that prey on the innocent for their own selfish gain. You are nothing more than a sick pervert who likes to get his balls rocked by murder."

"I'm more powerful than those guys. I'll never get caught," he gloated.

"Sexual gratification is nothing more than a pervert with a taste for torture. And one day real soon, you will be arrested and put in prison, because there is no way I will defend you."

"Women are easy to seduce and easier to kill. The agent woman wasn't my idea; that was Gertrude's. She thought by killing her it would throw the detectives off the trail. And it did. The rest, well they were sluts spreading dirty diseases. This last slut only took me an hour. One hour to buy her a couple of drinks, get her in my car, and go off to her place for some fun. What does that tell you, Doctor?"

"Being gullible and trusting was their only mistake."

"She won't do that again, will she?" He laughed, staring down at his jeans.

"I guess not. You ended her life."

"I did." He puffed out his chest.

"You manipulated Sadie into believing that you were a good guy? It's nothing to puff your chest out about. She was young and naïve, and you took full advantage of her, just like your parents did to you."

"You're wrong, Doctor. I made all that shit up so I wouldn't have to go to jail. I fooled the infamous Dr. Ellen Smith. I never had sex with my mother while my step- daddy watched. What kind of people do you think we were?"

Ellen felt like all the air had been sucked out of her lungs. Lightheadedness invaded her mind. She shuddered. Had she been tricked?

"That little tramp got in a car with a man she barely knew."

"You're telling me that you weren't abused?"

"I wasn't abused, Doctor. I told you—everything I said was to stay out of prison. I fooled you. End of story."

Ellen knew she wasn't going to get anything else out of Roger, for the time being anyway.

"How old was Sadie, or did you even bother to ask?" Ellen bit back a tear.

"Twenty. Her pubic hair wasn't as coarse as the others. Hot little body." He licked his lips.

"You disgust me. How did you take her life?"

"A little stabbing. Don't worry, she died quick." He was clearly proud of himself.

"The detectives are onto your little game."

"Those idiots couldn't get through a snowstorm with a plow."

"This time you're going to prison. And I won't influence the jury's decision."

"Come on, you'll be on the stand spouting out all your knowledge about psychopathic insanity bullshit. The jury will send me back to River Edge because I'm insane, remember?"

"You lied to me, remember?" Ellen smirked.

"It won't matter."

"I won't defend you this time. This isn't about insanity any longer. The courts frown upon premeditated murder."

"The system doesn't place the mentally ill in cages; it isn't human," he argued, ignoring her threat. "Oh, I spoke with a friend of yours." He swiftly changed direction of the conversation. "And who would that be?" Ellen tried to hide her alarm.

"Relax. It was a telephone conversation."

"Which friend?"

"The famous writer. I called to see how she was doing since no one's heard from you."

"Did you tell her I'm okay?"

"Not quite." He shrugged.

"What happened?"

"That girl's got some hot temper. And you say I need counseling?"

"Tell me what she said."

"She called me a maggot, piece of shit—"

Ellen burst out laughing. She knew how Franki would react to his mind games. "She called you names."

"It's not funny."

"To know Franki, it is."

"She told me you'd better not be hurt."

"It's a little late for that. She's one girl you shouldn't defy. You believe you're dangerous?" Ellen cocked her head, arching a brow.

"Is that a challenge, Doctor?"

"No, a promise. She'll cut your fucking heart out and shove it down your throat given the chance. You've killed two of her loved ones already. Franki doesn't take too kindly to that. You see, Roger, Franki's had a troubled childhood too."

"Maybe I should make an example out of her?"

Even though Ellen's stomach plummeted, she forced herself to laugh again.

"Something funny?"

"She'd slit your throat before you had the chance to do her harm. The one thing she has on you is loyalty and love. Oh, and if I forgot to mention, she survived years on the streets."

"And that makes her stronger?"

"No, just more dangerous. She has something to fight for. Don't let her beauty deceive you."

"Fine!" He groaned.

"Now what do you plan to do with me?"

"Set you free."

"I'm free to leave?" she asked, excited.

"You can leave tonight. I don't want you found right away. I need time to find a new hangout. This shack is old and smelly thanks to mouthpiece out there on the floor."

"Nightfall works. Why did you kidnap me?"

"It wasn't my idea. I know you don't believe that I'm capable of feeling, but I do like you, Doctor."

"What about Gertrude?"

"Let it rot. The system stamps me mad, and she sets me free to hunt humans."

"Did she ever mean anything to you?"

"No. Gertrude was a desperate woman searching for a desperate means of revenge. Funny how it all worked out. She's dead, I'm free, and you're alive."

"Did you plan to kill her from the start?"

"Since I first laid eyes on the ugly bitch. She had a bad disposition." He started laughing hysterically.

"It smells in here." Ellen turned up her nose.

"Do you need to use the bathroom?"

"Yes."

"Up then." He motioned her off the bed. "Hurry. All this killing makes a man tired."

Ellen gave him a surly glare.

"I would strongly advise you to get rest too. You have a long walk back to Victoria."

"In my condition?"

"Yep."

"Where are we?"

"The country. I have faith you'll survive."

"Christ, I can hardly breathe let alone walk."

"That's why I suggest rest."

"You are despicable."

Ellen made her way down the hall to the bathroom. This time Roger turned around, respecting her privacy.

"I'll be a few minutes."

"That's gross. I don't need a play by play please."

"You call something as natural as having a bowel movement gross, and the carnage you leave behind isn't? You are crazier than a shit-house rat."

He made the mistake of glancing over his shoulder.

"Turn around so I can do my business," she ordered.

"Don't be too long. I'm tired."

"I'll be as long as it takes." Ellen sat on the toilet, grunting her heart out, knowing it made Roger cringe.

Minutes later, she flushed the toilet.

"Whew!" He fanned his face. "Can't say your shit doesn't stink."

"No worse than the rotting corpse out there."

"A few more hours, Doctor." He helped her back to the bedroom.

A notorious serial killer had spared her life.

Chapter Seventy-One

Ellen was awakened as promised. Her eyes felt thick from the deep humidity that had settled in the room. A flush of adrenalin raced in her veins; this was it. At last she was free. A streak of light crossed the floor from the hallway. The disgusting odor wafting off the dead body had become so putrid she could feel acid climbing up the back of her throat. She swallowed hard, pushing its bitterness back into her stomach.

"It's time to go."

She gagged, slipping on her low-heal pumps. They weren't exactly hiking shoes, but they'd have to do. Ellen had no clue how long it would take her to get home. The one thing she was certain of was she needed to get away from this house and breathe in fresh air.

"I need to use the bathroom, and can I have a bottle of water to take with me?"

"No. Time is your freedom, Doctor."

Ellen glared at him. "And yours will be shortly lived, I assure you. Roger, you can't send me without water. I'll die."

"Survival of the fittest."

"I'll get home," she said, determined.

"I know you will. That's why you're still alive."

At the front door, Roger gave her a kiss the on the cheek. The mere touch of his lips against her cheek made her skin crawl.

"You're okay, Doctor Smith," he said, smiling.

"For god's sake, turn yourself in. Nobody else needs to die. Roger, it's not your fault you're sick."

"I was born this way."

"You know better."

"You get home now." He opened the door.

Ellen stepped out into the cool night air. She coughed and choked as she gulped in the crisp air. She took one last glance back at the number on the house, 412, before making her way out into the darkness. The moon was hiding behind a thick wall of moving clouds. She stopped at the end of the driveway, listening intensely for any sign of life that could point her in the right direction. Thick black air was all around her. Her faith would be tested this night. She made a left turn into the darkness of nothingness. She struggled for balance as she hiked the gravel road. It was like walking blind.

A few yards down the road, she tripped over a rock and went down hard. Her palms stung from tiny pebbles imbedded into her skin. It was too black to see if she was bleeding or not. She cursed as loud as she could, hoping someone would hear her. No luck. She pushed herself back up to her feet, trying to get her wind back. Although she slept most of the day, her physical strength was being tested due to the injuries.

She had no idea if she was heading further into the country or toward the city. Every joint, bone, and muscle ached. It was more and more difficult to breathe because of her broken ribs. Already exhausted, she would not quit. Every twenty or thirty steps, she stopped and rested. Faces of the people she loved made her press on. This was going to be one hell of a reunion. *And a hot shower.* She smiled through swollen lips.

Suddenly, Ellen spotted headlights coming toward her. With all the energy she could muster, she waved wildly for the driver to stop. The car slowed to a stop.

"Help me please. I need to get to Victoria."

"Doctor, really."

Her heart heaved, recognizing his voice. "Where the hell am I?" she screamed at him.

"Hang onto that anger, and you'll find your way home."

Ellen dropped to her knees and began to cry. She was shattered. "Roger, please? I don't know if I'll make it." She begged for the first time.

"You can do this," he coached.

"I'm in the middle of nowhere. I don't even know if I'm going in the right direction."

"Have faith."

The second Ellen realized Roger was going to do nothing for her, she rose up to her feet like a woman on a mission. "Fuck you, asshole."

He laughed. "That's my girl."

She started walking. Without a word of encouragement, he drove off, and she watched the taillights vanish into the darkness. She was alone again.

Ellen couldn't remember ever hating someone as much as she hated Taut. A while later, she began staggering, not knowing if she was on the road or shoulder. Out of breath and hurting all over, she could go no more. Once again, she fell to her knees and cried out. This time she didn't get up.

By the time Ellen opened her eyes, the darkness had turned to light. Her body shivered with warmth. She'd made it through the night. The daylight would guide her to safety. The weather was already starting to get hot. Ellen had to find a farmhouse soon, or surely she would pass out from dehydration. In the next couple of hours, the temperature would ascend into the double digits. After surviving the night, she would be damned if she was going to die on some dirt road where no one would find her.

She was daydreaming of sitting on the swing, outside in the garden with Sandy and Franki. Then down she went. A cloud of dust flew up, blinding her. She tasted dirt that was making her cough. Her eyes burned, and her throat was so parched that she retched. She tried to spit, but nothing came out. Dizzy and nauseous and determined as ever, she got to her feet.

Another mile down the road, Ellen collapsed. Her ankles were engorged over her shoes. She so badly wanted to take off her shoes, but it would take her forever to travel gravel barefoot. Tiny wheezes were all her lungs could take. It took a few moments before recapturing her equanimity. She looked out, spotting a farmhouse approximately a football field away. Ellen rubbed her eyes with dirty hands, adding more dirt to her already blurred vision. With the last bit of strength, she started limping to the mailbox. She'd made it, but once more she buckled. The sun was so hot she could feel her skin cooking beneath her clothes. The skin on her face felt like it was on fire. Ellen began to cry; she needed to get to the front door of the farmhouse, but how? *I'll crawl*, she thought. Inch by inch, she pulled herself over dirt and sharp stones. It hurt like hell, but she did it. Then she heard what sounded like a dog. Dragging herself up the porch steps; she began pounding on the door with everything she had left.

Finally the farmer opened the door. He looked aghast when he saw Ellen.

"Help me please," she cried.

Jessie the German Sheppard licked Ellen's face with love. She tried to laugh, but nothing came out of her throat.

"Ma'am, are you ..."

"Help?"

"Oh Christ, what do you need?" He pushed Jessie back in the house.

"Wa ... ter," Ellen whispered.

The farmer flew to the kitchen and got Ellen water. He held the glass to her mouth while she guzzled.

"What's going on, Marve? I heard the dog barking his fool head off earlier." His wife's hand flew to her mouth when she eyed Marve hunched over the injured woman.

"Oh my good god!" Mary screamed at the bloodied sight on her porch.

"It's okay, dear. Help me get her inside." Marve and Mary gently carried Ellen to the couch and softly laid her down. The dog immediately plopped down beside the couch. Mary removed Ellen's shoes.

"Thank you."

"What's your name, ma'am?" Marve asked softly.

"She's that woman, Marve—you know?" Mary said.

Marve gave a restless stare.

"Ellen Smith," she said, gaining strength in her voice.

"She's the doctor that's been missing."

"I need to use your phone."

"You need a hospital," Marve said.

"Please. I need to call Captain Barlow," Ellen said.

"I'll call him. You rest." Marve disappeared into the kitchen to call 911.

"Emergency 911."

"My name is Marve Peerson."

"Mr. Peerson, what seems to be the problem?"

"I found that doctor that's missing. She needs a hospital, but she won't go until Captain Barlow is notified."

"You do understand it's a felony for pranking this office."

"What the hell. I have the doctor in my living room on my damn couch, lady. Now put me through to that captain fellow."

"Hold the line, sir."

"Glad I'm not dying here. Gosh." Marve heard a click.

"Police department. Detective Dan Kape speaking."

"My name is Marve Peerson. I have the doctor that's been missing. She's on my couch and needs medical attention. She wants the captain to know she's here."

"You say you have Doctor Smith in your living room?"

"You guys all deaf? I said yes already." Marve took the phone from his ear and stared into the earpiece, exasperated.

"I need the address please."

"She needs to go the hospital, not visitors." Marve rolled his eyes.

"That won't be necessary. We're sending an ambulance, sir."

"Oh! Why didn't you say that to begin with? She's at 1200 Ilses Road, a mile and half down Ilses Road. Got it?"

"We'll be there as soon as we can."

"Hurry." Marve hung up and strolled quickly back into the living room.

"You must be pretty important 'cause they're sending the cavalry."

"Whom did you speak with?"

"Dan Kape."

Ellen smiled warmly. "Thank you both." Ellen broke down crying. Her ordeal was finally over.

"Come on now. You're all right." Fighting back his own emotion, he handed Ellen a tissue. "Need some more water?" He sniffed.

"Please."

"Ma, go get the doctor more water."

Mary winked at Ellen before getting up. "He's good at giving orders, I'll tell you that."

Marve pulled up a chair, getting closer. That weather-beaten leather skin couldn't hide the tenderness of his heart.

"How you feelin'?"

"Thankful."

"Looks like you took a pretty bad beating."

"I did." She smiled through swollen lips.

"Looks like he got the best of the fight."

"He tried."

The farmer admired her feistiness.

A few minutes later, Mary appeared carrying a tray with water, juice, fresh fruit from their garden, crackers, and cheese. She sat the tray on the coffee table and began gently wiping the dirt from Ellen face and hands. The dog instantly sat up when he smelled the food but was ordered to lie back down just as fast.

"Thanks."

"You and the other woman are the only two survivors."

"Do you know her name?"

"Rachelle Baum," Mary answered.

Ellen sucked on a piece of orange that never tasted so good.

"Is he as scary as they say?" Mary asked nervously.

"He's the epitome of evil."

"I think the cops should hang him high in a tree for everyone to see," Marve said.

"Some say he's not human," Mary said.

"He's psychologically sick for sure."

"Hang him high. Hell, I'll donate a tree."

Ellen winced, chuckling at Marve's dry sense of humor. Yet she believed he'd be the first in line to witness Taut's execution.

"Is it true that their brains ain't right? 'Cause if it's true, all the more reason to get rid of 'em. Why should taxpayers have to fork out their hard-earned money to keep these types alive? When we already know they can't be made right?"

"Because we're human. Being human separates us from guys like Taut, the pig farmer, Bernardo," Ellen said.

"Well that's all fine and dandy but—"

"Enough, Marve. Can't you see she's tired?" Mary scolded her husband.

"Sorry, ma'am."

"It's okay. I do understand how you feel."

"Can I ask one more question?"

"Sure."

"Does he have a partner?"

"Had. He killed her."

"So it was that nurse?"

"Yes."

"And he killed her?" Marve was looking even more puzzled.

"Yes."

"Remember, I got trees and a rope." He shook his head and left to get more coffee.

Chapter Seventy-Two

Dan bolted down the hall to the captain's office. He swung open the door without knocking.

"They found her, sir."

"Who?" John asked. startled from the abrupt interruption.

"Ellen. Doctor Smith."

"Where?" He jumped to his feet.

"Twelve hundred Ilses Road."

"Way out there."

"We can radio an ambulance on our way."

The two rushed out the door, meeting Jim who was coming back from taking a leak.

"Jim, let's go. They found Ellen."

"Holy shit, she's alive!" Jim screeched, running on his partner's heels. "How is she?"

"Peerson said she's injured and needs a hospital."

"I'll call right away. Address?" Jim keyed in numbers as he ran. Jim radioed an ambulance with his cell phone.

Captain Barlow took his car. Dan and Jim left in his Camaro. Two cruisers followed close behind. This time, lights flashed and sirens screamed as they sped through the streets, heading out to the country.

Dan just happened to glance in the mirror, seeing the ambulance in tow. Excitement filled their souls.

On the way, Jim suggested Ellen's friends be called. Dan thought that was a great idea and began thumbing his first call.

The phone rang twice before sleepy Franki answered.

"Miss Martin?"

"Yes."

"It's Detective Kape here." Franki sprung up, suddenly wide awake. "I have good news. Your friend Doctor Smith is alive."

"Thank God." She breathed a sigh of relief. "Can I see her?"

"I'll let you know when."

"Thank you, Detective. I'll phone Sandy."

"Talk to you soon."

"Bye, Detective." Franki threw the phone beside her and leaped on Steve, telling him the good news. Afterward, she called Sandy. They laughed and cried as Franki shared the good news. They couldn't wait to see Ellen again.

Chapter Seventy-Three

The circus had come to the country. The sirens echoed through the trees and could be heard for miles. Dan couldn't see the caravan of media behind the ambulance with the swirling dust. But he'd know soon enough. He did spot the helicopter buzzing overhead. The detectives saw brake lights through a cloud of dust. Jim braked and followed Captain Barlow down the long driveway. By the time the reporters drove up, the team was already on the step.

Marve ushered the law enforcement inside before Jessie decided to protect his territory by chewing a leg off an eager journalists. Ellen sat upright, sipping water with a handmade afghan wrapped around her shoulders.

"Ellen." John held her hand, sitting down beside her.

"John." She smiled with swollen lips and a fractured cheekbone.

"Am I happy to see you, woman. How are you?"

"I look worse than I am, really."

"I beg to differ."

"You would."

"Marve Peerson." He extended his hand to John.

"John Barlow. You found Ellen?"

"Yes, sir." He put his shoulders proudly back. "Found her on the porch. I wanted to take her to the hospital, but she wasn't havin' any part of that until she talked to you."

"She's stubborn."

"Got that right. Mary, you got nothin' on this lady."

The room came alive with loud, happy laughter.

"I'm Dan Kape, Mr. Peerson. We spoke earlier on the phone."

"Call me Marve, and this is my wife, Mary."

All three launched into friendly handshakes. Dan politely made his way over to Ellen.

"Ellen." He leaned down, kissing her hand.

"Dan." She winked.

"You scared the hell out of us."

"I wasn't having a lot of fun either." She tried to laugh.

Jim joined the circle around Ellen.

"May I?" He leaned down, gently giving her a welcome back.

"What I want to know is how in the hell did you get away?" Jim asked.

"He let me go."

"The serial killer just let you walk away?"

"Yes, last night."

"What—did you drive him nuts?" John asked, winking.

"I tried."

"You're pretty beaten up," Dan said.

"I'll live."

"Is that your blood?" Dan pointed to the dark stains on her shirt and pants.

"It's mine."

"Thought so."

"I got off easy, guys. Gertrude Caller is dead."

"No loyalty among animals." Jim straightened his tie.

"The ambulance is here, Ellen."

"I don't need an ambulance, John." She protested.

"Like hell you don't."

"No time, guys."

"Bullshit, Doctor," Dan corrected.

"This time you're outvoted," Jim said.

"They're on their way in," Marve informed, looking out his window.

"Listen, guys. I know where the house is."

"You aren't going anywhere until the medics check you out. If they say you need a hospital, then you're going to the hospital. That's an order."

"I have a cracked rib, no big deal, and a few cuts and bruises," she lied.

"This isn't negotiable."

"I'm the only one who can show you where his hideout is."

"And you'll be no good in a coma either. You have some serious injuries, Ellen, and you're not as young as you would like to believe."

"John, please—we're squandering valuable time."

Marve showed the attendants in. All five men moved out of their way. It was obvious Ellen needed to be hospitalized. She yelped as they laid her back onto the stretcher. Andy, the good-looking medic, placed Ellen in a neck brace first. Once the examination was complete, everyone listened for the verdict.

"Doctor Smith has two broken ribs that I can find. An X-ray will show more. I believe her arm is fractured above the elbow. She's staved and dehydrated. She needs stitches in her forehead and lip and has a slight fracture in her cheekbone. Her feet are distended as we can all see. And this doctor has a whole lot of cuts and bruises. We'll know more after she's examined at the hospital. In my opinion, we should be taking her with us."

"Yeah, well, that's your damn opinion." She struggled to get off the stretcher. "Get this contraption of my neck. Give me something for the pain. I'll go to the hospital as soon as John and I are finished. I'll even stay overnight for observation."

"Can she survive a couple more hours?"

"She made it this far. I don't know how."

"Mary, can I have more water to go please?"

"You can have whatever you want."

"I need my head examined to even be thinking you should come along," John said, shaking his head.

Ellen was out of the neck brace, anxious to get going. Mary loaned her a pair of sandals. This time, vengeance was in her eyes.

All four stepped out onto the porch.

"Ellen, you stay close. They'll be on you like a pack of wild dogs. Dan, stall them with little information. Enough to get us cleared of this place."

"Gotcha!"

The captain tucked Ellen under his arm and whisked her to the car. The detectives watched the car drive away and started walking toward the gaggle of journalists. He was instantly bombarded with questions. A dozen questions into the news symposium, Jim whispered in his partner's ear, "Time to go, buddy."

They headed toward the Camaro.

The reporters hurried to where Marve and Mary were standing. They had a moment in the spotlight as Jim took off out of the driveway.

Chapter Seventy-Four

The team raced down the gravel road, hoping against hope to apprehend Roger at the shack. This nightmare needed to end. The medics gave Ellen an injection of analgesics to help her pain. Glancing across the front seat, John smiled, breathing in a sigh of relief. He was amazed that the old woman was still sucking air.

"How many miles do you think you walked in order to get to the farmer's place?"

"It felt like a thousand walking it."

"You amaze me, old lady."

"I'll take that as a compliment." Ellen wheezed, trying to laugh.

"I'm still mad as hell at you."

"I knew this was coming."

"How did he manage to snag you? You of all people?"

"Stupidity on my part. Long story short, I got out of my car when he pulled up behind me."

"Hold up a sec," John interrupted.

"You heard me."

"You got out of your car just like that?" he said, snapping his fingers.

"I thought there was something wrong with my car. He was flashing

352

his high beams at me. So I pulled over to the shoulder, and yes, I got out. He told me I had a problem with my backlights. That's when I followed him to have a look. Just as I bent over, he cracked me across the head. The next thing I knew, I was blindfolded, hands bound behind my back, and eventually gagged. Roger tossed me into the backseat and drove me out here. The rest is evident. Look at me."

"What else?"

"This murdering rampage started with Gertrude Caller. She ordered Roger to murder these women, knowing the police would ask me to come aboard with the investigation. Her real motive was revenge all along. You see, John, I fired her some years back for attacking Franki Martin. And in her insane twisted mind, she believed that the late Doctor Blake loved her, but ..." Ellen took a breath. "Blake never got the chance to tell her back because I sent him to prison."

"It's a miracle you're alive. Want to hear my bad news?"

"Give it to me."

"We have until midnight to catch Taut. The suits are on the way."

"Midnight?" She looked at her watch. It was 10:15.

"That's not the worst part."

"I'm listening."

"And we're off the case. We're to turn over all evidence and walk away."

Ellen took a sip of water. "I sure as hell haven't gone through this abuse to be kicked out on my ass. Don't worry, John. Roger will be apprehended by midnight tonight. Besides, Mayor Cleaver and I have a little deal."

"I'm counting on it. Where's the nurse?"

"Dead on the living room floor."

"We'll need a coroner."

"And a shovel to scrape her up. She's been decaying fast."

"Only you'd know." The captain glanced across at his friend.

"Thanks for not giving up." Tears were stinging her eyes.

"Thank you for not giving in." He winked as they drove on.

"How is Rachelle?"

"Critical. Ellen, I saw the carnage with my own eyes. There is no way she should be alive right now. No way." Captain Barlow shook his head at the still vivid memory of Rachelle Baum lying in the hospital bed, bandaged from head to toe.

"Do you think she'll make it?"

"Based to her injuries, no, I don't. How in the world did you make it all the way to the farmer's house?"

"God's help. Plus I'm stubborn."

"Amen to him, and amen to you." He patted her hand.

As they rounded the corner, Ellen looked out and screamed for John to stop. John slammed on the breaks, skidding to a stop. Ellen's seatbelt locked, sending another wave of unbearable pain through her body. Jim punched his brakes before sliding into the rear end of Captain Barlow's vehicle. A naked woman had been dumped in the middle of the road. Ellen was the first one out.

"What the hell is this all about?" Dan looked across at his partner, mystified. All Dan could see was a giant cloud of dust. The detectives climbed out of the Camaro and began making their way through the powder of dirt when they heard the captain's bellow through the trees.

"Fuck. Fuck!" He slammed his hand on the roof. "Is it the nurse, Ellen?"

Ellen turned toward John. "No!"

"Oh, he's pissed." Jim rubbed his eyes.

"Let's go find out why," Dan said.

"Maybe it's a deer," Jim said, hopeful.

"Not by the look on his face, it ain't."

The detectives stood next to the captain.

"Sir?"

Captain Barlow looked up, tears running down his face. Dan eyed the beat-up corpse in the middle of the dirt road. Dan rushed over to Ellen, who was hunched over the body.

"Is she dead?"

"Does she look dead to you?" Ellen snapped at Dan.

"He knew you'd take us to the house. That's why he left the body here," John stated.

"He wanted us to find this one." Dan announced.

"Why?" Jim asked putting his sunglasses on.

"Because he can. He believes he's unstoppable." Dan helped Ellen to her feet.

"He's worse than Jack the Ripper ever was," Dan said.

"Jack never got caught, did he?" Ellen declared.

Dan paced in circles in front of the captain's car, smoking his cigarette with cold chills shooting up his spine, pins and needles at the truth of her words.

"That poison is going to kill you, Dan."

"Not before I get this prick, Ellen."

Dan popped the trunk and retrieved a blanket to cover the body.

"We're going to continue down the road. I want you two to stay until the coroner shows up."

"How will we know where you are?" Jim asked.

"Keep driving until you do."

"Yes, sir."

Ellen didn't feel so good. Her body felt chilled as the sweat pooled in her palms. But there was no way she was saying a word. A mistake like that would cost her an emergency hospital visit.

"The house isn't far from here."

"How do you know? It was pitch black when you left."

"Will you just trust me?"

The captain drove another ten kilometers when Ellen yelled, "Turn here." John drove up the hidden gravel path.

Minutes later, the Camaro flew in behind where they had parked. Beads of sweat rolled down Dan's face, dropping onto his gray T-shirt. He was the first to unsnap his holster. Ellen was ordered to stay put. The captain gave them a silent order to surround the house. This was a surprise he didn't want to go wrong. Captain Barlow positioned himself in front of the door. Raising his foot, he gave the door a kick. It splintered on the hinge.

Using his shoulder, Dan wasted no time getting inside the backdoor. The fetid scent of rotting organs hit them like a gale force wind. He had to retreat back outside to catch a gulp of clean air. Guns drawn, the detectives quickly searched the premises. Roger had fled like expected.

The grotesque figure on the living room floor turned their stomachs. The deafening sound of blowflies swarmed the body as maggots crawled in and out of the gaping wounds. There was a large pool of blood beside her head. This time Jim gagged while Dan made an exit for the door before he puked.

Ellen got out of the vehicle.

"It's nasty in there." Dan whistled.

"I know. I lived in it."

John looked at Ellen as she entered. "Is this Gertrude?"

"That's her."

Jim came walking out from one of the back bedrooms carrying bloodstained clothing. "Sir, I found these in the back bedroom."

"Identification?"

Jim fished in the pockets. "Ah and what do we have here." He pulled out a small, yellow change purse. He unzipped the zipper and pulled out a card. "Angel Snow. Born December 2, 82."

"Name ring a bell, Ellen?" Jim asked.

"No."

"Jim, call forensic. I want this place searched," the captain instructed.

"Got it." Jim was happy to get out of there.

The captain put his arm around Ellen's shoulder. "Let's wait outside. I think you've suffered enough trauma in this place."

The country seemed so peaceful and perfect. Birds were playing and singing in the trees. The sun glistened in between the trees. It seemed too beautiful a setting to be tainted by horror.

John's phone rang. He checked the number and smiled. "My loving wife." He beamed, placing the phone to his ear. "Isabella."

"Daddy! Daddy!" Aaron was screaming his name, frantic.

It was his little girl.

"Aaron, where's Mommy, baby?"

"The bad man took her, Daddy!"

Those words made John go weak at the knees. His daughter was near hysterics.

"Aaron, where's Alix?"

"Hiding!" Aaron cried.

"Daddy's coming home, baby. Aaron, stay on the phone with me; don't hang up."

"Daddy, I'm scared."

"I know. baby. Aaron, I have to tell my guys something. Don't hang up, okay?"

"He hurt Mommy."

"Where is Mommy hurt?"

"She's bleeding."

John's heart sank with fear.

Captain Barlow took the phone from his ear briefly. "The son of a bitch has my wife. I have to get home."

Ellen was already in the car before John finished his sentence.

"We're coming," Dan stated.

"Stay here and wait for forensics."

"I'll call Derk; he's just down the road. He'll be here when he gets here. I'm not waiting for him. C'mon, time is fucking ticking. Besides, that piece of shit isn't going anywhere. And we have enough forensic evidence to nail this bastard!" Dan yelled at his supervisor, shocking him back to reality. "We'll meet you there, sir." He slammed the passenger door while Jim squealed down the driveway. Rocks and dirt flew up behind both vehicles as they sped down the gravel road. They had hours—if that—to catch this psychopath or Isabella would surely die a horrible death.

Chapter Seventy-Five

The captain's heart was pounding fiercely. Ellen looked across the front seat, noticing beads of sweat sliding down his face. There was no mistaking that whatever dread she felt, his tripled in comparison. Everyone on the team knew Isabella's fate if they didn't find her in time. He would gut her like a pig.

At that very moment, John looked across with tears in his eyes. "Ellen, I don't want to know, but I need to know."

"He will kill her, John." Her words were like ice pellets stinging against his chest.

"How long do we have?"

"Three hours at most."

"That's it?" he screamed out in pain and frustration.

"The rules have changed. The game is between you and him now. You find him, your wife lives. Pray she doesn't beg for her life. Or he will finish her before the three hours is up, I assure you."

"My wife's life depends on us finding him?"

"And every other vulnerable woman."

"Where would he take her?"

"I'm not sure."

"Come on, Ellen, please tell me something. This is the woman I love, the mother of my children we're talking about here. You're the only one that's had the opportunity to go inside his head."

"He's a creature of habit. He'll go to where it's familiar or he'll move on all together. There is no straight path for him."

"I want round-the-clock surveillance on that place."

"Where are your men going to hide?"

"In the fucking house if they have to."

"Calm down."

"This is calm."

John got on the radio and called for backup to his home. There he would give further instruction. What instructions, he didn't know just yet. His first priority was his daughters.

Chapter Seventy-Six

Isabella had been stabbed once in the right breast. Defensive wounds crawled up her arms. She fought hard to get away, but Roger overpowered her like she was a little ragdoll. She could feel her left eye swelling beneath the duct tape. She strained to see something, anything that could inform her as to where she was. The car stopped; Roger popped the trunk and pulled Isabella out. He proceeded without pity to drag her into the woods. Splinters of wood and dirt pierced the bottoms of her feet. Isabella had no idea where this madman was taking her. Behind the tape, tears welled up in her eyes. The last frightful scene played in her mind of her babies screaming out in terror as she shrieked, "Hide!" Roger stole her away. Her lime-green tank top was soiled scarlet where she'd been stabbed.

Isabella had taken self-defense training, but even with all her knowledge and expertise, Roger was too powerful an enemy to take down. His strength and endurance was of three men.

After dragging her a fair distance, he stopped. He threw her to the ground like she was nothing. Her head fell against a tree trunk. She could feel the dampness of the forest floor against her cheek. The sweet scent drifted up her nostrils, giving her a small reprieve from her pain. She stayed still, exhausted from the beating. She knew she'd have to remain calm if she was going to make it out alive.

Roger kicked her over onto her back, tearing off her top. In one swift motion, he cut her bra off. Her bare breasts were now subjected for this monster to view. She felt sick to her stomach as his wet mouth devoured her injured breast. She turned her head and thought about her little girls and wonderful husband.

"Beautiful Isabella." He squeezed her left breast like a romantic lover. "What would the captain think of you now?" His laugh made her shiver to the bone.

She could feel his snake hands touching her all over. Then, without any warning, Roger unclipped his knife and slowly dragged the blade down the length of her body. It stung like salt in a wound. Blood bubbled up through the incision. Her breath heaved hard from the torture. She dreaded what was to come next. He intended to commit the devil's deed. Roger raped Isabella.

They were far enough into the woods where they couldn't be seen, but close enough to spy on the house. He knew the cops would keep an eye on the shack. He was surprised to see none of the detectives. All he could see were men and women in white suits, traipsing in and out of the house. Roger was proud of himself for killing Gertrude. He showed her who was in control. The other whore he killed hours ago was just another notch on his belt.

Isabella started trembling violently, her body going into shock. She fought hard to stay awake. But no matter how hard she tried to hold on, she couldn't. Everything suddenly went black.

Again she came to, hearing birds chirping in the trees above. She was alive. She listened. All was quiet around her, except for the wildlife going about their business. *Where is the monster?* Isabella thought. Every second that ticked by felt like hours. She waited, straining to hear a noise, like footsteps crunching on the underbrush. Nothing. Her heart began to pound like it was about to jump out of her chest. After a few more seconds, she struggled to her feet and made a break for it. It didn't matter that she was blind and naked; Isabella wanted to live. Fear was not going to get the best of her. She made it about twenty yards when she was knocked forcefully to the ground. Roger pounced like a lion, the cold steel of the knife embedded at her throat.

"Run again and you die. Understand?" he whispered in her ear.

Isabella muffled, "Yes."

He yanked her up on her feet and proceeded to drag her back into the woods. "Where is that big bad-ass husband of yours? Maybe he doesn't care as much as you think he does." Roger liked taunting Isabella.

Roger was full of shit, and Isabella knew it. Her husband was doing everything in his power to find her and bring her home.

Chapter Seventy-Seven

John squealed into his driveway. Squad cars were parked a half-mile down the block. Blue and red lights flashed, warning something was very wrong. Dedicated officers whispered low, waiting by their cars for orders. John ran toward the front door. Zori, Isabella's older sister, was nervously standing in the doorway with his two girls. John picked up his girls and held them close. The flashing lights on the squad cars stole Alix's attention. She appeared frozen.

"Zori, let's bring the children inside."

"John, I'm taking the girls with me. It's not safe here."

"Sure, but I have to speak with them."

"Jesus, John, haven't they been through enough?"

"Zori, please."

"You have to find my sister, John."

"I will." He said it louder than he intended to. "I promise, but I need to know what my kids saw. They may be the only link to finding her."

He tried to mask his shock as he entered the house. In the living room were broken vases and flowers strewn all over the couch, floor, coffee table. Pictures smashed, lamps broken and turned over on their sides. Isabella put up a hell of a good fight; that much was evident.

"Come on, girls, let's go upstairs." John carried his girls up the flight of steps to their bedroom.

The detectives entered the home, eyeing the disaster in the living room. This investigation had stepped up to a whole new level. Now it was very personal. Dan spotted the blood droplets on the white carpet. Blood was not a good sign. He could feel his chest getting tight.

The detectives put on their latex gloves before searching the premises. During the search of the kitchen, both detectives were stunned by what they saw. Directly in view, a knife stained with blood sat on the counter. He wanted them to find the weapon. Jim noticed a note next to the knife and picked it up.

"That fucking monster."

"What's it say?"

He read it aloud.

To Captain Barlow:
This has been a stabbing good time. The next time you see your lovely wife, it will be on a cold steel slab at the city morgue. Happy hunting. See you in hell.
RT

"Son of a bitch!" Dan yelled, slamming his hand down hard against the countertop. "That heartless, heartless bastard."

The detectives were feeling the pressure to catch this guy like a bomb about to explode.

The captain handed over his children to their aunt.

"These nice gentlemen are going to escort you girls to Aunt Zori's house. She's going to take good care of you two while Daddy goes and finds Mommy. Okay, babies. Give Daddy another hug. I love you both." He held his girls one last time before giving them over to their aunt.

The detectives came around the corner from the kitchen.

"You need to read this." Jim handed him the piece of paper. Captain Barlow read the note with grave pain in his eyes.

"We have to find this animal before he butchers my wife."

Chapter Seventy-Eight

All four entered the station in silence. McCalley was at his desk talking with Mayor Cleaver. Cleaver rose up to greet John. He stuck out his hand. "I'm sorry, John," he said sympathetically.

"She's still alive, and we'll find her."

Cleaver nodded.

Dan nudged his partner in the shoulder, eyeing the two men wearing dark suits standing close to Cleaver.

"Let me guess?"

"Yep, they have arrived."

"Hey, Cleaver!" Dan shouted at the mayor.

"Detective Kape."

"Don't think for one second because these heroes are here that we're going anywhere."

"They're here to help, Detective," Cleaver announced confidently.

"Then tell them to stay the fuck out of our way."

"That's not possible."

"Oh yeah?" Dan got up in the mayor's face, just itching for a fight. He had pent-up aggression and was looking for any excuse to release it.

"Dan!" Ellen yelled. "This is not helping anyone."

Dan stepped back as Ellen touched his shoulder.

"You're lucky, asshole."

"Meeting in the conference room, now. Move!" Captain Barlow barked.

Dan took Ellen at the elbow, leading her as quickly as she could move to the war room. Dan glanced over his shoulder at the agents right behind him. This was for a very important briefing.

"I ain't going anywhere, Ellen."

"You won't have to. Trust me."

"You okay?"

Her complexion was growing whiter by the second.

"I've seen better days." She winked.

Agent Derrick Brillow and Agent Brice Marshall walked around the room looking at the photographs of the dead women that Roger Taut had destroyed. Everyone in the room listened attentively as the captain spat out the evidence collected so far. The prime suspect in the kidnapping of Isabella Barlow was Roger Taut, identified by his daughter, Aaron Barlow. Then the captain assigned orders to the other three teams before closing the meeting. The entire time, Dan glared across the table at Cleaver. The little prick wasn't so tough now that he was face to face with the guys he'd threatened to kick off the case.

Within minutes, the room was cleared.

Chapter Seventy-Nine

Roger decided it was time to leave. It was too dangerous for him to be out there; the cavalry would be coming just as soon as the body was removed from the house. He pulled Isabella backward across the wooded carpet. The bottoms of her feet were raw and bleeding from splinters of twigs that had dug into the soles of her feet. Roger popped open the trunk, throwing her inside.

Pictures of her life flashed across her mind. It was explained in martial arts that if abducted and brought to a second new location, chances of your survival were minimal. The car started moving.

The next thing she knew, she was being yanked from the trunk of the car and pulled down a flight of steps. The musty smell of the cellar assaulted her senses. Then she was thrown to the cold cement floor.

"I'm going to remove the tape. Scream, you die."

Her eyes burned as he ripped away the tape from her eyes. The inside of her mouth felt like glue. It took awhile before her sight returned. It didn't stop her from straining in search of a door, window, something, but it was too dark. He kept her hands bound behind her back, making sure she couldn't defend herself.

"Where am I?"

"It doesn't matter."

"Am I going to die?"

"Yes." He spoke so calmly it was frightening.

"Roger, I want you to think of my little ones. If you kill me, they won't have a mom. Every little girl needs their mommy."

Roger hauled off, striking her across the face. Her pity was manipulative and offensive. On her knees, she begged him to stop hitting her. Then without another word, he left.

Isabella quickly huddled up against the wall, shaking and terrified. Wonderful memories of good times with her family flooded her mind with peace. In time, the shaking subsided. Falling in love with John was the best thing that ever happened to her. They had a deep love that no one could take away. Then a sadness slipped in when she thought about her two little girls. How would they get through without a mom? Who would get them ready in the morning for school and give them bubble baths and comb their hair and read books at night before they went to sleep? Isabella began to cry. She deserved to be with her family. She reached into the depths of her being for strength to keep going. She had to believe that John would come and rescue her. He couldn't raise their babies on his own. He was way too busy catching bad guys. The girls needed her. She smiled, closing her eyes to rest.

Hours later, Isabella jumped, hearing footsteps on the stairs. Without reason, Roger violently attacked her again. It was evident he had no intention of killing her yet. He was having way too much fun. She flinched at the cold steel slowly moving down her face. It took every bit of strength she had not to scream out. It would be fatal if she did.

"You're pretty tough, chick. You handle pain well." Isabella turned a deaf ear to his babble, determined not to cave into this madness. Her girls needed her.

"John will find me."

"Before or after you're dead? Would you like to gamble on the odds?"

The words flew from his mouth like daggers.

"Do it, you fucking coward. Get it over with!" She shouted at him. "Kill me. That's why I'm here, isn't it?"

"I'm going to make you feel so much pain, you'll beg me to take your life. I can torture you for days, bitch. That husband of yours believes I've taken you back out to the country. He's probably out there right now searching for your body."

"Don't be so sure of that." She spat blood from her mouth. Roger threw her to the floor and put the boots to her already battered body. When he finished, he rolled her onto her stomach. She braced herself to be assaulted again. He could ravage her body, but he couldn't take the love she had for her family. This brutal sexual assault left her bleeding. Her insides burned as trickles of blood rolled between her legs.

"You're delicious, Isi. Almost as good as my mother was."

Isabella passed out.

Isabella could hear John's voice telling her to be strong. He would find her and bring her home. Aaron and Alix needed her. She could feel herself desperately clinging to the last thread of life. She wasn't sure how much longer she could hang on. "Save me, John," she whispered into the dark, cold cellar.

Chapter Eighty

Five o'clock that afternoon, Captain Barlow stormed into the conference room, standing in front of the room. Every person that had worked on this case stood ready for instruction. Dan and Jim stood at the back of the room, arms crossed. Ellen was busy exploring old files and studying the map of where all the victims had been found. Something was missing. She took a deep breath of air. This was too simple to have been missed. The clue unraveled itself around the middle of the investigation.

"John!" she shouted across the room.

The captain didn't hear her.

"John!" she yelled louder.

This time he heard her, along with everyone else in the room. "Ellen, what is it?"

"Get over here and look at this."

All three hustled to the other end of the room.

"The central location of all these murders is right here." She pointed to the one red tack. "He's not taking her to the country, John. That was to throw us off."

"Sorry, I'm not following."

"I know where Isabella is," Ellen reported.

"Where?" Dan asked, energized.

"The most obvious place, guys. He's hiding her at Gertrude's old place on Sower. By placing the last body on the road, he made it look like he wouldn't return; knowing a search of her place had already been done."

Captain Barlow barked more orders as he ran through and out of the building. The sirens screeched with their lights flashing as they blew through the city. Every officer wanted this animal caught.

After his shower, Roger sat at the table eating beans from a can. Placing the skank in the middle of the dirt road was absolutely brilliant. He outsmarted his adversaries. He had it all; the captain's wife in the cellar was all he needed now. He could torture her for as long as he wanted until he'd go out and find another. Once he finished his beans, he sat with a rope, tying a knot for the new game he intended to play.

Suddenly he jumped at the alarming noise of wailing sirens coming closer. Roger peeked out the dust-covered blinds, seeing a stream of squad cars. Guns drawn, they were busting to take the notorious serial killer down.

Captain Barlow and his detectives covered the front door. Officers Barkley and Bently guarded the side cellar door. Officers stood guard in the driveway. Detectives Matt Cure and Lissner took the back entrance.

In one kick, the door crashed against the wall. It was dark inside with the curtains drawn. Each police officer hoping to have the chance to end this bastard's misery with a bullet in his brain and save the day.

Isabella thought she was dreaming. She thought she could hear heavy footsteps above her. The tape muffled her cries for help. She was on her feet, scared but ready.

Dan saw a flash moving from the hallway to the bedroom.

"He's in there," Dan whispered.

"Roger, come out with your hands up!" Captain Barlow ordered.

"Come in here, and she dies!" Roger screamed.

"You're trapped, Taut. There's no way out!" Jim hollered.

"You're surrounded. It's over." Captain Barlow said with authority.

"I'll kill her, and you know I will."

Officers Bently and Barkley had gotten in the cellar door and found the switch. Barkley gasped upon eyeing Captain Barlow's wife. She was cowering in the corner, naked, bleeding, and battered.

"Isabella Barlow," Officer Barkley spoke softly. "I'm a police officer, ma'am."

She turned around in shame.

"I'm going to get you a blanket, ma'am. But I need you to stay there." He dashed out to his car and grabbed a blanket. He stopped and grabbed Ellen on his way back. Isabella was still standing in the corner, trying to hide herself. Ellen took the blanket from Barkley.

"Isabella, it's Ellen. Officer Barkley is going to cut you free—okay, sweetie?" The moment Isabella's hands were free, she threw her arms around Ellen and cried. Ellen flung the blanket around her. The two women sat together on the floor in silence. Ellen could feel Isabella tremble.

"You two stay right here and don't move," Bently ordered, closing the cellar door.

The captain was still negotiating with Taut when the two officers came to the hallway to inform John his wife was downstairs.

It was time to take him down.

On the count of three, all three rushed the bedroom, knocking Taut to the floor. Dan and Jim had the glory of cuffing the serial killer while Captain Barlow ran to find his wife. He yelled her name, taking three steps three at a time.

"John, she's okay. Isabella is right here," Ellen said.

"Isabella."

"John, she's hurt pretty bad. She needs a hospital now."

He took his wife into his arms, holding her close. Tears sprang to his eyes. That's when she screamed and collapsed.

"I've got to get you both to Morial." The captain carried his wife as Ellen limped behind. These two women had made it against all odds.

Ellen stood beside the Camaro as the detectives proudly led Roger Taut out of the house, his hands cuffed behind his back. Ellen quickly intercepted.

"I told you they'd catch you. You horrible monster."

"Doctor, we meet again." He smiled.

"Don't you doctor me, you maggot." Ellen hauled off and smacked Taut across the face as hard as she could.

"Good shot, Ellen." Dan patted her gently on the shoulder, at the same time moving her away from him.

"I bet that felt good." He laughed.

"Get this piece of shit out of my sight."

The officers were happy to throw Taut where he belonged, in the back of a squad car. He was taking his last ride. The officer left the window open enough for air. Not that this criminal deserved any special treatment after the devastation he'd left behind.

Captain Barlow took the two women to Morial, leaving his detectives to stand on the lawn congratulating each other on a job well done. No one expected what was to come next.

"When we get this mess cleaned up, I'm going for few cold ones." Dan rubbed his whiskers.

"I'll join you," Jim answered, beaming.

No one noticed the man sneak over to the cruiser and put the muzzle of the gun into the opening of the window. "Go to hell!" he screamed before firing two bullets into the side of Roger's head, killing him instantly. Rachelle Baum had died an hour ago.

Detective Dan Masker was the first to tackle Austin Silverspring to the ground. Austin didn't fight back. Dan got the cuffs on him and pulled him up on his feet. "I would rather give you a fucking medal, but unfortunately I can't." He put him in the back of the cruiser and ordered Officer Barkley to get him down to the station.

Special thanks

My husband, Serge, for without his love and support, these manuscripts would have remained on my desk.

To my son, Matthew, for the sacrifices he has made during this crazy ride as a writer.

My dear sister Janet, for on dark days, makes me laugh with humor only the two of us understand.

My sister, Colleen, who acts as my cheerleader for giving me such inspiration and confidence to carry on.

My Teacher, Mrs. Hickey, for pressing upon me the true importance of words turned into imagination

To the entire team at iUniverse for their patience and diligence, couldn't have done it without you.

To Victoria, B.-C., for having such a beautiful city to inspire writing.

My higher power for this wonderful gift bestowed upon me.

Less not I forget all the amazing friends and strangers alike that took the time to read my first novel, "Breach of Sanity", and gave me the desire to continue on my writing journey and complete this novel, "Judas Playing Field".

CPSIA information can be obtained at www.ICGtesting.com
Printed in the USA
LVOW100111140613

338287LV00006B/37/P